For Nicholas.
Your strength and resilience knows no bounds.

Playlist

Can't Tame Her Zara Larsson	**I'm Not Here to Make Friends** Sam Smith
Dirty White Boy Foreigner	**Shake That** Eminem
Dr. Feelgood Mötley Crüe	**Sunshine On My Shoulders** Bob Denver
Gimme More Britney Spears	**Two Out Of Three Ain't Bad** Meat Loaf
Houdini Eminem	**We're Here For A Good Time (Not A Long Time)** Trooper
I Want To Know What Love Is Foreigner	**Working For The Weekend** Loverboy

A CHERRY MILLS MYSTERY

EVERY MOVE THEY MAKE

Lee Gabel

FRANKENSCRIPT

Frankenscript Press
Box 717, #105 - 1497 Admirals Road
Victoria, BC, Canada V9A 2P8

Every Move They Make (Cherry Mills Mysteries #1)

Cover illustration and design by Lee Gabel
Cover images supplied by DepositPhotos

Body font (ITC Galliard Pro) by International Typeface Corporation
Folios, heads and caps (Zapf Humanist 601) by Bitstream Inc.

ISBN 978-1-998869-01-5 (ebook)
ISBN 978-1-998869-02-2 (paperback)
ISBN 978-1-998869-03-9 (hardcover)

Want to find out more about Lee and the books he writes?
Please go to:
LeeGabel.com/links or visit his bookshop at:
Bookshop.LeeGabel.com

$$- 1 -$$

THE FRONT DOOR burst open and sent an echo down the entryway to every room in the house, followed by an angry *slam* and a heavy *thud*. Elise's purse presumably flung against the bench by the door.

In the living room Teigan and Mattix exchanged looks, both with mouths full of popcorn stopped mid-chew.

"Wait for it..." Teigan held up a finger and munched her mouthful of popcorn slowly.

Several seconds passed before the stomps began, up the stairs, one of Elise's trademark moves.

"Wait..." Teigan continued her play-by-play as Mattix waited with a guilty grin. "Almost there."

The thumping switched to creaking floorboards. Teigan tracked the travelling sound with a pointed finger at the ceiling until they both heard Elise's bedroom door *slam* closed.

Teigan snapped her fingers. "The meltdown has landed."

Mattix glanced at the television and sighed. The opening credits of the movie had just finished. "I guess the dance didn't go well."

If Teigan wore glasses, she'd be looking over the rims. "Brilliant deduction, Sherlock. Rain check?"

"Of course." Mattix looked at her optimistically. "Or maybe things aren't as bad as they sounded."

Being parents to two teenagers, Teigan and Mattix rarely got time for themselves in their own home, let alone the living room with its big screen TV. They usually sequestered themselves in their bedroom to give their kids run of the house. It was the least they could do. Soon enough they would be moving out, leaving the house empty and longing for teenage hijinks again.

Teigan and Mattix had been looking forward to Diamond Bay High School's annual Spring Fling dance just as much as their kids. But an evening of snacks, Netflix, and possibly chill had just frozen over.

Teigan pulled herself out from the warmth of the love seat in the living room and stepped over Elise's purse, jacket, and shoes that lay strewn at the base of the stairs. Nearing the second floor, Teigan recalled fondly the times when "hot mess" referred only to dinner time.

Elise had always been more volatile than her older brother. It had been six months since Newton had displayed what could be classified as a meltdown. He was a senior at Diamond Bay this year and had his eighteenth birthday coming up in July. Perhaps being two years older than Elise meant that his emotional maturity had developed more. Or maybe he was bottling up his feelings. It was hard to tell. Newton kept his cards close to his chest. Elise, on the other hand, liked to play emotional fifty-two pickup.

Teigan approached Elise's bedroom door, positioning her ear close, listening for sounds of distress.

"I know you're there, Mom," Elise said through the door. "I can hear you breathing."

Teigan drew back, sensing her annoyance. "Just checking up on you, hon. You want to talk?"

"No. Just leave me alone."

Now was not a time to negotiate. "Okay." Teigan turned to

leave, then paused. "You're welcome to join me and Dad for a movie. We just started it. And we have pop—"

"I *don't* want to be part of your *love-fest!*"

"O-kay," Teigan whispered to herself. She padded back to the stairs with slow, deliberate steps, like she was leaving a lioness's den. Slow because she could read her daughter like a book, and she knew what was coming.

True to form, Elise's bedroom door cracked open. "Mom?"

Teigan turned to see Elise standing in her bedroom doorway, her simple yet elegant midnight blue halter-neck dress that they had picked out together a week earlier backlit by her bedroom light. It was easy for Teigan to flash forward and see the woman her daughter would become.

Elise's cheeks were wet with tears. She did want to talk. It was written all over her face.

Teigan took her daughter in her arms. "Oh, sweetie. What happened?"

Elise buried her face into Teigan's shirt. "Hazy ditched me."

Elise and Haislee (Hazy) Kirkland had been best friends since kindergarten. They had been through everything together and usually were inseparable.

"Did you two have plans? For after?"

"Yeah. She said she had a stomachache, but she disappeared and she's not answering my texts now."

"You've called her?"

Elise pulled back and rolled her eyes at her. "Nobody ever calls anyone anymore, Mom."

"Right. What about... Facetime?"

"You mean Snapchat. She's not answering anything."

Teigan pulled Elise in for a hug. "I'm sure she's fine. Maybe her battery died."

"Yeah, maybe."

"Give it some time." Teigan started down the stairs. "Elise?"

"Yeah?"

"That dress is stunning on you. You have a real sense for fashion, just like your grandmother, because you certainly didn't get it from me."

Elise smiled, probably for the first time since returning home. "Thanks, Mom. I'm going to change. As hot as this dress is, it's a little scratchy."

Teigan nodded. "Offer's still open, okay? Movie and popcorn."

Elise retreated into her bedroom and closed the door. No slam this time.

Teigan plopped herself back down beside Mattix, her chin on his chest, gazing up at him. "Miss me?"

"Terribly." Mattix kissed her. "Ship out of danger?"

"She'll be fine." Teigan rolled over and grabbed the remote, restarting their movie. "Haislee's M.I.A."

Mattix snagged a handful of popcorn and handed the bowl to Teigan. "Haislee has become a bit of a wildcard lately."

"What do you mean?"

"She's been less reliable," Mattix said. "Flaky. Late for hangouts, that kind of thing."

"Do you not remember what it was like to be a teenager?" Teigan raised a brow at him. "Add social media and all that shit on top of everything. It's amazing that teenagers get out alive these days."

"That's fair."

Teigan scooped up a handful of popcorn. Just as she filled her mouth, the phone rang in the kitchen. She glanced at Mattix.

He shook his head. "Let it go to voicemail."

The phone rang twice more, then went silent.

"See?" Mattix grabbed some popcorn.

The iPhone Radiate ring tone floated down from Elise's bedroom, then muffled talking. "That's probably Haislee now," Teigan said.

The phone in the kitchen rang again. Teigan moved to get up, but Mattix held her back.

"Elise," he called out. "Could you get the phone, please?"

Teigan stared at him with a quizzical look. "Why?"

"Our kids should be serving us now," Mattix said, his eyes on the television. "They're old enough."

"You're serious?"

Mattix smiled and chuckled to himself. "Partly. The extension is twenty steps from her room. Hardly a hardship." He yelled up at Elise again. "Elise? Can you *please* get that?"

Elise's bedroom door squeaked open followed by soft footsteps along the upstairs hallway and into the master bedroom.

"See? They can be useful to us." Mattix winked at her.

Teigan huffed at him. "Lise? Who was it?"

The staircase creaked in its usual spots, but Teigan's question remained unanswered.

"Elise?" Teigan shot Mattix a look of concern. He paused the movie and both shifted forward in the love seat, immediately attentive.

Elise entered the living room. She wore an orange T-shirt and sweatpants, but her face was white as a sheet. She held her cell phone in one hand and the upstairs extension in the other, in front of her body, like she was unsure what to do with it.

"Hon, who is it?"

Elise swallowed hard and her words came out weak and gravelly. "It was the hospital. Something's happened to Newt." She gave the phone to Teigan with a trembling hand.

Teigan placed the phone to her ear as all of her worst fears fought to cloud her thoughts all at once. She pressed seven on the keypad to replay the message.

"Let me listen." Mattix reached for the phone, but before he could take it, Teigan hung up, redialed, and waited.

"Hello, yes, this is Teigan Coleman. You just called regarding my son Newton." A pause. "Yes. I'm his mother."

She listened, her eyes shifting nervously between Mattix, Elise, and random points in the room. She raised her free hand to her mouth, her fingers trembling now too, as if to stifle a scream.

Teigan continued the call, answering questions only she could hear. "Not that I'm aware of."

The person at the other end of the call, presumably a nurse, continued talking.

"Yes..." Teigan's voice sounded robotic. "Okay." The caller hung up. Teigan's hand dropped to her lap, still gripping the phone.

Mattix moved around to face her. "Tee? What's happened?"

Teigan looked up at Elise, then to Mattix. "Newton's in a coma. A suspected drug overdose."

"What?" Colour drained from Mattix's face. "That's impossible. Newton doesn't do drugs."

Or did he? Teigan's mind struggled to recall any warning signs but instead ended up in the dark recesses of her imagination. *And if Newton had access to drugs, what else was he into?*

The three stared at each other, frozen by confusion and dread.

Elise broke the silence. "Wait. What if it's a prank?"

Teigan locked gazes with her daughter and shook her head slowly. "You and I know that was no prank."

Teigan stood, followed by Mattix and Elise. There was no need for further discussion. They piled into their Nissan Pathfinder with one destination, their minds consumed with worry and fear and for Teigan, guilt.

Newton would always be her first born. Her sole job was to keep him safe and she had failed, despite her considerable skills.

I should have done more, I could have done more, she screamed inside her head. Before they arrived at the hospital, Teigan made a solemn vow to herself and to Newton.

I will do more because I have the power to do so.

– 2 –

THE SUMMER PRECEDING Newton's senior year at Diamond Bay High School had ended up being one of the worst in recent memory. He worked at his local Baskin-Robbins, one of the many businesses that formed the brilliantly named Main East Plaza. The aging complex was situated parallel to Main Road East in Cherry Mills, a residential neighbourhood in Hamilton, Ontario. To the students of Diamond Bay, the mall had one name: Main Eats, because eating was all you could really do there.

Newton's ice cream-slinging employer apparently had 31 lives as well as flavours and had escaped the COVID pandemic that killed over half of the plaza's original businesses.

Scooping ice cream wasn't all bad. In fact, it was pretty good as jobs go. His hours were flexible and the store was a brisk walk or a short bicycle ride away. The neighbourhood of Cherry Mills was small, but diverse enough to keep Newton's life interesting.

Consistently warm summer temperatures in the high 70s meant a lot of business from girls in shorts and tank tops. And many of them went to either Diamond Bay High or McMaster University. Newton flexed his scooping arms as he built up his people (flirting) skills, something which social media was doing its best to destroy. He liked to think that they were coming for ice cream partly because he saw himself as easy to talk to and fairly good looking. "It's not bragging if it's true," he often told himself. But he made sure to keep his ego in check, unlike his friends Richard and Dustin.

Richard Baum had been Newton's best friend since middle school. The two of them had much in common, video games (particularly retro consoles) and music from the '80s and '90s being their main interests. Richard had big dreams but little follow-through. He saw himself designing his own video games and assumed Newton would compose the music. The assumption had formed the first crack in their friendship.

Every single idea that Richard came up with would be put on hold when something bigger and better popped into his head. Not a single game was ever finished and Newton never had a chance to compose anything. Still, their friendship weathered these disappointing setbacks until Dustin Stoaks attached himself to the friend duo in Grade 11.

Dustin held himself in high regard and made it clear to anyone within earshot that he had the answer for everything. In contrast to Newton and especially Richard, Dustin's family was loaded. He lived with his mostly absent parents in an obnoxiously large mansion in Rockwood West, a small affluent neighbourhood bordering on Cherry Mills. The house had a private driveway and porte cochère, a pool, a tennis court, and a well-tended garden. Newton often wondered where the Stoaks went for vacations, because their house was like a resort to begin with.

Confidence was Dustin's middle name and that was a good thing. Only during the past two years had girls appeared on Newton and Richard's radar. Dustin wasn't classically handsome (he'd disagree), nor was he tall and fit (he'd disagree), but his reputation as a player kept Newton, Richard, and others within his circle of influence so they could experience the "one percent." Because if Dustin could get girls, so could they.

"I get laid at least once a week," Dustin often told them. "By the end of the year, so will you, if you stick by me, listen, and learn."

What many forgot (or chose to ignore) was most, if not all, of the girls were interested in one thing, and that wasn't Dustin. It was what Dustin had access to, whether it was money, booze, or drugs. Because rich people had connections that regular people didn't. Wisely, Newton took Dustin's success with girls with a grain of salt. However, Richard was all in. He had found his leader.

The three of them began to hang around together on a regular basis. Dustin was generous towards Richard with both his time and money, but with Newton there always seemed to be strings attached. He offered friendship only when he wanted something from Newton.

"Give me your notes, braniac," Dustin would say, his greedy hands beckoning after goofing off in the classes they shared. "I've got a mod for Grand Theft Auto to show you later." Newton saw through Dustin's attempts to soften his demands. Teasing a special video game or some other exclusive content was hardly an incentive, but Newton let it slide to keep the peace. And it worked for a while.

After the Grade 11 Spring Fling dance, Dustin suggested picking up some Party Packs from Mary Brown's Chicken and taking it to the afterparty at Pyckman Quarry. Urban development in Hamilton required vast quantities of cement. Pyckman Quarry's seemingly unlimited supply of limestone, cement's principle ingredient, ensured a long and profitable business lifespan. It also provided a consistent and relatively secluded spot for teenagers to raise hell without having to worry about police. The owners of the quarry could have installed security lighting and cameras but never did. Maybe the owners had partied there as teenagers, too.

"If it's anything like last year, the place is going to be fuckin' jumpin'." Dustin gripped the steering wheel of his black 2023

Cadillac Escalade. He looked at Richard in the passenger seat rocking his head back and forth to Drake on the stereo. "So how much chicken is that?"

Richard shrugged. "Fuck if I know."

Dustin eyed Newton in the back seat through the rearview mirror. "How much? Gimme a number."

Newton had no idea, but he could find out. "How many people are going?"

"Oh yeah," Dustin said. "You guys weren't there last year because back then you were fuckin' losers. Then you met me."

Newton bristled. "How many?"

"My parties are epic. You know that. Let's say a hundred?"

Newton pulled out his phone, called up the website for Mary Brown's, and performed some quick math in his head. Easy math. "Get eight Party Packs."

Dustin laughed and tossed his gold Amex card at him. "Take care of it, calculator boy."

"Right away, cash-stuffed dough-boy." The words were out before Newton had a chance to stop them. He had committed the double cardinal sin of joking about Dustin's money and his weight.

Richard stopped rocking his head and glanced at Dustin. Newton felt the heat from Dustin's humourless eyes through the rearview mirror.

"Relax," Newton said. "I meant it in the best way possible."

Dustin punched the off button to the stereo, plunging the SUV into heavy silence. "Did you, *Newt?* Did you *really?*"

"Come on. I was joking." Newton shrugged. "Calculator boy made a joke."

"A joke. Right," said Dustin. "Get on that chicken. I don't want to have to wait."

Dustin smiled, but his eyes told a different story. Anger? Annoyance? Something still simmered behind them. Newton distracted himself by placing the order.

"And don't be memorizing that credit card number, *Newt.*" Dustin kept his eyes on the road and spoke without swearing. Profanity usually flowed from his mouth like a faucet on full. It was part of his larger-than-life personality. The fact that he was holding back, that was the biggest red flag of all.

– 3 –

IF DUSTIN AND RICHARD had left the afterparty at Pyckman Quarry in a wheelbarrow, they would not have remembered. Newton had limited himself to two beers, which he drank early in the evening, and chased them down with a *lot* of fried chicken. As it turned out, not many who turned out for the party had wanted to eat chicken. Take-out boxes and torn bags filled with partially eaten food littered the parking lot.

The food and passage of time meant that Newton was sober when the three of them left the quarry in the wee hours of Saturday morning. Dustin and Richard were both drunk and high. Newton suspected marijuana from the number of bongs he had seen at the party. Any other recreational drugs thrown into the mix was anyone's guess. He had steered clear.

The only impairment Newton faced was his body's thirst for sleep. His body would win, and soon. Getting everyone home in one piece was the order of the day, or in this case, morning.

Before the party, all three had agreed that they'd crash at Richard's afterward because his house was closest to the quarry. With great difficulty, Newton poured Dustin and Richard into the back seat of the Escalade and dug the keys out of Dustin's pocket.

"You tryin' to give me a handy, *Newt?*" Dustin slurred his words with a slack-eyed grin.

Newton ignored him, closed the passenger door, and climbed behind the wheel. The Escalade felt huge, what he imagined driving a tank would feel like.

He had started learning to drive the previous September, earning his G1 license quite quickly. But driving his two friends home that night would break several laws, the biggest one being on the road between midnight and 5am.

Newton took out his phone, all ready to text his parents, then jammed it back into his pocket. In this case it would be better to ask for forgiveness than for permission if shit hit the fan. If he drove the speed limit without drawing attention to himself, he wouldn't have to ask for either.

Fifteen tense minutes later, with Newton's nerves on high alert for any sign of police, he rolled the Escalade to a stop in Richard's driveway. Breathing a sigh of relief, Newton killed the engine and texted home that he'd be staying at Richard's for the night.

"Good party?" Teigan texted back.

"Was OK. Super tired tho." Newton's thumbs typed in a frenzy even though he was exhausted.

"Want a pickup tomorrow? If so, when?"

"Let u kno, k?"

Teigan sent back a thumbs up.

The lights in Richard's house were still on, but not out of concern. Divorced from his wife Charlie for most of Richard's life, Peter Baum was a night owl who liked to watch porn on his big screen TV. Newton would never forget the sleepover at Richard's house during Grade 9 when he accidentally wandered into the living room at three o'clock in the morning and saw Peter masturbating in his La-Z-Boy. Peter had no idea he had been caught; his headphones had blocked Newton's surprised gasp. There were few things more cringey than seeing your best friend's dad jerking off to porn.

Newton had long suspected that Peter had a porn addiction. He also believed the constant exposure to porn had warped Richard's view of flirting, dating, and dealing with teenage social situations in general. Both subjects were cans of worms that would forever remain unopened.

Newton knocked on the door to Richard's house. The flickering lights inside the house from the TV stopped and he heard stumbling and a broken dish. After what seemed like a curiously long time, Peter came to the door wearing a housecoat.

Jesus Christ, he's going to flash me.

It was the first thought into Newton's head. He choked back the nervous laughter in the back of his throat.

"Newton!" Peter said. "Good to see yah. I thought you guys were going to be out all night."

I bet you did.

"No, Mr. Baum. Richard and Dustin are a little wasted. Well, a lot. I thought it'd be better to get them home safe."

Peter glanced at the Escalade parked in the driveway. Newton saw what he thought of as disappointment creep across the man's face.

After another awkwardly long pause, Newton continued. "Uh, can you help me get them inside?"

Peter snapped out of whatever thoughts he was having. "Yeah, yeah."

Newton opened the passenger door and grabbed Dustin by the shoulder. He groaned but didn't wake. Peter took the other arm and directed him inside. To Newton's surprise, Dustin's legs partially worked but doubted that he'd be able to support himself.

"Bag any tasty chicks?" Peter looked at Newton over Dustin's hanging head.

Newton returned an uncomfortable glance. "You'll have to ask them in the morning."

"No, I meant you."

Newton shook his head without making eye contact. "Not unless you count Mary Brown's Chicken."

"Man, what I wouldn't give to be a teenager again," Peter said. "There's some fuckable girls at Diamond Bay, that's for sure."

How is this guy for real?

The man hadn't changed since Newton first met him over six years ago.

They dropped Dustin on Richard's bed, and a few minutes later, Richard took the spot next to him.

"Are you crashing here, too?" Peter asked. "I mean, that's totally okay."

"I was hoping to." Newton looked back at Richard and Dustin snoring on Richard's bed. "For just a few hours."

"Yeah, yeah. No problem."

Newton locked the Escalade and returned to the house. Peter held out a blanket and a pillow.

"You can take the couch if you want."

The thought of sleeping anywhere in Peter's "love den" gave Newton the creeps. "I'll take the floor."

Peter gave him a questioning look that seemed to say, "You're crazy."

"I'll be asleep so fast the floor won't make any difference."

"Suit yourself."

Newton spread out the blanket on the floor at the foot of Richard's bed and wrapped himself in it. Despite the lack of a mattress, sleep took hold within minutes. He dreamed of the police pulling him over and throwing him in jail for reckless driving.

– 4 –

THE SOUND OF THE JAIL DOOR slamming closed and locking woke
Newton with a start. It was a little after nine in the morning. For
a moment he didn't know where he was. Then he caught the scent
of coffee and bacon wafting from the kitchen and his dream of
being arrested melted away.

That was Peter's thing. Coffee and bacon. Newton wasn't sure
if it was an everyday occurrence, or just something Peter did on
the mornings after sleepovers to make it seem like he was a cool
dad. It only partially worked. The morning bacon feasts were one
of his only redeeming traits. Peter would never be truly cool.

Newton imagined his dad making waffles back home and
texted his mom for a pickup. As much as he liked coffee and
bacon, he liked weekend waffles more.

Newton stared at the ceiling, mottled with water stains. He
was glad he had spread out half of the blanket on the floor the
previous night. The dirt and dust under Richard's bed had collected
in fuzzy layers.

Richard had the most difficult life out of the three of them.
One parental income hit hard. Hanging out at school or at parties,
it mattered less where each of them came from than where they

were going. But in all the time he had known Richard, Newton had never felt at ease in Richard's house.

The coffee and bacon did their job and made his stomach rumble, but it was the desperate need to pee that got Newton off the floor. Richard and Dustin were still dead to the world. He contemplated taking a photo of them sleeping in the same bed so he could make jokes later, but thought better of it. Conveniently still in the clothes from the previous night, he made his way to the bathroom.

In his head, Newton heard Dustin's voice: "Drain the vein. Make the bladder gladder." It was one of his dumb sayings that actually made sense.

After washing his hands, he entered the kitchen to see Peter shovel a huge pile of cooked bacon off a baking sheet and into a bowl containing even more cooked bacon. The quantities seemed a little insane.

"Help yourself," Peter said.

Newton thanked him and had eaten two pieces of bacon when he spotted a collection of balled-up tissues next to Peter's La-Z-Boy. He thought of what he must have interrupted last night and immediately lost his appetite.

Peter furrowed his brow at him. "You okay?"

"Still a little queasy." It was mostly a lie, but the tissues tipped the scales.

"Right." Peter nodded. "Grease and hangovers. Sorry 'bout that."

Newton felt his phone vibrate in his pocket. He had set up a custom vibration for every member of his family and knew that his mom had arrived. He breathed a sigh of relief and waited for the doorbell.

$$- \; 5 \; -$$

Teigan parked her white Nissan Pathfinder behind Dustin's Escalade and found herself wondering what Newton thought of his friends driving expensive cars like that. As far as she was concerned, a luxury SUV didn't belong in the hands of a seventeen year old. What made it worse: Dustin hadn't earned it. He had been given everything he ever wanted on a silver platter.

Newton hadn't been interested in driving until recently, but it still wasn't much of an interest. He was content being an expert on the HSR (Hamilton Street Railway). Common buses had replaced the streetcars and trolley buses back in 1992. But things change, and once Newton found a steady girlfriend, Teigan suspected a driver's license would soon become a priority.

Teigan took a swig of coffee from her travel mug, ignoring the pleas of her bladder, and texted Newton. "Extraction team in place. Stand by."

She pocketed her phone. Richard's house was one story with no basement. The exterior needed a new coat of paint, and the detached garage looked like it had been added several years after the main dwelling had been built. The last time she had seen the garage door open, it had been packed to the rafters with crap.

That's what happens when you don't have a basement.

Peter had parked his precious 2022 Toyota RAV4 hybrid next to the garage, exposed to the elements. Teigan didn't think that was a good idea for a vehicle with a battery. In fact, she didn't think electric vehicles were a good idea at all. They could have her gas-powered SUV when they pried the steering wheel from her cold, dead hands.

The RAV4 was leased. And when Peter traded up to get the "latest and greatest" electric model, he made sure everyone knew about it.

"Want to know how much money I saved this month by *not* buying gas?" Peter would ask. Nobody cared but he told them anyway, repeatedly if he got the chance. In the words of Shania Twain, one of Teigan's favourite singers, "that don't impress me much."

Teigan rang the doorbell. A moment later, Peter pulled open the door. He wore a ratty and stained housecoat with a torn tissue hanging from one of the pockets. His legs were bare, except for socks with holes big enough for multiple toes. His housecoat hung open in a loose "V," exposing a smattering of gray curling chest hair. Teigan didn't like chest hair as a rule but thinning chest hair seemed somehow worse. His bare chest meant that he wasn't wearing a shirt either. For a fleeting second Teigan thought his housecoat would slide open and scar her for life.

Then the smell hit her, a wall of bacon that nearly made her gag. Subtle bacon smells were good, welcomed even, but when you come away greasy without touching or eating anything, not so much.

"Teigs! Lookin' good!" Peter flashed his brows. "Come in." He stepped aside and swept his arm toward the dark interior of the house. He had started calling her "Teigs" back when Newton was in Grade 6 and had just become friends with Richard. For some reason, he had linked her name to Cheryl Teigs, a supermodel popular in the '70s and '80s, and it stuck. Teigan hated the comparison.

"Thanks, but I really can't stay," Teigan said. "Pick up only."

"Come on. How about a coffee and some bacon?"

Teigan swallowed hard against her repulsion. "Well—"

"Hey, Mom." Newton gave her an urgent look, definitely ready to go.

That makes two of us.

"Actually, can I use your bathroom?"

"For sure," Peter said. "You remember the way? Straight ahead, right, then left."

"I remember." But even if Teigan hadn't remembered, Peter's house had a layout that held no secrets. You knew where everything was from the front door. Still, it wouldn't hurt to reacquaint herself with the floor plan, especially if she needed to revisit the house later. Even with an eidetic memory, refreshing the details made the memories more vivid.

Teigan strolled past the living room, which was partially sunken and carpeted with hideous blue shag. An immense La-Z-Boy recliner sat directly in front of a large screen TV. Balled tissues littered the carpet.

"That's an eighty-five inch screen," Peter called out as she walked. "OLED. Got it at Costco."

I don't give a shit.

Most of the walls were bare. Those that weren't held photos with dumb pithy sayings, as if someone had printed out a bunch of bad memes and hung them up. Except at the end of the hall. A family portrait had been hung there; Peter, Richard, and a woman that Teigan assumed must have been Peter's wife at one time. He had never mentioned her name in the six years that Newton had known Richard. To the left of the portrait were two bedrooms. To the right was the laundry room and bathroom. She entered, closed the door, and did her business.

After washing up, she peeked into the medicine cabinet. Teigan had read recently that four out of five people snooped that and she was one of them. There was nothing unexpected, except for the tubes of Preparation H and Astroglide. What a combination.

Teigan peeked back down the hall and saw Peter in the kitchen laying raw bacon onto a cooking sheet. She crossed to the two bedroom doors.

The first room contained a queen bed with strewn sheets, a dresser, and a mound of laundry in the corner, presumably dirty. The small window on the back wall provided barely enough light to cut through the darkness.

Teigan moved on to the second room. In terms of layout, it was a mirrored carbon copy of the first. Posters, an even mix of rock and roll and scantily clad women, covered the walls. Classy was not the first word to come to mind. Richard and Dustin lay asleep on the bed, or so it first appeared.

"Have I died and gone to heaven?" a voice said.

Teigan squinted into the gloom of the bedroom and saw that Dustin was staring directly at her, scanning her from head to toe. She turned and headed back down the hall.

"Aw, come back," Dustin called back, barely audible now. "Take care of my..."

Teigan froze.

Did he just say, "early morning wood"?

Whatever it was, she was sure it was inappropriate.

"Sure you can't stay?" Peter grinned at her and ran his greasy fingers through his prematurely white hair, which had been thinning and receding in uneven patches for some time.

"Afraid not," Teigan said. "Maybe next time."

"Take some for the road." Peter collected some bacon and began to wrap it in paper towel. "How's business going? Sales *trickling* in from your *little* venture?"

During the pandemic, Teigan had started a drop-shipping business from home, selling cool gadgets and toys that people couldn't do without. It caught on and now earned more than her previous accounting job. And it certainly wasn't a *trickle*.

"Business is great," Teigan said. "I anticipate a quarter million in sales by the end of the fourth quarter." She had exaggerated the numbers to make him envious.

"That so?" Peter said. "I've got this great idea for a product. I could build it for cheap and make millions. But I better not say too much. You might pounce on it. Or maybe I could license the idea to you and you could make and sell it. It'd be a win-win." He winked at her. Peter was not the brain trust of Cherry Mills, that was certain.

"Yeah, maybe."

Peter handed her a toweled pouch of bacon, the grease already soaking through. "You could use a little..." He let his eyes roam. "Curves on your curves."

Teigan bit her tongue and took the greasy packet, wishing she was wearing gloves. "Thanks." She made a hasty exit and found Newton waiting in the car.

"What took you so long?"

"Peter began to talk." Teigan handed the wrapped bacon to Newton.

"I don't want it."

Teigan looked around, then set it on the console between the seats. "He told me I needed *curves* on my *curves*."

"What the *hell*, Mom. He said that?"

Teigan nodded, started the SUV, and backed out onto the road. "Is that what you call *skinny-shaming*?"

"I don't know," Newton said. "The guy's an asshole." He looked at his mother and shrugged. "Sorry, but he is."

"Is Richard like that?"

Newton paused to think, then shook his head. "No." He rolled down his window, took the wrapped bacon, and tossed it out.

"Read my mind."

Teigan and Newton drove home with all the windows open, their stomachs primed for weekend waffles.

– 6 –

EVERYTHING BEGAN TO CHANGE after the "Mary Brown Incident." Dustin offered Newton minimal interaction in and out of school. Most of the time it was the cold shoulder. When he did pay attention to Newton, a slow character assassination among his peers was Dustin's end game. And he was exceptionally good at it.

During an English presentation in front of the whole class, Newton made the mistake of trying to break the ice with a relevant joke.

"Saying 'I'm sorry' is the same as saying 'I apologize,'" Newton said. "Except at a funeral."

The teacher and a couple of students chuckled but the rest of the class barely responded. They were watching the clock, waiting for the weekend to begin.

"You better apologize for that joke," Dustin said from the back of the room, inducing snickers from other students. "Because we're not laughing *with* you. We're laughing *at* you."

The dig got more reaction than Newton's original joke and threw off his concentration, which pleased Dustin to no end.

Afterward, Elise found Newton standing at his locker with his forehead resting on the door. "Hey Newt. You okay?"

Newton sighed, opened his locker, and collected a few books to place in his backpack. "It's nothing."

Elise positioned herself so that she could make eye contact with him. "Bruh, who do you think you're talking to?"

Newton remained tight-lipped.

"It was Dustbin, wasn't it?" *Dustbin*. That was Elise's nickname for him.

Newton looked at her. "Right, as always."

"What happened this time?"

It was hard for Newton to get the words out. "He embarrassed me in English class."

Elise regarded him with concern and kindness. "Why are you friends with that jerk?"

"I don't know. He just worked his way into my life."

"Like a parasite," Elise said. "He's a sociopath. You know that, right?"

Newton closed the padlock on his locker. "Whatever."

"Elise!" Haislee bounded toward them from down the hallway.

Elise waved at her. "I got to go, but remember this, big brother." She poked at his chest with an index finger. "You're a good guy. And Dustbin's an asshole. Don't you forget it." She skipped toward Haislee and Newton watched them go. A subdued smile rose on his face.

Haislee leaned in. "What's up with Newt?"

"Nothing." Elise didn't make it a habit to gossip, especially about her brother. Haislee would have had a field day with it. "Let's go."

Haislee spun around, took enough steps backward to send a quick wave to Newton, then completed her three-sixty. Both girls disappeared around a corner and out of sight.

As the weeks wound down toward the end of the school year, Richard avoided Newton more and more. By the time Grade 11 wrapped up, Newton found himself cut off from the best friend he had known for six years. To add salt to the wound, Dustin invited Richard to spend the summer with him at his uncle's place in Los Angeles.

"I'm gonna get you laid, dude. Pop your cherry on a hot California chick," Dustin told Richard on the last day of class. "Guaranteed one hundred percent." He made sure to say it within earshot of Newton, just to rub it in a bit more. Newton knew it was mostly unreliable Dustin bullshit, but it still hurt. Not seeing Richard for the entire summer was going to hurt more.

His job at Baskin-Robbins became welcome distraction. He took on as many shifts as he could manage. *Maybe I'll find a girlfriend over the summer,* Newton thought. *That'll show them.*

The weeks flew by. Newton greeted regular customers eagerly, even remembering some of their favourite ice cream flavors. There was one girl that he was particularly smitten by: Juniper Thompson (he had consulted his Grade 10 yearbook to determine her last name.)

Juniper wore her brunette hair in a ponytail and rarely wore makeup. That didn't matter to Newton. He already thought she was a knockout.

If the store wasn't busy, Newton would sit with Juniper at one of the small circular tables lining the front window. She'd eat her ice cream cone (cookies and cream), and he'd watch her eat it. Their conversation came easy but never got too deep. He desperately wanted to ask her out on a date, to a movie or a picnic, anything really. But he couldn't find the nerve to follow through. By the end of August, Newton wondered if they would ever move out of the friend zone.

To make matters worse, Dustin and Richard showed up at the store on the Friday evening before Labour Day. The pretentious rumble of his Escalade alerted Newton of their arrival.

"Didn't know you guys were back," Newton said. "How was L.A.?"

Dustin scanned the tubs of ice cream behind the freezer glass, working his way toward the end where Juniper and Newton stood. "Two months of sex, drugs, and rock and roll." He slapped Richard's shoulder. "Even Dick dipped his wick, ain't that right?"

Richard laughed and nodded. Newton couldn't tell if he was playing along or putting on a show for Dustin.

Newton gave Juniper a look of embarrassment. "Sorry," he said quietly.

Dustin leered at Juniper, then at her ice cream cone. "Cookies and cream, huh?" He leaned onto the freezer's countertop. "So, *Newt*, have you filled her *cookie* with *cream* yet?"

Richard averted his eyes and said nothing.

Juniper scowled at Dustin. "Perv." She backed away from the freezer and made a beeline for the door.

"Juniper!" Newton ran out from behind the counter and caught up to her in the parking lot outside. "Sorry about that. Dustin's gross."

"Get some better friends, Newton." Juniper walked away.

"They're…" Newton choked on his words. "They're not my friends," he whispered. The truth was out, if only to himself.

When Newton returned to the store, he saw that Dustin had helped himself to a bowl of ice cream. That meant he had gone behind the counter, an area off limits to customers.

"You guys need to leave." Newton shot an angry look back and forth between Dustin and Richard. "Right now."

Dustin licked his plastic spoon. "Cookies and cream's pretty fuckin' good." He slapped a ten dollar bill on the counter and strolled to the exit. "Come again!" He threw his half-eaten bowl of ice cream in the garbage and left. Richard followed close behind, avoiding Newton's gaze.

The Labour Day long weekend came and went. Newton sent a text to Richard and asked if he wanted to hang out, maybe play some video games. Usually, at least before this past summer, Richard responded to his texts right away. Now it took hours, if he responded at all. He knew Dustin was probably behind the delays but couldn't prove anything. Newton's attempts to sort things out with Juniper failed too. His texts remained unanswered. It appeared that she had ghosted him.

Monday, the night before the first day of Grade 12, Newton lay in bed, his frustration and anger mounting. Most days, he could rein it in and distract himself. But not today. He had been punished for something that wasn't his fault and the casualty had been Juniper's friendship, something that had grown strong over the summer, at least he thought so.

Dustin Stoaks strikes again.

Newton's anger got the better of him. "FUUUUCK!" He picked up the nearest object within reach, a Magic 8 Ball from his headboard, and threw it hard across the room. Scooping ice cream had given him muscles he didn't know he had.

The Magic 8 Ball struck the opposite wall and left a considerable dent in the drywall. He had expected the toy to shatter. That would have been very satisfying and would have gone a long way to diffusing his rage. But it just rolled out of the crater in the wall and dropped to the floor.

"Can't even do THAT right." Newton sprang off the bed and grabbed the black plastic sphere. Navy blue dye seeped out of the side through a crack that spanned one side. It had already collected in a dark pool on the laminate flooring, probably staining it permanently, and now an expanding blue blotch marked his hand.

"Goddammit!" Newton ran downstairs to the garage, leaving a trail of blue drops behind him. He grabbed a hammer and placed the Magic 8 Ball on the driveway. Out of curiosity, he turned the ball over to read his final fortune.

"Outlook not so good," the window in the bottom reported.

Newton grumbled and shook the ball, spreading blue ink drops all over his hand and the concrete around him. He turned the ball over again.

"Outlook not so good."

He shook the toy again, causing more ink to drip down his

arm. Same message. Impacting the wall in his room had jammed the fortune.

"You're terminated, fucker." Newton placed the Magic 8 Ball on the driveway and brought the hammer down on the top of it as hard as he could.

The existing crack on the side of the sphere gave way to the secret chamber inside holding the ink, exploding it in a shower of navy blue drops.

"Newt?" It was Teigan. She stood on the porch in front of the house. "What—"

"Mom?" Elise bounded from the front door and stopped short, narrowly avoiding bumping into Teigan from behind. "What the... What happened?"

Teigan narrowed her eyes at Elise and shook her head once. Message received loud and clear.

Newton sighed. "Don't worry. I'll clean it up."

"There's some drops inside, too." Teigan tried to make eye contact, but Newton wasn't having any of it. "Want some help?"

"I *said* I'd clean it up." He hadn't raised his voice but spoke sternly enough to make sure there was no misunderstanding.

Teigan and Elise retreated into the house. Newton collected the convex remnants of the Magic 8 Ball and dropped them in the garbage. Then he unwound the garden hose from the side of the house and washed away the ink.

A stain remained. Of course it did.

"Fuck my life." Newton found a scrub brush and managed to scour most of the blue ink out of the concrete. He recoiled the hose, returned the hammer, and retraced the path he had taken from his room.

Newton discovered that Teigan had already cleaned up most of the drips. He poked his head into the living room where Teigan, Mattix, and Elise were all watching television. "Thanks, Mom."

Teigan smiled at him and nodded. "I bet a shower would feel nice."

"Good idea." Newton climbed the stairs to the bathroom he shared with Elise. He closed the door and looked at himself in the mirror. Blue ink dots covered his face, as if he had radioactive freckles. He sighed, undressed, and stepped into the shower.

The warm water on his skin *did* feel nice. Plus this meant he wouldn't have to shower in the morning. He could relax a bit before leaving for the first day of his last high school year. Moms just know.

Newton stepped out of the shower. The ink stains on his hands looked a little lighter but it would be a while before they were completely gone. And that could only mean...

Using his towel, Newton cleared the mirror of condensation and, to his horror, discovered that the blue ink dots on his face remained. He washed his face until it was red and raw. The dots remained.

Lesson learned. Smashing a Magic 8 Ball is bad Karma. Newton put on his pajamas and went to bed early. Maybe the whole long weekend had been a dream, or more accurately a nightmare, and all he had to do was sleep it away.

But it wasn't a dream. The dots on his face were still there in the morning. At the breakfast table, everyone noticed, especially Elise, but no one said a word, even though Newton could tell that questions and suggestions were on the tips of their tongues.

He skipped breakfast, grabbed his backpack, and left the house without saying goodbye. Newton considered riding his bicycle, but walking would take longer, delaying the inevitable onslaught of mockery by his so-called friends. He felt like he was walking to his own execution, and in a way, he was.

$$- \; 7 \; -$$

Choosing to walk to Diamond Bay High School had been a mistake. It would have been better for Newton to ride his bicycle and face things head on. That was the way he was with most things. Rip the Band-Aid off the situation. But his worries won out. The stains on his hands and face felt permanent, even though he knew the thought was ridiculous. Instead of feeling excited about the new year, his brain rolled through undesirable scenarios all the way there. All of them led by Dustin.

That jackass holds too much space in my head rent free.

Diamond Bay sat on twelve acres of land smack in the middle of Cherry Mills. Norway Maple and Eastern White Pine lined the school grounds in sparse copses. The two-story brick and mortar building stretched the length of the grounds, with no extra room for a track or soccer field. Some argued that was a good thing. Newton was one of them. He preferred indoor sports.

Built in the late 1960s, Diamond Bay served between 700 and 1,000 students and had gone through two renovations in its lifetime, the last in 2004. After almost twenty years of use, exterior bricks had cracked and internal structures had "exceeded their expected useful life" (as reported in the school newspaper the previous year.) There was little doubt the school was due for a huge face-lift.

Newton was glad he wouldn't be around to see it. University or college was in his future. If the renovations actually happened, no doubt he'd hear all about it from Elise.

He followed Edgerton Street as it curved north, residential homes on one side and the Cherry Mills Community Forest on the other. No matter what the Cherry Mills town council did to make the forest more inviting, it always gave Newton the creeps, especially in fall and winter when the lack of foliage made the trees look like skeletal hands reaching up from the grave.

Ahead, he could see Diamond Bay's red brick exterior and its large steel lattice portico supported by two large concrete pillars. Students collected in groups in front of the main doors and spilled out onto the front lawn.

Newton felt his stomach tighten. He pulled out his phone and with an ink-stained hand composed a selfie. Zooming into the photo, the constellation of blue spots on his face remained as unchanging as the stars in the night sky.

What was I thinking? That they'd magically have faded away?

Newton pocketed his phone and continued onward. No point in delaying his fate any longer than necessary. His thoughts floated back to a summer with Juniper. Most of it, except that last day, had been good. Great, in fact. He liked her and he was certain she liked him back. The brief encounter last Friday couldn't have destroyed all that, could it? The thought bolstered his resolve.

He broke from the sidewalk and cut across the lawn toward the front entrance of the school. He thought he heard whispers already and did his best to ignore them.

Juniper stood with a couple of her friends near the bank of entrance doors. He waved, his blue hand instantly forgotten and out for all to see. She raised her hand slightly, as if to return the greeting, when—

"Hey *Newt*." On the opposite side of the entrance stood

Dustin, Richard, and a couple other students Newton only had vague memories of. Dustin and his entourage hadn't been on Newton's radar when he had approached the school, so they must have begun following him at some point.

Dustin sauntered over and slapped his hand on Newton's shoulder. "How's it hanging?"

Newton shook him off. "Good."

"Good?" Dustin took a closer look at Newton's face. "What's wrong with you?"

"Nothing." Newton shot a look at Richard and caught a smirk on his former friend's face as he cast his eyes to the ground.

Dustin gave Newton a visual once-over. "What's up with your hands... *and* your face, despite being ugly as fuck?"

Here it comes.

"You been giving Papa Smurf a handy?" Laughter rose up from Dustin's fans, egging him on.

Newton decided his best strategy was to not give Dustin an audience. He glanced at Juniper and saw that she, her friends, and everyone in the immediate area were now watching the show, most starved for entertainment. Some even had their phones out in anticipation. But not Juniper. She had a sorrowful look on her face.

Dustin caught the exchange. "Ah, *there* it is. The hot goss." He grinned at Juniper, exposing his perfect white teeth. "You poppin' her *blueberry?*"

"Shut up," Newton said through clenched teeth as he folded his arms across his chest.

Dustin returned his attention to Newton. "Or do you got blue balls to match your hands? I hear she's a frigid bitch. No wonder you scoop ice cream for a living."

Juniper pulled open one of the doors at the entrance and ran into the school. One of her friends followed her.

Newton grabbed the lapels of Dustin's leather jacket with both fists and pulled him close. For a moment, fear and surprise flickered in Dustin's eyes before they fell vacant again.

"You just don't know when to stop, do you?"

Dustin sneered. "I keep doin' what works."

"But you're *too stupid* to know when it doesn't." Newton pushed Dustin backward and let go. He stumbled and bumped into Richard before regaining his balance.

Newton scanned the impromptu audience with a steely gaze, ending on Richard, then pulled open the front door and walked inside, his head held high. His twelfth year of school had begun and Dustin had failed to get to him as badly as he thought he might.

Fuck the ink stains. They're temporary. And so is Dustin.

$$- 8 -$$

Newton had expected more harassment from Dustin and his little group of followers. To his surprise, he was left alone for the remainder of the first day, despite sharing a few classes with them. Maybe Dustin had wised up and realized that Newton wasn't going to be pushed around anymore.

Wishful thinking.

Dustin was dumb in some ways, but Newton knew not to underestimate him. He could be devious when he needed to be. Avoidance was the best strategy.

The first day back was always a meet and greet. At his homeroom he was assigned his locker and given a padlock for it. *First floor, number 0023. A prime number. Good.*

All the Grade 12s had their lockers on the first floor, something about the lower grades having to climb more stairs to get to their things. Membership had its privileges. Newton tested the combination on the padlock a couple of times before finding his locker and securing it.

He joined the bustling crowd of other students as they found their classes for the semester and teachers gave a rundown of what the class would cover. It was also a time to reconnect with friends you hadn't seen over the summer. That didn't apply to Newton this year.

With the exception of Juniper, Newton's dust-up at the front of the school this morning had eliminated any potential friendly conversation. He could relax and play on his phone. His latest obsession: *Monopoly Go!* His goal was to get as far as possible in the game without spending any real money. But he didn't let his guard down completely.

The bell rang at noon, followed by end of day announcements. The day always ended at lunch on the first day. He collected his things and made a trip to his locker to deposit the books he had collected during orientation.

As he exited the school, Newton spotted Juniper and a couple of her friends standing near the concrete support for the entrance portico. They didn't have any common classes, but she was the only person he considered approachable today. Even though she had ghosted him, he still wanted to talk face to face, maybe get a reason why.

He adjusted his backpack on his shoulder and waved to get her attention. Juniper looked at him, causing the rest of her friends to look, too. Some of her friends even smiled.

Probably because they know the drama.

Juniper returned a half-hearted wave and leaned in to say something to her friends. They nodded, gave her hugs, and marched away from the school.

Newton jammed his hands into his pockets. "Hey."

"Hey." Juniper offered the briefest of glances.

"How was your first day back?"

"Good. You?"

"Good too," Newton said. "I got Barker for math, so that's really good."

"You're lucky." Juniper looked back in the direction her friends had left.

"Look, I'm really sorry about what Dustin said this morning,"

Newton said. "And for what he said at Baskin-Robbins last week. It was super shitty."

Juniper avoided making eye contact. "Yeah, it was."

Their conversation stalled uncomfortably. Newton longed for the ease they'd had before Dustin entered the picture, instead of this awkward exchange.

"Hey, I know I've texted you a lot and you haven't answered." Newton took a breath. "I just want to know why?"

Juniper finally looked at him, her eyes captivating him as they had all summer, but also holding sorrow. "I'm just not in a good place at the moment. Guy friends are off the table." She turned to walk away and Newton followed.

"Can I at least call you sometime?"

"No," Juniper said without stopping.

"I know Dustin's an ass, but—"

Juniper turned and Newton saw anger on her face instead of sadness. "Just drop it. Okay?" She continued down the walkway and Newton saw her friends emerge from behind a tree near the road.

Newton nodded but she never saw it. He grimaced, his mouth suddenly sour with the taste of anger, even hatred, toward Dustin.

He leaned against the concrete pillar and watched Juniper leave with her friends. The last possible friend option had disintegrated right before his eyes.

Newton was confident he'd make new friends over the coming year, but it would have been so much better to have friends already.

As if the Devil had a conduit to his thoughts, Newton glanced over his shoulder to see Richard standing behind the glass doors to the school, watching him. He was surprised to find that he was alone and for a fleeting moment he thought that Dustin had cast him aside.

Richard pushed through the doors and strolled out toward Edgerton Street.

Maybe Newton had a chance to repair that friendship. They

had six years of history behind them. Surely that counted for something. He had to try. Newton followed him.

"Richard," Newton called out. "Can I talk to you for a sec?"

Richard ignored him and seemed to quicken his pace.

"Come on, Richard." Newton matched his pace and walked beside him. "You owe me a—"

Richard stopped and faced him. "I don't owe you anything."

Richard's abruptness surprised him, but Newton continued. "We've been friends a long time. What the hell happened?"

"I don't like who you are anymore."

"What do you mean?"

"You *know* what I mean," Richard said. "I've seen the way you act at work, the way you *flirt* with all the girls that come in."

"I'm just being myself," Newton said. "I'm just being friendly. Plus, what's wrong with flirting once in a while?"

"Once in a while? You creep on girls *all* the time."

"Creep on... What? That's bullshit."

Richard crossed his arms. "Oh really? I saw you with Juniper. Just now. Saw you creeping on her so bad she had to run away to her friends."

Newton took a step closer. "So you heard our conversation?"

"Didn't need to," Richard said. "The creep factor was on full display."

"Says the guy who hangs around with the biggest creep there is."

"This has nothing to do with Dustin."

Newton laughed. "Even *you* knew who I was talking about." He looked at Richard for a moment. "You chose that piece of shit over me. Six years of friendship means that little to you?"

Richard stared back at him blankly. "If you stop *being yourself,* then maybe we still got a chance." He broke away and strode toward the street. "Have a nice life."

Newton stood, dumbfounded, and watched him go. The confidence he felt in the morning after standing up to Dustin had evaporated into a mixture of confusion and sadness. However, his feelings were short-lived. No one else had an issue with his behavior except Richard. And even six years of friendship was no reason to change anything about himself. He liked the way he was.

$$- \; 9 \; -$$

THE WARMTH OF THE SUN had restorative effects. On the walk home from school, Newton couldn't help but hear Bob Denver's "Sunshine On My Shoulders" echo in his mind. It had been one of his grandfather's favourite songs and Pops had played it often when the family came for a visit at Wintergreen Retirement Residence. The lyrics had made an indelible mark in his memories. September heat radiated across his shoulders and, while Newton wasn't completely happy like in Denver's song, he wasn't exactly sad either.

Things are going to be okay.

Newton dug out his headphones from his backpack and started a playlist of 1980s music. Pops had introduced him to songs of the '60s and '70s, but it was his parents who had masterfully schooled him on the music of the '80s.

"Music went downhill after the '80s," Mattix and Teigan would tell him often. "Especially after autotune was invented."

But Newton didn't take their word as gospel at first. He did his own research, listening to thousands of songs over the past couple of years and developing his own personal taste. There would always be outliers from the '90s and beyond, but when push came to shove he tended to fall back to music of the '80s. It was difficult to isolate just one song or band as his favourite.

Elise was the one holdout in the family. She and her friends thrived on music from the Millennium. Newton had no patience for it but as long as they both wore headphones, disaster was averted.

Newton's headphones blasted Loverboy into his ears. "Working For The Weekend" became his temporary mantra as he rounded the bend in Radcliffe Crescent and saw his house in the distance. His safe space. The beat's tempo lifted his spirits and inspired him to quicken his pace. His music held a powerful, sometimes unstoppable force.

He could still see the faded blue ghost of his Magic 8 Ball on the driveway. Newton glanced at his hands and reassured himself that the stains on his hands and face were truly temporary.

Newton pushed open the front door. "Yo."

"Yo, yourself," Elise said, her voice echoing back from the kitchen.

Newton pulled his headphones to his neck, kicked off his shoes, and dropped his backpack. He noticed there was an extra pair next to Elise's. Probably Haislee. He made a beeline for the fridge.

"Hey, Haislee." Newton plucked a carton of orange juice from the fridge door.

Haislee flicked her eyes up and held on him for a second too long, before settling back on what Elise was viewing on her phone. "Hey."

Newton squeezed the carton's spout open and raised it to his lips. "Where's Mom?"

"Up in her office, where else?" Elise glanced up at Newton. "And don't you dare—"

Newton smirked at her and drank straight from the carton.

"Bruh! Other people drink from that too, you know. Gross."

Newton wiped his mouth, set the carton down and leaned on the countertop. "Less dishes to wash, right Haislee?"

"Um, right."

Elise raised an annoyed brow at Haislee. "Whose side are you on?"

"Your's of course," Haislee said. "I just don't want you to get rough, dishwater hands... 'cause... *you know.*"

The two girls looked at each other and burst out laughing.

"Nice." Newton grinned. "How'd the first day go?"

"Same shit, different year," Elise said.

"And we got Palmer for math," added Haislee.

"Damn! *Harry* Palmer." Newton laughed. "Beware of that dude." He raised his hands up and wiggled his fingers, then waved them up and down, mimicking the curves of a woman's body. "He's got rushin' hands and roamin' fingers."

"Ew, bruh." Elise wrinkled her nose up but kept her eyes on her phone. "Did not need to know that."

"You did." Newton cast a serious look at them both. "Promise me you'll report that douche if he touches you in any way."

"Um...," Elise began.

"Promise me. Both of you."

Elise and Haislee met his gaze. "We promise," they said in unison.

"What about you?" Haislee asked. "Anything interesting happen today?"

"Apparently you guys live under a rock," Newton said. "Dustin got up in my grill, just before school."

Finally something more interesting than Elise's phone. "What happened?"

"Stood my ground. Almost fucked him up."

Elise gave him a sideways look that said *I've heard that before.* "What does *that* mean?"

"It means I could have knocked his teeth out, but I pushed him instead. Once." Newton put the cap back on the orange juice. "I beat him with words. It's probably all over Insta."

"What about Richard?" Elise always asked the questions that cut right through all the bullshit.

Newton shook his head. "He made his choice."

"Sorry."

He shrugged, returned the juice to the fridge, and left the kitchen, headed for the stairs.

Elise called back, "Mom said to take out the garbage."

Newton sighed and reversed direction back through the kitchen, pulling on his headphones as he went. Through the garage, at the side of the house, sat two rolling bins: the gray one for garbage and the green one for organic waste. He believed they should only have one big garbage bin since it probably all went to the same place anyway.

He rolled the bins to the curb and returned to the side entry to the garage. He opened the interior door from the garage to the house, turned the corner, and bumped into Haislee.

"Jesus Christ, Haze!" He pulled his headphones off. "You scared the shit out of me."

"Sorry." She blinked up at him with a quirky, lop-sided smile. "What're you listening to?"

"Foreigner."

Haislee shrugged indifference.

"They were huge, like, thirty years ago. Still are." Newton removed his headphones and placed them on Haislee's ears. He watched her listen as a sly smile curled at the corner of her lips.

She slid the headphones off and placed them back around Newton's neck. For a moment it felt like they were at a freshman dance as Haislee let her hands linger lazily on his chest. The smell of whatever shampoo she'd used that day still clung to the earpads.

"A dirty white boy, huh?" Haislee grinned and looked up at him, locking her eyes on his. They held an unmistakable glint that made his stomach buzz in a good yet dangerous way. "Looking for trouble? We should go out, 'cause I got *ideas*."

The heat Newton felt was different from what he felt with Juniper, and it scared him. "You're fifteen."

"And you're seventeen," Haislee said. "Two years is nothing."

"You're my sister's best friend." He shook his head slowly. "Not gonna happen."

Haislee broke her gaze and stepped aside. A mixture of embarrassment and anger flushed her cheeks.

"Sorry," Newton said.

"Whatever." Haislee looked to the floor.

"Haze?" Elise called from the kitchen. "Where'd you go?"

Newton took one last look at Haislee. "Sorry." He returned the headphones to his ears and carried on through the kitchen.

Elise stopped him. "Have you seen Haislee?"

Newton pulled one earpad aside. "Huh?"

"Haislee?"

He pointed his thumb back over his shoulder. "The bathroom, I think." Newton climbed the stairs to his room and closed the door.

The earpads of his headphones still held Haislee's scent. Newton had known for a while that Haislee liked him more than just as the brother of her best friend. This was the first time she had let her true feelings show in such an overt way and that had taken guts. But he had to shut her down and risk upsetting her because it was the right thing to do.

Or was it?

– 10 –

ELISE RAISED HER PHONE. "I found the video Newt was talking about."

Haislee stood next to the bathroom door and looked a little flushed. Elise noticed right away.

"Haze? You okay?"

Haislee straightened herself up and ran her fingers through her blond hair. "Yeah, just felt a little crampy."

"Shit. Want something for it?"

Haislee shook her head. "I think I'm good for now."

"Okay." Elise led the way back to the kitchen. "You gotta watch this. It's sick." She laid her phone down on the counter and pressed play.

The Instagram video showed Dustin and Newton in front of Diamond Bay High School, with a bunch of onlookers surrounding them, one of them Richard. The sound quality was awful. They could barely make out the words but luckily their actions spoke louder.

Elise singled Richard out in the background. "There's Weak Dick." She had come up with Richard's nickname back before summer holidays began.

Haislee nodded and managed a small, forced smile. But Elise was too focused on her phone to see it this time.

The handheld video showed Dustin getting in Newton's face, Newton pushing back, then turning to enter the school.

"Wait." Haislee dragged her finger across the screen to scrub playback, then let the video play again. "Who's that? Looks like he's talking to her, too. Or about her."

"Dustbin?"

"Yeah. Who is that?"

Elise scrubbed back and pinch-zoomed the screen. "I don't know."

"Send it to me." Haislee scrutinized the video. "If he wasn't so cringey, he'd almost be fuckable."

"Who? Dustbin?" Elise's jaw dropped. "Bruh! You did *not* just say that."

Haislee shrugged. "On looks alone, maybe."

"No." Elise shook her head and placed her hands on Haislee's shoulders. "Just no."

"You're biased though. We got to keep our options open."

"Dustbin is *not* an option," Elise said. "Even if he was, which he *isn't,* I'd never be able to look at Newt again. Neither would you."

Haislee fell silent for a moment. "Lise, I think I better go."

"Cramps again?"

"Yeah." Haislee grabbed her backpack and her purse and headed for the front door. Elise followed her. "I'll see you tomorrow."

"Yeah," Elise said. "Who's Palmer gonna hit on first?"

"*Not* us." Haislee pulled Elise in for a hug. She cast her gaze to Newton's closed bedroom door on the second floor. "Love you," she said softly.

"Love you, too." Elise stepped back and pulled open the door. Haislee stepped out onto the porch, then to the driveway. She turned to wave and Elise waved back.

Elise returned to the kitchen and picked up her phone. She watched the video one more time, at Dustin, Newton, and the mystery girl in the background.

She could ask Newton who the girl was. He must know. This girl seemed to be part of whatever had been said this morning. But now was not the time.

Elise forwarded the video to Haislee's Instagram account. If anyone could figure out who that girl was, it'd be Haislee.

$$- \; 11 \; -$$

HAISLEE'S HOUSE WAS PART WAY down Tipperary Street, only two blocks away from Elise's. Without a back alley running between the row of yards, getting back and forth between houses took longer than it should.

When away from home or running an errand, her dad (and occasionally her grandfather) always joked that it was "a long way to Tipperary, to the sweetest girl I know." The song had been made famous by marching British soldiers in the First World War. She had always thought the song was silly and embarrassing (especially her dad's tone deaf rendition) until recently when she looked it up. Soldiers sang the song to help them remain connected to where their home and families waited for their return. Approaching her sixteenth birthday had given her a deeper understanding.

Always a latchkey kid, Haislee unlocked her front door, stepped inside, and locked it behind her. She immediately texted her family message group that she was home.

Her mom, Grace, sent back a thumbs up, then added, "Homework?"

Haislee texted back, "None. 1st day." But that wasn't entirely true. The little red notification above the Instagram app icon showed a "1." That meant homework of a different kind, the kind she liked best.

Haislee didn't refer to herself as a tech goddess, but lots of other people did. Elise was one of them, and it wasn't without merit. She knew her way around computers and smart phones. Her tech knowledge would make the members of the Audio/Visual squad at school get down on their knees and proclaim, "We're not worthy!" Everyone knew it was a joke, but really it wasn't. Haislee walked the walk.

As expected, the video she had watched at Elise's house was sitting waiting for her in her Instagram inbox. She clicked play and watched, but the audio from her iMac speakers sounded tinny. She grabbed her Sennheiser headphones, plugged them in and threw them over her ears. Her memory flashed back to her recent interaction with Newton, but she pushed forward, scrubbed the video back to the beginning and let it play.

After a couple of viewings, Haislee paused the video on a frame with the best view of the mystery girl. She captured the screen and called up Google Lens. After cropping the image to remove everything except the girl's face, she let Google Lens do its thing.

Dozens of images flashed up alongside the image. All were close, but none were an exact match.

Haislee returned her attention to the original video and looked at the comments. As she scrolled, she could see the scales tipped in Newton's favour. That didn't surprise her. Newton was a good guy. The comments didn't offer much else.

She returned to the video and played it again, this time keeping her eyes closed to help her focus on what she was hearing. Still, the ambient noise overpowered the dialogue between Newton and Dustin.

Haislee saved the video to her iMac, stripped off the audio into a separate file, and loaded it into Audacity, her favourite audio processing software. She tried using a collection of filters to remove the noise while leaving the conversation intact, but it didn't work at all. The audio frequencies of the conversation were too close to the ambient noise and the filters ended up removing everything. This wasn't a Hollywood movie where they had a magical enhance button.

As much as Haislee knew about software and technology, sometimes going old school was the best alternative. She dug into her bookcase, pulled out her Diamond Bay 2022 yearbook, and scrutinized the Grade 11 student pages one photo at a time.

The photos were small, about the size of a passport photo, twenty-five to a page. The detail in the face was scant but enough for identification. Newton's photo jumped out at her immediately.

She refreshed her memory on the girl's image, but page after page resulted in no match remotely similar.

The odds of finding a match dwindled page by page. Still, Haislee continued her search. She was nothing if not thorough. The notion that the girl might be new to the school this year was not lost on her, but she had to be sure.

Haislee flipped to the last page, and there, in the middle row, ironically under Dustin's photo, was the girl in the video.

Juniper Thomas.

Juniper had short purple hair in her yearbook photo, which contrasted with the long dark (Brown? Black?) hair in the video. The cropped and enlarged image from the video had pixelated the details.

Haislee searched Instagram and found Juniper's public profile. She scrolled through the images and found them typical of most teenage girls, including herself. Then she landed on one of her sitting and eating an ice cream cone in Baskin-Robbins. Haislee recognized the store's decor and the parking lot layout through the window behind Juniper.

"That's at Main Eats," Haislee whispered to herself, despite being in her room alone with the door closed.

That Instagram post had multiple photos. Haislee swiped

through them. Most were variations of the first, with Juniper laughing, having what looked like a good time. The last photo stole her breath like a sucker punch. She heard herself gasp.

There on the screen of her iMac was a selfie of Juniper and Newton, heads together, both smiling, both eating ice cream. Juniper wasn't looking at the camera, but at Newton.

Haislee knew what a look like that meant. Instead of the thrill of winning a hunt, instead of surprise, Haislee felt anger, jealousy, rage even, as she narrowed her eyes at Juniper's face.

Haislee's phone chimed. A text from Elise flashed on the screen.

"Hey grrrl! Who's the girl?" her text read. Haislee stared at Elise's text long enough for Elise to follow up. "Haze?"

Haislee tapped, "No idea. Must be new." Her thumb hovered over "Send" for a second before hitting the button. A *swoosh* and a "Delivered" notification confirmed it.

"Wanna hang out later?"

"Still crampy," Haislee texted.

"♥ Hugz. Call me 18r."

Haislee gave Elise's text a thumbs up and tossed her phone aside. She wasn't sure why she had lied to her best friend, except that there must be more to the story. She wanted answers.

$$- \ 12 \ -$$

TWO WEEKS LATER, the incident between Newton and Dustin had faded from the memory of most students at Diamond Bay. Haislee had bookmarked the video and rewatched it a few times since, trying to decipher what Newton and Dustin were talking about. The video itself was no longer an obsession. But there was something connecting Dustin, Juniper, and Newton, and her curiosity kept gnawing at her.

Haislee exchanged a few books at her locker and headed to her last class of the day, Math with Palmer. The best part of the class was sitting in the back with Elise and thinking of ways to raise shit without getting caught.

She spotted Juniper heading down the stairs toward an exit. Curiosity sprinkled with leftover jealousy convinced her to follow. She wouldn't miss much of Math class, and what she did miss she'd get from Elise. They covered for each other.

Juniper was already out of the school and halfway to Edgerton Street. Was she in a hurry or just a fast walker?

Haislee ran to catch up. "Hey."

Juniper turned to see this unfamiliar student jogging toward her.

"Are you Juniper?"

Unfamiliarity switched to caution. "Yeah." Juniper sharpened her glare. "Who are you?"

"I'm Haislee... Kirkland. I'm in Grade 10."

Juniper gave her the once-over, then turned to continue on her way.

"I... I'm friends with Elise," Haislee said. "Sister to Newton. Newton Coleman."

Juniper turned back. "What do you want?"

"I saw that video, from the first day of school," Haislee said. "You know the one?"

Juniper stepped closer. "What do you *want*?"

"I want to know what Dustin said that upset you."

"You don't ask for much, do you?"

"I know you and Newton are friends," Haislee said. "I thought maybe I could help."

"I don't need your help."

"But I—"

"Look..." Juniper trailed off as her eyes focused on the parking lot behind Haislee.

She turned to see what Juniper was looking at and saw Dustin leaning against his black Escalade in the student parking lot.

Juniper poked Haislee's shoulder to get her attention. "It's not safe. And stay away from *him*." Her eyes flicked at Dustin, then she continued toward Edgerton.

"Wait." Haislee took a step to follow, then stopped. She glanced over her shoulder to see Dustin lumbering toward her. She had heard enough about Dustin from Elise to know to steer clear of him. But Dustin intercepted her halfway to the school's entrance.

"Do I know you from somewhere?"

"You've probably seen me with Elise Coleman... I'm Haislee."

Dustin smiled warmly but the way his eyes floated over her cranked up his cringe factor.

Haislee narrowed her eyes at him. "You must know who I was talking to, right?"

Dustin nodded subtly. "Yeah. Juniper Thomas."

"How do you know her?"

Dustin shrugged. "I don't know. She was probably at one of my parties. They're legendary, you know."

"What were you and Newton taking about on the first day of school?"

"You really cut to the chase." Dustin laughed. "How the fuck should I know? That was weeks ago."

"Two weeks, to be precise," Haislee said.

"Whatever. I don't keep track of what I say." Dustin jammed his hands in his pockets and stepped closer, eyeing her again. "You should come to one of my parties. Bring Elise. I guarantee you'd have a fuckin' blast."

It was Haislee's turn to look him over, except she could never pull off the creep factor as well as Dustin. "I'll think about it." She took a step backward. "Got to get back to Math class."

"Palmer?"

"Yeah." Haislee grinned. "How'd you know?"

"He fills his classes with babes." Dustin grinned back. "Be careful during Trig, when he's talking about Pi and shit."

"Why?"

"If you don't pay attention, you might discover his hand down your pants, checkin' out your curves and angles." Dustin laughed.

Eww. Gross.

"Later, Haislee Kirkland," Dustin said.

Haislee pulled open one of the doors to the school and had stepped inside before realizing that Dustin knew her last name. That meant he knew who she was all along. Alarm bells should have gone off in her head but instead she felt excited. And her reason for talking to Juniper in the first place was quickly forgotten. Maybe the reason wasn't as important as she thought.

A senior knew who she was.

Maybe Haislee was too quick to judge Dustin. She didn't even know him. Barring what Elise had said about him, the guy seemed okay for the most part. She had a feeling a Dustin Stoaks party was in her future. If he was still friends with Newton, then she'd see Newton at those parties. And she'd be able to keep Juniper away from him. But how would she convince Elise to go with her?

– 13 –

THE DIAMOND BAY Grad Winter Formal took place on the last day of school before Christmas break, a Thursday. Being the middle of December, the temperatures hovered close to freezing and a couple of inches of snow had already fallen and stuck around.

The dance was just for the Grade 12 students, a "perk" for sticking it out so long in Hamilton's public school system.

Newton was going stag. He hadn't met anyone that had captivated him quite the way Juniper had, although he hadn't been looking either. Maybe he'd see her at the dance, but he didn't hold high hopes.

The previous week he had accompanied Teigan to Tip Top and bought his first suit. It hadn't needed any alterations. The salesperson had said that was rare, but Newton wasn't sure if that was the truth or a sales line. He decided it didn't matter. He had looked good in the angled full-length mirrors.

Now he stood in front of his bathroom mirror and adjusted his tie. He still looked good. "Gonna turn some heads tonight, motherfucker," Newton whispered to himself. He glanced at his phone. Time to go.

All week, Elise had tried hard to conceal her envy. She thought the dance should be for everyone. As she watched him come down the stairs, she was practically bursting.

Her mouth fell open. "Bruh!"

"What?" Newton examined himself, looking for something out of place.

"Nothing." Elise smirked at him. "Just total fire."

Newton smiled. "Thanks."

Haislee poked her head around the corner of the living room. She ran her eyes over his suit, then back to his eyes. "Yeah. A def rizzler."

Newton swallowed hard and returned a guarded grin. "It's just a suit."

"Whatever you say," Haislee said in a dreamy voice, fluttering her eyelashes. Elise noticed and gave her a playful slap. Haislee retreated back to the living room.

Newton slipped into his dress shoes and tied them.

"Mom! Dad! You're going to miss it." Elise called toward the kitchen.

Teigan and Mattix met Newton in the entranceway. They both smiled warmly at their firstborn.

Teigan teared up, as she had done at Tip Top, but it was more real now. "So handsome." She smiled and placed her hands together in front of her mouth as if she was praying.

Mattix stepped up to Newton, took him into his arms, and patted his back. "I'm proud to call you my son."

Teigan quickly swiped her tears away with her index fingers. "I need a picture."

Mattix turned on the entranceway light and Teigan framed Newton on her phone and snapped a picture. "So handsome," she said.

"Mom, stop." Newton glanced toward the living room and saw Haislee watching. He felt his cheeks warm.

"You sure you don't want a drive?"

"Yeah," Newton said. "It's not *that* cold. And the sidewalks were clear when I came home. Should be fine."

Teigan nodded and gave him a hug. "Be safe. Text us if you need anything."

Newton nodded. "I will." He pulled open the door and stepped onto the porch.

From inside, he heard Haislee's voice call out, "Don't do anything I would do!" Then giggles.

Mattix and Teigan stood in the doorway while Newton walked down the driveway to the sidewalk.

"Have fun!" Teigan called as they both waved. Newton waved back.

The cool December air invigorated him and he found himself mulling over the past four months of school. The fall semester would end in January and then it would be five more months until he could say goodbye to Diamond Bay High School forever.

His thoughts drifted to Dustin and Richard and how things had changed. He knew Dustin would be at the dance. His ego never missed an opportunity to be the center of attention. Richard would be close by.

Newton's mind wandered. A few years ago, Mattix showed him an old Looney Tunes cartoon that featured a bulldog named Spike and a Jack Russell terrier named Chester. The two dogs had a master-slave dynamic. Chester followed at the heels of Spike and agreed with anything Spike said. It was Spike's way or the highway. Two cartoon characters from the 1950s had perfectly captured the friendship (if you could call it that) between Dustin and Richard. Newton smiled at the simple yet accurate comparison. Richard would always side with Dustin and Newton believed that was the only reason Dustin kept him around.

Newton's plan to avoid Dustin as much as possible over the past four months had worked, and by association that meant he didn't see much of Richard either. They had shared the last class of the day, English, but even with one common class, Dustin kept his distance and his insults to himself.

It felt very out of character, considering Newton had hung out with Dustin and Richard all through Grade 11. Dustin's bravado had become commonplace and expected any time he was around.

Newton knew narcissists like Dustin didn't change their personality much, if ever. As the semester played out, the three of them circled each other like hesitant predators, wary of each other but unwilling to strike first.

Maybe it's okay to let my guard down a bit.

Newton could see the Christmas lights wound around the entrance pillars of the school, made to look like two glowing candy canes. There were a few students standing outside the entrance talking and passing around a vape stick. He nodded at the one smoking and the boy smirked and nodded back.

After heading inside, Newton heard laughter from outside. They could have been laughing at him, but he preferred not to know.

Newton presented his ticket and entered the gymnasium. The space had been effectively converted into a winter wonderland, with colourful Christmas lights, streamers, hanging glittering snowflakes, and a mirrorball hanging over the center of the floor.

Most people milled about on bleachers lining the edges of the basketball court dance floor. Welcoming music played, but the modern songs would soon take over. If the deejay took requests, Newton would be spending most of his time trying to get some 1980s representation.

Newton scanned the darkened gym, looking for familiar faces, specifically one face.

Juniper.

Even if he never got a chance to talk to her, seeing her would make his night. But so far, no such luck. He pulled out his phone and passed the time playing *Monopoly Go!*

The evening stretched out song by song, recognizable to everyone except for Newton. He saw no one he wanted to dance with, and no one asked him. He lost interest in reviving some '80s music and began wondering why he had come.

"What's up, bruh?"

Newton glanced back to the bleacher seat directly behind and saw Dustin smirking back at him. He could have chosen to sit almost anywhere else, but hadn't. As expected, Richard sat nearby.

Newton closed his eyes and shook his head slowly.

Dustin moved down a row and sat next to Newton. Richard followed.

"Still got a raging case of blue balls?" Dustin stared at him, waiting for a response.

Nice try, fucker.

Newton ignored him, stood, and stepped down toward the dance floor. Dustin wasn't going to ruin this for him, even though the evening had been a total bust.

Dustin cupped his hands around his mouth to amplify his voice. "Papa Smurf still got your tongue?"

Newton stopped, turned around, and climbed the bleacher steps until he stood facing Dustin. "We've managed to avoid each other so far this year. Let's keep it that way."

"Chill, bruh," Dustin said. "I come in peace. I swear."

Newton wasn't buying it. "Merry Christmas, Dustin." He took pleasure watching Dustin's smug smirk falter.

Newton looked at Richard. "Happy New Year." He resumed his descent toward the dance floor, a smile breaking on his face.

Despite not getting in the face of the deejay, one of Newton's favourite songs, "I Want To Know What Love Is" by Foreigner, rose up from the speakers. Everyone on the dance floor paired up to slow dance, not leaving any room for the "Holy Ghost" as Pops would have said.

As his classmates moved, between gaps in their slowly moving bodies, Newton spotted Juniper on the opposite side of the gym.

She wore a sleek, sleeveless dress with spaghetti straps, purple and flowing, and it sparkled with tiny sequins. He was convinced that she had smiled at him. He smiled back.

Newton pushed his way across the dance floor, in and around other dancing couples, until he stood where he thought he had seen her. But Juniper was nowhere in sight. He spun around, looking everywhere.

"Did you see her?" Newton asked the nearest couple. "Juniper?"

The couple shrugged and drifted away, swaying to the beat. Juniper had vanished as quickly as she had appeared, and Newton was beginning to think he had imagined the whole thing.

He had also been wrong. Seeing Juniper for the briefest of moments hadn't made his night like he thought it might. It was just the fucked up cherry on top of a fucked up year.

Newton navigated along the edge of the dance floor and found the exit. He had seen and heard enough. It was time to put this part of the school year to rest.

"Newton!" A voice called out.

Newton turned and saw Dustin and Richard on the bleachers watching him leave.

"Happy New Year," Dustin said, then raised his hand and made a "V" with his index and middle fingers. "Peace."

Newton said nothing. Part of him thought he was imagining Dustin's parting words too.

Am I that *desperate for friendship that I'm seeing things that aren't there?*

He headed into the hallway, out the front doors, and into the crisp December air. He felt more alive at that moment than he had during the previous three hours. He dismissed Dustin's farewell as disingenuous. It was safer that way.

It began to snow lightly during Newton's stroll home. He longed for his headphones to immerse himself in music that he actually cared about. Instead, he started to hum "I Want To Know What Love Is," adding the odd lyric to the still quiet of the night.

Later, he would dream of Juniper and her purple dress sprinkled with stars and wonder why she disliked him so much.

$$- 14 -$$

WORKING FROM HOME had its advantages: unlimited coffee, an
'80s playlist at full volume, working in your pajamas (or nothing
at all). And unfamiliar sounds amplify in an empty (or nearly
empty) house, which made teenage shenanigans difficult to pull
off.

Teigan's daily runs and the occasional trip to buy office supplies
or groceries provided ample opportunity for teenage make-out
sessions. She chose to believe nothing happened during those
absences (ignorance truly *was* bliss), but she'd be first to admit
to the brilliance of teenagers who wanted something, or to
experience something.

Teigan had just returned from her afternoon run. The roads
and sidewalks had still been reasonably clear and the temperature
hovered a few degrees above freezing. A light jacket over a T-shirt
and cold-weather leggings did the trick keeping her warm until
her circulation had picked up. Once the snow hit in January, she'd
have to revert to the local gym, not her first choice due to the
barbies and roid-heads.

She emptied the mailbox and stepped inside, her cheeks
glowing rosy in the warmth. Teigan kicked off her shoes. The
house sat silent as it usually did on a Friday afternoon. Elise was

still at Haislee's house and Newton was working, according to the location app on her phone. She wasn't looking forward to the new normal when her kids started dating. Her own teenage days held many fond memories, although her parents would probably disagree. Now with teenagers of her own, the tables had been flipped.

Part of her wanted to spy on her kids, beyond watching them on an app, and relive her own youth through them. She could do it, too. She had a finely honed ability for surveillance. But Newton and Elise deserved their own secrets, as long as those secrets didn't place them in harm's way. That boundary would remain uncrossed.

Mattix had taken the week off, so she expected to hear him puttering around the house working on something.

"Matt?" Teigan flipped through half a dozen letters, all bills or requests for donations. "Hon?"

The final letter in the stack was addressed to Newton in careful, bubbly handwriting. There was no return address, no stamp, and no other identifiable markings.

Teigan turned on the lights in the entranceway and held the letter up to their brightness. The paper inside was opaque and revealed no clues as to who it was from or what it said. She felt a brief pang of guilt for trying to look but dismissed it, thinking any parent would have done the same.

Mattix poked his head out from their bedroom upstairs. "Did you call me?"

Teigan was still scrutinizing the mystery letter. "Yeah."

"Sorry. Had headphones on," Mattix said. "What are you looking at?"

"It's a letter to Newton." Teigan set the envelope on the stairs so he'd see it when he got home. "Sender unknown."

Mattix descended the stairs. "You want to steam it open, don't you?"

Teigan shrugged and smirked. "Maybe. But no. I'd never do that."

"You would if you knew you could get away with it."

Teigan widened her eyes at him in surprise.

"What? I'd probably do it too." Mattix met her at the foot of the stairs and kissed her.

"Stop. I'm all sweaty."

Mattix smiled. "I like it when you're all sweaty." He took the rest of the mail from her and placed it on the top of the newel post. "Do you realize we have the house to ourselves?"

Teigan mirrored the glint in his eye. "But we've got your New Year's party tonight."

"Not for a few hours." Before Teigan could protest, Mattix pulled her into a fireman's lift and carried her up the stairs. "I must save you, m' lady."

Teigan squirmed and laughed on the way up. Near the top step, she managed to slide down facing him and secured her legs around Mattix's waist, her arms around his neck. He looked at her with that little devious smile she loved so much.

He entered their bedroom and they both crashed onto the bed kissing. They had their clothes off in what seemed like seconds.

Teigan and Mattix spent the next hour enjoying their own afternoon delight. Afterward, now *both* sweaty and satisfied, they showered together, then finished getting ready for their party.

"Sex is wasted on the young," Teigan said, her arms around his neck.

"Yeah, hundred percent." Mattix kissed her. "Although the kids would disagree."

Sounds of the front door opening and closing echoed from the entryway and up the stairs.

"Hello?" Newton called out.

Teigan stepped out of the bedroom in an elegant red off-the-shoulder cocktail dress. "Hi, honey."

"Whoa, Mom. You look great."

Teigan waved him off. "Your Dad and I have his work thing tonight."

"Oh yeah. Right. Happy New Year two days early."

Mattix followed Teigan down the stairs, dressed in a black tuxedo with a red bow tie that matched the colour of Teigan's dress. "What am I, chopped liver?"

Newton smiled as he untied his shoes and hung up his jacket. "Looking good too, Dad."

"Good shift?"

"Yeah. Guess so. Not too busy."

Teigan picked up the mystery letter and held it out to Newton. "This arrived for you today."

Newton took the envelope and flipped it around. Teigan was certain that she saw a spark of recognition when Newton looked at the handwriting on the front.

"Any idea who it's from?" Teigan asked.

"No." Newton climbed the stairs slowly, as if on autopilot, examining the letter in his hands. "When do you guys leave?"

"Soon," Teigan said. "I'll leave money for pizza."

"Okay. Thanks." Newton's voice floated down from the second floor. Then he entered his room, closing the door behind him.

Teigan wanted to know what was in that envelope as much as Newton did and she wanted to watch him open it. The pull inside her head to know what she couldn't see would always be there, a constant battle. But maintaining his trust and having him know that she respected his privacy mattered to her more.

Newton didn't mention a thing about the mystery letter all weekend, nor had his demeanour changed in any significant way.

By the time New Year's Day arrived the following Monday, Teigan had not forgotten the letter but deemed it unimportant. It had become a non-event. She hoped that the remaining school year would be a non-event too.

$$- \; 15 \; -$$

THE FIRST DAY BACK to school after Christmas break was much like the days before. Newton kept his head down, did his work, kept interactions to a minimum, and avoided Dustin as best he could. But even with four grades represented at Diamond Bay, it was still difficult to disappear. If someone wanted to find you, it didn't take long.

It was the last day of the fall semester. Newton had completed his final exams the previous week and the remaining few days were considered free classes, where students could catch up on overdue work if needed. Attendance was still mandatory.

His mom had been bugging him about researching universities and colleges, but that hardly seemed important now. It would all work out in the end. Newton spent his time browsing social media, listening to music, and playing *Monopoly Go!*, not necessarily in that order.

Next week meant new classes and maybe new friends, if he could stay away from Dustin and Richard, although that hadn't helped much for the first semester. Newton found it hard to engage with his classmates when the dastardly duo was nearby. Still, it was a new beginning and he wanted to stay positive.

Newton stood at his open locker and grabbed his jacket and backpack, preparing to go home.

"Hey *Newt*." Dustin's potent cologne, probably Chanel or Prada, invaded the immediate surroundings like an unstoppable virus. He had preceded his greeting with several quick raps on Newton's locker door, then opened it flat against the locker beside. Richard stood close by.

Newt. The short form of his name was reserved for friends and family only. Dustin and Richard were neither and he hated hearing it come out of their mouths.

"You're a hard guy to find," Dustin said.

Newton rolled his eyes and looked at him as if saying "Oh, really?"

"What's the *hot goss, Newt?*" Dustin flashed his brows and his perfect white teeth.

Newton took the high road and decided to remain civil. "I don't do *gossip*."

"Damn," Dustin said. "You have a good Christmas at least?"

Newton looked at him. "Why do you care?"

"I dunno. Just tryin' to be better."

What a load of bullshit. Newton slung his backpack over a shoulder. "The break was fine."

"*My* Christmas was fan-fuckin'-tastic, thanks for asking," Dustin said. "Spent it in Cabo, smashin' chicks every night. Even Rich got his dick wet."

Newton cast his eyes at Richard. "You went with him?"

Richard straightened up, puffed out his chest, and nodded. "It was tight."

"Hella tight." Dustin bumped fists with Richard. "So I was thinkin', Newt. It's a new semester, new beginnings. Let's bury the hatchet."

"Interesting choice of words," Newton said.

"You know what I mean." Dustin stepped closer. "Be my wingman."

Newton stared at Dustin with disbelief. His miasma of expensive cologne had permeated Newton's taste buds as well as his nostrils, almost choking off his words. "What?"

"You heard me."

"What about *him?*" Newton motioned at Richard.

"You can never have enough wingmen," Dustin said. "Am I right?" He sent a punch to Richard's shoulder.

Richard gave an affirming nod and rubbed his shoulder.

"I think I like flying solo." Newton paused, then said, "Thought you'd jump on that with one of your witty comebacks. Maybe you have changed."

Dustin shrugged and crossed his arms on his chest, a stupid grin on his face.

Newton shifted his eyes from one to the other, closed his locker, and locked it. He took a few steps toward Richard and leaned closer. "Keep being yourself. You know... bragging about *smashing chicks*. Because that's not creepy *at all*."

Richard's face flushed red and he looked away. Newton had successfully hit a nerve and headed for the exit.

"The offer remains open, *Newt,*" Dustin said. "See you next semester. Maybe we'll have some classes together."

Newton pictured Dustin's smug face smirking back at him. He raised his arm backward and flashed his middle finger.

Richard's ultimatum from back in September came rushing back, causing Newton to relive it as if it had just happened.

"Fucking hypocrite," he said to himself, teeth clenched in anger. He punched through the exit doors and into the cold air. It was snowing again, just as it had the previous week. Fat snowy flakes, the size of quarters, helped cool him down. Newton focused on next week, a new semester. Maybe he'd share a class with Juniper.

– 16 –

Luck was on Newton's side for once. Although he had taken several of the same subjects as Dustin and Richard, he wasn't in any of their classes during his final semester in public school. Avoidance of the two would be even easier. And the icing on the cake: Juniper was in his International Cinema elective.

Maybe there was a God – or something – looking out for him.

As the first few weeks of the semester advanced toward spring break, International Cinema became Newton's favourite class. He loved movies almost as much as he loved music from the '80s and had signed up for it last year on a whim. He learned about the history of not just Hollywood, but of the international films and directors that shaped the films of today. Plus, he got to see Juniper for an hour five days a week. Talking to her remained elusive except for the most basic of pleasantries.

The day before Valentine's Day, McMaster University had arranged an open house for the senior students from several high schools. Three standard school buses had been parked in front of Diamond Bay when Newton arrived that morning. Instead of attending first class, everyone piled into the waiting vehicles and were given buttons signifying what school they were from.

Twenty minutes later, the caravan parked next to a fleet of

other school buses and a mix of students made their way to the L. R. Wilson Lecture Hall. Concentric rows of seating, divided into three sections by two stepped aisles, expanded back from three massive video screens. The space reminded Newton of pictures he had seen of the United Nations Assembly Hall, except here it was modern white and blue.

Once settled, every seat was occupied with potential students. It was obvious where Dustin and Richard sat. His voice spewing off-colour jokes carried in the open area.

Sitting near the middle, Newton scanned the rest of the hall for Juniper. If she was here, she blended into the sea of faces. One tall boy with closely cropped hair sat on the aisle and gave him a wary look. Feeling self-conscious, Newton sunk back into his seat.

"Hey *Newt.*" Dustin whispered loud enough to be heard from where he sat with Richard, two rows behind.

Against his better judgment, Newton swiveled in his seat and looked back.

"How's that *McMasterbating* degree going?" He laughed and egged Richard and others to join in. "Have you passed the *blue ball* test yet?" Dustin roared. Some students from other high schools laughed, but most didn't. Newton faced front and let the jokes slide off, reassured that Dustin was in the minority.

Bury the hatchet, my ass.

Several presenters spent the next hour giving a brief and engaging overview of everything McMaster University had to offer. Even Dustin knew to keep his mouth shut.

The presenters followed up with an hour devoted to questions. Newton's mind buzzed with possibilities that he had not considered. Could a Bachelor of Fine Arts be in his future? He was already on the right path with his International Cinema class at Diamond Bay. Maybe his mom was right (of course she was). More research was needed.

The information session wrapped up and the students began

to file out of the lecture hall along the stepped aisles on both sides of the central seats.

Newton merged with the line of students ahead of him. Progress toward the exit was slow, but he was too busy thinking of the future to care.

A scuffle ahead of him took him by surprise and by the time Newton heard the words "back off, motherfucker," it was too late. Someone ahead had pushed someone else, forcing a student he didn't know to back into him. Newton lost his balance and stumbled backward over one row and landed hard, connecting with the arm rest of a swivel seat in the next row. He felt (and heard) something snap on the left side of his body.

The pain was electric white. Newton screamed as he hit the aisle steps and clutched his side.

"Oh shit," someone said, then laughter. Students towered around him, a sea of faces, mostly familiar, some in shadowed hoodies, most agape with concern. Richard and Dustin poked their heads in front of the taller students. Later, Newton thought Dustin had enjoyed seeing him in pain. His eyes had held a certain glee, but it was difficult to be positive looking back through the veil of Tylenol-3.

One of the presenters rushed forward and pushed students aside to provide Newton with ample space. They called 9-1-1 and diverted the rest of the exiting students around him.

Everyone takes breathing for granted until something impedes it in some way. Waiting for the ambulance, Newton took in rapid shallow breaths to minimize the pain radiating from the left side of his chest.

The presenter that had called 9-1-1, a middle-aged woman wearing glasses, jeans, a plain T-shirt, and a white relaxed blazer, scanned the remaining few exiting students. "Does anyone know this young man's name?"

She was met with either blank, gawking stares, or head shakes of "no."

She looked down at Newton. Her shoulder-length rusty hair spilled down around her face. "Hey there. I'm Kate. I'm going to hang out with you until the ambulance arrives. Is there anyone I can call?"

Newton tried to talk but it hurt too much.

"Sorry. Bad idea," Kate said. "Got a phone?"

Newton pointed to his right-hand pocket. Kate wasted no time carefully digging out his phone. She held it to his face to unlock it. She opened the contacts and showed them to him.

"Call Mom? Blink once for yes."

Newton blinked once and Kate dialed. Teigan picked up on the second ring and Kate informed her what had happened and that she had nothing to worry about.

Midway through the call, paramedics arrived. After assessing his condition, they carefully moved Newton to a spinal board and attached a pulse oximeter to his index finger. They placed ice packs along his left side and as a precaution fastened foam blocks on each side of his head. An oxygen mask was snugged up around his nose and mouth and they wrapped him with a blanket. Lifting from opposite ends, the paramedics carried him to the gurney they had parked at the door.

Kate finished her call and provided the paramedics with Newton's basic identification. As the paramedics rolled him out to the waiting ambulance, she tucked his phone into the blanket. "Newton, I let your mom know that you're in good hands. She'll meet you at the hospital." Kate paused. "I hope this isn't a black mark on McMaster. We hope to see you in the fall."

Newton blinked once but he didn't think it registered as a "yes." With his head immobilized, he couldn't see if Kate had responded or anything else around him except the chilly sky above. He wondered how many students had seen what happened and how many were from Diamond Bay.

There's probably a video on Insta already.

The ice packs had done wonders for reducing the severity of

his pain. Now that he was tucked in, secure, and en route to the hospital, Newton allowed himself to relax. He was pretty sure he wasn't bleeding, and he didn't sound like a deflating balloon with every breath. Whatever the official diagnosis, he'd be ready. It couldn't be that bad.

– 17 –

DURING THE DRIVE to the hospital, one paramedic remained in
the back, monitoring Newton's vital signs.

"Newton, how are you feeling?"

"Hurts," Newton said. "Ice helps."

"Good." The paramedic glanced at the portable patient
monitor. "You're going to be fine."

The overhead fluorescent lights in the ambulance treatment
bay flickered. Newton could hear the lights buzzing over the
ambulance's engine noise, the sirens, and the traffic outside.

"Do you know someone named... Stoaks?" The paramedic
held up a scrap of lined paper in front of Newton's face.

Scrawled in orange ballpoint were the words, "Stoaks did it."

Newton squinted at the paper, following the cursive orange
loops. "Uh, yeah," Newton said. "Goes to—" He winced as a
bolt of pain shot through his left side.

"Sorry. Don't talk." The paramedic noted an increase in
Newton's pulse. "Just listen. This might be useful, if you want to
press charges." The paramedic folded the small scrap a few times
and slipped it into his T-shirt.

Newton tried to work through his recent memories of the fall,
but the details were fuzzy and fading fast.

Someone saw *Dustin shoving people? But who?*

Teigan was waiting at the hospital as expected. The paramedics unloaded Newton and rolled him through the sliding double doors into the ER. Broken bones required immediate treatment. One paramedic tracked his vital signs on a portable monitor. The other informed the attending physician what had happened. After determining there had been no spinal injury and no evidence of flail chest, the paramedics removed the foam blocks and the oxygen mask from Newton's head and face. He was given two Tylenol-3 tablets and sent for X-rays.

Teigan and Newton found themselves back near the ER, waiting for results. She perched on the edge of his bed and took his hand. "I'm so glad you're going to be okay. What happened?"

Newton took a moment to think back, then shrugged. He spoke slowly and softly. "It was after the presentation. We were all leaving and someone ahead of me got pushed."

"Did you see who it was?"

Newton closed his eyes and pictured the crowd of Grade 12 students crowding around and looking down at him, Dustin and Richard included. Despite this memory, he still had no idea who the instigator was. The handwritten note suggested Dustin was involved, but he couldn't prove anything.

"I wasn't really paying attention," Newton continued. "Somebody bumped into someone else and they knocked me over into one of the seats. Like dominoes. And..." He motioned to the left side of his chest. "Hurts like a sonofabitch."

"I bet," Teigan said. "How was the presentation?"

"Actually super good." Newton's eyes lit up. "I always thought McMaster was a stuffy old university, but there's lots of cool stuff there. There's this program called iArts, integrated arts I think, where I could expand on my film class."

"Sounds interesting."

"I still have to do more research, though." Newton saw Teigan grinning at him and immediately knew what she was thinking.

"I know, I know." He chuckled briefly, then winced. "Jesus. Hurts to laugh."

"Sorry," Teigan said. "You can do anything you put your mind to, you know."

Newton nodded. "I know."

The attending physician exited from the ER and approached them.

"Newton Coleman, correct?"

"Yup," Newton said. "What's the damage?"

"You're lucky," the physician said. "Just a minor fracture to the sixth rib on your left side. There doesn't seem to be any other injury."

"What's next?" Teigan was all ears.

"Not much. With minor fractures to the rib cage, time and care is all that's needed. You'll be all healed in five or six weeks. Avoid overexerting yourself, but gentle stretching is recommended. Above all, listen to your body. Don't overdo it. Pain is a signal that there's something wrong."

"Do we need any special pain meds?" Teigan asked

"The worst of it is over. Tylenol or Advil, taken as directed, is fine to manage the pain," the physician said. "My advice: take it easy for a few days. Move slowly. Use a cold pack for fifteen minutes a few times a day. Oh, and try to avoid laughing, coughing, or sneezing. Other than that, you're golden."

"I can handle that," Newton said. "Thanks, Doc."

The physician nodded. "Take care."

"Let's find your clothes and get out of here." Teigan helped Newton off the bed and they sought out a nurse to assist them.

– 18 –

TEIGAN TRIED HER BEST to minimize the bumps and vibrations on the trip home, aware of every speed bump, stone, and crack in the road. But some of the icy ruts were unavoidable. She slowed whenever she saw them, but hit either a rock or some frozen buildup, shaking the Pathfinder.

She looked over at Newton and saw him wince, pulling in a short breath. "Sorry."

Newton shook his head. "It's okay. We'll be home soon enough."

"How're you doing, otherwise?"

"Alright, I guess," Newton said. "I think they gave me Tylenols with a little extra something. The pain isn't that bad, if I don't move too quickly."

"Probably Tylenol-3. They have some codeine in them to knock pain on its ass."

Newton looked at her, alarmed. "It's not addictive is it? Like oxy?"

"Codeine's a narcotic too and you could get addicted if you took enough," Teigan said. "But it's a lot weaker than oxy. One dose of codeine isn't going to do it."

Newton relaxed. "Good. The less drugs the better."

"Newt, there's nothing wrong with taking some Tylenol or

Advil when you need to. Less pain means less anxiety. You'll heal faster."

"I know, Mom."

"Don't get any ideas. You're going to take it easy," Teigan said. "Okay?"

"No ideas. Check. But that reminds me. Can you go by Baskin-Robbins? I have to change my hours."

"Can't you give them a call?"

"I'd prefer to talk to Barry in person," Newton said. "Makes a better impression."

Teigan agreed and adjusted her route home to include a stop at Main East Plaza. She pulled into a parking space close to the entry. Newton unfastened his seatbelt and pushed the passenger door open with his right foot.

"I could go get him." Teigan shot him a look of concern. "Save you the trip?"

"I'll be okay, Mom." Newton smiled through a flash of pain in his left side. "I'll go slow."

It was hard for Teigan to let him go unaided. She watched Newton move, one slow and careful step at a time, to the sidewalk, then to the door. She was positive that he was hurting, despite the Tylenol-3, but he disguised it well.

Once inside, Newton gave Barry a short wave. Barry Todd was the kind of business owner that liked to be involved in the store's operations a couple of days a week. He felt it wasn't right that his employees should have to run the business on top of their own assigned jobs.

Barry had been chatting with Tabitha, another employee a few years older than Newton, when he noticed Newton's gait was different.

"Newt, what's going on, buddy?" Barry stepped out from behind the freezer counter and closed the gap between them so Newton wouldn't have to.

Newton and Tabitha exchanged a wave. "Long story short, I fell and cracked a rib." He pointed at the left side of his body.

"Jeez-louise, that sucks," Barry said. "You're gonna take it easy, right?"

"That's what I wanted to talk to you about." Newton thought about sitting but the effects of the Tylenol-3 were waning. The pain had edged back into his ribs. "I definitely can't work until at least next Monday."

"Newt. Listen to me." Barry looked him square in the eye. "Take all the time you need. Your job will be here waiting. Okay?"

Newton nodded. "Thanks, Barry."

"No worries, eh?" Barry took his right arm and began to help him to the door, then stopped. "Hold on. I have something for you."

Barry jogged behind the freezers to the back office, returning moments later with something small and white in his hand.

"Found it on the floor this morning." Barry extended his hand. In it was a white envelope with Newton's name written on the front. "Maybe you got a secret admirer."

Newton took the envelope. After a quick glance at the handwriting on the front, he jammed it into his front pocket. "Maybe. Anything to make this day better."

Barry helped Newton back to the Pathfinder, even though Newton said he could do it himself. "Good employees deserve good treatment."

Teigan popped her head out from the driver's side. "Thanks, Barry."

"No worries, Mrs. Coleman." Barry waited until Newton had settled in the passenger seat, then closed the door. He twirled his finger until Newton rolled down the window. "Take care of yourself, Newt. And I want to hear *all* about your secret admirer later."

Newton nodded and gave Barry a thumbs-up as Teigan backed

out of the parking space. She merged back onto Main Road East and continued the rest of the way home.

"Tell me about this secret admirer." Teigan grinned and raised her brow in anticipation.

"Not much to tell." Newton kept his eyes on the road ahead. "When I was in the store, Barry told me someone called for me earlier, but they didn't say who they were and they didn't leave a message."

"Was it a *girl?*"

"Yeah." Newton flipped down the passenger visor and looked at himself in the small mirror. His attempt to hide his smile was not lost on Teigan.

"That's interesting. And something to look forward to."

Newton looked at her. "What do you mean?"

"For when you go back," Teigan said. "Maybe you'll be the one to answer the phone next time."

"Yeah, maybe."

Teigan turned off Radcliffe and into their driveway between two monolithic mounds of dirty snow. The city's plows had chosen to pile the snow of the surrounding block onto their driveway. Mattix had to clear the driveway after every snowfall.

"Looks like we beat everyone home," Teigan said. "Will you let me help you into the house?"

Newton smiled. "Yeah. Sure, Mom."

Once inside, Newton kicked off his shoes. "I'm going to my room for a while."

"Remember what the doctor said," Teigan said. "Try to stay upright."

"Got it, Mom." Newton climbed the stairs, one step at a time, using his right leg to do the work. Once in his bedroom, he piled a couple of his pillows against his headboard and managed to sit reclined against them. He sensed his pain level increasing, but now that he wasn't moving, everything felt tolerable, at least for a while.

He pulled the envelope out of his pocket. Newton flipped it around. This one was smaller than the first one that had come to the house. He held it to his nose and detected a faint trace of perfume or maybe soap.

Newton looked across his room to where he had hidden the first envelope. He wanted to open the one in his hand, but didn't want to move and hide it afterward.

In the end, curiosity won out. He slid his finger under the sealed flap and pulled out a single, purple sheet of paper, folded in half twice. After reading it, he placed everything back into his pocket. He'd hide it later.

$$- \; 19 \; -$$

NEWTON WAS BACK at school the following Monday. His left side still hurt, but with alternating doses of Tylenol and Advil, he was able to minimize the pain. On top of missing three days of school the previous week, he had also missed the Valentine's Dance.

He had kept up with his studies through Google Classroom, but the dance was a once a year event, and the last Valentine's Dance at high school. Newton liked to think he would have gone stag if he hadn't been injured, but reality set him straight. He had acquaintances but no friends. The dance would have been an exercise in frustration and disappointment. Unless Juniper had gone. That would have made up for everything, but now he'd never know.

I could ask around, see if she went.

Newton dismissed the thought. He trusted no one enough to ask. Anything that would make him seem like less of a creep was the better option.

He was sitting in his first class ready to tackle trigonometry when the P.A. speakers crackled to life. One of his fellow classmates, someone he didn't recognize, began reading a few school news items and a sports report. They tried their best to emulate an FM radio announcer and ended up sounding strained and weird. But the announcements concluded in a way Newton hadn't anticipated. Nor would he soon forget.

"And finally," the student's voice said. "We'd like to welcome Newton Coleman back after breaking a rib at McMaster University last week. We're glad you're okay."

Newton groaned and shielded his eyes. If he could have slid under his desk, he would have, but it hurt too much. Trig be damned. All eyes were on him now.

The teacher began clapping, which encouraged the rest of the class. Newton thought the attention was unwarranted. His rib was fractured, not broken. Fact checking the school announcements wasn't high on the list of priorities.

A blond girl next to him (Gabriella? Briella?) leaned across the aisle and whispered, "You're in The Bullet, too."

Every Monday of the week, the *Diamond Bay Bulletin* was printed and distributed to drop boxes scattered around the school. The kids called it "The Bullet" because the publication was efficient at killing your social standing. Except if you were a jock. Jocks were immune.

"What? Ugh." Newton sighed and offered a pained smile. "Thanks." He hid his eyes behind his hands.

"Must hurt, huh?" Gabriella gave him an expectant look.

Newton looked at her, nodded, and recovered his eyes. Now he'd have the equivalent of a giant social spotlight trained on him for the entire day.

But the day had a surprise in store for him. His other classmates didn't make fun of him or get in his face. Most wanted to wish him well and were glad he was okay.

At lunch, Newton grabbed a copy of "The Bullet" and found the news item on him. It was more of a footnote, a postage stamp-sized blurb on the corner of the back page under the headline "One Last Thing..."

The blurb read, "Our hearts go out to Newton Coleman, who broke a rib at the McMaster University open house last week.

Give him a hand if he needs it and don't make him laugh. Get well soon, buddy. The Spring Fling Dance is right around the corner. Hugz. *The Bulletin Crew.*"

Newton read the blurb again, then flipped back to the front to read the masthead. Juniper was listed as one of the "Bulletin Crew," responsible for writing and layout.

Maybe Juniper wrote that blurb.

The assumption brought a broad smile to his face and he slipped the thin publication into the pocket of his binder. Newton had his International Cinema class at the end of the day and he promised himself to ask.

That meant enduring Chemistry. The topic today covered molecular bonds and structure. Every time the teacher drew a molecule on the whiteboard, with lines signifying the bonds between elements, all Newton could think of was slow-moving clock hands.

He was first out the door at the bell. Struggling through his pain, he found his seat at the back of his film class. Newton eagerly watched for Juniper to arrive, but at the same time tried to look cool.

The pain in his side had begun to flare. Pulling his backpack to his lap, he retrieved his Tylenol and a bottle of water and swallowed a dose.

"Hi, Newton."

Newton looked up just as he was setting his backpack on the floor to see Juniper had taken her seat across the aisle from him.

"Sorry about your rib," she said.

"Thanks."

Juniper faced forward, waiting for class to begin.

Newton clenched his teeth and drew in a breath. He hated the awkward feeling of their chats now. He wanted the ease of summer back. But it was now or never. "Hey, did you write that thing in *The Bulletin?*"

Juniper looked at him and smiled, just a little. "It was a group effort."

But whose idea was it?

Who actually wrote it?

Who decided where it would go?

Are you going to the Spring Fling with anyone?

Newton decided to save his questions for a later opportunity. "Thanks again. Meant a lot."

"You're welcome." Juniper shifted her attention back to the front of the class.

Time flew in International Cinema. Teigan had always said to pay attention to courses that felt effortless; that was a good sign. The end-of-day bell rang, and the students packed up their books and shuffled out. Had Newton moved quicker, he may have had an opportunity to talk to Juniper more. But even though the Tylenol he had taken an hour ago had just kicked in, he still moved slowly. He didn't want any setbacks.

Newton stepped into the hallway and made his way to his locker. He exchanged a few items, rearranged the contents of his backpack, and locked his locker. He was heading for the main entrance when Juniper came bounding down the steps from the second floor and nearly bumped into him.

"Hey." Newton cast a glance back up the stairs. "You've got a locker upstairs? I thought all seniors got lockers on the first floor. You know, a perk of membership."

Juniper wore a backpack as well but held a few books in front of her chest like a shield. Her ponytail bobbed and swayed against her shoulders with each step.

"It's a long story," she said.

They continued down the hallway toward the main entrance.

"Hey, did you go to the thing at McMasters last week?"

"Yeah," Juniper said.

"I looked for you," Newton said. "I didn't see you."

"I was way at the back. I saw you."

Newton nodded. He thought about asking her if she had seen who had pushed him, then decided against it. "What'd you think?" He opened the main entrance doors and they stepped into the cool February air. Snow and ice crunched under their feet.

"It was great. I'm seriously considering their iArts program. They offer a lot of interesting stuff."

"Hey, me too." Newton looked at her and their eyes connected, much like they had last summer. "I had no idea McMaster was so cool."

As Newton and Juniper walked toward Edgerton Street, Dustin's black Escalade slid into view from the student parking lot. Dustin and Richard leaned against the front bumper talking.

Dustin waved. "Newt!"

Newton shifted his eyes only minutely, keeping his attention on Juniper. "Maybe we'd share some classes."

Juniper tightened her grip on her books. "Yeah, maybe. I got to go. See you tomorrow." She hustled toward the street.

Newton could have caught up to her if he had wanted to, but his rib threw up a cautionary flag. "See yah." He looked back at Dustin and Richard and decided that avoiding a direct attempt at contact might end up being worse than the contact itself.

He walked over to where they stood. "Hey," Newton said.

Dustin motioned at Newton's side. "How's your rib doing? Healing up?"

Newton shrugged. "Slowly."

"Must suck," Dustin said.

"Broken bones usually do. Plus I can't lie down or sleep. So yeah, it sucks." Newton glanced at Richard, who immediately looked away, then back at Dustin. "Did you see who pushed me last week?"

"Hey, want a lift home?" Dustin hooked his thumb toward Edgerton. "Me and Richard are going that way anyway."

Newton shook his head. "No. I'll manage."

"You sure?" Dustin scrutinized the icy sidewalk. "You wouldn't want to slip and hurt yourself more."

"I won't slip." Newton turned and followed the sidewalk to the street.

"Later, Newt," Dustin called out.

Newton did not wave or look back, but overheard subdued laughter. Without context, it was pointless to speculate on what was so funny, but his mind went there anyway and his thoughts began to taint the good day he had just experienced.

The Escalade's engine rumbled to life. Newton could hear the slow crunching sound as the tires rolled over the scattered patches of ice and snow in the parking lot.

The oversized SUV rolled beside Newton on Edgerton Street, matching his walking speed. The driver's side power window slid down.

Dustin hung his arm on the open window and leaned toward Newton on the sidewalk. "Last chance, *Newt*."

"No, I'm good." Newton focused on potential slippery spots ahead on the sidewalk.

"Are you?" Silence hung between them for several uncomfortable seconds. "Of course you are." The power window hummed closed and the Escalade pulled away, its exhaust following like a billowing storm cloud.

Newton swore he heard laughing again, but dismissed it. He focused on his brief interactions with Juniper, which had been a few positive steps forward in a sea of distance.

– 20 –

AFTER FOUR WEEKS, Newton's broken rib had almost completely healed. He was taking Tylenol and Advil sporadically, most days not at all, and sleeping lying down had become doable again. He could scoop ice cream, but he still hadn't gotten the go-ahead from his doctor for more vigorous activities. Spring Break would be here in a week, and after that, the Spring Fling dance. He felt confident that he'd be able to dance without pain.

Newton collected his binder and companion books and followed Juniper out of their International Film class. He had decided that morning to ask Juniper to the Spring Fling dance, but he hadn't found the nerve to follow through yet. Film class was the best place to ask her, but with the school day having just ended, his chances were dwindling by the second.

Newton quickened his pace so he could be walk beside her. "Hey."

Juniper offered a brief glance and a small smile. "Hey."

"Any plans tonight?"

Juniper shrugged and held her books close. "You know, homework. The usual."

Newton focused on her eyes and lashes until he had to look

away to make sure he didn't collide with another student. "What subjects?"

"I got to decide on an art project for my Capstone," Juniper said. "What's your Capstone about?"

"I haven't completely decided yet, but it's probably going to be about film and movies." Newton saw the main entrance quickly approaching. Now or never. "I've been thinking. Would you—"

Juniper passed the stairs leading up to the second floor. "Hold that thought. I got to get some things from my locker."

"I'll go with you."

Juniper shook her head. "It's okay. I'll just be a sec." She sprinted up the stairs, weaving around the crowd of students coming down.

Seconds turned into minutes. Newton checked his phone for any texts that could have explained Juniper's delay. There were no messages waiting for him.

After five minutes had passed, Newton decided to head to the second floor to look for her. But before his foot hit the first step, he heard a familiar voice call his name.

Newton turned to see Dustin and Richard strolling toward him. "Talk about bad timing," he said under his breath.

"Wassup, dawg?" Dustin raised his hand in preparation for a bro-hug, something Newton had no intention of reciprocating.

"Nothing," Newton said, although he really wanted to walk Juniper home.

"Me and Rich were heading to my place to play video games," Dustin said. "Wanna come?"

Richard rocked on his feet and smirked.

"Nah," Newton said. "I got Capstone homework."

Dustin waved him off. "Forget that bullshit Capstone. I'm going to say one thing, then I'll let it go. But you're going to go for it."

Newton dropped his backpack and waited.

Dustin drew out his hands like a magician performing a final reveal. "Forza Motorsport."

Last year, before Dustin forced himself between Newton and Richard, the three of them would have Forza racing contests. They could have played the game at Richard's or Newton's place too, but Dustin had a dedicated games room off his bedroom. The space had a massive widescreen television, surround sound, leather seating, and every accessory imaginable, including a racing simulator cockpit.

Newton hadn't seen a lot of Dustin and Richard since January, and especially now, not having common classes with them in the second semester. But driving games, especially Forza in the driving simulator, that was fucking fun. He made an exception.

"Okay, but I left something upstairs," Newton said. "Give me five."

Newton turned to head up the stairs and Haislee launched herself at him from the next step up. She hooked her arms around his neck and swung herself around. "Surprise!"

Newton stumbled backward. Had Dustin and Richard not been there to break Newton's fall, he may have injured himself again.

"What the hell, Haislee!" Newton was on the cusp between annoyed and angry.

Elise ran down the steps. "Hazy, stop!"

Newton placed his hands on Haislee's waist and moved her away, but not before she planted a kiss on him, half on his cheek, half on the corner of his mouth.

Haislee released her hands. "Just saying hi. I haven't seen you much lately."

"Um, hi," Newton said.

Elise joined Haislee at the bottom of the stairs. "Sorry," she said to Newton, then to Haislee, "Bruh, don't be gross."

"What?" Haislee grinned at Elise, then stole a look at Newton.

"He's my *brother,*" Elise said.

"But he's not *my* brother." Haislee sauntered by Newton, smiling and dragged her fingertips lightly across his chest as she went.

Elise caught up to Haislee and grabbed her arm, then looked back at Newton. She mouthed the word "sorry."

Newton smiled and shrugged back at Elise. He watched the two girls exit the school, Haislee throwing her head back and laughing.

Newton turned back to Dustin and Richard. They looked back at him, their mouths agape.

"Dawg," Dustin said. "That was almost better that Forza. That chick with your sister... Haislee? She's fuckin' hot. Am I right, Rich?"

Richard laughed. "Totally."

"In fact they're both—"

"Stop." Newton said. "Don't be pervs."

"Whaddaya mean?" Dustin laughed. "She was practically suckin' you off right in front of us."

Newton held Dustin's gaze with serious eyes and said nothing.

"But you got a point." Dustin's eyes wandered to the front entrance where the girls had left. "Don't mess with jailbait, eh?"

"I wouldn't know," Newton said. "Anyway, let me go grab that thing. I'll be back."

Dustin motioned to the front entrance. "Hurry up. We'll be outside in the Caddy but we're not gonna wait long."

Newton sprinted up the stairs to the second floor. He scanned the hallway, now mostly clear of students. He walked past rows of closed lockers and empty classrooms.

Now standing at the opposite end of the hallway, Newton looked back the way he had come. There was no sign of Juniper. The girl's washroom might have been a possibility, but he couldn't bring himself to step inside and check.

Newton still had few more days to ask Juniper to the dance.

He felt both relieved and angry with himself that he had missed this chance.

He sprinted back down the stairs and met Dustin and Richard, already in the Escalade with the motor running. Newton climbed into the back seat and fastened himself in.

Dustin backed out of the parking lot and eyed Newton in the rear view mirror. "Find what, or *who,* you were looking for?"

"Yeah," Newton lied.

Dustin gunned the engine and peeled out onto Edgerton Street. "I'd give anything to drive F1 for real."

Newton gripped the door handle with white knuckles. "I think there's a place east of here, maybe forty-five minutes away."

"Are you shittin' me?"

"No," Newton said. "I remember looking it up a while ago, around when you got your racing simulator, at a place called Laurel Lane Estates. I think."

"Newt for the win," Dustin nodded at him through the rear view mirror.

Richard selected a streaming radio station from the Escalade's console. "Dr. Feelgood" by Mötley Crüe blasted from the speakers.

"Shit, bruh." Dustin lowered the volume using the controls on the steering wheel. "The '80s called. They want their music back. Fuck." He punched in a favourite, "Top Rap Songs of 2024," and Eminem's "Houdini" replaced Mötley Crüe.

$$- \; 21 \; -$$

"I'LL JUST BE A SEC," Juniper had said. As she ran up the stairs to Diamond Bay's second floor, home to the freshmen and many of the Grade 9 and 10 classrooms, she wondered if Newton would be waiting for her when she returned. If she was reading his signals right, he would be. But Juniper had misinterpreted signals in the past.

For as long as she could remember, Juniper had had troubles interacting with other people her age, both girls and boys... especially boys. One short-lived boyfriend was all she had to show for the past four years at Diamond Bay. Her parents had told her that there was no need to rush things, that she'd probably find *her people* after high school. It was likely true, but it was also hard for a teenager to hear.

Juniper snaked around the students descending the stairs on their way out. She wanted to wish them all away, but the universe seemed to always know when she was in a hurry and threw obstacles in her way to slow her down.

Finally on the second floor, she proceeded toward her locker midway down the hall. The numbers of younger students Juniper needed to avoid dwindled the farther she walked.

Maybe Newton wouldn't wait for her. Maybe she was all wrong

about things. She'd never belong with people her own age. Juniper felt her heart begin to pound and knew an anxiety attack was imminent unless she could calm herself down. She stepped into the girl's bathroom and locked herself in a stall. Juniper took two breaths at a time, a large deep one followed by a short one, then exhaled through her nose. She kept her mind focused on the image of Newton downstairs, waiting for her. Once she was sure that her heart wasn't going to burst out of her chest, she stepped out of the stall, washed her hands (habit), and resumed her path to her locker.

Two girls, probably in Grade 9 or 10, walked past her going the opposite direction. Normally she avoided eye contact with people she didn't know, but one of the two girls looked familiar. They locked gaze. The other girl knew her, too.

Juniper reached her locker and glanced back at the two girls. The one she had recognized was leaning into the ear of the other, whispering something. They both laughed as they headed toward the stairs.

She exchanged a few books with the ones she was carrying and closed her locker. Juniper dug out her phone and tapped out a message to Newton. "On my way. Hope you're still there."

Juniper's thumb hovered over the "Send" button, then reconsidered and backspaced over the message. "Too desperate," she said to herself as she pocketed her phone.

She headed for the stairs and pictured Newton waiting for her. As Juniper stepped off the top stair, she heard laughing echo back up the stairwell.

Great. More people I'm going to have to avoid.

She rounded the mid-floor landing and spotted a girl with her arms around Newton's neck, the girl she had just recognized. And she was kissing him. And behind them stood Dustin.

As if it was second nature, Juniper stepped back and out of sight. She felt her heart begin to race again as questions flooded her mind.

Do I walk down now? What do I say?

Who is that girl? Does Newton have a girlfriend?

Why did Newton talk to me, then? Is he playing me?

Is Newton friends *with Dustin now?*

Juniper's beating heart overrode any rational thought. She bolted back up the stairs and down the hall to the staircase at the opposite end. She flew down them two steps at a time and exited onto the field by the school.

She ran as fast and as far as she could until her lungs burned for relief, trying her best to avoid the remnants of snow and ice, before dropping her books and sitting down on the curb of the sidewalk. She hung her head between her knees and cried.

"It's not fair." A tear rolled off her nose and disappeared into the grass. "It's not supposed to be like this." Juniper looked back at the school, balled her hands into fists, and narrowed her eyes as anger simmered behind them. "It's *not* supposed to be like this."

$$- \ 22 \ -$$

Ten minutes later, Dustin pulled into a circular driveway in Rockwood West. An ornate concrete fountain stood in the center. Newton always wondered why three people would need such a massive house to live in. But questioning the motives of the rich was often a waste of time.

Dustin parked under the porte cochère, then ran up the stone steps and unlocked the large oak front doors. "You know the drill. I gotta restock, so I'll meet you up there."

Newton followed Richard through an open gathering area and up a grand staircase. "Restock?"

"He's got a fridge and pantry up there, remember?" Richard kept his eyes forward, minimizing their engagement. "That way, he doesn't have to leave if he doesn't want to."

Newton scrunched his brows in thought. "That sounds sad, doesn't it?"

"Sounds *awesome*."

In Dustin's bedroom on the second floor, Richard approached a full-length mirror between the bed and wardrobe. Using a hidden handle, he slid the mirrored pocket door open. Including the games room, the square footage would easily eclipse Newton's house, probably Richard's too.

"I never get tired of this place." Richard grinned as he walked into the ensuite games room and flicked some wall switches. Mood lighting faded up, highlighting multiple console games, a computer with three monitors, limited-edition signed game posters, and a simple bar kitchen. Surround-sound speakers were expertly positioned around the tops of the walls.

The racing simulator was clearly the focal point of the room and faced a 200-inch flat screen television that covered one entire wall of the room. Two leather couches flanked the simulator.

Dustin entered the room with a couple of paper bags full of snacks and two six-packs of beer. He pulled off three cans, then threw the rest in the fridge. In a bowl already waiting on the bar countertop, he emptied an entire family-sized bag of chips.

"If you're gonna use the simulator, wash your hands first," he said. "Or I'll fuckin' *kill* ya." He tossed a beer to Richard and Newton, and opened his own, slurping off the fizz. "Drink up, boys."

"Is the TV new?" Newton asked.

"Couple months old," Dustin said. "Great for games, but holy fuck, you haven't seen porn until you've seen it in Ultra HD."

"Amazing tech in the hands of an idiot," Newton whispered to himself.

Richard popped the seal on his beer, took a drink, then belched. "Nice."

Newton studied the can. A rainbow-coloured alligator breaking a chain with its toothy jaws stared back at him. "DECEPTIVE CREATURE IPA" in all caps wrapped around the top of the can in a bold, modern font. Newton cracked the beer and swigged a mouthful.

"Not bad at all," Newton said.

Dustin shotgunned the rest of his beer while Forza Motorsport loaded. "Time to fuck shit up." He took his seat in the simulator and began driving. Newton sat in one of the leather couches and Richard in the other.

Even though Newton was excited to be playing Forza, he still felt a little isolated in the group, like he really didn't belong. It was difficult to relax. He hoped the beer would help with that as he felt its far-reaching warmth spreading.

It didn't take Dustin long to total his 1993 Jaguar XJ220. He offered the cockpit to Richard and went to the fridge to get another beer.

Richard set his beer down on the small coffee table in front of the couch, took the controls of the simulator, and started his race.

"So *Newt...*" Dustin opened his second beer and planted himself on the couch beside Newton. "About this Haislee."

"What about her?" Newton kept his eyes on the screen. Watching Forza was almost as good as playing it.

"Got any *hot goss* on her?" He flashed his eyebrows. "Emphasis on the *hot.*"

"No," Newton said.

"Jesus. Your sister hangs with her. You musta heard or seen *something.*" Dustin drank.

Newton shook his head. "Even if I did know something, I'd never betray my sister's confidence."

Dustin groaned. "Bruh! *Buzzkill.*" He popped the Forza disc out of the player.

"Hey!" Richard glared at Dustin in protest. "I was going to get a world record."

"Change of plans." Dustin inserted a different game disc. The logo for Grand Theft Auto 5 faded up on the screen. "Let's fuck some whores."

Dustin's affinity for the sex workers in Grand Theft Auto 5 was a well known fact to both Newton and Richard. Some might even say Dustin was obsessed.

For Newton, his interest in any aspect of the game had faded long ago, and he wanted no part of it now. "Guys, thanks for the invite, but I got to split." He set down his beer and stood.

"Come on," Dustin said, his words a little slurred. "Let Lola bust your nuts."

"I prefer the real thing," Newton said.

Dustin looked Newton over. "You gonna have to walk, 'cause I can't drive you now."

"No problem." Newton headed for the door. "Later."

"Remember! Stay away from that bitch Haislee," Dustin called back. "She's *jailbait*."

Newton was already out of Dustin's room and headed for the grand staircase, when he stopped, his mind working scenarios in his head.

Coming here had been a mistake, but would he reopen old wounds if he left? Newton surprised himself when he discovered that he didn't care. Dustin and Richard were not friends anymore but acquaintances. Officially. And with that realization came a soaring sense of freedom. He had taken the first step in finding better friends.

$$- \ 23 \ -$$

NEWTON SPENT SPRING BREAK working at Baskin-Robbins. He had secured a shift almost every day, mostly to cover for the employees taking holidays, but he also wanted to make up for lost time. His cracked rib had set back his budget. It had set back a lot of things.

He had hoped that Juniper would visit the store during the break. It was so much easier to talk to her without the distractions of school. She added colour to his life and he missed it. But she never appeared.

Early in the first week back to school, decorations and posters for the Spring Fling began appearing on the hallway walls and windows.

By the end of the first week back, he still hadn't asked Juniper to the Spring Fling. She had been acting aloof in International Cinema, even sitting in a seat closer to the door so that she could make a quick escape at the end of class.

Friday arrived. With the dance that the evening, Newton decided to take a page from Juniper's playbook. He sat in the front row of film class, next to the door, ready for a quick escape. If he was fast, he could get his things at his locker and be ready to ask her as she passed by. What he hadn't anticipated was an interruption by Dumb and Dumber.

The bell rang and Newton was off like a shot. He made a beeline to his locker, exchanged what he needed for the weekend, and grabbed his coat. He was watching the door to the International Cinema classroom, craning his neck around moving heads and bodies, waiting for Juniper to emerge.

Dustin punched the top of Newton's locker door with his fist. "How's it hanging, *Newt?*" Richard stood behind with his hands jammed in his pockets.

Newton didn't answer immediately, instead choosing to keep his eyes on the exodus of students.

Dustin smirked at him. "You going to the dance?"

"Uh, what?" Newton gave Dustin a second of his attention. "I'm kinda busy."

"Tonight. You going?"

Newton kept his eyes on the hallway. "Yeah."

"Got a *hot* date?" Dustin flashed his brows. Newton barely registered the gesture. "Jackass isn't even paying *attention,*" Dustin said, his aggravation building.

Newton spotted Juniper, walking in his direction, holding her books close to her chest like she always did. Their eyes connected, then she shifted her gaze ever so slightly to Dustin. She refocused on the stairs ahead and increased her pace.

Newton ran after her. "Juniper."

She kept walking.

"Juniper, wait." Newton reached out and touched her shoulder lightly. "Please."

Juniper faced him, blankly. "What do you want?"

"I just..." Newton couldn't read her face like he was used to. It was like she was looking at nothing. There was no excitement or happiness. The sparkle in her eyes had dulled. If he asked her to the dance now, he felt as if he'd lose her forever. He couldn't risk it. Instead, the truth bubbled out.

"I miss you," Newton said.

Juniper's eyes widened just slightly and just for a moment. His words had surprised her.

"Maybe I'll see you tonight?" Newton managed a small smile. He thought he detected something change in her face, but whatever it was faded just as quickly as it had appeared.

Juniper said nothing as she turned and headed up the stairs. Newton briefly considered going after her but decided he had done his best. The ball was in her court.

As Newton walked back to his locker, Dustin was laughing and slow-clapping. Richard snickered next to him.

"Epic crash and burn," Dustin said. "No loss, though. I hear she's a slut."

Before Newton realized what he was doing, he had Dustin's shirt collar gripped in one fist, his forearm across his chest, forcing him against the lockers. "What'd you just say?"

Surprised, Dustin pushed back. "Get the fuck *off* me."

Newton let him go and grabbed his backpack. "She's not like that."

"Word on the street says she is." Dustin looked Newton over. "Guess your microscopic dick ain't up to her standards." He nudged Richard and they both started laughing.

Newton slammed his locker door closed and locked it. "You guys enjoy memorizing *dick sizes*? Now *that* is some *hot goss*." He hoisted his backpack over one shoulder and headed for the main entrance without even a glance backward. The lack of snickering as he left was music to his ears.

The real fallout of the afternoon hit Newton as he walked home. There was no one else he wanted to ask to the dance. Even if there was, it was too late. It looked like he'd be going stag. Again.

He clung to the hope that he'd see Juniper there, but he also knew not to put too much weight in it. That thread could break at any moment.

– 24 –

GOING TO THE DANCE without a date wasn't the worst thing in the world. Elise was going with Haislee, which according to her wasn't considered a real date. But she had picked out a great dress with Teigan during Spring Break: dark blue and sleek, it hung around her neck and left her shoulders and back exposed. It was almost as good as the dress Juniper had worn to the Winter Formal. *That* image Newton would never forget. He looked forward to seeing it again... if the Universe was on his side.

Newton, on the other hand, decided not to wear his new suit. He picked out something more casual, dark dress pants with a sky-blue button-up shirt and a matching dark tie. He wore his everyday shoes because dancing in dress shoes gave him blisters.

After a quick and easy dinner of homemade macaroni and cheese, Teigan insisted on driving both Elise and Newton. She picked up Haislee on the way, her outfit hidden under her coat.

The two girls giggled and whispered in the back seat as they fiddled with their phones during the short trip to the school.

Teigan glanced at Newton as she turned onto a side street. "You've been quiet tonight."

Newton shrugged. "Not much to say. Don't want to get my hopes up."

"Hopes up for what?"

Newton sighed. "Nothing." He watched the streetlights pass by the window.

Teigan knew not to pry. If it was important enough, Newton would share when he was ready. "Well, you look very nice," she said, smiling. "You never know what, or who, the future holds."

"Thanks, Mom."

Teigan turned onto Edgerton. As expected, the school was busy with arriving vehicles, but a lane had been reserved for drop-offs. Teigan pulled up to the curb and Newton, Elise, and Haislee piled out.

Teigan leaned toward the open passenger door. "Have fun! Be smart. If you need a lift, I'm only a call away."

Elise and Haislee were already out of earshot, but Newton poked his head into the SUV. "Got it, Mom." He motioned to the girls walking to the entrance of Diamond Bay. "I'll make sure they know, too. Bye." Newton closed the door.

Teigan watched Newton jog up to the girls and escort them inside. "Now there's a real gentleman," she said to herself. The longing to relive her youth tugged at her. She pictured the gymnasium decked out with Spring decorations, fancy lights, and loud music.

It would be so easy to take a quick peek inside.

A honk from behind broke her reverie and Teigan pulled away, leaving the school receding in her rear view mirror. She felt proud of the young adults that her kids were becoming. But the feeling was bittersweet too. They'd soon leave home and form their own families. Time could be unkind.

Teigan turned into the driveway and shut off the engine. As she stepped out of the SUV, she realized that she and Mattix had the house to themselves. She switched her thoughts to how to busy themselves for a few hours.

$$-\ 25\ -$$

As soon as Newton, Elise, and Haislee entered the darkened gym, the girls split off into the crowd to find other friends to hang out with. Newton scanned the dance floor and bleachers for one familiar face but couldn't find her.

The whole Spring Fling environment reminded Newton of the Winter Formal, except green. Green decorations, green mini lights, and the same mirror ball with green spotlights on it, reflecting thousands of flying green diamonds everywhere. If he had to choose, the Winter Formal would win, hands down.

He nursed too many cups of watered down punch on the bleachers in hopes of spotting the elusive Juniper. But as he had expected, she was a no-show.

Surprisingly, Newton didn't see Dustin and Richard either. That, and the music, was the best part of the evening. By nine-thirty, he was ready to leave. Living close to the school meant that walking was always an option.

He pulled out his phone and saw that his battery was almost dead. Newton groaned and quickly texted Elise, "Going home. Phone dead. L8r." Moments after tapping "Send," the screen on his phone went black. He left the gym and headed outside, wondering why he even bothered coming in the first place. Deep down he had known Juniper wouldn't be there.

"S.S.D.D.," Newton said to himself.

Same shit. Different dance.

It was several degrees above freezing. The moon hadn't graced the night sky yet and the stars glittered above like silent observers in the vast darkness. Newton sighed, unable to shake his feeling of loneliness. His breath floated away in a cloud of condensation.

Halfway home, he heard a familiar voice call his name from behind.

"Newt!"

Haislee?

Then Newton heard the familiar grumble of large SUV. Specifically a *black* Escalade.

Then it couldn't be Haislee, could it?

His curiosity won out. Newton turned and was immediately blinded by the high beams of the Escalade. He shielded his face and could make out Haislee waving from the back passenger window, her phone in the other hand shooting video.

The Escalade rolled past and slowed. Dustin smirked at him and rolled down the driver's side window. Haislee paused to tap at the screen of her phone, then continued her excited waving.

"Hey, Newt." She gave him a shy smile.

"Hey, yourself." Newton shifted his gaze at Dustin. He could also see the shadow of Richard in the front passenger seat. "Where you taking her?"

"Huge afterparty at Pyckman." Dustin kept his eyes on the road ahead while he spoke.

"You should come," Haislee said.

Newton faced her. "Where's Elise?"

"She went home early." Haislee folded her arms on the open window and rested her chin. "Stomachache."

Newton considered texting Elise to confirm, then remembered his phone was dead.

"Come on, Newt." Haislee opened her eyes wide and fluttered her lashes at him. "It'll be fun."

"Yeah, make a fuckin' decision," Dustin said. "I can't sit here burning gas all night."

Newton had nothing to lose. Plus Haislee was a friendly face. He pulled open the passenger door. "Slide over." Haislee excitedly shifted her seat as Newton buckled himself in and closed the door.

"Newton Coleman is in *da house!*" Haislee leaned over and framed a selfie of herself and Newton.

Dustin powered up the windows. "Got to make a pit stop first." He accelerated down the street, then made a familiar turn. Newton knew exactly where Dustin was headed and it wasn't toward Pyckman Quarry.

Ten minutes later Dustin pulled into his long, circular driveway. The mansion loomed in the distance, accentuated by strategically positioned spotlights along the roofline. At night it looked like a Disneyland attraction.

Haislee's jaw dropped. "Holy shit. You live *here?*"

Dustin rolled the Escalade to a stop in front of the main entrance and grinned at her in the rear view mirror. "Yup. *And* I party here. You haven't lived until you've experienced a Dustin Stoaks party."

Newton looked out the window and rolled his eyes. Haislee looked up in awe at the multi-paned windows on the second floor.

"Why aren't we partying *here,* then?"

"The night's young, Haislee," Dustin said.

Haislee giggled. "My friends call me Hazy."

"Okay, *Hazy.*" Dustin motioned at Richard. "Let's go." He stepped out of the Escalade but poked his head back for a moment. "We'll be back in five. Don't go anywhere."

Dustin and Richard closed their doors and entered the mansion.

Haislee turned to Newton excitedly. "Have you been inside?"

"Yeah," Newton said. "But don't get too worked up. It's just a house with more stuff and space than three people would ever need."

"Speak for yourself." Haislee returned her gaze to the house and took another photo. "Dustin doesn't have a girlfriend, does he?"

Newton reached out and put his hand gently on Haislee's shoulder. "Be careful around him, Haislee." he said. "The only person he cares about is himself."

She shifted her gaze to Newton's hand. He withdrew it immediately like it had been burned. Haislee locked her eyes with his in the darkness of the SUV. "You had your chance."

"Come on," Newton said. "You know it's an age thing. Nothing personal."

Haislee studied him. "So if I was your age, would you be into me?"

Newton returned her stare. Thoughts of Juniper had him fighting for the right words. The sound of the front doors closing echoed in the courtyard and diverted both of their attention to Dustin and Richard. They carried a cooler between them and a loaded insulated duffel bag in each of their free hands.

"Thought so." Haislee spoke at the window. "Like I said, you had your chance."

"Don't say I didn't warn you," Newton said.

"I don't want to talk about this anymore." Haislee twisted in her seat to record video of the back cargo area. "Let's just party. You can do that, right?"

Newton nodded, but Haislee didn't notice. Her phone held all her focus.

Dustin opened the back hatch, then hopped into the driver's seat while Richard loaded the supplies. He made a point of sniffing the air. "Do I smell... *sex?*"

Haislee laughed. "Fuck, no."

Dustin glanced back at Newton and Haislee in the back seat and laughed. "Sweet burn." The SUV's engine roared to life.

Richard climbed into the passenger seat as Dustin revved the engine.

"Time to get wasted, bitches!" he said as he peeled out of the circular driveway.

– 26 –

BY THE TIME the Escalade arrived at Pyckman Quarry, the afterparty was in full swing. At first glance, it seemed like there were more teenagers in attendance here than at the dance. Maybe news of the party had spread through social media, like a mini *Project X*. Or maybe it was because the area was smaller, more densely populated. Newton didn't care. He looked forward to experiencing the group energy of young people who had zero fucks left to give.

The headlights of haphazardly parked vehicles exposed a shoulder-high chain-link fence, the only barrier between safe ground and a plunge to dark water below. One of the vehicles had music pumping from its speakers loud enough to cover the entire area.

Teenagers were everywhere, milling about, sitting or laying on the ground, on the hoods of cars, in truck beds making out, smoking weed and drinking. A fire burning from a steel drum sat in the center of it all like a bonfire fueling an ancient ritual.

Newton was positive he could have scored many different kinds of drugs if he set his mind to it, but none of that interested him.

Dustin found a spot to park. He popped the back hatch and

jumped out of the Escalade. He slid one of the insulated bags to the edge of the cargo space, unzipped it, and pulled out a six-pack of Coca Cola and a bottle of Bacardi. Haislee followed him with her phone's camera.

"Booze then beer, you're in the clear!" He cracked the seal on a Coke, took a long drink, then refilled it with rum. He handed the can to Haislee. "Ladies first."

Haislee gave Newton a quick glance before grabbing the can. She held the can in front of her for a selfie photo, then took a drink. "Woo-hoo!"

Dustin tossed Richard and Newton each a can of Coke, then took one for himself. Richard opened his, took a swig, and presented his can for refill. Newton did the same, even though his bladder was protesting due to the amount of punch he had drunk from the dance.

Dustin filled Richard's can and had barely begun pouring rum into Newton's can before it overflowed out the top. "Don't be a pussy. Make more room!"

"Make more room! Make more room!" Haislee cheered.

Newton dead-eyed him as he sipped the spilled rum off the top of the can and followed up with a long pull. He flashed a grin for Haislee's video as he held the can out for Dustin to top it up.

"Now you're talkin'," Dustin said. "We'll make a man outta you yet, *Newt*."

Dustin filled up both his can and Richard's before raising it above his head. "Here's to getting fucked up!"

Everyone cheered except Newton. Instead, he left to soak in the atmosphere and find a place to empty his bladder. He approached the chainlink fence and looked out into the darkness. He could almost make out the water below. Newton followed the fence until he was just out of reach of prying eyes and burning headlights. He set his Coke on the ground, unzipped, and relieved himself.

Newton closed his eyes and felt relaxation fill his body. Once finished, he kicked his can over and listened to it gurgle down toward the quarry water.

"The pause that refreshes," someone said behind him.

Newton had grown to love that voice, even though the secrets behind it had been crazy-making so far. He decided to play it cool and kept his eyes seeking the darkness of the quarry. "I was wondering if you'd show."

Juniper stepped up beside him at the fence and latched her fingers on the chainlink. She wore a long dark coat that hid the rest of her body. A small purse hung from her shoulder. "Wondering?"

Newton shrugged. "Hoping."

The two stood there without talking, just taking in the night and trying to ignore the mayhem of the afterparty and absorb it at the same time. It didn't hurt to have a friend nearby.

Newton turned to her, Juniper's face lit just enough by the dim ambient mixture of headlights and firelight. "Can I tell you something?"

"Sure," Juniper said.

"My dad has this saying," Newton said. "If you like someone and they like you back, you'll know. If they don't, you'll be confused."

Juniper's lips curled into a small smile. "Sounds like your dad is a smart guy."

"Yeah, he is. But my point is... you're confusing."

"I'm *complicated*," Juniper said. "I've got history and issues just like everyone else. They just get to me more often." She paused and looked down at her fidgeting hands. "I do like you. But you might want things to go faster than I'm comfortable with."

"I can take things slow." Newton looked to the stars. "I mean I'm graduating high school and I don't have a girlfriend. That's about as slow as you can get." He returned his gaze to her face.

"I guess you excited something in me. I liked it and wanted more. Does that make sense?"

Juniper nodded.

"So what do we do now?"

Juniper scrunched her shoulders as she thought. "Be friends that are more understanding of each other?"

"I can do that."

Juniper looked back at the afterparty and the parked vehicles. "And get better friends. Dustin, Richard, you're better than that."

Newton grinned. "I'm ahead of you on that one. They're just acquaintances now."

"Then get better acquaintances."

They both laughed. Juniper reached for Newton's left hand with her right. Newton looked at their hands, then back to Juniper.

"What does *that* mean?"

Juniper dug briefly into her purse and pulled out a long, cylindrical object, difficult to discern in the shadows.

"What's that?"

"So many questions." Juniper stepped closer.

"I'm just trying to understand what's going on," Newton said.

"Right." Juniper held up the object. "This is a tattoo marker. A *temporary* tattoo marker. I don't want to get you in shit with your parents."

She removed the cap, took Newton's hand in her left, then poised to write on the back of his left hand. Juniper looked up at him with wide eyes. "Trust me?"

"Yes."

"Don't worry. I'll be quick."

"Or take your time." Newton grinned at her. "I don't mind."

Juniper let her eyes drift over his face, then got to work. Three seconds later, she recapped the pen and returned it to her purse.

"Shit, when you said you'd be quick, you weren't lying." Newton looked at his left hand and saw a small heart shape written in purple ink, drawn with a single unbroken line, ending with a tail that resembled a "J." He recognized the symbol in an instant and it shook him to his core.

"So you'll know we're friends tomorrow," Juniper said, "if we, you know, pass out tonight or something." She rose up on her tiptoes and kissed him softly on the cheek.

"*That's* where you've been hidin'!" Dustin stepped out from behind a parked car and strutted toward the fence.

Juniper gave Dustin a look of angry annoyance, before forcing a smile at Newton. "Bye."

"Juniper, wait!" Newton was set to follow her but Dustin stopped him.

"What's the hurry?" Dustin glanced back in the direction Juniper had taken. "What you been doing out here, besides hitting on Beckys?"

Newton closed his eyes and took a breath to calm himself. "Just came out here to take a piss."

"Was she holding your dick?"

Newton ignored the question and looked out over the quarry.

"Well now that she's gone, we can kick this party up a notch." Dustin unzipped his fly and began to urinate.

Newton headed back toward the vehicles and firelight and passed Richard walking the opposite direction toward Dustin. "*Dick* can hold your dick," he called back.

"Bruh!" Dustin said. "Newt made a joke. Someone call the papers."

Richard unzipped as Dustin finishing up. "Hurry up. It's time to switch to beer."

Newton spotted Haislee leaning against the Escalade, shooting video reels and chatting to a guy who was standing very close to her. "You okay?" He motioned at the guy.

Haislee gave Newton a confused look and shoved her phone in his face. "You should be mingling!"

Newton thought about how long it would take to walk home from here. He pulled out his phone to calculate the distance and the dead battery icon stared back at him. He stepped up to the back of the Escalade and began rummaging in the back for beer.

"The *fuck* are you doing?" Dustin pushed Newton aside. "Do I go through *your* fridge without asking?"

"You don't go through my fridge *at all*," Newton whispered to himself, smiling.

"What was that?" Dustin scrutinized Newton as he pushed one insulated bag back and pulled the second bag forward, along side the cooler. "Didn't think so."

Richard returned and leaned against the SUV next to Dustin. Haislee, and the guy she was talking to, stood beside Richard. She aimed her phone at herself, then spun it around the crowd gathering around Dustin's Escalade.

"You all have a nice buzz goin' on, thanks to *me*," Dustin said. "Time to kick back with some beer." He unzipped the nearest insulated bag and pulled out two cans of DECEPTIVE CREATURE IPA. "Now *that's* what I'm talkin' about!"

Dustin tossed a can to Haislee and her new friend. She recorded a selfie video of them tapping cans and drinking. Dustin held out a can to Newton. "Come on, bruh. Take it. Consider it a peace offering."

Newton was fed up with Dustin. He couldn't hide it anymore and Dustin knew it. But the beer looked refreshing, more refreshing than an overly strong rum and Coke.

"Jesus, dude," Dustin said. "I don't got all night." He passed the can to Richard. "Hand deliver this to Mister Prima Donna."

Richard took the can, walked over to Newton, and presented the beer. Haislee followed the action on her phone.

Newton took it. "Do you do everything he says now?"

Richard returned a glower. "No. Of course not."

Dustin continued to throw beers out into the crowd, then took the last one for himself. "Here's to the start of a fucked up night!"

Everyone cracked the seal of their beers and tapped their cans.

Newton's can fizzed foam over the lid and he slurped it off. He pulled several swallows and sighed. The first beer always tasted the best. But he had to find some better people to drink with.

– 27 –

NEWTON HAD SPENT the past ten minutes looking for Juniper. Why would she draw on his hand if she wasn't going to stick around? There was still much to talk about. Important questions needed answers. Of course, he knew the answer: Dustin. For someone who claimed to be God's gift to women, Dustin sure knew how to repel them.

He stumbled past some partiers who were rapping badly (yelling) to "Shake That" by Eminem and planted himself against the front grill of a Jeep Cherokee. Newton squinted at the label of the beer in the firelight, the can more than three-quarters empty now, noting the alcohol content: 6.8%. It was a lot stronger than the beer he usually drank, and it had his head swimming already.

"What kind is that?" Seemingly out of nowhere, Juniper reached from behind Newton, grabbed the can, and examined it.

"Jesus, you must be m... magical." Newton was having difficulty finding the right words. "You just... disappear and reappear... like a ghost."

She leaned against the Jeep next to him. "Just avoiding Dustbin and his douche parade."

Newton laughed a bit too loud. "My sister calls him that. Dustbin."

"Yeah. It fits." Juniper sniffed the spout of the can, threw her head back, and emptied the contents of Newton's beer with a few large gulps.

"Hey, I was... drinking that!"

"You can finish mine." Juniper handed him a partially empty can of a different brand of beer.

Newton held the can up to his face and tried to focus. "This is only... five cer-pent." He turned to her, slack-eyed. "You ripped me off two... cer-pent."

"Don't think you needed that extra two *percent*." Juniper pushed herself off the Jeep's grill. "But I need another. Don't move. I'll be right back." She disappeared back into the crowd behind him.

Newton raised his can and let loose a burp that had snuck up on him. "Not gonna move." He took another ample pull, shrugged, and swallowed.

A Black girl in a red puffy jacket, with her hair hanging in tight box braids, sidled up beside him. She was smoking an overstuffed joint.

She nodded at the Cherokee's grill while moving to the beat of the music. "That chick your girl?"

Newton looked at her through heavy eyelids. "Just friends... at the mo."

"Mind if I hang?"

Newton raised his beer at her, as if to say, "cheers."

"I've got to tell you something," the girl said.

"Really?" Newton drank from his beer then looked at her dark skin awash in the flickering orange fire glow. "Do I know you?"

"Not yet." The girl grinned and took a drag from the joint, waited a moment, then exhaled slowly. "I've been checking you out for a while."

"Me?" Newton tapped his chest. Beer splashed out of the can and onto his coat. "Like, here?" He pointed ambiguously at the crowd of partygoers.

"Here. There."

"For a *while?*" Newton returned a boozy smirk.

The girl nodded. "You're Adam, right? You go to Diamond Bay?" She narrowed her eyes at him and looked him over. "Broke your rib?"

Newton laughed and finished his beer with a grimace, then threw the can into the fire. He had preferred the IPA that he had started with. "Close. I did break a rib, but my name's Newton."

"Aw, fuck. That's right." She shielded her eyes for a moment, embarrassed. "Spliff's buzzin' me. Newton, Newton, Newton…" She tapped her head with her finger, then inhaled.

"Two out of three ain't bad." Newton said. "Good song, too."

"What?" The girl frowned at him.

"Never mind." Nobody got his '80s music references. He leaned closer, somewhat involuntarily. "What's your name?"

"Semira." She held out the joint. "Wanna hit?"

The effects of the beer had hit their pinnacle. Normally Newton avoided marijuana, but he had been good for so long, one drag couldn't hurt. He had trouble focusing on the joint between her fingers and it took two attempts to grab it. He inhaled, his inexperience in full display, and immediately coughed the smoke back out.

Semira laughed and took the joint back. "Relax." She tapped his lips, and whispered, "Open up." Newton followed her instruction. Semira inhaled and brought her lips close to his. She exhaled as Newton inhaled, more smoke this time, and he managed to hold it for a bit longer before he coughed.

Newton waved his hands back and forth in surrender. "That's it. I can't—"

Semira planted her lips on his and kissed him hard, pushing him backward onto the hood of the Cherokee. Initially surprised, Newton eased into the kiss. When they both came up for air, he smiled at her.

"Wow. What kind of weed is *that?*"

"The *good* stuff." Semira locked onto his eyes with hers. "Wanna... go somewhere?"

Newton wasn't a complete moron, and he wasn't completely wasted either. He knew what Semira wanted, and part of him wanted it too. But he was having trouble thinking straight. "I, uh..." His eyes shifted past her face, past the steel drum with fire licking its sides. Juniper stood glowering at him, holding a beer in her hand. Her lips crept into a slow, vindictive smile. Then a crowd of partying teenagers swallowed her up again.

"Juniper? Wait!" Newton stood to give chase, then careened to one side, unable to maintain his balance. His surroundings blurred, and the music, the rap, the singing, and talking all melted together into a low hum.

His thoughts muddled. Had he even seen Juniper to begin with? Was it a figment of his overactive imagination?

"Newton?" Semira was shaking him.

Or was it someone else?

Newton's world turned as black as the water at the bottom of Pyckman Quarry.

– 28 –

SEMIRA CROUCHED NEXT to Newton and shook him, but he remained unconscious. She placed her ear next to his mouth, then sat up. "Help! This guy needs HELP!"

Dustin sat on the Escalade's back bumper, regaling Richard and a small group of devotees with stories of his sexual prowess. "What the fuck is goin' on?" Annoyed, he nodded at Richard. "Check it out."

Richard disappeared, then returned a moment later, his face flush with panic. "It's Newton. He's passed out."

Haislee overheard Richard and poked her head up from the back seat of the Escalade. She pushed off the guy she had been making out with and kicked open the door, her spiteful anger at Newton suddenly forgotten. She opened the camera app and began recording.

A crowd had surrounded Newton. Dustin pushed through and knelt. He grabbed the front of Newton's coat, pulled him up, and shook him.

"Come on, Newt." Dustin stared at Newton as if his touch held magic, but a flash of panic appeared on his face when Newton didn't respond. He shook him again, then began slapping Newton across the face. "Stop being a dick. Don't ruin this."

"What the fuck, bruh!" Semira pushed Dustin back.

"Back off, bitch." Dustin scowled at her and slapped Newton again. "We got to wake him up."

"By slapping him?" Semira pushed Dustin back, harder this time. He fell back onto his ass. "You're a fucking moron."

"Fine." Dustin stood. "You figure it out." He trudged back to the Escalade.

Richard stopped him. "What happened?"

"What do *you* think?"

Richard held Dustin's gaze.

"*WHAT?*" Dustin grabbed Richard's collar and pulled him nose-to-nose. "It's not *my* fault that he can't drink worth shit." Dustin closed the back hatch and opened the driver's side door.

Richard followed him. "Yeah, but—"

"You comin'? Or are you gonna stay with the rest of these *losers?*"

Richard hopped into the Escalade, closed the door, and buckled himself in.

The rise and fall of sirens cut through the night.

"COPS!" someone yelled.

"It's a raid!" another partier called out.

The afterparty devolved into chaos. Dustin and Richard were among the first to peel out of the parking area. Everyone else scattered, some into the surrounding foliage, others into the rides they came in. Minutes later, there was no one left at the quarry except Haislee and Newton.

She crouched, unzipped Newton's coat, and listened to his chest. "Help!" Haislee yelled into the emptiness, despite the approaching sirens. She had to do something. But what?

Recalling her basic first aid, she began alternating between chest compressions and mouth-to-mouth resuscitation. Haislee had fantasized countless times about how Newton's lips would feel on hers, but not like this.

Newton's body convulsed. Alarmed, Haislee sat back on her

heels as she watched vomit start to dribble from his mouth. Without thinking, she rolled him on his side, his mouth close to the ground, so he wouldn't choke.

What if he died, even though she had done everything she could to save him? She'd have been the *last* one to touch him. It'd be *her* fault. She'd be the prime suspect and it would *ruin* her life. She ran into the shadows, her jacket pulled over her head, just before the ambulance's headlights pinpointed where Newton lay.

"He'll be okay," Haislee repeated to herself as she ran through the darkened trees, pumping her legs as fast as they would go. "He's got to be okay."

$$- \ 29 \ -$$

It took Haislee almost an hour and a half to get home, alternating between running and walking. Her feet were screaming. She loved to dance and instead of heels, she had made the smart choice to wear flat shoes with ankle straps to the Spring Fling. They were black and classy.

"Sexy, too," she had thought when she had picked them out with her mother a couple of weeks before the dance.

If she had worn heels, she would have had to walk home, bare feet on cold pavement, and it would have taken twice as long. Her feet would have been a mess. Instead, the worst she'd face would be a couple of blisters on her heels.

She could see her house ahead, following the curve of Tipperary Street. The salvation of her bedroom lay behind one of the darkened windows on the second floor.

A flickering glow shone through the front bay window. It was almost midnight and her parents were still up. That would make her salvation trickier, but still doable. She ran up to the side of the bay window and peeked carefully through the bottom corner. For the briefest of moments, Haislee thought she'd catch her parents having sex on the couch.

Eww.

Or she could decide to not look. However, her current reality demanded she know who was up. She rose up on her toes and spied through the window.

Grace and Sam lay stretched out on the couch, their feet propped up on an ottoman and a big bowl of popcorn between them. On a side table was an open pizza box and two remaining beers from a six-pack. They had gone to Main Eats and picked it up. Her parents didn't believe in food delivery. They were weird that way.

Haislee let out a sigh of relief. She wouldn't have to bleach her eyes and memory, but she *had* to know what they were watching. She shifted her position and peeked the other direction.

She could only afford to watch for a few seconds. Otherwise, to the neighbors across the street, she'd look like a prowler. She probably already did. The only actor Haislee recognized was the hunkalicious Bradley Cooper.

Her feet cramped and she dropped to her heels again. Haislee skulked around the side of the house, through the side gate, to the back door. She dug out her key and let herself in. She could hear the muffled sounds of the movie in the front family room.

Haislee slipped off her shoes and tiptoed to the stairs. There would be a brief moment as she rounded the bottom of the stairs when she'd be in full view from the living room, but her parents would be facing the television.

I'll make it if I'm quiet.

She held her breath and took the first step, then the next. One by one Haislee ascended the stairs. Once her eyes passed the second floor landing, she could see her bedroom straight ahead. Almost home free.

Creeeak.

Haislee had been sneaking up and down these stairs for most of her teenage life. She had memorized the steps that made noise and devised a method of walking to avoid them. She imagined herself avoiding the Shai-Hulud in *Dune*. But this time, she forgot.

Maybe it was her physical exhaustion or the adrenaline from seeing Newton passed out. Whatever it was, the second step from the top released a single groaning creak that revealed her presence.

The television muted. "Haze?" Grace called from the family room. "Haislee, is that you?"

Haislee's brain refused to work, so she decided to go with the truth, God help her. She threw her shoes and purse at her bedroom door and tore off her jacket, leaving it in a heap just beyond the top of the stairs.

"Yeah?"

"I didn't know you were home." Grace appeared at the bottom of the stairs. "Anything wrong?"

Perhaps, the entire truth wasn't a good idea. Haislee improvised as she descended one slow step at a time. She rubbed her forehead for good measure.

"I got a stomachache at the dance and came home early. You guys weren't here, so I went to bed. I totally forgot to text the family chat." Haislee shrugged. "Sorry."

At the base of the stairs, Grace felt Haislee's head and neck, then looked her over. "Sweetie, you're all clammy. How are you feeling now?"

"Better," Haislee said. "I don't know what happened, but sleep helped."

"It always does." Grace looked back at Sam on the couch. He was passing time scrolling something on his phone. "Want to join us? There's popcorn and some pizza left."

Haislee relaxed, her salvation achieved. She raised a brow. "And there's beer, too..."

"Nope," Sam said without looking up from his phone. "That's not the beverage you're looking for."

Haislee made a line to the pizza and grabbed a slice. It was a deluxe vegetarian from Hawt House Pizza. She took a bite and nearly melted. It tasted so good. She devoured the slice and took another.

"Slow down, Mogwai," Sam said. "You know what happens when we feed you after midnight."

"Real funny, Dad." Haislee pointed at the paused image on the television. "Whatcha watching?"

"Licorice Pizza," Grace said.

"P. T. Anderson wrote and directed it," Sam added. "It's pretty good. Come. Sit."

"That's okay." Haislee walked toward the kitchen. "I'm going to go back to bed." She placed the slice of pizza on a plate and grabbed a Black Cherry and Vanilla sparkling water from the fridge.

As she climbed the stairs again, her mom called out, "Got a plate?"

"On it." Haislee smiled to herself, then whispered. "I'm so good."

"Night, sweetie."

"Night, Mom. Night, Dad," Haislee said. "Love you." She heard the movie start playing again.

"Love you too." Sam said.

Haislee set her food on her desk and collected her jacket, purse, and shoes. After almost ninety minutes of walking and running, her flat shoes had stood up pretty well.

She finished her pizza and lay back on her bed. Haislee could still see Newton's unresponsive face in her mind. She hoped he'd be okay. She had done what she could with the time she had, but part of her doubted her decision to leave.

She pulled out her phone, poised to text Elise back, then decided against it. She had felt sick, after all. Better to maintain that story. Haislee threw her phone onto her bedside table and rolled onto her side.

She closed her eyes, hoping that sleep would come and wash away everything bad that had happened tonight. But Haislee was a realist. She knew it was wishful thinking, never to come to light.

Her phone chirped. She wondered if it was Elise texting her.

Maybe it was bad news. She tried to ignore it but found herself wondering what the text said and who had sent it. There are few things with greater pull for a teenager than an unread text from someone.

The plan was to fall asleep and read the text in the morning but Haislee's best attempt to resist failed. Her phone made a pre-emptive strike and chirped to remind her that the text was waiting, demanding that it be read. Immediately. Then it chirped again. Someone had sent another text. Two texts a few minutes apart were waiting. It was something that Haislee could not ignore.

She rolled onto her back and grabbed her phone. As expected, two text notifications floated on the screen. She unlocked her phone and called up the messages app. The two texts were from a number she did not know.

The first text read, "Stoopid wh0re."

Followed by, "Delete the party videos NOW or I'll kill you."

Haislee copied the phone number into Google. The search revealed nothing. She hopped back to the messenger app.

"Who is this?" Haislee tapped out.

Whoever it was on the other end responded, "FAFO."

Fuck around, find out.

Haislee wasted no time. She knew that anything released to the Internet had a high likelihood of becoming permanent and irrevocable. She loaded Instagram and found the photos and videos that she had posted earlier. She called up the post submenu and her finger hovered over "Archive." That was the non-destructive option that would have hidden the post from the public. Instead, Haislee scrolled the menu all the way to the bottom and tapped the red trashcan icon, deleting the post from Instagram forever. It felt strange. She could count on one hand the number of times she had deleted her videos, and for the second time in one night, she had chosen self-preservation. She powered down her phone and slid it back onto the bedside table.

But the guilt of leaving Newton like she did began to slowly eat away at her. How would she tell Elise? Would she tell her at all? Haislee didn't know.

– 30 –

THE AMBULANCE ROLLED to a stop close to where Newton lay, with its headlights focused on his body. The driver gave her partner a concerned but knowing look. It was never a good sign when they rolled up on a deserted party scene, leaving the victim alone. Without the person who called in the incident, the paramedics had no idea what had happened, how long the victim had been unconscious, if they'd taken special medication, or worse.

Everyone, including the paramedics, knew Pyckman Quarry was a popular place to party. Despite that fact, Cherry Mills didn't see a lot of extreme drug or alcohol misfortune. But time remained the persistent enemy in an ambulance call. The paramedics leaped into action, not wanting this young person to become a sad statistic.

The driver ran to where Newton lay and dropped to her knees. "Hey, buddy. Hey. You awake?" She spotted the vomit and swept his mouth clear of remainders with a gloved finger. She clapped her hands in front of his face, but Newton remained unresponsive. She pulled out her penlight and checked his eyes. Pinpoint pupils stared back at her and his lips had a tinge of blue.

She pulled open his coat and applied a sternal rub in an

unsuccessful attempt to raise consciousness. The second paramedic joined her with the jump bag.

"How's he looking?" The second paramedic unzipped the jump bag and began preparing equipment.

The first paramedic pulled her stethoscope from her jacket pocket, inserted the eartips, and placed the bell on Newton's chest, stretching past the collar of his shirt to get contact with his skin. She listened carefully. "Not good. There's a weak pulse and his respiratory rate is tanking."

The second paramedic gave the surrounding area a cursory survey. Alcohol bottles and cans lay strewn about, but no drug paraphernalia. "Damn, he's like a black box." He pulled out a manual ventilator and handed a Narcan preloaded syringe to the first paramedic.

"Tell me about it." As she assembled the syringe, a silver Toyota Camry with a magnetic police cherry on top rolled next to the ambulance. Jackson Konishi, a Hamilton Police detective, stepped out and approached the medics but left them ample space to work.

Jackson dropped to a crouch position. "Whatcha got?"

"Probably accidental OD. On what, who knows. He was alone when we arrived."

The first paramedic tilted Newton's head back and inserted the Narcan atomizer into his nostrils, injecting the medicine one nostril at a time.

The first paramedic placed the ventilator over Newton's nose and mouth and began squeezing the pump. Within a minute, Newton began to stir.

"Easy now, buddy." The second paramedic locked his gaze with Newton's. "Everything's going to be okay. Just relax."

Back at the ambulance, Jackson helped the first paramedic carry out the stretcher and engage the wheels. "Jesus, that Narcan is magic."

"We're not out of the woods yet," the first paramedic said as they rolled the stretcher toward Newton. "We've got about thirty minutes before whatever he took overpowers him again. He might already have permanent brain damage. Hard to tell." They lowered the stretcher.

"Good news. Pulse and breathing are strong," the second paramedic said.

"Excellent. Let's get him loaded," the first paramedic said as she grabbed Newton's legs. The second hooked his hands under Newton's arms. "On three. One. Two..."

The paramedics hoisted Newton the short distance onto the stretcher, wrapped him in a blanket, and secured him with straps. They rolled him to the back of the ambulance and loaded him in. The second paramedic followed the stretcher in, maintaining a constant rhythm on the ventilator.

"I'll follow you," Jackson said.

The first paramedic nodded at him as she closed the back doors and climbed into the driver's seat.

Fifteen minutes later, the ambulance rolled into the Emergency entrance of Cherry Mills Medical Centre. Jackson met the paramedics at the door.

The second paramedic held out a small piece of paper as he continued to squeeze the ventilator. "You're going to want to see this," he said. "I found it in the treatment bay en route. Must've fallen from his jacket."

Jackson took the paper. "You sure it's from him?"

The second paramedic nodded. "We keep our rig clean."

"Rolling paper..." Jackson walked with the paramedics as they guided Newton into the hospital.

"Yeah, probably Zig Zag," the second paramedic said. "Keep it. I have a photo we can use to contact family."

"Thanks." Jackson scrutinized the paper. The handwritten words on it, scrawled in purple ink, read, "Newton Coleman, Radcliffe Cr."

Jackson tucked the paper into his jacket pocket and watched

the paramedics roll Newton into the ER. He had more questions, but it was time to let the medical professionals do their job.

$$- 31 -$$

Mattix turned into the parking lot of Cherry Mills Medical Centre and scanned the lot for an open space.

"Just go to the main entrance and let me out." Teigan had already unfastened her seat belt.

"I'm coming too," Elise said.

Mattix pulled into the main entrance off Victoria Avenue South. Teigan and Elise hopped out.

"I'll text you if we move from Emergency." Teigan shared a scared and concerned look with Mattix.

"Go," he said. "I'll find you."

Teigan and Elise ran into the Emergency entrance and approached the registration desk.

"We got a call that my son Newton Coleman had just been brought in," Teigan said. "They said it was a drug overdose, but that's impossible. He doesn't—"

"One moment, please." The nurse's finger flew across her computer keyboard behind the front desk. "Could you spell Newton's last name?"

"Jesus Christ, who misspells Coleman?" Impatience rose in Teigan's voice as she spelled her last name.

Elise touched Teigan's arm. "Mom, they're just doing their jobs."

Teigan swallowed hard and nodded, then wiped a tear away with a quick swipe of her hand. "Sorry, you're right."

"Any specific questions, you'll have to speak to the attending physician." The nurse handed some information to an ER volunteer, who disappeared through the double doors that led to the treatment area. "Please take a seat. A doctor will see you as soon as possible."

"I can't sit, dammit." Teigan paced back and forth.

"Mom." Elise broke through Teigan's distress for a moment and hugged her. "It's going to be alright."

Mattix entered the waiting room. "What's going on?"

"We're waiting to talk to a doctor," Teigan said. "But I want to see Newt now."

Mattix stepped in and took Teigan in his arms. His thoughts were going nowhere good and words eluded him.

A doctor stepped through the swinging double doors separating the treatment bays from those waiting for treatment. He looked at his clipboard. "Coleman?"

Teigan broke away from Mattix's embrace and all three crossed the small waiting area to meet the doctor. She read the name tag on his lapel: Dr. Marcus Gaffney.

Dr. Gaffney stood tall, broad, and confident, his Black skin and short natural hair bearing a stark contrast to the wash of fluorescent lights and white walls. He held out his hand and shared a firm handshake with all three.

"There's no easy way to say this," Dr. Gaffney said. "Your son Newton has suffered a drug overdose. Of what, we don't know yet. We've run a tox screen and should get results soon."

"Is he going to be... okay?" Teigan locked her eyes with Dr. Gaffney's.

"We've stabilized him, but whatever he took has caused him to slip into a coma."

"Oh God." Teigan's knees wobbled and Mattix caught her. Elise took a step backward to prevent her from falling.

"I won't sugar-coat this," Dr. Gaffney said. "Drug overdose is very serious. But he was brought to the ER within hours and that allowed us to get a jump on whatever was in his system."

Mattix shook his head in disbelief. "How does this happen? Our son doesn't do drugs. Or even alcohol for that matter."

"I'm not saying this is what happened in Newton's case, but sometimes it's just one bad decision, perhaps a tainted drug supply," Dr. Gaffney said. "Do you know where he was tonight?"

"There was a dance at his high school," Teigan said.

Dr. Gaffney jotted a note on Newton's chart. "Maybe there was an afterparty. That happens quite a lot."

Teigan and Mattix turned to Elise. "Do you know anything about an afterparty?" Teigan asked.

"No, Mom." Elise struggled to hold back tears. "I left when Haislee ditched me because of her stomachache."

"We're doing everything we can," Dr. Gaffney said. "We plan to move Newton to the ICU on two."

"Can we see him? Now?" Teigan wrung her hands.

Dr. Gaffney looked at the Coleman family crumbling in front of him. "I can take one person back for a few minutes."

Mattix spoke without hesitation. "Tee, you go."

Teigan looked at him with red-rimmed eyes, then at Elise.

"I agree with Dad," Elise said.

Teigan swallowed hard. "Okay." She took her husband's and her daughter's hand in hers and gave then a brief squeeze.

Dr. Gaffney led Teigan through the double doors, through the hustle and urgency of other nurses and doctors, to a curtained bay in the Acute ward of the Emergency Department. He pulled the curtain open and motioned inside.

"Just a few minutes."

Teigan stepped in and Dr. Gaffney closed the curtain behind her. Newton lay in bed, his hair tousled, his eyes closed, and his chest gently rising and falling. It was almost like how he looked on any given morning. Except here, modern medical equipment kept him alive.

He had been intubated to help him breathe and a ventilator maintained a constant supply of oxygen to his lungs. His pulse blipped on the vital sign monitor, repeatedly drawing out an electronic version of his lifeline.

All this equipment and expertise held Newton's life stable for now. But Teigan knew how precarious life could be. She also knew that it had taken time to get him to the hospital.

Would he be the same when he woke?

Would he wake up at all?

She stood next to the bed, picked up his right hand, and kissed it lightly. Newton's hand was warm and Teigan hoped that would never change.

"Why, Newt?" Impending tears burned against her eyelids. "You don't do that stuff. It makes no sense."

Dr. Gaffney pulled the curtain aside. "Mrs. Coleman. It's time. We need to move him to the ICU." He extended a gentle hand to escort her out, and presented a small package of tissues. "We are doing everything we possibly can to help Newton find his way out of this."

Teigan looked back as the curtain swung shut and saw a team of nurses prepping Newton for transportation. She used a tissue to wipe her eyes and nose. "He's a fighter."

"I'm sure he is." Dr. Gaffney pushed through the double doors into the waiting area. "Once he's settled, visiting hours are 9am to 8pm. Try and get some sleep."

Mattix and Elise were on their feet in an instant. He took Teigan's hand and squeezed it. "Any change?"

"He's headed up to the ICU now," Teigan said.

Dr. Gaffney nodded at the three of them, then returned to the busyness within the ER.

"When can we see him, Mom?"

"Tomorrow morning," Teigan said.

The three of them stepped into the chilly night air. The stars twinkled above. It was a night that Newton would have appreciated.

"I'll get the car." Mattix hustled past the hospital's main entrance and disappeared around a corner.

Elise hugged Teigan. "I'm scared, Mom."

"I know. Me too. But Newt will be fine."

"Promise?"

"I promise." After seeing Newton hooked up to all the life-supporting equipment, with wires and tubes running every which way, Teigan hoped the universe could honor that promise.

No one talked on the drive home. Slightly different versions of the same worried thoughts ran through each of their minds.

Mattix said nothing, instead focusing on the road.

Teigan turned to the side mirror. Elise sat in the shadows of the back seat, glued to her phone, her face lit up from doom-scrolling.

Probably Instagram, her go-to favourite.

At one point, raucous cheering rose up for a moment before she zeroed the volume.

"Sorry," Elise said without looking away. Her face held stony concern. Or was it anger?

Teigan adjusted the passenger visor mirror to get a better look at her. "Everything okay, Lise?"

"Uh, what?" Elise's eyes flicked up to connect with Teigan's for a moment before the magnetism of her phone pulled them back. "Oh. Yeah. Fine."

Teigan watched her for a moment longer before sinking back into her own thoughts. The questions and scenarios kept returning to why.

Why drugs, Newt?

It was only later when she realized that the better questions were *how?* and *who?*

– 32 –

THE MORNING COULDN'T COME soon enough. Mattix and Elise chose accompanying Teigan to the hospital over work and school. If there ever was a special circumstance, this was it.

The three of them arrived at the reception desk of the Intensive Care Unit at exactly 9 a.m. Teigan half expected a joke about punctuality to lighten the mood. Instead, the nurse at the desk asked them to sign in and quietly directed them to room 223.

"No food or drink, please," the nurse said. "And please be respectful of our other patients by keeping your voices down." The ICU door unlocked with a buzz.

The ICU followed a rectangular layout, with four connected corridors that surrounded work areas, offices, and a conference room, and rejoined at the reception desk. Twenty-eight patient rooms branched off the opposite side of the corridors, ensuring that they all shared at least one common wall.

Teigan was first to room 223. The door was mostly closed, allowing the casual passerby a sliver of a glimpse into the room. Beside the door, the observation window blinds were drawn. She pushed open the door in a wide, silent arc.

Newton lay in a bed centered against one wall, flanked by the ventilator and the vital signs monitor, and facing a work center and sink. A pulse oximeter surrounded his right index finger like a snake beginning the process of consuming its prey whole. A blood pressure cuff encircled his left bicep.

Beyond the bed, a row of chairs sat in front of a large exterior window. A private bathroom opened from the corner of the room, between the exterior window and the work center.

Mattix placed his hand gently on Teigan's and Elise's shoulders as they entered. The sounds Teigan had heard in the ER from the monitor and the ventilator seemed amplified in the smaller room.

An IV stand held a bag of clear fluids, connected to Newton's arm by a long tube. An additional tube with a stopper connected to one end snaked its way around his head, left ear, and disappeared into one nostril, affixed with tape. Another tube emerged from under the sheets and terminated at the top of a bag hanging from the end of the bed. It contained yellow fluid.

They walked around the bed to the row of chairs, but sitting was the last thing on their minds. Teigan approached the side of the bed and took Newton's left hand. It was warm but lifeless, just as it had been in the ER. She kissed it and squeezed it gently. As she expected, there was no response.

Mattix glanced at Newton's vital signs on the monitor's screen. Everything appeared steady and normal, and the complete opposite to how his son looked, in the starkly white bed.

Elise struggled to hold back tears and grabbed Mattix's hand. He wrapped his arms around her.

"This is bad," Elise said. "Like, *really* bad."

"I know." Mattix fought back tears of his own. "But we're going to get through this. Newt's strong." He pulled back, held Elise's shoulders, and locked his gaze with hers. "We need to be strong too. Can you do that?"

Elise nodded and wiped her eyes. Mattix placed his arms over Teigan's and Elise's shoulders and pulled them together. Seconds drifted into minutes as they stood by Newton's bedside, each of them lost in their own thoughts, perhaps of prayer, of hope, or of worry.

Elise's phone vibrated in her pocket. She pulled it out, unlocked it, and immediately began typing.

Teigan looked over at her. "Do you need to do that now?"

Mattix nudged Teigan and gave her a short, subtle shake of his head. His look said, "leave it for now."

"Sorry." The tear tracks on Elise's face were still fresh. "I got to deal with this."

Teigan sighed and backed down. Elise stepped out into the corridor and almost collided with a doctor coming in. She stepped aside to let the doctor pass by, then leaned herself against the doorframe. She felt her phone buzz in her hand again and she looked at the screen, poised to reply.

"Where R U?" Haislee had texted moments earlier.

"Y do U care?" Elise had replied before heading into the corridor.

"Come on. U know I care."

"At hospital," Elise tapped back.

The icon that indicated Haislee was replying, the annoying thought balloon with three dots, appeared for a moment, then disappeared. Elise couldn't wait for a response.

"Where the FUCK were U last nite?" Elise texted.

No response.

"Newt OD'd." Elise's thumbs worked the digital keyboard furiously. "Say something."

"Sorry. Almost got busted," Haislee sent back. "Newt OD? WTF!"

"He's in a coma," Elise texted.

"JFC," Haislee's text said.

"Anything I should know?"

The reply icon floated for an uncomfortably long time. Finally, "No."

"U sure?"

"Told U no last nite," Haislee texted. The reply icon floated, disappeared, then reappeared. "Felt sick. Left the dance. Went to bed."

"Really? Your Insta post says different."

Elise stared at the screen, waiting for more. She wanted a reason to believe Haislee, but the videos Elise had watched last night in the car were pretty clear. Haislee had been at the afterparty. But Elise also knew that texting left a lot to the imagination.

Tired of waiting, Elise texted back. "Doc's here. Got 2 go." Then she added, "NEED 2 TALK." She turned her phone to silent and slipped it back into her pocket.

– 33 –

THE DOCTOR LET Elise pass by, then directed her gaze at Teigan and Mattix. The look of concern never left her face. "Mr. and Mrs. Coleman?"

"Yes." He extended his hand. "Mattix, and this is Teigan."

The doctor shook Mattix's hand firmly, then Teigan's. "I'm Doctor Avery. I'll be overseeing Newton's treatment and recovery. But first, let me say how sorry I am. This sort of thing shouldn't happen to anyone, let alone teenagers."

Dr. Avery removed the stethoscope hanging around her neck, positioned the eartips, and placed the bell on Newton's chest. She noticed Teigan and Mattix watching her closely.

"I know we're monitoring vitals..." Dr. Avery motioned at the vital signs monitor. "But I like to check for myself every once in a while. We can't put all our faith in machines." A moment later, the stethoscope was back around her neck. She picked up Newton's chart hanging at the footboard. She jotted a note and set the chart back down.

Dr. Avery walked around the bed and pulled a chair for herself. "Please."

Teigan and Mattix sat and took each other's hand.

"Obviously you're aware that Newton has suffered a drug

overdose, resulting in coma," Dr. Avery began. "We received tox screen results early this morning, and—"

"Please don't let it be fentanyl," Teigan said. "Or heroin, or crystal meth, or—"

Dr. Avery reached out and took Teigan's free hand. "Please. Let me finish."

Teigan shot a panicked look at Mattix, then back at Dr. Avery. "What is it? What did you find?"

Dr. Avery took a fortifying breath. "We found alcohol in Newton's blood and trace amounts of THC, the active ingredient in marijuana. But more concerning were extremely high levels of GHB and Rohypnol."

Teigan and Mattix shared a look of confusion.

"Roofies," Elise said from the doorway.

Dr. Avery looked over at her and nodded. "Yes."

"They're date-rape drugs, Mom."

"We know what it is, but..." Teigan trailed off and looked at Newton underneath a snarl of tubes and probes.

"Somehow he was dosed with both drugs," Dr. Avery said. "However, Newton's got a lot going for him. He was admitted quickly and his heart rate is strong. Someone was looking out for him before the paramedics arrived, so there's an excellent chance of little to no brain damage."

Teigan placed her face in her hands. "This can't be happening." Mattix placed his arm around Teigan's shoulder.

Elise approached the footboard and grabbed it to steady herself, her knuckles turning white.

"GHB and Rohypnol are controlled substances that can do great harm," Dr. Avery said. "Please understand, I am required by law to report their use, especially with minors, to prevent further risk to others. The police will want to talk to you as well."

"Who helped Newton?" Mattix asked. "Before the paramedics arrived?"

Dr. Avery shook her head. "That's something the police will

have to determine." She stood up. "Now, I have other patients to see to, so if you have any other questions, you can direct them to a nurse or write them down and I'd be happy to answer them later on."

Dr. Avery walked to the door and stopped. "This is easy for me to say, but please try not to worry. Newton will get the best care available. This is what we do here." She paused to reinforce her concern, then disappeared down the corridor.

Teigan looked up at Elise. "Did you talk to Newt at the dance last night?"

"No," Elise said.

Teigan persisted. "What about Haislee? That was her texting you, right? She likes Newt."

"Yeah, Hazy texted me, but she doesn't know anything."

"How do you know for sure? It's easy to lie in text. Did she talk to Newt?"

"Mom. Stop!"

"Whoa, whoa." Mattix raised a brow at Elise. "How about I get you to school."

Elise shrugged.

"You need a distraction," Mattix said.

Elise glanced at Newton, then at his vital signs monitor churning out data with every heartbeat. "Nothing's going to distract me from this."

Mattix took Teigan's hands. "I'm assuming you're going to stay?"

Teigan looked at him with red-rimmed eyes and nodded.

Mattix stood, moved bedside, and kissed Newton's forehead. "Come back to us, Newt," he whispered. "Promise me." He walked to the door. "Lise. Let's go."

Elise hesitated for a moment, then dropped to her knees, and hugged Teigan. "I'm sorry, Mom."

"Me, too," Teigan said. "Now go. I'll keep you both in the loop."

Elise joined Mattix. He closed the door to a sliver, just as it had been when they arrived.

Teigan shifted her chair closer, grabbed Newton's left hand, and rested her head on the edge of the bed. No matter how she tried to deny it, Newton was in mortal danger, all because of date rape drugs. But one thing that she could not deny was that *someone else* had given the drugs to him.

– 34 –

THE HOURS MELTED away as Teigan maintained her vigil next to Newton. She watched nurses come and go, performing their assigned duties. They checked his vital signs. They emptied the bag that collected his urine. They fed him a beige slurry through his nasogastric tube and replaced the bag of fluids hung above the bed. This would be Newton's routine for the foreseeable future.

By mid-afternoon, Teigan's stomach was growling fiercely and she could feel a headache on the horizon. The ICU's no food or drink policy meant she'd have to leave. But any moment away could mean a moment missed, a moment where Newton might need her.

Teigan decided to take a quick break. She'd be no good to anyone if she wasn't completely present. She let the nurse at the reception desk know that she'd be back in a few minutes and left the ICU.

Guilt washed over her every minute she was gone. Her sweet boy, her first-born needed her. As Teigan headed for the elevator to the first floor, she passed by a small waiting room. Against one wall were several vending machines. One held refrigerated perishables like sandwiches and Danish pastries, another held snacks and candy, and the last one, a coffee machine.

"Thank God for small miracles," Teigan said to herself before realizing it. She needed a huge miracle, but this would do for now. Maybe it was a sign that the universe was looking out for her and for Newton.

She selected a strong coffee with an extra shot, black. The machine ground and whirred inside, and deposited its hot brew into an awaiting paper cup. Teigan sipped it and felt relaxation flow through her body, dissolving her headache.

She moved to the refrigerated vending machine and bought a chicken sandwich and a blueberry muffin. Teigan planted herself in one of the waiting room chairs and devoured her meal, not caring about best before dates or how many preservatives were in them. To be honest, for vending machine fare, it wasn't that bad.

Teigan washed everything down with the rest of her coffee. It had been less than a day and she was already a recognizable fixture in the ICU. Signing in wasn't necessary anymore. Teigan gave a small nod to the nurse at the reception desk. A buzz and click opened the door to the ward and she hurried back into room 223.

An Asian man with wavy black hair stood at the footboard of Newton's bed, examining his chart. His black khakis, sport jacket, and white shirt and tie screamed law enforcement. He was about Mattix's build and looked about the same age.

Teigan stood at the doorway. "Can I help you?"

"You're Teigan Coleman?" The man raised a brow.

"Yes," Teigan said, eyeing him cautiously. "And you are?"

"Jackson Konishi, Hamilton Police, Investigative Services." He pulled his jacket aside and exposed the badge clipped to his belt, then extended his hand to shake.

Teigan accepted and shook firmly. "Do you mind if I take a

closer look?" She motioned at his badge. "You can never be too careful these days."

Jackson nodded. "Understood." He unclipped his badge and handed it to her. "I specialize in drug-related cases."

Teigan examined the badge and gave it back. "My son doesn't do drugs. Someone else did this to him."

"Never meant to imply anything." Jackson clipped his badge back onto his belt. "People usually don't take GHB and Rohypnol voluntarily."

Teigan walked around him and reclaimed her seat by Newton's bed.

"Mrs. Coleman, I'd like to ask you a few questions, if that's okay." Jackson hooked his thumb at the door. "It won't take long, but if it's a bad time, I can come back."

"I suspect it's going to be a bad time for a while," Teigan said. "Let's get it over with."

"I'll try and be quick, Mrs. Coleman," Jackson said. "My intent is to find out who did this to your son and stop them from doing it to others."

Teigan nodded. "And please call me Teigan."

"Noted. Speaking of which, do you mind?" Jackson flashed a pad and a pen.

"Not at all."

"Okay. Now that we're on a first name basis... Teigan, I know things are fresh, but walk me through last night if you can. The sooner we can nail down a timeline, the better."

Teigan sighed and rubbed her forehead. "You know about as much as we do."

"Trust me," Jackson said. "You'll always know more than me about this."

Pushing through her worry, Teigan recalled everything she could think of from the previous night, starting with dropping Newton and Elise at the Spring Fling dance and ending with Elise returning upset about Haislee.

"Then a bit later the hospital called," Teigan added. "We left immediately after that."

"What time was that?"

Teigan thought for a moment. "Probably between nine-thirty and ten. Maybe later, I can't say for sure. I wasn't tracking the time at that point."

"Has Elise communicated with Haislee since last night?" Jackson flipped a page in his notebook.

"I'm not sure," Teigan said. "But I assume so. She's at school now."

"I'll want to talk to Elise and Haislee at some point. I'd give you and your daughter plenty of notice."

Teigan nodded. "That's fine. Haislee's parents are pretty easy going, too. In fact, they're like family."

"It's great when that happens." Jackson paused. "I've got some tougher questions. Do you know if Newton had taken drugs of any kind in the past?"

Teigan stiffened at the question. "I told you before. My son doesn't do drugs."

Jackson tilted his head at her. "All teenagers do drugs at some point."

"Not Newt. He's dead set against them, a hundred percent."

"Okay..." Jackson tapped his pen on his pad. "Does Newton associate with anyone who takes drugs?"

Teigan shook her head. "Not that I'm aware of. But the school isn't huge. There's bound to be kids he knows that do."

Jackson jotted down something on his pad. "What about enemies? Is there anyone who'd want to hurt him like this?"

"You mean intentionally drug him?"

"Yeah."

"Every kid has a bully," Teigan said. "But there's no one I know that would do *this*. Newton did have a falling out with his best friend last year, but he's over it," Teigan said. "I think they still talk. They just don't hang out."

"What's the friend's name?" Jackson watched Teigan reach for Newton's hand.

"Richard Baum." Teigan spelled out Richard's last name.

"When you say 'they talk', do you mean in a friendly way?"

"I assume so." Teigan glanced at Newton under the snarl of wires and tubes. "He doesn't say much about it anymore."

"I hear you," Jackson said. "Teenagers hold a lot in these days."

"Do you have kids, Jackson?"

"One on the way. Due in…" Jackson performed a quick mental calculation. "About three months. But I'm already stressed out."

"Get used to it." Teigan could sense Jackson's happiness and excitement and appreciated that he dialed it back due to the circumstances. "A piece of advice. Keep your kids away from social media for as long as possible. It's a dumpster fire."

Jackson nodded. "I can imagine. Thank you." He wrote a few words onto his pad. "Can you think of anyone else that would be worth talking to?"

"There is another person." Teigan's eyes darkened. "Dustin Stoaks. He tends to be friends with Newton only when he wants something from him. So I would call him more of an acquaintance."

Jackson raised a brow. "Son of Whitaker and Colette? Lives in Rockwood West? Parents own Stoaks Cadillac?"

"You seem to know a lot about him."

"Not really." Jackson underlined a word on his pad. "They're just a very influential family."

"Influential, as in gets *special treatment* by law enforcement?"

Jackson locked his gaze with hers as annoyance flashed across his face. "I'll pretend I didn't hear that. Anyone else of note that I should talk to?"

"I don't think so."

Jackson removed a business card from his jacket pocket and handed it to her. "Teigan, if you think of anything else, give me a call, any time. You never know what might come up."

"I will."

Jackson stood and presented his hand once again. "No need to stand."

She took it and they shared another strong handshake. "Actually, I do have a question."

"Shoot," Jackson said.

"Where did they find Newt?"

"Pyckman Quarry. It's a popular party spot."

Teigan nodded wanly. "I know. I partied there as a teenager. I'm sure you probably did, too."

"I did."

"Doubt it's changed much in all these years."

"I was there at night," Jackson said. "But I bet you're right." He flipped his notepad closed and slipped it and his pen back into his jacket pocket. "Thanks for speaking with me. I *will* get to the bottom of this." He channeled every ounce of sincerity he could find. "And Newton is going to be okay."

Teigan returned a strained smile. "I hope you're right, on both accounts." She watched Jackson close the door behind him and was left with her thoughts to mingle with the sounds of Newton's life-saving equipment.

Again, she sought out his left hand and the warmth it radiated. If anything could be considered an anchor that stopped her from sinking too deep into this new hell, it was Newton's hand.

Teigan raised his hand, careful to not bump the IV cannula, and lightly kissed his knuckle. She felt the edge of the tape securing the IV to his hand roll slightly, sticking to her thumb. Teigan examined the tape to make sure that it didn't need replacing.

Creeping out from under one edge of the semi-translucent tape was a pen mark she hadn't noticed until now, and it piqued Teigan's curiosity.

She set Newton's hand down by his side and bent over to try and get a closer look. She took a photo with her phone and tried to use filters to isolate the rest of the marks, but with no success.

The only way would be to peel back part of the tape to expose the skin.

Starting at one corner and going very slowly, Teigan pulled back the tape until the marks stared back at her. A doodle would be a better word.

The purple pen mark formed a heart shape with a little curled tail at the bottom. It reminded her of the beginnings of a henna tattoo. Teigan took another photo before sticking the tape back down again.

She called the photo up on her phone and pinch-zoomed it to display the doodle within the confines of the screen. Being on his left hand, Newton could have drawn the heart himself, but he had never intentionally done anything like this since he was old enough to hold a pencil. Unless she didn't know her son as well as she thought she did.

$$- \ 35 \ -$$

A BONFIRE BURNED in a shallowly dug hole approximately thirty feet from the quarry's edge. But despite the fire, overwhelming cold and darkness surrounded Teigan.

Pyckman Quarry looked just as she remembered it. And why wouldn't it? She was reliving a memory, but not a complete memory. Only a shell of one. Despite her exceptional recall, most details had faded, leaving only the simplest of images behind: the fire, the chainlink fence, the trees, and the deep cut in the earth that led down to stagnant water. Teigan imagined the insatiable hole in the ground now. Larger, hungrier, and unforgiving.

She walked toward the fire and spotted white lines in the gravel next to it. As she approached, the lines moved and crisscrossed each other until they formed the shape of a body, resembling a chalk outline for the deceased at a crime scene, but drawn in paint.

Is this where the paramedics found Newton?

Teigan dragged her foot across the lines to disrupt the shape, to erase its existence. The lines remained exactly where they were, unchanged.

She got down on her hands and knees and dragged her fingers across the lines. Gravel moved under her hands and pebbles stuck under her nails, but the lines held their form. It was as if they were being projected from above.

Teigan slammed her fists down on the sharp gravel. "No! He's not dead, dammit! He's strong! He's—"

Blinding light blasted her face and caused her to fall backward. She braced herself with one hand and shielded her face with the other.

Confusion turned to horror as she realized that the one bright light was actually two, rapidly approaching.

Headlights!

Teigan scrambled to her feet to run but the chainlink at the edge of the quarry stopped her.

"DANGER! DECEPTIVE CREATURES! STAY OUT!" screamed the block-lettered warning sign in front of her face. The fence seemed to wrap around her on three sides, blocking every direction she tried.

She turned and faced the looming headlights, gripping the links of metal with white fists.

"Noooo!" Teigan screamed into the headlights and at whatever (or whoever) was behind them as the impact flung her through the fence and down into the dark open pit of the quarry. She hit the water and—

Teigan jolted awake in the chair next to Newton's hospital bed. Her hands gripped the chair's arm rests. Pyckman Quarry had seemed as real in her dream as the last time she had partied there as a teenager. Teigan wondered if she'd see the same chalk outline, the same warning sign, the same black water if she visited the quarry now.

Or maybe I already have.

As she dismissed the thought and blinked away the remnants of her dream, she realized that there was a third person in the room.

She glanced across the bed and saw a tall male individual, standing at least Newton's height, maybe taller. A large navy blue hoodie hung off his strong and broad-shouldered frame and the hood shielded his face from view. His hands alternated between relaxed and white-knuckled fists.

Teigan slid the chair back as she stood, trying to get more space between them. "Excuse me. Can I help you?"

The person stood motionless and did not respond.

"Hello?" Teigan tried to shift her head to see the individual's face, but he anticipated her move and adjusted his stance to maintain his anonymity. "Who are you? What do you want?"

For a brief moment Teigan thought she was hallucinating or still dreaming. She pinched the skin between the finger and thumb of her left hand with the other. Pain shot up her arm.

Not a dream.

"Say something, right now or I'm going to get security." Teigan spoke firmly but there was a waver of fear in her voice, barely noticeable.

"I'm sorry." The person dropped their head, turned, and headed out the door in long, intentional strides. He hooked his hand on the edge of the door and closed it as he left.

Teigan stood for a moment, not quite sure what to make of the situation. The voice of this individual didn't sound familiar to her, but an apology indicated that Newton might have known this person.

With her fears abated, she ran to the door and pulled it open. "Wait!" Teigan scanned the corridor in the direction the person had gone and found it empty. She ran to the reception desk. "Did you see a person walk by just now? Tall, blue hoodie?"

The nurse behind the desk thought for a moment. "I do remember someone passing by, but I wasn't paying much attention. People come and go all the time during visiting hours."

"Did they sign in?" Teigan leaned over the countertop to get a glimpse at the nurse's workspace. "Can I look at the sign-in sheet?"

"I'm afraid not." The nurse scrunched her brow. "Is something wrong?"

"No. It was just an unfamiliar face. Spooked me a bit."

The nurse pulled a binder out from a shelf under the desk and flipped it open. Her finger traced out the entries of the day so far. "I don't see any sign-ins in the past hour. Does that help?"

Teigan managed to spot Jackson's upside-down signature at the bottom of the list but no one else afterward. "Yes and no."

The nurse pursed her lips in mild confusion. "All right. Is there anything else I can help you with, Mrs. Coleman?"

Teigan shook her head. "Thanks though," she said and walked back to Newton's room. It couldn't all be in her mind. She focused on recalling her brief interaction with the unknown person.

Did he sneak in behind Jackson or was he already here?

Something kept pulling on her memory, something familiar but without enough substance to make sense. It was just one more question in a long list that needed answering.

– 36 –

THE END-OF-DAY BELL RANG. Elise rushed out of her history class, squeezing past slower students ahead of her. She should have stayed home. She couldn't keep her mind on anything other than Newton's condition and Haislee's Instagram videos. She rushed to her locker, exchanged some books, then ran to where Haislee's locker was located. She stood on the opposite side of the hallway and waited.

It didn't take long. Elise spotted her best friend running down the hallway toward her locker, her eyes locked on her destination, unaware of anything else. Perhaps Haislee was rushing to avoid talking, but there was no chance of that happening. Elise would make sure of that.

Haislee pulled open her locker and frantically dug through the contents inside.

Elise wove her way through the crossflow of students and propped herself up on the locker next to Haislee's. "Going somewhere?"

Haislee looked at her, crumpled, and lost it. She threw her arms around Elise's neck and began to cry. Elise stumbled a step backward.

"I'm sorry, Lise." Haislee spoke through her sobs. "I'm sorry.

I should've told you. But I can explain." She released Elise and faced her. "I fucked up, but I can explain."

Elise looked left and right, then pointed at the doors at the end of the hallway, the opposite direction to the main entrance. "Not here."

Haislee grabbed her things, wiped her nose on her jacket sleeve, and followed Elise. "How's Newt. Is he okay?"

"No." Elise slammed her hands on the crash bar of the door at the end of the hallway, as if for emphasis. "He's not *okay*." She broke away from Haislee, down the stairs to the first floor, then outside. She turned on her. "What the FUCK, Haze?"

"I'm sorry," Haislee said between sniffles. "How many times do I have to say it?"

Elise crossed her arms on her chest. "Talk. Don't leave anything out."

"I'm sorry I ditched you at the dance, but Dustin offered to drive—"

"You went with *Dustin?*" Elise's eyes blazed with anger. "Are you *crazy?*"

"Look, you were in the bathroom," Haislee said. "Dustin showed up and offered to take me to the afterparty. I figured you wouldn't want to go, so I made up the stomachache thing."

"You could've asked me."

"Honestly, Lise?" Haislee stared back at her. "You would've gone with Dustin?"

"Well, no, but you could've asked."

"Just so you could say no," Haislee said. "Then judge me for going without you. That's exactly why I *didn't* ask."

Elise shook her head angrily. "That's all bullshit anyway. Did you see anything weird?"

"Bullshit? Fuck *you*, Elise." Anger began to rise in Haislee's voice now. "That *bullshit* says more about you than it does about me."

Elise took a moment to breathe. "Did you see anything weird? At the party?"

Haislee scrunched her brows. "Weird? Like how?"

"Like drugs," Elise said. "Roofies."

"What? No." Haislee's eyes widened. "Is that what happened to Newt?"

"Someone dosed him."

"Fuck..." Haislee sat on the grass. "You saw my videos, right?"

"Yeah, right after leaving my brother in a coma," Elise said. "First you lie to me, then you ditch me, then you don't return my texts."

"I turned my phone off."

"The *tech goddess* turned off her phone?"

"I don't care if you don't believe me." Fresh tears welled in Haislee's red-rimmed eyes. "It's the truth."

"Spare me." Elise paced back and forth on the grass in front of Haislee.

A moment of silence passed. Haislee looked up at her. "I tried to save him, you know."

Elise stopped pacing. "What?"

"Everyone ran but I *stayed*. I did CPR on him until the ambulance arrived."

"*Then* you ran."

"I didn't want to get in trouble." Haislee shook her head subtly. "You would've done the same thing."

"I would've *stayed*," Elise said. "He's my brother. He's your friend, and you left him."

"And if he dies, that's *my* fault?" Haislee waited for an answer that never came. "Maybe it is." She broke down again and hung her head between her knees.

Elise softened. Both of them were angry and hurt. She sat next to Haislee and placed her arm around Haislee's shoulder. "I'm sorry I was such a bitch, but we aren't hiding things from each other now, are we?"

"No." Haislee looked at her. "I'll never lie to you again."

"Me, too." Elise managed a small smile. "Did you tell the police what you told me?"

"That Jackson dude?" Haislee shook her head. "No. I stuck to my lame-ass stomachache story. Do you think it would help? I can call him."

"It might. You never know what the police will dig up about someone."

"Okay," Haislee said. "I owe Newt that much."

The two teenagers hugged. Despite clearing the air with Haislee, Elise still knew that the truth didn't affect Newton's condition now. But it might reveal who was responsible.

Dustin sat in the racing simulator and Richard reclined on one of the leather couches. Grand Theft Auto 5's immersive Los Angeles cityscape flew by as Dustin drove his sports car through every pedestrian he could. He called it the "second-best side-quest," the first being fucking the digital prostitutes for free.

Richard piped up unexpectedly. "You think Newton's going to be okay?"

Dustin recoiled in the racing simulator. "What? *That's* what you're thinkin' about?"

"Well, it was weird. That's all."

"What's weird about it?" Dustin focused on the massive screen in front of him. "He drank and smoked too much. Obviously the pussy couldn't handle it. Other than that, I don't give a shit."

Richard shrugged. "I guess so."

The doorbell rang.

Richard glanced at Dustin. "You expecting anyone?"

"No." Distracted, Dustin's sports car wrapped itself around a telephone pole and the digital driver inside smashed through the windshield. The screen faded to grayscale and the word "wasted" floated above the scene in red. "Fuck!"

Dustin crossed the room to his computer desk and pulled up

the security video feed on the front entrance. An Asian man stood staring at the door, looking nonchalant.

The doorbell rang again.

"Okay, okay, wait for fuck's sake." Dustin stepped to the intercom next to the game room door and pressed the talk button. "Hello?" He turned to watch the Asian man's response.

"Hi. Jackson Konishi, Hamilton Police. I'd like to speak with Dustin Stoaks." He flashed his badge directly in front of the camera. He had known exactly where it was all along.

"The police want to *talk* to you?" Richard spoke in a rapid, panicked whisper.

"Be *quiet*." Dustin scowled at Richard, annoyed. "And why are you whisperin'? He can't hear us unless I press 'talk.'" Dustin did exactly that. The speaker crackled for a second. "What's this about?"

"I'd like to speak to Dustin regarding an incident last night at Pyckman Quarry," Jackson said.

"Holy shit," Richard said, still whispering. "He knows about the party. Shit. Shit. Shit. I better not get expelled."

"Will you *shut* the fuck up? Okay?"

Richard stared back at him, stunned, and nodded.

"Quiet." Dustin glared at Richard and pressed talk. "I'll be right down," he said and walked through his bedroom to the upper hallway.

Richard followed. "Wait. What are you going to tell him?"

"I don't know. Roll with it, I guess."

"Tell him to talk to your lawyer first." Richard's eyes darted with panic. "You got a lawyer, right?"

"Yeah, but why? That makes me look guilty. We don't have anything to be guilty of... right?" Dustin narrowed his eyes at Richard as he walked. "Are *you* hiding something from me?"

"Huh? You're crazy." Richard said. "We were both there, at the same time. But maybe we could say we weren't. I mean—"

Dustin stopped. "You're full of stupid ideas today. There's got to be video of us there, especially because of that Insta-crazy bitch Haislee. Startin' to regret inviting her. I'll say we were there but didn't see anything. That's pretty much the truth, right?"

"I guess, but police are trained to spot lies."

"Whatever." Dustin waved him off. "Stay here and don't make a sound. Got it?"

Richard nodded.

Dustin pointed back at the computer monitor with the live security video feed on it. "Watch my skills at work."

– 38 –

DUSTIN SAUNTERED DOWN the stairs. He could see Jackson through the vertical windows that flanked the front door. If his mother, Colette, had been home, there would have likely been a fire burning in the river-rock fireplace, warming the gathering area and immediate surroundings with an inviting glow. She liked keeping a welcoming home. Dustin on the other hand couldn't give a damn. He was usually in his room and a fire downstairs didn't affect him in the slightest. Except today. A fire would have been a nice touch.

Dustin opened the door and gave Jackson his best smile.

"Dustin Stoaks?" Jackson eyed him carefully.

"None other."

"Jackson Ko—"

"Konishi. I remember," Dustin said. "From when you told me, like, literally sixty seconds ago."

Jackson displayed his badge again. "Just so we're official."

Dustin said nothing. He wondered if he made Jackson nervous. He liked to think he had that effect on people.

"May I come in?" Jackson made a move to enter the house, but Dustin blocked him.

"I'm not allowed to let strangers into the house when I'm alone."

"Alright. But what I've come to talk to you about may be of a personal nature, perhaps something you'd want to keep private."

Dustin stepped outside and closed the front door to a sliver but didn't latch it. He pointed past the porte cochère to the circular driveway and expansive gardens surrounding it. "I'm not worried. There's no one around who's goin' to hear."

Jackson nodded. "Suit yourself." He retrieved his notepad and pen. "Do you have an issue with me taking notes?"

"What if I did?"

"Then I'd stop," Jackson said. "Simple as that."

Dustin hesitated. "Fine. Let's do this."

"Okay." Jackson clicked his pen. "Where were you last night between the hours of 8pm and midnight?"

"I was at Pyckman Quarry for a while, but left early," Dustin said.

"How early?"

Dustin shrugged. "I don't know exactly. Maybe nine-thirty? I wasn't keeping track."

"Were you there with anyone?"

"Of course. I don't go to parties alone," Dustin said. "Or I host them myself."

"Who were you there with?" Jackson stood poised with his notepad and pen.

"Richard."

"Last names too, if you don't mind."

"Richard Baum."

"Anyone else?" When Dustin hesitated, Jackson continued. "Was Newton Coleman with you?"

"Yeah," Dustin said.

"Was there drug use last night?"

"Probably, but I don't do that shit." Dustin hung a thumb off a belt loop. "You're not tryin' to get me for drugs are you? 'Cause if you are, I'll piss for you right now."

"Maybe later, depending on how this case develops," Jackson said. "Do you sell drugs, Dustin?"

"What? No!" Dustin recoiled in offense. "If anyone was going to get drugs from me, not that I've ever done that in my life, but if they were, they'd get it for free 'cause my parties are legendary."

"Legendary." Jackson nodded. "Were you consuming alcohol?"

"Everyone was drinking something. I handed out a bunch of beer to people."

"Was one of those people Newton?"

"Sure," Dustin said. "I gave a beer to him, to Rich, and to a bunch of people I didn't even know. That's how I roll. You'd know that if you'd been to one of my parties."

"Right." Jackson underlined something twice on his notepad. "Do you know what happened to Newton last night?"

Dustin paused to think. "He passed out. I tried to revive him."

"*You* tried to revive him?" Jackson narrowed his eyes. "How?"

"I slapped his face."

Jackson paused his writing. "Slapped?"

Dustin realized immediately that he had said too much, but knew that the odds were good that someone had recorded the moment on video. His bet was on Haislee. "Saw it in a movie once. Probably the wrong thing to do, 'cause people shoved me out of the way."

"Then what happened?"

"We heard sirens and everyone ran."

"Including you."

"Yeah," Dustin said.

"You didn't stay to help Newton? Your friend?"

"We're not besties, if that's what you're gettin' at. Anyway, other people were helping him, so I left."

"Do you know where Newton is right now?"

Dustin furrowed his brows for show. "At the hospital? That's what people are saying at school."

Jackson nodded his head subtly and flipped back in his notes. "Initially, you said you left early, but now you're saying you left when everyone else did."

"Whatever, man," Dustin said. "I left first. Before everyone else."

Jackson eyed him. "No plans to leave town any time soon, Dustin?"

"I wish, but no," Dustin said. "I got school and grad's coming up."

"Alright." Jackson exchanged his notepad and pen in his jacket pocket with a business card. "If you think of anything else."

Dustin glanced at the card dismissively.

Jackson descended the steps under the porte cochère that led to the circular driveway, then stopped and turned. He locked his gaze with Dustin's dark, lifeless eyes. "Oh, one more thing. Do you know where I can find Richard?"

Dustin shrugged. "Try his house."

"Yeah," Jackson said. "That was my first stop. Wasn't there."

"Sorry. Can't help you." Dustin watched Jackson start his car and follow the circular driveway off the property. He pushed back through the front door to find Richard just inside. "Didn't I tell you to stay in my room?"

"I wanted to listen and the security video didn't have audio," Richard said. "Besides, I was super quiet."

"And if he *had* heard you, we'd be fucked."

"Why? Practically the entire graduating class was at Pyckman."

"I said I was *alone,* numbnuts." Dustin glared at Richard. "It only takes one lie to screw everything up." He headed back up the stairs, Richard following close behind.

"We better make sure your story matches mine." Dustin stopped at the second floor landing and looked back at Richard. "Because he's going to want to talk to you next."

Richard gulped, his anxiety spiking. He followed Dustin back into his room. It should be easy. Just tell the truth. Get it right. But there was the truth, and there was the truth as told by Dustin.

JACKSON GOT INTO HIS CAR, stopped the audio recorder app, and slipped his phone into a stand on the dash. The Camry started rough until he gave the engine some gas. He followed the roundabout and turned out of the Stoaks' driveway, headed back to Cherry Mills and glad to be leaving Rockwood West.

Maybe it was the opulent homes and lifestyles, or the undercurrent of unfriendliness that he experienced when his investigations led him there, but he always felt uncomfortable visiting the upper-class Rockwood West subdivision. He let go a relaxing breath as more familiar neighbourhoods passed by his car.

Jackson hadn't visited Richard's place yet. That had been a line designed to make Dustin nervous and Jackson was unsure if it had worked. Dustin appeared unfazed by his questions and except for the timeline discrepancy, leaving early versus first, Jackson suspected that Dustin was being truthful. He'd confirm through social media channels later, but right now, he wanted to speak to Richard.

While stopped at a red light, he pulled up Richard Baum's address into his map app and plotted a course. Ten minutes later, Jackson pulled into the driveway of a rundown house on Meridale

Lane. The comparison between Dustin and Richard, the haves and have-nots, was stark and not lost on Jackson.

He rang the doorbell and waited. The blue sky took on a darker hue as the evening wore on. Dinner time was close, and Jackson's stomach rumbled in response. This would be his last stop for the day.

Jackson heard thumping steps approach the door before it opened with a creak. A man with sparse, curly graying hair and wearing a tattered housecoat stood in the doorway. There were bits of dried food stuck to the threadbare patches, at least Jackson thought they were food.

The man blinked aimlessly at him as if he had never seen an Asian-Canadian before. "Is this the home of Richard Baum?" Jackson asked.

"Yeah." The man continued to blink, giving a first impression of low intelligence.

"Jackson Konishi, Hamilton Police." Jackson flashed his badge. "Are you the legal guardian of Richard Baum?"

"Yes. I'm his father, Peter." He rewrapped his robe and cinched the belt in an attempt to look more presentable. It didn't work. "What's this about?"

As Peter reworked his robe, the overwhelming scent of cooking meat and body odor spilled from the door. Jackson struggled against a gag. "An incident took place last night that I'd like to speak to him about."

"Do you mean the afterparty? At the quarry?" Peter raised a brow at him and grinned yellowing teeth. "I heard it was rad."

Jackson breathed through his mouth as he pulled out his notepad and pen. "Okay to take notes?"

Peter shrugged. "Sure."

"Great. Who told you the party was *rad*?"

"Rich told me," Peter said. "Or maybe it was Dustin. Maybe both. I can't remember." He tipped his hand like he was drinking. "Had a bit too much."

"Dustin stayed here last night?"

"Oh yeah. Dustin says over pretty regular. He and my boy are best buds." Peter spoke like this was something to be proud of. "Not sure why, though. Have you seen the kid's house? The fucker lives in a mansion."

"It's a different world."

"You're telling me." Peter scowled. "I'm just going to have to invent something everyone wants and make a million dollars. Move out there too. That'll show 'em."

Jackson nodded. "When do you expect Richard home?"

"He told me he was hanging out at Dustin's today, so I dunno," Peter said. "He might stay the night. Hey, you want some coffee and homemade jerky?" He stepped aside to make space for Jackson to pass.

"No, thank you," Jackson said. "Perhaps another time. So... Richard is at Dustin's house right now?"

"Probably." Peter flashed his stained teeth again in a crooked smile. "You should go talk to him there. And check out Dustin's crib while you're at it."

Jackson nodded. "Thanks. Good idea." He pulled out his business card and handed it to Peter. "Just in case, please ask Richard to call me when he gets a moment."

"Will do, Detective..." Peter squinted at the card. "Konishi. Say, is that Japanese or Chinese? I can never tell."

If Jackson had a quarter for every time he'd heard that ignorant question, he'd be able to retire. "I'm Canadian. My grandparents were Japanese." Jackson pocketed his pad and pen and returned to his Camry. "Have a good night."

"Ever think about converting to electric?" Peter pointed to Jackson's car.

"Not on my salary," Jackson said. "Good night, Mr. Baum."

Jackson slipped behind the wheel and closed the door, cutting off Peter Baum's spiel on electric cars mid-sentence. He gave the man a wave through his closed window to avoid looking rude.

During the short drive home, Jackson's brain began to analyze the information he had collected so far. He had been doing the job so long that it became second nature. His brain just kicked in and he was powerless to stop it.

Inconsistencies had already appeared in Dustin's story. He had lied. Richard had likely been at his house all along. Jackson contemplated heading back to Rockwood West to confront them, but he already knew they were hiding something. Extra time would add anxiety to the mix, which never helped anyone when they were hiding something.

It had been almost twenty-four hours since Newton's overdose. While the recreational use of GHB and Rohypnol was on the rise again after two decades, using both together in amounts sufficient to cause overdose felt more like a personal attack and less like a dosing mistake.

As Jackson wound his way home for the night, he formulated a plan. The teenagers of today were smart, with their devices and social media, but he was smarter.

$$- 40 -$$

IT HAD BEEN almost a week. Teigan had become a permanent fixture at the ICU at Cherry Mills Medical Centre, although she still had to adhere to visiting hours. Teigan brought her laptop with her. The idea: Keep her business running as seamlessly as she could while staying close to Newton for as long as possible. If he experienced a turn for the worse, she wanted to be there.

The first few days were a complete failure. Teigan got nothing done. Worries consumed her.

What if Newton dies?

What if Newton has brain damage?

What if Newton wakes up and he's not the same teenager I remember?

What if Newton never *wakes up?*

Teigan found herself eating poorly and catching short naps whenever she could. The nurses on the floor sympathized with her predicament, having seen similar situations play out countless times before. But their recommendations to go home and take care of herself fell on deaf ears.

Running a business is not easy, as Teigan quickly discovered when she started GadgetGot during the 2020 pandemic. But a drop-shipping business took a little less day-to-day upkeep than most businesses once the infrastructure was in place. And having no inventory was a blessing. GadgetGot survived her lack of attention during Newton's initial days at the ICU. The business was more forgiving than she had anticipated.

Now that Teigan had settled into a routine, she found cracking open her laptop and getting some actual work done was easier. She knew the nurses and doctors were doing everything they could for Newton. Even the repetitious sounds of the vital signs monitor and the ventilator had become unobtrusive background noise, much like a babbling brook or wind rustling the leaves on a maple. Or at least that's what she tried to imagine. The ventilator sounded gross most of the time.

Taking a taxi to the hospital every day was too expensive, so the third day Teigan rented a red 2019 Honda Civic from ZipZoom (securing a cheaper corporate rate), despite Mattix's push to drive her back and forth. The family had never needed two cars until now.

"I want to be able to leave at a moment's notice," Teigan had argued. "And I don't want to be a burden." Mattix let the issue go, as disagreeing would have been pointless.

Working on her business in Newton's room kept her mind busy. Newton's routine remained unchanged. Nurses moved his body gently to avoid bedsores and to prevent his joints from becoming stiff. The procedures that required privacy (bathing, removing fecal matter) were usually taken care of after visiting hours. On the odd occasion of a bathroom emergency, Teigan took a short break to let the nurses complete their duties undisturbed.

Teigan made a point of touching and talking to Newton frequently as she worked. Newton never responded, but the nurses said that including him was beneficial to his recovery. Her first born deserved as much as she could give.

After a week had passed, Teigan's worries began to creep back into her head. With Newton's medical status unchanged, she began to lose faith that he'd come out the other side. Seven days had felt like a month, even with passable vending machine sandwiches and black coffee.

Black like the water in Pyckman Quarry.

Mattix entered the room at six o'clock, the time when the family usually sat down and ate dinner together. Dinner time at the Coleman house was device-free and meant for reconnecting and talking about interesting events that took place during the day. Teigan staying at the hospital each day had fractured many of their family routines, dinner time being one of the most important.

Mattix held a vase with a beautiful bouquet of mixed flowers. "Hey, Tee." He leaned in to kiss her, then looked at Newton. "How's he doing?"

"Stable, but unchanged," Teigan said.

Mattix placed the vase and bouquet on the work center countertop so that Newton would see it when he woke up. He took Newton's hand in his, surprised by its warmth, and kissed it lightly. Pulling a second chair over, he sat and found Teigan's eyes. "Tee... Let me buy you dinner."

"But visiting hours don't end 'til eight."

Mattix took her hands in his. "Yeah. But you know the nurses have your contact info. You know they'll call you if things change. You know this. We both do."

Teigan let her eyes drift away from Mattix to Newton, her son, hanging on to life by wires and tubes. "But I'd never forgive myself if..."

Mattix leaned in and wrapped his arms around her. Teigan sobbed softly against his shoulder, her eyes watching the slow rise and fall of Newton's chest in time with the ventilator.

"You must be exhausted," he said. "Let me take care of *you*. Please."

"Okay," Teigan whispered.

Mattix helped her pack up her things and led her to the door. Teigan looked back at Newton. It was no different than when she had to leave at the end of visiting hours each day, but this time she was choosing to leave with time left on the clock. It felt different. It felt wrong.

"They'll call if they need us," Mattix said. "Come on. Dinner awaits."

Mattix escorted her to the Pathfinder and helped her climb in. He hopped behind the wheel and navigated out of the parking lot.

"Wait. What about my rental?"

"It'll be fine overnight," Mattix said. "I'll drive you here tomorrow morning."

"Sounds like you've got everything figured out."

Mattix gave her a quick look and smiled. "Not everything. Just a few important things."

Teigan fidgeted with the handle to her laptop bag. "Do you know if that detective spoke to Elise yet?"

"The one from last week?"

"Yeah. Jackson... something," Teigan said. "I have his card in my purse somewhere."

"Elise didn't mention anything specific, so if he did, it probably didn't amount to much." Mattix gave Teigan a quick look. "Elise couldn't have been at that party, could she?"

"She was with us, remember?" Teigan said.

"What if she was there *before* coming home?"

Teigan shook her head emphatically. "She wouldn't lie about that."

"Teenagers are more secretive these days," Mattix said.

Teigan sighed. "I don't need any more worry right now."

Mattix pressed his lips together and silently cursed himself. "Sorry. Has that detective updated you?"

"No," Teigan said. "He hasn't been on my radar. For obvious reasons."

"Maybe we should talk to him."

Teigan squeezed the top of her purse until her knuckles turned white. "Can we talk about this later?"

"Of course."

She looked out the passenger window to orient herself. "Where are we going?"

Mattix formed a tentative grin.

"Please, nothing posh." Teigan blew her nose into a tissue. "I'm just not in the mood."

"Trust me." Mattix turned onto King Street West. Soon a familiar beacon rose up ahead from behind the tall buildings on the right side of the street. Familiar and loved by the whole Coleman family, the restaurant sign glowed in the darkening sky in white, orange, and brown.

Teigan looked across the console at Mattix. "A&W?"

Mattix's trademark grin reappeared. "I figured you'd want some comfort food."

"Hell, yeah." Teigan felt a rush of mixed feelings descend upon her, mostly good ones. She wiped a tear from her eye.

"Inside or in the car?"

"Inside's fine."

Mattix parked and they both got out. He secured a booth by the window. "Sit tight. I'll order."

"But you don't know what I want," Teigan said.

Mattix tilted his head and grinned slyly at her. "Bitch, please." They both laughed.

Teigan passed the time trying to think of other things besides Newton. Why hadn't Jackson updated them? Had he talked to Dustin? Had the school addressed Newton's overdose? Because the school hadn't approached them at all, as far as Teigan knew. Was there something she should be doing instead of maintaining a vigil? All these questions in her mind fought for airtime, but Newton kept winning out.

Mattix returned with a tray containing two Mama Burgers, two orders of onion rings, and two root beers in frosty glass mugs.

Teigan took a sip of her root beer and sighed. Its cool, sweet, and slightly spicy flavour sent a wave of relaxation through her body. It was almost as good as coffee. She unwrapped her burger. "You got a Mama Burger, too?"

Mattix nodded. "Of course."

"But you always get a Papa Burger."

"We're celebrating mamas tonight," Mattix said. "And at this moment you're the best mama on the planet."

Teigan began to take a bite, then stopped. Her tears soaked into the napkins on the food tray.

"Oh, Tee. I didn't mean to upset you."

"No, it's okay." Teigan took his hand and kissed it. "I just feel incredibly guilty, being here, indulging myself, while Newton's back at the hospital slowly fading away."

"Newton's not fading," Mattix said. "He's going to get through this."

"How do you know?" Mattix's face swam in her teary vision. "You can't."

"I just have a feeling." He gave Teigan's hand a gentle squeeze. "And I'm going to keep faith in that feeling."

"Does that mean I have no faith?"

"No, Tee. Of course not." Mattix leaned forward and rested his chin on his clasped hands. "It must be very intense at the hospital. Maybe less time there would be good, to separate yourself a little."

"But that'd be abandoning Newton," Teigan said.

"Not if you're advocating for him in other ways, like talking to the police, and the school." Mattix's eyes held steady with hers. "We could do it together. I can take time off work."

Teigan whole body shuddered. "Maybe."

"Promise me you'll think about it?"

Teigan nodded. "Okay."

"Would you like to go home?"

"No," Teigan said. "Let's finish our meals."

As they ate, they made a plan. The school and the police department were the first things on their list. Because Mattix was right. Someone was responsible and they deserved answers.

– 41 –

Main East Plaza was deserted at seven-thirty in the morning. Haislee stood in front of Mainline Burgers with her arms wrapped around her body. Even though the morning sun was breaking free of the surrounding trees, April mornings in Cherry Mills were still chilly. It didn't help that her designer puffer jacket actually was quite thin and didn't provide much warmth. She stood and shivered on the curb, facing an empty parking lot and paying the price for wearing the latest fashion.

Haislee checked her phone. "7:45" in cold white numbers stared back at her. Soon she'd have to leave. Being late for school might raise suspicion and that was the last thing she needed.

A silver Toyota Camry turned into the parking lot. It had to be Jackson. What were the odds of anyone else showing up to Mainline Burgers this early on a weekday? The sedan rolled into a parking space near the center of the lot.

Haislee stepped off the curb and approached the sedan with caution. Once she saw Jackson's face, she was able to relax. Inside the sedan, Jackson leaned across the console and opened the passenger door.

"Get in," he said.

Haislee did as instructed and slid into the heated leather

passenger seat. The interior was pleasantly warm as well. She imagined her cheeks glowing a rosy pink.

Jackson left the engine running and raised two cardboard cups sealed with lids from MontJava. "Mochaccino or hot chocolate?"

Haislee reached for the mochaccino and flipped up the lid. "Thanks." She took a tentative sip and relaxed into her seat.

"I know we don't have much time." Jackson set down the hot chocolate and pulled out his pen and notepad. "Mind if I take notes?"

Haislee nodded as she drank her warm caffeinated elixir.

"Okay." Jackson turned in his seat to face her. "You have some information for me?"

Haislee met his gaze. "I'm not going to get in trouble, am I? Like, I can't get in trouble."

"Look, Haislee. That really depends on what you tell me."

Haislee stared at the sign to Mainline Burgers through the windshield. "I didn't have a stomachache that night. That was a lie I told to Elise... and you."

Jackson jotted notes. "Okay."

"I was at the afterparty. Dustin drove me."

Jackson raised a brow. "Dustin Stoaks?"

"Yeah," Haislee said. "Richard was with him."

"Any reason he asked you?"

"I don't know. I mean, maybe he likes me, but I just wanted to get to the party." Haislee sipped her coffee. "So I went."

"Why didn't Elise go with you?"

"She's not as much of a party girl as I am," Haislee said. "Plus she doesn't like Dustin."

Jackson nodded. "Why?"

"Newton and Dustin have drama." Haislee glanced at Jackson and watched his hand scribbling in his notepad. "They're friendly, but they, like, stopped being friends last summer. I guess Lise didn't like how Dustin treated him."

"Is there any reason why Dustin might want to harm Newton?"

Haislee shrugged. "I don't know. Don't think so."

"Okay." Jackson scanned his notes. "Dustin drove you to the afterparty. Then what happened?"

"Well, we didn't go straight to the party," Haislee said. "Dustin picked up some alcohol at his place, then we went to the party."

"Alright, then what?"

Haislee took a fortifying sip of her mochaccino. "We just drank and, like, partied. Then Newton passed out and everyone freaked. Dustin tried to revive him by slapping his face. Dumbass. I..." She took another sip. "I did CPR on him until the ambulance came. Then I ran."

Jackson finished writing a note, then fell silent and nodded slowly.

"So am I in trouble?" Haislee blinked at him.

"Well..." Jackson took in a deep breath. "You didn't tell me the truth the first time. Why should I believe you now?"

"Because I should've stayed with Newton." Tears began to well in Haislee's eyes. "Now he might die. Or never wake up. That's on me. I just want to, like, make things right."

Jackson locked his gaze on Haislee. "Did you drug Newton?"

"What? No!" Haislee shook her head emphatically. "Never."

"I believe you," Jackson said. "Instead, you tried to save him. So, no, you're not in trouble. But next time you talk with police, if there is a next time, tell the truth. It helps the investigation move forward faster. It's the truths that end up exposing the lies. Understand?"

"Yeah." Haislee tilted her mochaccino to capture the last sip and placed the empty cup in the console drink holder, beside the hot chocolate. "Are you, like, going to drink that?"

Jackson stowed his pen and notepad and handed her the second drink. "Can I give you a lift to Diamond Bay?" Before

Haislee could protest, he added, "I'll drop you off a few blocks away."

"Yeah, that'd be good. Thanks."

Jackson put the Camry into gear and turned out of the parking lot onto Main Road East.

"This doesn't look like a cop car."

"I don't need a computer," Jackson said.

"Too bad. I love tech." Haislee examined Jackson as he drove. "Do you wear a gun?"

"All officers of the law carry a gun." Jackson kept his eyes on the road ahead.

"How is the investigation going anyway?" Haislee set the hot chocolate on her knee.

"I can't discuss an active investigation," Jackson said. "But your additional *truthful* information will prove to be very useful." He pulled the sedan over a few blocks from the school. "I'll drop you here, if that's okay."

"Yeah, fine." Haislee opened the passenger door, stepped out, then leaned back into the car. "I hope you get whoever did this."

"So do I," Jackson said. "Go take care of your friends. And Haislee?"

"Yeah?"

Jackson's gaze was dead serious. "Don't lie anymore."

Haislee nodded and closed the car door. She watched Jackson perform a U-turn and drive away in the opposite direction from where they'd come.

As she began the short walk to the school, Haislee thought back on the information she had given Jackson. He hadn't once asked about social media or videos of the party. She hadn't offered, either. That wasn't lying, was it?

The morning bell rang as she hustled toward the main entrance of Diamond Bay. Just inside the doors and off to one side to avoid the crowds of students, Haislee pulled out her phone and texted Elise.

"Just talked 2 Jackson," she tapped. "Told him everything."
Everything except the videos...
Haislee hit send. The lie came easy this time.

– 42 –

TEIGAN WOKE THE NEXT MORNING with her stomach twisted in knots. Coffee was the only thing her stomach agreed to keep down. Mattix on the other hand polished off a bowl of cereal, toast with peanut butter, and coffee.

"I've taken the entire day off just in case," Mattix said.

"Just in case of what?" Teigan slipped on her shoes and jacket. It was early April, and the morning air still held a chill.

"Snakebite?" Mattix shrugged. "Maybe we'll need it after what we find out."

"What are we going to find out, Matt?" Teigan eyed him carefully. "Do you know something you're not telling me?"

"No, of course not. Forget I mentioned it."

"Not going to happen," Teigan said. "Now that's all I'm going to think about."

Mattix hung his head and sighed. "I'm sorry. I was just trying to prepare."

They told Elise what was going on, then moments later found themselves heading for Diamond Bay High School. The route was familiar. As a family they had traveled this way to numerous concerts and events. The reason for the trip today cast a shadow over everything.

Arriving early had its advantages. The parking lot was almost empty and Mattix found a spot close to the front entrance. Plus there was less likelihood that they'd be spotted by students that might know them.

Instead of turning right and following the familiar path to the gymnasium like they had on numerous occasions before, Teigan and Mattix carried on forward. The entrance to the main office of Diamond Bay faced the left side of the central hallway, aptly called the heart of the building.

Teigan and Mattix stepped inside the anteroom of the office and checked in with Miss Pringle, the receptionist.

"The Colemans to see Principal McCarthy," Teigan said.

"Do you have an appointment?" Miss Pringle looked over the rims of her glasses at them.

"No, but all we need is a few minutes of his time," Mattix said.

"Mr. McCarthy is a very busy man." Miss Pringle picked up the phone. "Contrary to popular belief, high school principals have many duties, and their time is not to be taken for granted."

"We'd never do that," Teigan said. "It's just... we're looking for details about our son's accident last week and—"

Something clicked and a flicker of recognition flashed across Miss Pringle's face. "*Newton* Coleman. Of course. You must excuse me." She held the phone against her ear, dialed an extension number, and waited for a moment. "Morning, Grey. Newton Coleman's parents are here. They'd like to speak with you." Miss Pringle listened and nodded. "I know, but... Alright." She hung up the phone.

Miss Pringle's gaze found Teigan's for a second but returned to her computer screen like her life depended on it, her fingers busying themselves over the keys. "He'll just be a moment. Please take a seat."

Mattix settled into an uncomfortable, boxy chair. "It's like we're celebrities."

"For all the wrong reasons." Teigan sat beside him and took his hand.

They barely had a chance to relax before Principal Grey McCarthy entered the anteroom from a warren of offices and hallways branching off the reception area.

Principal McCarthy stood a few inches shorter than Mattix with dark brown hair slicked back. His two-piece suit and button-down shirt and tie strained at his waistline, threatening to burst at any second. To Teigan, he looked like a compressed Don Draper from the television show *Mad Men,* under pressure and half as handsome.

Principal McCarthy jutted out his hand. "Mr. and Mrs. Coleman."

Mattix and Teigan shook his hand in turn, Teigan already turned off by the weakness of his grip.

"Follow me, please." Principal McCarthy led the way back to his cluttered office. On one side of his desk a stack of books and folders balanced precariously beside a thermos and a mug with "World's Greatest Principal" written on it.

Probably bought the mug for himself. Teigan continued to scan the office. The shelves looked dusty and unorganized, like the publications there hadn't been touched in months. The atmosphere in the office held the essence of stale body odor, coffee, and something else (tuna salad?)

Mattix and Teigan took the two chairs in front of McCarthy's desk, which were more comfortable than the ones in reception, but not by much.

McCarthy closed his office door, then sat forward at his desk and clasped his hands. "Before we begin, let me say how sorry I am for Newton's... situation."

"Thank you," Teigan said.

"I assume this is about Newton?"

Both Teigan and Mattix nodded.

"Rest assured, I'll help in any way I can," McCarthy said.

Teigan glanced at Mattix and he gave her a subtle nod. "We want to know if there have been any developments at the school."

"If you've heard anything," Mattix added. "Like rumours, or through social media."

"So far, nothing. But all our staff at Diamond Bay have their ear to the ground I assure you," McCarthy said. "They'd let me know if they heard something."

"What *have* you done?" Teigan sat on the edge of her seat.

"As we have done in the past when the school encounters a traumatic event, we hold an all-grade assembly," McCarthy said. "We make sure students know how to access emotional help if they need it."

"What if they know something about what happened," Mattix said.

"Like a tip," Teigan continued.

"Our students know that they can drop anonymous tips into our suggestion box, just beside the office entrance," McCarthy said. "Plus we had a reminder about Newton in this week's bulletin. Students can also send an anonymous message through social media if they choose."

"And?" Teigan asked.

"Like I said before," McCarthy said, "Nothing yet."

Teigan balled her hands into fists. "But someone *must* know something. *Everyone* was at that party."

"Including lots of kids from other schools," McCarthy said. "It may have begun as an offshoot from the Spring Fling, but word about parties spread fast."

Mattix narrows his eyes at McCarthy. "So have you contacted any other schools?"

"Not that I'm aware of, but..." McCarthy grabbed a pen and jotted something on a piece of paper. "I'll get that done today."

Teigan locked her eyes on McCarthy's. "My son isn't out of the woods yet. He could die or remain in a vegetative state for the rest of his life. I want you to treat him like you'd treat your own child. Go above and beyond. We want to know who did this."

"I don't have kids, Mrs. Coleman," McCarthy said. "But we share the same goal."

"Well, either *you* get some results, or *we* will."

The tension hung heavy in the small office. McCarthy took a calming breath. "We'll continue to do everything in our power to find out more. You have my word."

Mattix and Teigan stared back at McCarthy, until Mattix broke the silence. "I think we're done here." He stood. "Thank you for your time," he said curtly and escorted Teigan through the door.

McCarthy stood. "Let me walk you out."

Mattix turned back. "Thanks, but we'll find our own way."

Teigan and Mattix pushed through the crowds of students walking to class. Ahead they spotted a black Escalade pull in two parking stalls away from their Pathfinder.

Mattix glanced at Teigan. "Don't do anything you'll regret later."

Teigan tilted her head at him. "Give me some credit, huh?"

"Yeah, yeah. Just saying."

Dustin and Richard slid out of the giant SUV and passed by Teigan and Mattix on their way into the school. They talked to each other quietly.

"Mr. and Mrs. Coleman?"

Teigan and Mattix turned to find Dustin waiting behind them. Richard stood a few feet farther away and avoided their stares.

"We've heard about what happened to Newton," Dustin said. "We hope he's okay."

Both Teigan and Mattix felt disarmed by Dustin's words, but it was Teigan who spoke first. "He's hanging to life by a thread."

Without a beat, Dustin said, "If there's anything we can do, just name it."

Teigan exchanged a look with Mattix, then resettled her gaze on Dustin. "Actually, I'd like to talk to you about what happened at the party."

"Sure, but now's not a good time... obviously." Dustin looked back at the school entrance. "DM me on Insta later and we'll set something up."

Richard fidgeted with his hands and kicked imaginary sand back and forth. Mattix eyed him up and down which made him fidget more.

"I'll do that," Teigan said.

Dustin rejoined Richard and the two teenagers continued toward the school.

"I don't like those two," Mattix said.

"What's to like?" Teigan tugged on Mattix's coat sleeve. "Come on. Let's go."

They both hopped into the Pathfinder. The cab of the SUV eliminated most of the exterior noise once the doors were closed.

"We seem to be on a roll," Mattix said. "Next stop, police?"

"You call that a *roll*? More like a disaster."

"It could've been worse. They could've stopped us at the door."

Teigan stared out the windshield, focusing on the front entrance that Dustin and Richard had passed through only moments ago. "If they had done that, they would have suffered my wrath."

Mattix glanced at her and nodded. "True. You *are* a force to be reckoned with. So what do you think?"

"Let's do it. See if Jackson has any new information for us," Teigan said. "Then we'll get lunch and you can drive me back to the hospital."

Mattix nodded and backed out of the parking stall. Teigan tried to focus on questions for the detective but found her mind floating back to an image of Newton in his hospital room. It had been a week with no news from police, a fact that left an undercurrent of anger in the back of Teigan's mind, one that she'd have to keep in check.

"Maybe we should give the detective a heads up that we're on the way," Mattix said. "He might not even be there."

Teigan nodded, pulled out her phone, and dialed. The call connected and she put Jackson on speaker.

"Matt and I are on our way," Teigan said. "We'd like to speak with you."

"Did you discover anything new I should be aware of?" Jackson's electronically filtered voice piped from the phone's speaker.

"Funny. That's exactly what I was going to ask you. But I'd rather do that in person. See you in about ten minutes." Teigan hung up on Jackson before he could respond.

"I know you're annoyed, but—"

"That's putting it lightly," Teigan said.

"We'll catch more flies with honey than vinegar." Mattix gave her an appeasing smile.

"Are you going to be full of clichés today?"

"Ouch." Mattix laughed. "Breathe, Tee. I'm not your enemy."

"Sorry." Teigan raised his right hand from the stick shift and kissed it lightly. It had become increasingly more difficult to remain hopeful as time marched forward. She crossed her fingers that Jackson would offer more actionable information than McCarthy had.

$$- \ 43 \ -$$

Mattix pulled into a parking lot next to the Hamilton Police Service on Wilson Street. He lucked out with a parking spot not too far from the Investigative Services Division building. After paying for a ticket, they both walked to the front entrance.

Mattix caught Teigan's eye. "United front, okay?"

"Okay."

They found each other's hand and stepped into the building. Jackson was waiting for them at the reception desk. He had dressed exactly the same as the first time Teigan had talked to him: white collared shirt, tie, and khakis, but this time without his jacket.

Jackson held out his hand in greeting. "Teigan and…"

"Mattix."

The three of them shared firm shakes all around.

"Good to finally meet you, Mattix."

"Likewise."

Jackson presented his arm toward the metal detectors and the elevators beyond. "Sorry, but it's policy." He stepped through the detector without setting it off.

Teigan handed her purse to an officer standing beside the detector. He opened it and began poking through it. Teigan's cheeks warmed with unwarranted guilt. She decided she didn't like this place and would be glad to leave. She walked through the metal detector and set off a thought-rattling alarm. A second officer waved a metal detecting wand around her body and isolated the buttons on her jeans, her earrings, and her wedding ring.

"Careful," she said to the second officer. "They're deadly weapons."

The second officer stared at her blankly, returned her purse, and waved Mattix through. The alarm went off again, and the second officer isolated his watch as the culprit.

"My apologies," Jackson said. "Never can be too safe." He led them to the elevators and slammed his fist on the up button.

An elevator arrived and the three of them stepped inside.

"How old is this building?" asked Mattix.

Jackson thought for a moment. "Four years thereabouts, almost as old as it took to build."

"Cost a pretty penny, if I remember correctly."

"$26 million," Jackson said rocking on his feet.

Teigan stared at the closed doors as if she was trying to open them with her mind. "Our tax dollars at work."

"Money well spent, as far as I'm concerned," Jackson said.

The elevator doors slid open and Jackson led them down a long hallway. He paused at his office. "Let me grab my notes."

"Why not have the meeting here?" Teigan stepped into the doorway and gazed into the small, sparsely decorated office with one window. There wasn't a plant in sight but on one wall hung a corkboard with photos, news clippings, and bits of paper tacked to it. Imagining working here eight hours a day gave her the shudders.

"Everything's all set up in the conference room." Jackson pulled his notepad out of the inner pocket of the jacket hanging from his chair. "This way."

Jackson opened a door several offices down the hallway to a

windowless room lit with overhead fluorescents. "Please. Take a seat. Can I offer anyone coffee?"

"No thanks," Mattix said. Teigan shook her head and they both took seats along one side of the long conference table. Jackson sat at the head of the table.

"Let's cut to the chase," Teigan said. "It's been a week with no updates. What can you tell us?"

Mattix placed his hand lightly on Teigan's hoping that it would have a calming effect.

"Since it's an open investigation, there's not much I can share," Jackson said. "But I talked to your daughter…" He flipped through his notepad. "Elise. She didn't offer anything new."

"When did you talk to her?" Teigan asked. "She didn't mention anything to us."

Jackson glanced at his notes. "Last Friday at Diamond Bay High School. I also talked to her friend Haislee and later confirmed her whereabouts with her parents. Her stomachache checked out."

"What about Richard Baum? And Dustin Stoaks?"

"I'm sorry, Teigan. They were at the afterparty, but their stories check out too," Jackson said.

Mattix felt Teigan's hand tense into a fist.

"Look, the party had broken up by the time I arrived on the scene, leaving me with little to go on. No one is talking. Those that *are* talking, their stories fit, and most of the partiers can't be identified."

Teigan glared at Jackson. "Why?"

"We simply can't identify them."

"What about social media?" Mattix asked. "Teenagers post about parties all the time."

Jackson shook his head. "A dead end."

"You're obviously not looking very hard. Teenagers these days will post anything for likes and shares." Mattix narrowed a questioning look at Jackson. "What about their Finstas? Did you check those?"

"Finstas?" Jackson jotted the word down.

"Fake Instagram profiles," Mattix said. "That's where the juicy shit is."

"I'll look into it."

"Damn right, you will," Teigan said. "On second thought, how about you give us Newton's phone. I think we'd run a better investigation than you."

"Newton's phone is evidence in an ongoing investigation. I shouldn't have to tell you this." Jackson sighed and rubbed the bridge of his nose. "However, I have a few more leads I'll be following up on. Other than what I've already told you, the investigation isn't open for further discussion."

"But we're the PARENTS for fuck's sake," Teigan said. "We deserve to know."

"I can promise you that when I have something to share, you'll be the first to know," Jackson said. "If I share everything now, it could jeopardize the investigation. You don't want that."

"You know what I don't want?" Teigan's eyes blazed across the table at him. "I don't want my son to die. I don't want him to wake up a vegetable. I want my son back! Exactly the way I remember him."

"I want that too, Teigan," Jackson said. "I really do. Unfortunately, the only person who really knows who was near him at the party is Newton."

Silence descended on the room. Mattix caught Teigan's attention, his eyelids moist with tears.

"Tee, let's go. Okay?"

Teigan nodded as she struggled to hold back her own tears.

"I'll see you out," Jackson said. "And before you say no, it's standard policy."

Teigan and Mattix stood. "Fine," he said.

There were no pleasantries or idle chit chat on the way back to the front entrance. Jackson paused just before the exit gate. "Teigan," he called out.

Teigan had her hand on the door, but stopped and looked back.

"I'm on your side," Jackson said. "Don't forget that."

Mattix placed a hand on her shoulder. "Let's get some lunch."

Once they returned to the SUV, Teigan's frustration and worry got the better of her. She sat in the passenger seat, covered her face with her hands, and cried.

Mattix sat with her, sharing the enclosed space and the sound of her sobs, until he could bear it no longer. He stepped out of the vehicle, walked around to the passenger side, and opened the door. He knelt and pulled Teigan close. She made no attempt to resist as he wrapped his arms around her. Mattix had been married long enough to know that there were no words he could say that would soothe the current pain. Sometimes listening was enough.

Soon Teigan settled herself and pulled away. Her eyes said, "thank you." Mattix returned to the driver's seat, retraced his path back to the exit of the parking lot, and began looking for a good place for an early lunch.

After several blocks, Teigan piped up. "If you don't mind, can you just take me back to the hospital?"

Mattix looked at her, concern crossing his face. "Can we at least get lunch first? You got to get some proper food in you."

"The vending machine sandwiches have been pretty good, actually."

"If you like sandwiches loaded with preservatives that were made a month ago."

"It's not that bad," Teigan said. "And you know it."

"Fresh and juicy burger... or stale ham and cheese." Mattix tilted his head side to side. "You're right. It's a toss-up."

Teigan sighed. "Come on."

"I'm kidding, Tee," Mattix said. "I just want the best for you, especially now. That includes sandwiches." When Teigan didn't respond, he added, "Of course I'll take you to the hospital. And since I have a day off, I'd like to come up to the ICU with you. It's been a couple of days since I've seen Newt. Rain check on lunch?"

"How about we share a vending machine sandwich instead?"

"Rain check *and* a vending machine sandwich." Mattix turned onto Victoria Avenue South. "No substitutions."

"Deal."

After finding a parking space in the hospital parkade (Mattix hadn't been quite as lucky as at the police station), Teigan and Mattix found themselves sharing a roast beef sandwich beside the vending machines before going back in Newton's room. For Teigan, it was like any other of the past seven days – business as usual. But seeing Newton had clearly rattled Mattix.

He took one of Newton's hands. "Are they feeding him enough? He looks like he's lost weight."

"He gets a nutritional slurry several times a day," Teigan said. "If you stay long enough, you can watch."

Mattix kissed Newton's hand and leaned close to Newton's face. "As much as I love you, buddy, I'm not sure I can watch that."

"That's his present reality, hon," Teigan said.

Mattix began to pace at the foot of Newton's bed. "Tee, I think I'm going to go. I'm of no use here."

"It's hard, isn't it?"

"Yeah." Mattix nodded his head gently. "But I'm not giving up hope. You know that, right?"

"I do."

"I feel it'd be better for me to keep the home fires going," Mattix said.

Teigan forced a smile. "You do that."

"If you need me, promise me you'll call."

"I will. I promise."

Mattix leaned in and kissed her. "I love you."

"I love you, too," Teigan said despite feeling hollow inside.

A moment later, it was just Teigan, Newton, and the whirr and hum of his life-saving machines in the room once again.

Teigan fought her initial disappointment in Mattix by acknowledging his willingness to step up at home, giving her the time and space she needed. But after talking with both the school and police this morning, she knew in her heart that maintaining a vigil at the hospital wasn't the best use of her time. She leaned back in her chair and focused on the vital signs monitor. The bouncing heartbeat line lulled her to unwanted but needed sleep.

Teigan awoke to the sounds of the toilet flushing and hand washing. Betty, Newton's regular day nurse, appeared from the adjoining bathroom with his empty drainage bag. She hooked it back up to his urinary catheter and rehung the bag.

"Good afternoon, Teigan," Betty said. "Sorry to wake you."

Teigan sat up and stretched. "I must have dozed off. Everything okay?"

Betty glanced at the vital signs monitor and nodded. "Same as this morning."

"Betty, can I ask you something?"

"Of course." Betty gave her a gentle smile. "Although I can't guarantee the answer you want."

"Am I wasting my time here?"

"By staying at your son's side?" Betty shook her head emphatically. "No. I believe Newton knows you're here, and that's comforting for him. But staying here is only one way to care for him."

"What do you mean?"

Betty paused at the door to the room. "Whatever you decide to do, Newton will understand. He knows you're doing everything you can."

"Thanks, Betty."

Betty nodded at her, then disappeared down the corridor. Teigan sat up and placed her hands together in front of her mouth, in thought as well as prayer. She let her eyes wander over Newton and the tubes and wires and machines keeping him alive, as she had done countless times over the past week.

Teigan had been left with no other choice. She knew what she had to do and she hoped Newton would understand.

$$- 44 -$$

Mattix stood at the kitchen sink mindlessly cleaning up the breakfast dishes Elise had left behind. Looking out the window at the back yard, he could see all the signs of Spring coming: new leaves on the trees, budding flowers, even the grass looked revitalized. New life.

He had existed more in his head since Newton's overdose and found he wasn't paying as much attention to his surroundings, both at home and at work. He was thankful for the time off today. He couldn't remember the last time he had taken a mental health day off work, apart from vacations. He realized he had needed it. Keeping things running smoothly at home was a full-time job too.

But he also felt tremendous guilt. Teigan had been staying at the hospital all day, every day since Newton had been admitted to the ICU. He couldn't even manage half an hour. Pathetic.

Mattix glanced at the dishes in the sink and thought about how much Elise wanted to be seen as an adult, like her big brother, yet she failed at the most basic life skills like loading a dishwasher. He knew those skills would come in time, but Mattix found himself wanting Elise to hurry. She'd need to grow up fast if Newton—

The front door swung open and Mattix's heart skipped a beat. He spun where he was standing. From the right spot in the kitchen, there was an unimpeded view of the front lawn and Radcliffe Crescent. He spotted a red car at the curb. The odds that someone other than Teigan had entered the house were extremely slim, but Teigan was at the hospital.

With his hands still wet from watery milk, Mattix made a move toward the entryway. "Tee?"

"None other," Teigan said. "You wouldn't happen to be hungry, would you?"

"Now that you mention it..." Mattix found Teigan sitting on the stairs. "You okay? I thought you wanted to stay at the hospital."

"I thought I did too, but after our meetings this morning..." Teigan shrugged, then blindly raised a bag emblazoned with the A&W logo. "Papa Burger?"

"You read my mind." Mattix took the bag, squeezed in, and sat next to her on the stairs. He untied her shoes and slipped them off her feet. "Sometimes I think you're psychic or something."

Teigan looked at him with eyes that appeared startled for a moment before they softened. "You think so?"

"Yeah," Mattix said. "I swear you have some kind of sixth sense about things."

She closed her eyes. "Wait. I'm getting something." She placed her fingertips on her temple and nodded. "Yes. It's a clear message." She opened her eyes and faced him. "Your Papa Burger will be cold soon." A small grin slid across her lips.

"Amazing." Mattix kissed her, then stood and offered his hand. "Our very own Kreskin."

Teigan took his hand and he helped her up. She pulled off her coat and left it on the stairs. In the kitchen, she grabbed some plates and cutlery while Mattix unloaded the A&W bag.

He pulled out a Mama Burger, a Papa Burger, an order of fries, an order of onion rings, and two root beers. But there was one more item left in the bag, and it stopped Mattix cold. He knew what it was before seeing it. An apple turnover. He felt an immediate stinging behind his eyelids.

"I'm sorry, Matt," Teigan said. "I had to. If I can't be with Newt in person, at least I can be with him in spirit."

Mattix fought back his tears and nodded. "No, I get it. I probably would've done the same thing."

The hot apple turnover was Newton's favourite A&W side. He had often said how he could get through anything as long as he had A&W apple turnovers.

The two of them dug into the food without words for the first few bites.

"A&W two times in two days..." Mattix raised a brow at Teigan as he speared an onion ring with a cluster of French fries. "Is this becoming a habit?" He crammed the fried food into his mouth.

Teigan sipped her root beer to wash down her mouthful of burger. "I guess. If it needs to be."

Mattix took a large bite of his burger as he searched for the right words. They didn't *need* to talk. Teigan and Mattix were at a point in their marriage where silence was okay too, but this wasn't one of those times.

"What changed your mind? To come home?"

Teigan set her burger down. "After today and getting no help from the school and police, I figured we're on our own." She sipped her root beer. "Just like Newt's all alone fighting to get back to us, we're alone fighting for him. I can't fix him, so I'm going to pound the pavement and talk to people."

Mattix's gaze never wavered. "What can I do to help?"

"Keep running the house like you have been," Teigan said. "And go back to work."

"But I can do all that stuff too."

"We don't want to jeopardize your guaranteed income," Teigan said. "Revenue from GadgetGot is regular but it's not guaranteed. If I need help, I'll ask."

"Promise?"

Teigan nodded. "Promise."

Mattix sat back in his chair. "You're amazing. How'd I get so lucky?"

"You got good taste in chicks."

They finished their meals, collected the packaging, and threw it in the garbage.

"I think I'm going to have a lie down," Teigan said.

"Want *company*?" Mattix grinned and flashed his brows.

"Sure, if you're going to *sleep*." As if on cue, Teigan yawned. "I feel like I haven't slept in weeks."

"Challenge accepted," Mattix said.

"Come on, then." It was Teigan who offered her hand this time.

The two of them stretched out side-by-side on their bed and Teigan pulled a thick knitted afghan over them both. They found each other's hand and it didn't take long before sleep took hold too.

– 45 –

THE WARMTH OF THE AFGHAN pulled at the edges of sleep, but
Teigan's brain remained busy, piecing together the holes in
Newton's last conscious day on Earth. Social media was a black
box that she was sure Jackson hadn't followed up on. And there
were still many at Diamond Bay that she could talk to. But Teigan
had one more card up her sleeve that might end up being the key
to everything. Her dream of Pyckman Quarry just over a week
ago had stuck with her and had reignited an opportunity.

Buried in the back of her mind, filed but not forgotten, was
what she simply called her *magic power.* It was a gift she had told
no one about. Not her friends, her family, not even Mattix. It was
a secret she would take to her grave.

After beginning college, Teigan discovered that she possessed
the ability to visit places while sleeping. Some would describe it
as lucid dreaming, but there was one huge difference: she could
see things happen at those places in real-time. It was identical to
a physical visit to the place in question, except no one else there
could see her. It was also during college where she learned the
real name for her talent: astral projection.

With practice, Teigan found that sleep wasn't necessary. Taking
a moment to relax in a quiet place was enough to send herself

elsewhere. But there were rules. First, she couldn't project herself to a place that she hadn't seen before. She couldn't envision the Great Pyramids in her head and visit there. But she found that modern technology like Google Maps could offer clues for a partial visit. Second, the place needed to be stationary and grounded on Earth. She couldn't visit the interior of an airplane in flight or a car on a highway even after travelling in one.

Wandering into areas of a projection where her eidetic memory could not supply enough detail, her mind did its best to fill in what was missing. But sometimes there was nothing to draw on. Those "dead zones", if she stepped into one, catapulted her back to a wakened state, leaving her dizzy and nauseated.

Teigan knew all too well that in the wrong hands, the power to project could be abused and used to gain advantages over others. She had promised herself that she'd never use it to do harm. The things she'd learn from witnessing what happens behind the wrong closed doors could never be forgotten, especially with an eidetic memory.

But she had broken her promise – twice. She had used her power to discover her ex-husband's infidelity. Some may have considered it an invasion of privacy, but Teigan felt it was within her right to make a *surprise visit* to her ex-husband's workplace. He and one of the secretaries on his floor had been making good use of the couch in his office. Overhearing him tell his mistress that he never loved Teigan and "couldn't wait to divorce the bitch" shattered Teigan's heart, wounding her deeply, and it took all her will to not use those words against him during their divorce proceedings. That would have been like pouring gasoline on an already raging inferno.

But without using her power to expose the infidelity in her first marriage, she may not have met, fallen in love with, and married Mattix, an infinitely better man. She believed that was Karma rewarding her. Never once in their twenty-one years of marriage had Teigan considered using her power to check up on

Mattix. He was solid, trustworthy, and showed up when she needed him to.

Teigan wasn't quite so proud of her second use of her power. If she could take it back, she would. When Newton was thirteen, he developed a friendship with a girl from school named Naomi. They had partnered on a class Geography project. The COVID pandemic hadn't shuttered the world yet and Naomi became a regular visitor to the house for several weeks spanning October and November 2019. They spent a lot of time in his room, with the door "open a crack" as requested by Teigan.

One Saturday afternoon, curiosity and concern got the better of her and she projected into his room during one of their get-togethers. Teigan discovered no covert teenage fooling around, just two diligent students working together to get a good mark on their geography project. In this case, her surveillance was a breach of both trust and privacy. Ashamed of herself, Teigan vowed to never use the power again.

Now faced with dead ends from both the school and police, she thought about reawakening her magic power to project. It could help reveal information that could lead police to an arrest. But unless all the places she visited were open to the public, what she'd be doing would be considered an invasion of privacy.

But who would know except her? The secret would die with only her. Besides, no one would believe her anyway. This was an urgent problem. Whoever drugged Newton could do the same to someone else, possibly killing them.

I deserve answers, if not for me, then for Newton.

Would the power to project come back to her easily, like riding a bike? Teigan had to find out.

$$- \; 46 \; -$$

DESPITE INITIALLY RESISTING IT, Teigan had fallen asleep for a few hours. She woke feeling refreshed just after four o'clock in the afternoon. Mattix's familiar deep and regular breathing meant that he was still dead to the world. It was the perfect time to try projecting, and she had the perfect destination: Newton's hospital room.

She checked the landline by her bed for any voicemails and her cell phone for any messages or texts. All clear. Teigan lay back down on the bed, closed her eyes, and used Mattix's steady breathing like a metronome to time her own breaths. In through her nose, out through her mouth.

Astral projection was inherently different than lucid dreaming in one important way: the destination of a projection is just as real as being there in person. The physical parameters of the environment can't change, whereas in a lucid dream the dreamer can control everything, including the state, look, and feel of the environment. Plus, what happens in a lucid dream still remains a dream.

After spending a week in Cherry Mills Medical Centre's ICU, Teigan found it easy to picture the room with Newton's bed. She wondered if her special power to project was related to having an eidetic memory. Her ability to recall detail had always been good, but perhaps projection unlocked a subconscious eidetic link that allowed a near perfect recreation of a location in her mind. Teigan set the thought aside and focused on her current journey.

Newton's room, including the complicated medical apparatus keeping his breathing steady and monitoring his vitals materialized before her. The permanent objects held a shimmering quality, like a subtle mirage had mixed with a hologram.

But there were gaps. Objects, like Newton's chart, remained blurry with only a suggestion of tables and text on the top sheet. Things were falling into place. She hadn't given the chart a detailed look, so her projected destination lacked that detail.

She walked around the bed, between the empty chairs, and reached for Newton's hand. Her hand passed straight through to the mattress, and her fingertips felt buzzy, like when her foot fell asleep, but it wasn't at all unpleasant like having pins and needles.

Betty entered the room and walked around to where Teigan stood. Before she could step out of the way, Betty walked right *through* her. Teigan's whole body buzzed until Betty returned to the foot of the bed and noted something on Newton's chart.

This must be what it's like to be a ghost.

Teigan moved close to Betty and poked Betty's shoulder with her finger. It passed through Betty's body as if there was nothing there, releasing the same buzzy feeling wherever their bodies intersected.

Betty finished her notes, rehung the chart, and left the room. Teigan gazed at her own hands and tried to clasp them. They passed through each other, but without the buzzy feeling.

Teigan reached for the chart. Her fingers did not pass through it, but she could also not affect the chart physically in any way. The clipboard swayed in diminishing arcs as a result of Betty hanging it there, until it fell still.

Teigan had discovered another rule of her special power:

inanimate objects, although touchable, were permanently immovable. It made sense.

She squeezed past the first chair and sat down in the one closest to the bed. Other than being able to actually touch Newton and feel the softness and warmth of his hand, projecting herself into his room was the next best thing. And she was surprised at how quickly the knack of her power had come back to her.

Teigan glanced at the vase of flowers on the counter facing the foot of the bed. She'd need to top-up the water next time she visited. Her eyes roamed the room, settling on the window. The view from the second floor was high enough to see further across Hamilton's eastern cityscape. It wasn't anything like New York, but there was enough variance of buildings, lights, and foliage to make the view somewhat interesting.

A shadow caught her peripheral vision. She turned back to see a large form in the corridor casting a silhouette on the blinds of the observation window. And it was moving slowly toward the door.

Teigan froze, forgetting for a moment that she was invisible to anyone actually in Newton's room. She watched as the tall figure almost had to duck entering the room. Teigan remembered the navy hoodie in an instant, but his face... was not gone but distorted. It was as if his face had been painted on and, while the paint was still wet, given a swirly coat of flesh-coloured paint. He looked like he had stepped out of an episode of The Twilight Zone.

She ran around the bed to face this strange intruder. Teigan tried to look him in the eyes, even though his eyes were a blurred mess. Teigan stepped backward as she watched him reach out and place his large hand on Newton's chest.

The navy blue mystery figure stood like that a moment, before he reached forward to the vital signs monitor and ran a finger along one edge. He carried on to the ventilator.

"Wait," Teigan said, suddenly alarmed. "What are you doing?"

The figure placed his hand on the top of the ventilator, then down the side and a terrible thought formed in Teigan's head.

What if he turns off the ventilator?

What if he's the person that drugged Newton and he's here to finish the job?

"No!" Teigan shouted. "Get away from him!"

The figure did not flinch. Of course he didn't. Teigan wasn't physically in Newton's room and he couldn't see or hear her. She scanned the room frantically for some way to distract the person and her eyes settled on the vase of flowers.

She ran *through* the figure, her body buzzing as she did, to the back counter and lay her hands on the vase. It wouldn't budge.

Teigan looked back at the figure, still poised over Newton, his hand still on the ventilator.

Was his hand on the switch?

"GET AWAY FROM HIM, YOU BASTARD!" Teigan gripped the vase that seemed to be glued to the countertop. "GET AWAY FROM HIM NOW!"

The hooded figure turned his head in her direction as if he had heard her command, his bleary suggestion of eyes darkening, and—

Teigan's body jolted in her bed on Radcliffe Crescent. Her eyes fluttered open. To her left sat Mattix, propped up against his pillow, alarm and concern in his eyes.

"Bad dream?"

Teigan rolled on her side to face him. "A doozie." She reached for his hand. "But it was—" She caught herself and hoped that Mattix wouldn't spot her lie. "It wasn't real."

"What was it about, if you don't mind me asking?"

Teigan's mind reeled as she decided what details to share. "I was at the hospital... a stranger in dark clothes and no face was going to turn off Newton's ventilator." As she described her first projection in years, she realized it was more truth than fiction, and it sounded crazy. In other words, it was perfect.

"Jesus, Tee." Mattix caressed her face. "I'd be yelling at the bastard too. Remember anything else?"

"No." But Teigan remembered all of it, especially how the stranger turned his head toward her just before the projection dissolved.

"I'm glad it was a dream," Mattix said.

Teigan remained silent and nodded in response. In this case, the less she said, the better. It wasn't a lie if the words never came out of her mouth.

Mattix slid his legs off the bed. "I'm going to take a quick shower."

"Any requests for dinner?"

Mattix thought for a moment. "No, but don't start on anything until I'm done. I want to help." He pulled off his shirt and threw it into the hamper as he strolled to the bathroom.

Part of her wanted to tear off her own clothes and join Mattix in the shower, getting dirty as they got clean. But Teigan had a task before her that held far more importance.

$$- 47 -$$

ELISE WASN'T HOME from school yet. Teigan padded down the stairs and slid her phone out of her pocket. There was a text waiting for her that read, "@Hazys."

Teigan confirmed Elise's location, then tapped out a return message. "Home for dinner?" A second later Elise sent back a "thumbs up."

As shower noises hissed and bubbled through the ceiling from upstairs, Teigan moved to the garage to ensure greater privacy. She dialed the ICU reception desk at Cherry Mills Medical Centre. A voice she recognized answered the phone.

"Betty? This is Teigan Coleman calling."

"Teigan! Missed you today." Betty's voice buzzed in Teigan's ear. "What can I help you with?"

"Is Newton okay?"

"Yes, of course," Betty said. "We promised to call if his condition changed."

Teigan knew what the answer to her next question would be before asking it, but she asked anyway. "Has he had any visitors today? After I left?"

"Yes, actually," Betty said. "A tall, young man. He said he was a friend of Newton's."

"Did he leave a name?"

Teigan could hear Betty flipping open the logbook. "Looks like his name was…" Betty paused, then laughed. "Oh. He signed it as 'Aye Friend.' Literally *a friend,* just like he had introduced himself."

Teigan thought about asking about what the visitor was wearing, but she knew the answer already. "Thanks, Betty."

"Will you be back tomorrow?" Betty asked.

Teigan could hear the expectation in Betty's voice. "I'll be making fewer visits. My family needs me at home. And honestly, being there all day every day was getting too hard for me."

"Of course," Betty said. "Do know that the floor loves you."

Teigan felt her cheeks blush. "Thank you. The feeling is mutual." She heard Mattix descend the stairs. "And thanks for the information. I appreciate it."

"Take care, Teigan." Betty hung up.

Teigan slipped her phone into her pocket and met Mattix in the kitchen. He was already pulling ingredients from the fridge.

"Pasta and meatballs with a side salad." Mattix flashed a grin at her that faltered when he saw her face. "What's wrong?"

Teigan shook her head. "Nothing. Dream hangover, I guess." She hated keeping things from Mattix, so she offered a bit more truth. "I called the hospital to check on Newton."

Mattix froze. "And?"

"No change." Teigan slipped her arms around his waist and they shared a strong, silent embrace. Seconds turned to minutes before Teigan broke away and looked up at him. "Pasta sounds great."

It was a simple meal, easy to prepare, that always satisfied. Twenty minutes later, as they were plating the food, Teigan's phone dinged. She glanced at the screen and laughed.

"Looks like it's just us," Teigan said. "Elise is eating at Haislee's."

"Then that demands…" Mattix dug around in a drawer next

to the stove. "Candlelight." He had several battery-operated tea-lights in his hand. He turned them on and scattered them on the table.

"And some Malbec." Teigan grabbed two wine glasses and a partially consumed bottle of Chilean Malbec and brought them to the table.

The two of them sat. Teigan poured wine in both their glasses, then raised hers. Mattix mirrored her and waited, presumably for a toast of some kind.

Instead, Teigan set her glass down and burst into tears. Mattix sprang out of his chair, moved around to the opposite side of the table, and kneeled to hold her.

"Why are we celebrating?" Teigan sobbed against Mattix's chest. "The wine, the candles, it feels wrong."

For a long time, Mattix said nothing. Then, softly he said, "We're surviving, Tee. That's worth celebrating... but we don't have to. We can wait."

"What if he doesn't wake up? Or what if he does, but everything that makes him *our* Newton is gone? His future, wiped out in an instant because of one stupid action."

"What if..." Mattix eyes glassed over. "What if he survives without any complications?" He fought against his own burgeoning emotions. "I believe our son doesn't want to start over and will do *everything* in his power to get his life back, to get back to *us*."

Teigan took a shuddering sigh, wiped her eyes, and managed a smile and a nod. "Let's eat before things get cold. But I'm gonna table the toast."

Mattix gave her a quick hug. "Sounds good." He looked at the battery-powered candles flickering in the middle of the table and proceeded to turn them all off, pushing them aside. "Bad idea."

They had barely begun eating when Teigan set her fork down and held her head. "It's always on my mind now, Matt. All the time. And I just can't put it together. We know Newt's gone to parties before where drugs and alcohol were available. He's told us. I'm so thankful he's been so open. But those date rape drugs? This is the first time I've heard of them used in our little bubble."

Mattix squinted at her. "Bubble?"

"You know, Diamond Bay, and our surrounding community." Teigan chewed half a meatball and twirled her pasta through the sauce on her plate.

"I can remember GHB being used recreationally at parties, before we were married," Mattix said. "Probably Rohypnol, too. But it seems its use now is for sexual assault. We haven't heard much about it here because sexual assault goes largely unreported."

Teigan gave Mattix a questioning look mixed with concern.

"I've been reading up on it," Mattix said. "And before you ask, no, I've never used those drugs. And I've never sexually assaulted anyone. Ever."

"There was never any doubt in my mind, hon," Teigan said. "But if that assumption is right, about rape going unreported, then just the existence of those drugs in Newt's body means there's a market for those drugs in our community. Which means there's more sexual assault happening here than we know."

Mattix twirled pasta on his fork and speared a meatball. "I think that could be said about any community. Sadly, there's always a dark side." He chewed his pasta and sipped his wine.

The front door creaked open.

"Lise?" Teigan exchanged a curious glance with Mattix.

"Yeah, it's me," Elise said from the entryway. "Who else?"

"Everything alright?" Mattix waited for an emotional meltdown.

Elise sauntered into the kitchen. "Yeah, fine." Her shoulders slumped with a sigh. "Haze said 'yes' to me staying before clearing it with her mom. And her mom said *Noooo.*" She waved her hands in mockery. "Like an extra mouth to feed is *such* a big deal."

Mattix stifled a grin.

"There's enough left for you if you want to join us," Teigan said. "But you'll have to nuke it."

"Sure," Elise said. "I'm starving." She dished herself some food, reheated it in the microwave, and carried it to her place setting between them at the oval dinner table. She took a bite, then spat it out.

Elise felt the eyes of her parents on her. "What? It was too hot."

"Funny how microwaves make things hot, huh?" Mattix winked at her.

Elise smirked at Mattix as she took another bite, blew on it first, then shoveled it in. "What were you guys talking about? And it better not be about sex."

"We were talking about date rape drugs and sexual assault," Teigan said.

Elise paused her chewing for a moment. "Heavy," she said, then continued eating.

Teigan raised a brow at Mattix and he shrugged a "Why not?" back at her. "Do you know of anyone at Diamond Bay who's been assaulted? Or drugged then assaulted?"

"Uh…" Elise swallowed and set her fork down. "Um, sure. I mean rumours go around, like, all the time."

Teigan focused her gaze. "*All* the time? Is there any proof? Has anyone been charged?"

"Not that I know of," Elise said. "The people I've heard of are too scared to, like, report it, or take too long, and all the evidence is gone."

"How do you hear about these assaults?"

"Jeez, Mom. If I knew I was going to be interrogated, I'd have eaten at A&W or something."

"Sorry." Teigan reached out and touched Elise's hand.

"We're just trying to get some perspective on the kids in your and your brother's lives," Mattix said. "Maybe it can help us understand why he was targeted."

"Well, I guess I hear about stuff mostly through social media," Elise said. "Then gossip from there. Stuff spreads hella fast on socials."

Teigan adjusted her chair to face Elise. "Have you seen any pictures of the afterparty from last week?"

"Yeah, lots." Elise kept her eyes on her plate and ate more pasta. "But I didn't see any of Newt. I would've told you."

"Can I see some of them?" Teigan anticipated resistance.

Sure enough, Elise's guard went up, then in an instant, her demeanour changed. She pulled her phone from her back pocket and opened Instagram.

Teigan and Mattix flanked her as Elise began scrolling through her public feed. It didn't take long to spot a post about the afterparty. She tapped on the video to enlarge it. Playback lasted less than ten seconds and Newton was nowhere to be seen in the chaotic visuals.

Elise exited from the video, back to the creator's main page. Mattix's eyes narrowed on the creator's details above the grid of images.

"Do you have a Finsta, too?" He pointed at an account link in the creator's details.

Elise struggled to swallow her mouthful of pasta. "What do you mean?"

"Lise, I work in IT," Mattix said. "I know all about Finstas."

Teigan leaned forward to look at them both. "They sound familiar. Remind me what Finstas are?"

"A Finsta, or 'fake Instagram' is a separate account where people post things to only a select group of people, to keep things private or anonymous," Mattix said. "Is that about right, Lise?"

"Yeah." Elise returned to her home feed and refreshed it.

"I mentioned them to Jackson. Not sure why it's called 'fake', or why people post the link."

"That's just what they're called," Elise said. "And if they're posting the link, it's not a true Finsta." She pointed at the link. "That's just, like, a separate account."

"So, Dad asked you if you have a... Finsta." Teigan dropped to a crouch beside Elise's chair and looked up at her. "Do you have one?"

Elise put her phone into standby. "Yeah. Like, pretty much everyone does."

Teigan exchanged glances with Mattix. "Can we see it?"

Elise shook her head without hesitation. "No. It's like a diary. It's *personal.*"

"Okay," Teigan said. "Would you show us if it helped us find the person responsible for Newton's overdose?"

Elise looked at Teigan with surprise. "Mom! Of course. *God.*"

"Your mom and I didn't want to offend you," Mattix said. "But I know how deep the hooks of social media can go. Just know that we trust you, okay."

"Um, this is getting weird," Elise said. "Can we just, like, finish eating?"

"Good idea," Mattix said.

The three of them finished their meals without any further words. Newton's empty chair didn't help.

– 48 –

AFTER DINNER, TEIGAN RETREATED to her office and loaded Instagram in her web browser. She quickly learned that there were things that she couldn't do on the website. She'd need to use her phone.

To Teigan, social media was a necessary evil and one of the only places she could advertise GadgetGot. She wasn't a stranger to apps and technology, but she rarely used it "socially." Now she faced a crash course on Instagram.

She downloaded the app onto her phone and registered an account under her own name. Then the app asked if she wanted to sync her contacts. Teigan hesitated at first, but allowed the app to proceed for one reason. A list of people she knew who were on Instagram displayed on the screen. She scrolled down and saw that the list included Elise's account. She approved everyone but noted Elise's username.

Teigan added a second account with the username "dark. angela2005." If Elise had a Finsta, then so would she. Teigan suspected it would be useful to have one going forward. She did not sync contacts, but instead followed many of the suggestions provided to her.

Switching to her desktop web browser, Teigan looked at Elise's profile and began to check out her posts.

"Mom?" Elise stomped into her office.

Teigan hid her browser window but looked as guilty as the Cheshire Cat. She raised a brow at her daughter.

Elise placed her hands on her hips. "Did you just follow me on Insta?"

"Yes," Teigan said. "Is that a problem?"

"Yeah, it *is*, Mom." Elise fumed, angrier than Teigan could have ever expected. "Can you stop? It's, like, totally lame."

Teigan was ready to press the issue but thought better of it. As long as Elise's profile remained public, Teigan could still research her daughter's activity. And she didn't want Elise to have any reason to make her profile private.

"Sorry, hon," she said. "I think it automatically synced my contacts. I'll unfollow right away."

Elise blinked, her anger defused in an instant. It was clear that she'd been expecting a fight. "Uh, okay. Thanks."

Teigan found Elise's account, unfollowed her, then sent an in-app message to her. "Unfollowed. Sorry. xo." A second later, Elise sent her a thumbs up.

Teigan returned to Elise's profile and continued browsing her posts and noting the comments, going back in time until the Spring Fling. There was one user that commented on all Elise's posts, quickly and consistently. One click confirmed that it was Haislee's public profile. She repeated the process, watching for comment trends.

Teigan quickly realized that searching this way could take a huge amount of time. She couldn't help but wonder if Jackson was doing the same thing. If he wasn't, he should be.

Then another thought struck her. Teigan went to the list of people she was following and scrolled through them. The list included Newton's account too. She tapped on it and found Newton's profile was set to private. There was no getting around that electronic barrier. But what if his Instagram account held a clue to this whole mess?

Teigan went to bed early. She'd need all the energy she could muster for what she had planned the following day.

$$- 49 -$$

Teigan woke an hour earlier than she usually did and capitalized on the extra time. She showered, dressed, and made pancakes, scrambled eggs, bacon, and hashbrowns. As coffee brewed, the smells of this rare weekday breakfast brought Mattix and Elise down to the kitchen as well.

Mattix took in the spread. "Wow. What did we do to deserve this?"

"Nothing," Teigan said. "Just felt like it."

Elise yawned and rubbed the sleep from her eyes. "Please feel like it more often. This should be a regular thing."

The trio sat and ate, the events of the previous evening seemingly forgotten. Afterward, Teigan enjoyed a second cup of coffee on the porch while Mattix drove Elise to school and himself to work. It felt like an ordinary morning, the exception being the lack of Newton's upbeat disposition. But Teigan was on the case now. If she couldn't help Newton heal, the least she could do would be to find out who did it, with or without help from the police.

She had the house to herself. With the mess in the kitchen mostly cleaned up already by Mattix, Teigan laid down on the couch in the living room. She closed her eyes and began a series of deep, relaxing breaths.

She focused on the Hamilton Police Service Investigative Services Division building that she and Mattix had visited two days earlier and projected herself there. Its concrete and steel facade was still fresh in her memory, although her memories never went entirely stale.

Not being able to physically move objects remained a small obstacle. She slipped inside an open door as someone was leaving and walked to the elevators, passing (buzzing) through people as she went. Again, she waited until other people boarded the elevator car and joined the group going up. The doors closed and the sensation of the elevator floor moving up and compressing her body brought her out of her projection with a gasp. Then, remembering her projection to Newton's hospital room, she reminded herself of one of the cardinal rules.

Objects and environments that I interact with are immovable.

Teigan made a mental note to only use stairwells when acquainting herself with a building, especially when wanting to return in a projection. She pulled an afghan over her body and tried again, breathing deeply, and this time projected straight to the second floor, as if she had just stepped off the elevator.

She saw a group of men and women headed down the hallway toward the meeting room where she and Mattix had talked with Jackson. Her body fizzed every time it occupied the same physical space as someone else. Sporadically, the feeling was tolerable, but dealing with a crowd became annoying, almost uncomfortable.

Note to self: when projecting, avoid crowds.

Teigan reoriented herself and saw Jackson exit his office. She ran toward his office door, but he closed it just before she could slip inside. Teigan switched to plan B and followed Jackson to the meeting room the other detectives had congregated in. She gritted her teeth, preparing to endure the buzzy feeling of walking through him, but he shut the door before she was able to follow through.

Teigan walked farther down the hallway, following it around a corner. However, since she hadn't ventured that far in her physical body or had any idea what that area of the building looked like, the hallway disintegrated into a featureless rectangular tunnel that led into darkness and ended in abrupt dizziness and nausea. It was particularly strange to see people with blurred faces pass by and disappear into the hallway where her mind had no past memory.

She tried to break free of her current projection so she could restart it again, but found she couldn't do it on her own. Getting into a projection was easy but getting out of one turned out to be considerably more difficult. Her unconscious body had less power over her than her conscious one. The elevator was an option, since it moved and had worked before. And she could take the dark and dizzy path which could lead to throwing up on the living room couch. Back at the hospital, it had been intense emotion that had returned her home. If there was another way, she couldn't think of it.

Another note to self: when projecting, be specific.

Teigan returned to the elevator. She couldn't press the call button, so her only alternative was to wait. It wasn't long before the elevator opened and a clerk carrying a several folders emerged. Teigan walked inside the elevator, buzzing through the clerk and turning to face the hallway.

The elevator doors began to slide closed just as she saw the clerk enter Jackson's office. Teigan seized the moment, leaped forward, and squeezed out of the elevator before the doors sealed shut.

She ran for Jackson's office. The clerk had dropped one of the folders on his desk and was on her way out when Teigan shot through the door, passing through the clerk's body a second time. She was in. Finally.

Because Teigan hadn't seen the back side of Jackson's office door, it didn't exist in the projection. But she had seen the front side, and her subconscious finished the back side as if she *had* seen it. Brains were wonderful things. The back of the door was drab and featureless, probably close to the real thing. She watched the clerk latch the office door closed.

Now Teigan had the office to herself. Most of the details were generally clear, from what she could remember from her last visit with Mattix.

However, when she approached the cork board, she found she needed more detail to make sense of everything. The photos tacked to the board looked blurry, as if blowing up a thumbnail-sized photo to an 8"x10". Some of the board's contents were muddled beyond recognition, like a photo that had been double exposed. Perhaps things had been rearranged since she last saw them and appeared overlapped. But even with the blurred details, some photos were obviously not related to Newton's case, which made sense. Teigan cursed herself for assuming Newton was Jackson's only priority.

There was one piece of evidence on the board that jumped out at Teigan. A small square piece of white paper had Newton's name and street written on it in purple ink.

Newton Coleman, Radcliffe Cr.

At first, she thought it could it be a label for the photos underneath it. But despite the current blurriness of the handwriting, there was something familiar about it. Teigan took her time, memorizing every letter.

Teigan walked around Jackson's desk. Parts of the floor and the back half of his desk didn't exist in this projection either, since her earlier vantage point two days ago had been from the doorway. Again, the floor and the back of the desk *were* there, subconsciously imagined and reconstructed without detail. It was like the crappy imagery she had seen generative AI produce of objects that seemed to exist but didn't follow any logic or prescribed visual rules. She returned to the front of the desk, examining everything she could see.

Jackson burst through the door, startling Teigan. It took a moment for her to remember that he could not see her. He picked up the folder from his desk and flipped through it. Teigan considered looking over his shoulder, but knew it would be gibberish.

Jackson faced the cork board. "Shit. As if I need *another* fucking case." He threw the folder onto his desk for emphasis.

Teigan knew she had to talk to Jackson again. But her priority now was ending the projection, a skill she had not mastered yet.

She stepped out of Jackson's office and returned to the elevator. The doors opened as if she had commanded them to do so. Teigan stepped inside and waited for the doors to close, knowing the unpleasant feeling of being crushed between floors would soon overwhelm her. She took a large breath and held it, waiting, as if filling herself with air would make her more difficult to crush.

More people piled into the elevator, some overlapping her body, making it buzz uncomfortably. Her lungs burned for air. Teigan waited until the last possible second and was about to take a refreshing breath when she blinked and saw the familiar ceiling of her own living room. She looked at the clock on the mantle. It was almost noon.

Had holding her breath ended her projection? Maybe. It was something she had to test later, but at that moment, she had a task with far more importance.

Teigan ran to her office, grabbed a pen and paper, and wrote "Newton Coleman, Radcliffe Cr." on it several times, matching the cursive she had memorized in Jackson's office as closely as possible with each pass. It had to mean something, she just wasn't sure what yet.

$$- 50 -$$

DURING THE DRIVE to the hospital, Teigan struggled to concentrate on her driving. She had almost blown through two red lights already. It wouldn't do her or her family any good to be in an accident. But despite the potential consequences, Teigan found her mind seeking answers, surprisingly not to Newton's state of health, but falling back to the mystery person she had seen in her first projection.

Tall, navy blue hoodie, with a faceless face.

Teigan found a parking spot and killed the engine to her rental. She sat in the temporary isolation of the car and attempted to reconstruct the memory of her first projection and the mystery visitor.

"A friend," Betty had told her before.

But who?

Teigan liked to think that she knew most of who and what went on in her kids' lives, but there was no one she knew who fit the description of what she saw in Newton's hospital room. She wondered if Betty could identify the person after almost a day had passed.

She followed used the stairwell to get to the second floor ICU instead of the elevator. It was only after pulling open the fire doors to enter and exit the stairwell that Teigan realized that closed stairwells would pose problems in a projection as well. Her super power had some substantial flaws.

It had only been two days since Teigan had last visited Newton at the hospital, but it felt like weeks. She emerged from the stairwell, the fire door hinges releasing a tired squeal.

At the reception desk, Betty looked up from her conversation with another nurse and waved.

"Teigan," she called out. "Good to see you today."

Teigan nodded and managed a smile. "You too, Betty. How's my favourite teenager doing?"

"A bit better today," Betty said.

The second nurse handed a pen and a clipboard with the sign-up sheet on it to Teigan. "You know the drill."

Teigan took the clipboard. As she signed her name, she scanned the past entries. Sure enough, there in black and white a few entries before hers, was the name "Aye Friend." She returned the clipboard, then caught Betty's eye. "Fill me in?"

The two women talked as they turned down the corridor to Newton's room.

"Newton remains in stable condition," Betty said, "But—"

"I don't like buts, unless they're my husband's."

Betty laughed, then continued. "Not to worry. We've seen increased brain activity. Ever since Newton was admitted, his brain activity has been strong, but it's stronger now. A very good sign."

Teigan closed her eyes. Sometimes she forgot to breathe. It had happened more often than usual over the past week. She paused at the door to Newton's room and inhaled.

"Thank you, Betty," she said. "I wouldn't have been able to do this without you."

Betty returned a warm smile. "Don't sell yourself short, kiddo. You're practically staff by now. Not many moms can claim that title."

They shared a brief hug and parted. Teigan stepped into the room and Newton looked exactly the same. For a moment she envisioned a physical change to go with Newton's increased brain activity.

"What were you thinking?" Teigan whispered to herself. "Such a dumb—"

She glanced at the counter opposite Newton's bed. The countertop was clear. The vase of flowers that had existed there two days ago was gone. Surely the bouquet couldn't have shrivelled up in that time.

Teigan gave the room a cursory scan. There were few spots that could have accommodated such a large and vibrant bouquet and had they been moved, they would have stood out like a beacon in the fog. But there was no vase of flowers anywhere in the room.

Teigan stepped back out into the corridor. "Betty?"

Halfway back to the reception desk, Betty turned around. "Yes, Teigan?"

Teigan trotted back to meet her. She imagined Betty walked enough each day for the both of them. "The bouquet, in Newton's room. It's not there."

"Oh, I must apologize for that," Betty said. "Somehow the vase fell off the counter and smashed. Custodial cleaned it up but I forgot to tell them to save the bouquet."

"When did this happen?"

Betty furrowed her brow for a moment. "Come to think of it, it happened right after you called yesterday. Or maybe before. They were pretty close."

"And what about that young man in the navy blue hoodie?" Teigan practically vibrated with curiosity. "Was he there then, too?"

Betty nodded, slow at first, then affirmatively. "Yes! Now that you mention it, he left right when we heard the crash." She gave Teigan a once-over. "Is everything okay?"

"Yes, but are you sure? About the young man?"

"I can't be a hundred percent sure," Betty said. "Everything happened all around the same time. Is that any help?"

Teigan stared vacantly back at the door to Newton's room. "Maybe."

"Do you know who that young man is?"

"No," Teigan said. "But I think Newton might." She turned to Betty. "Thank you. For everything."

"Yes. Of course."

The two women parted ways again and Teigan returned to Newton's room. Once more, her eyes fell upon the empty countertop, then they shifted to Newton laying on the opposite side of the room. Whatever happened, Newton would have seen it all if his eyes had been open.

Teigan stood beside Newton and rested her right hand on his chest, just as she had watched the mysterious young man do in yesterday's projection.

"What did you see, Newt." Teigan whispered to herself. "*Who* did you see?"

The entire scene came back to her in a flood of images, and with it a realization. There weren't three people in Newton's room yesterday, but *four*. And she had been the only one who had touched the vase. That left one very important question:

Who moved the vase? Because it couldn't have been Newton.

Teigan suspected she already knew the answer, but it didn't make sense.

– 51 –

TEIGAN SPENT THE AFTERNOON by Newton's bedside. The news of his increased brain activity lightened her spirits considerably. To extend her optimism, she called up a special music playlist on her phone, one that she and Newton had built over the years. The songs spanned decades but had a definite bias for those released in the 1970s and 1980s.

She hadn't brought her laptop but instead used her phone to catch up on work emails. The sounds of the vital signs monitor and the ventilator continued in the background, expected and reassuring. Occasionally the tempo of the music and the ventilator matched, connecting the entire room together with Newton's favourite rock and roll bands.

It was a good afternoon. And to Teigan's surprise, she felt no guilt for not visiting in two days. She had a new direction now, even though it didn't help Newton directly. Once Teigan set her mind on exposing the perpetrators that had drugged him, she'd stop at nothing. It wasn't a matter of "if" but "when."

Teigan didn't know when Jackson left his office for home. Detectives were often called away from the office and home at strange hours. She pulled out her phone and dialed.

The line trilled once before Jackson answered. "Mrs. Coleman."

His voice lacked the warmth she remembered from her past interactions, and rightly so. Teigan had come down hard on him in their past meeting for simply doing his job.

Not fast enough.

"Look, Jackson," Teigan said. "I'd like to apologize for the way I spoke to you last time. I was out of line."

"I get it. This process can be frustrating, especially for parents."

"Can we talk? I can be at your office in fifteen minutes."

"I'll be heading out around then," Jackson said. "There's a Tim Horton's not too far from here, corner of King Street East and—"

"I know it," Teigan said. "I'll meet you there." She had grown fond of the Civic she had rented from ZipZoom. Having a vehicle of her own offered a freedom she hadn't experienced since starting GadgetGot. Pooling resources to reduce household expenses had always been a good idea, especially when starting a new business. But now, maybe a new car was in her future, one emblazoned with GadgetGot branding.

It took Teigan ten minutes to get to Tim Horton's. The Investigative Services Division of the Hamilton Police was at most four blocks away, so there was a good chance that Jackson had arrived already. She found a parking space off King William Street and headed toward the coffee shop on foot. It was close to dinner time, but a coffee and apple fritter would hit the spot.

"Mrs. Coleman!"

Teigan was halfway across the parking lot when she heard Jackson call her name. They had been on a first name basis, but being addressed formally, now and on the phone earlier, grated on Teigan's nerves and brought back all the anger and frustration she had felt the last time they had met.

"Mr. Konishi." Teigan crossed her arms against her chest. "Any updates for me?"

Jackson studied her. "Updates? Is that what this is about? You could've at least bought me a cup of coffee first. And I could've updated you over the phone."

"Well?"

"No updates," Jackson said. "Not in Newton's case or the other seven cases I'm working on. Now tell me why you wanted to meet in person."

An unexpected flash of anger welled up within Teigan and she fought to get hold of it. "There's a note on your bulletin board. When were you planning on telling us about that?"

Jackson narrowed his eyes at her. "You know I can't discuss an open investigation."

"Don't play dumb," Teigan said.

"Note or no note, I can't discuss—"

"You know damn well what note I'm talking about."

Jackson's face slackened, like he was trying to hide his surprise. Teigan noticed and it only stoked her anger more.

Jackson raised his hands in mock confusion. "So spell it out for—"

"You know, the square, white piece of paper with Newton's name and address written on it... well just the street name, not the number." Teigan locked her gaze on Jackson's. "*That* note."

Jackson's face paled.

"Yeah," Teigan said. "I thought so. I want to get the bastards who did this, but we should be working together, sharing information."

"It doesn't work that way," Jackson said. "Civilian involvement in a police investigation is dangerous."

"Then you leave me no choice." Teigan turned and stormed toward her car.

"What do you mean?" When Teigan didn't respond, Jackson ran after her and grabbed her arm. "What do you mean?"

Teigan yanked her arm out of his grasp. "You're a smart guy. Figure it out."

Jackson shook his head, annoyed and confused. "What's gotten into you? I have to follow procedure. I've been very clear about this."

"Talk to me when *your* child is hospitalized in a coma." Teigan's words held new sharpness, making Jackson wince.

"Mrs. Coleman," he said. "Teigan. Come on."

She opened the car door and got in, slamming it behind her.

Jackson tapped the driver's side window with a knuckle. After starting the engine, Teigan rolled down the window.

"How did you find out about the note?"

Teigan stared up at him for a moment. "Maybe if you were doing your job, you'd know." She closed the window and drove out of the parking lot.

As Jackson shrunk in her rear view mirror, Teigan slammed her hands against the steering wheel and cursed police protocol. Not getting her apple fritter was the icing on this shit sandwich. Teigan had already been moving toward her own investigation, but this interaction with Jackson left little doubt how she would proceed going forward.

– 52 –

TEIGAN PARKED HER CIVIC by the curb in front of their house on Radcliffe. She killed the engine and focused her eyes on the line of garbage bins lined up in front of the homes in the distance. Mattix had already taken in their bins, a job usually reserved for Newton. Thank God for Mattix picking up slack without question.

She took in several deep breaths to try and dissipate the residual anger running through her body. She didn't want to infect the rest of the evening with a bad mood.

On one of the garbage bins in the distance, an extra smaller bag of garbage sat balanced along one edge of the lid. It reminded her of the vase of flowers that Mattix had placed on the counter in Newton's room, the vase that had mysteriously fallen and smashed, according to Betty, in a scattered mess of glass shards and broken stems.

An idea popped into Teigan's head. She closed her eyes and started a series of deep breaths to relax her mind and body, in preparation for projection.

She had barely begun when a rap on the passenger window brought her out of her reverie. Mattix peered at her.

"Everything alright in there?" The window muffled his words.

Teigan wanted to say no. She wanted Mattix to leave her alone, but his earnest face won her over. She reached across the console and unlocked the door.

"Safe to approach?"

Teigan nodded. Mattix slid into the passenger seat and closed the door. A moment passed before Mattix broke the silence.

"What's going on?"

Teigan shrugged and rested her head on the back of the seat. "Nothing. Just thinking."

"About?"

She could feel Mattix's eyes on her and it made her want to squirm. Teigan shook her head and stared vacantly out the windshield.

The car clicked as it cooled and the two of them sat without words. Mattix knew her well enough to know that further questions would not be smart.

"Looks like you need your space," Mattix said softly. He opened the door, then twisted in his seat. "Dinner's going to be ready in about twenty." He placed one foot on the sidewalk.

"I spoke with Jackson," Teigan said, still focused on the trash bins farther down the street.

"I..." Mattix considered his words. "I thought we were a united front."

"We still are. I just... needed to speak with him."

"About what?"

Teigan balked. She had walked headfirst into a conversation she didn't want to have, because it meant she'd have to lie. She couldn't tell Mattix about the note she had found during her earlier projection, because that would mean having to explain *how* she learned about the note in the first place. That was a can of worms she refused to open.

"I wanted an update."

"Let me guess," Mattix said. "There wasn't one."

"Right. I got mad all over again." Teigan rested her hands on the steering wheel. "I told him we're going rogue."

Mattix furrowed his brow in confusion. "What does *that* mean exactly?"

"It means we're going to run our own investigation."

"Is that a good idea? I mean, the police are trained for this. They have procedures—"

"You sound like Jackson. Fuck procedure." Teigan stared at him. "Don't you want answers? That's our *united front.*"

"Of course I want answers," Mattix said. "But you've decided a lot of things today without talking to me first. That doesn't sound like a united front to me."

Mattix was right and Teigan knew it.

"Look, Tee. There are some things we're not good at. I think doing our own detective work is one of them. Let the police do what they're good at. And we'll do what we're good at."

"What's that?"

"Keeping our family together," Mattix said. "You and I, we're like epoxy. We're strongest when we're working together."

Teigan matched Mattix's gaze. "Only you would come up with a comparison like that." A small grin slid across her lips.

"I know, right?" Mattix flashed his eyebrows. "That was a good one." He took one of her hands and kissed her palm. "United front, okay?"

Teigan nodded. "Epoxy for the win... I'll be in soon."

Mattix winked at her. "Don't take too long. Lasagna is not a dish to be served cold." He closed the door and returned to the house.

She watched him go and guilt washed over her. Despite what they had just talked about and agreed upon, Teigan and Mattix had not *promised* to act as a united front. She was determined to do everything she could to deliver justice for Newton and no one, not even Mattix, could change her mind. If that meant doing some looking around on her own time, so be it. Newton deserved no stone unturned.

– 53 –

ELISE SAT AT HER DESK in her room working on math homework. There was a single clear path from the door to the desk, passing her bed on the way.

"Tidy up? Why? It's, like, functionally perfect as it is," Elise had told Teigan on many occasions. The way clothes lay scattered about, it looked as if a grenade had detonated in her laundry basket.

She had her phone streaming music to help her concentrate, but all it was doing was inspiring her to hum along and tap her feet. Quadratics, solving trigonometric problems, exponents, linear programming graphs, she hated all of it. To top it all off, an algorithm designed to be needlessly complex had generated the current questions she had to solve. They caused more frustration than actual comprehension. Elise was intelligent, but she knew her future did not lie within the sphere of STEM. She hoped her parents wouldn't be disappointed, but she couldn't get behind something she loathed so much.

But Elise didn't hate mathematics as a whole, if it was the right kind. Give her a workplace or business math course and she'd be all in. Something that would be useful in everyday life, something like what Teigan used when running GadgetGot. Elise never understood why schools taught the kind of math that most kids would forget over the summer break or a month after graduating.

Mattix called up from the kitchen. "Dinner in fifteen, Lise."

"Thanks, Dad."

Elise had three questions left, hopefully doable in the time left before dinner. Then she could eat and go do what she wanted. Mattix made a mean lasagna, and the smells of garlic, herbs, and spices were driving her stomach wild. On top of the music, it was hard to concentrate on anything.

The lead in her mechanical pencil broke. She clicked the end to advance more lead, and an insignificant piece fell out. Elise shook the pencil and heard nothing rattling inside its mechanical shell. She clicked the end several times to confirm.

Definitely out of lead. Crap.

She looked around her cluttered desk and could not find any replacement lead. "Mom?"

A moment later, Mattix answered from the entryway on the first floor. "She's outside. Can I help with anything?"

"Do we have any point-five pencil lead?" Elise continued to click the end of her pencil as if that would magically produce more lead.

"Um, good question," Mattix said. "Try Mom's office."

Elise leaped from her chair and wandered into Teigan's office just down the hall. Neat and orderly, with everything in its place, the space was a stark contrast to her room. Functionally perfect could have described her mom's office too, but it was also boring as hell.

Elise scanned the top of the desk and searched a few drawers before her eyes set upon a piece of paper sticking out from under a book on ecommerce. Normally she'd gloss over such a detail, but there was handwriting on the paper that looked familiar. She pulled it out to get a better look.

On a piece of Teigan's GadgetGot letterhead, Newton's name and their street was written all over the page, sometimes the name repeated, sometimes the street, sometimes both together. Elise recognized the handwriting instantly.

Haislee?

She ran back to her room, grabbed her phone, and returned to take a couple photos, one of the whole page and a few closeups. She selected them all and texted them to Haislee.

"Do U know what this is?" she typed below the collection of photos.

It took a moment to deliver, then Haislee texted back, "Um looks like my writing."

"NS," Elise tapped. "But on my mom's papers???"

"No idea," Haislee texted back.

Elise couldn't put it together.

Mattix called up to let her know that dinner was ready. "Oh, did you find the lead?" he added.

Elise returned the paper to where she had found it, then began nervously clicking the empty mechanical pencil with her thumb. "No," she said.

"You can ask Mom at dinner."

A couple of blocks away, Haislee sat in her room pinch-zooming on the photos Elise had sent her. The cursive looked like her handwriting when she was writing quickly. Her telltale letters, the "a" that looked like an "@," the "e" that looked like a backwards "3," the tail on the "n" when ending a word.

A text message notification from Elise flashed on Haislee's phone. It read, "R U sure U don't know what this is???"

Back at the Coleman house, Elise stood in the doorway to Teigan's office, watching and waiting as the three dots bounced inside Haislee's thought balloon. Then it morphed into the text message, "Totes sure," then, "Makes no sense."

Elise gave Haislee's text a thumbs up and pocketed her phone. She had three more math questions still to do and now she faced the biggest distraction of all: Why would Haislee's handwriting be on papers in her mom's office?

– 54 –

MATTIX'S LASAGNA WAS TERRIFIC. It always has been. It was one of the things that made Teigan sit up and take notice when they were dating over two decades ago. Both Mattix and the lasagna had gotten better with age.

One of the rules of the Coleman household states that whoever doesn't cook must clean up. Teigan took her place at the sink and began to scrub the pots and baking dishes that were too cumbersome for the dishwasher. As rules go, this one was easy to follow.

As Teigan scoured food remnants, she'd take periodic breaks to gaze out the window facing the sink. Their deck, which had been replaced a decade earlier, needed either a coat of paint or a total rebuild. She'd opt for the rebuild. They could afford it. But Mattix's frugal nature (and technical ability) tended to extend the lives of their appliances and surroundings long past their typical expiry.

The shed in the back yard needed repair too. Its shingled roof was missing at least a dozen shakes.

"An easy fix," Mattix had told her.

A rake leaned up against the side of the shed. Teigan couldn't remember if she or Mattix was the last to use it. She reminded herself to put it away after she finished in the kitchen.

As she scrubbed, her mind drifted back to the morning when Betty had told her about the vase of flowers in Newton's room, how they had fallen, and how she had failed to move them in her projection the day before.

Someone moved them.

Then a thought hit her.

Maybe it was me.

She dried her hands and headed upstairs. Mattix called to her from the living room.

"Want to watch something with me?"

Although the offer was tempting, Teigan had an experiment to run. "Maybe in an hour? I want to lie down for a while." She started up the stairs.

Mattix poked his head around the wall by the stairs. "Feeling okay?" His voice held mild concern.

Teigan looked back, smiled, and said, "Yeah, just tired." The lies, although small, had begun to pile up and it made her feel a little sick to her stomach.

Once in the master bedroom, she laid supine on their bed, propped up her head comfortably, and pulled a thick afghan over her body. The warmth and deep breaths would have her relaxed and projecting in no time.

Teigan closed her eyes and envisioned the back yard. It was easy to do. After twenty years, she knew the space like the back of her hand. But even despite being able to picture everything, small details were lost. The exterior of the house was smooth instead of textured stucco. Everything took on a slight plasticized look, glossy but less specular.

She approached the shed and reached for the rake leaning against it. Years of use had worn the wooden handle smooth to the touch. Teigan ran her finger along one edge, then ended by pressing her finger against the handle. As expected, the rake remained fixed, as if nailed or glued in place.

Teigan gripped the rake with both hands and tried to shake it free.

No dice.

She cast her mind back a day earlier to her first projection to Newton's hospital room and her run-in with the tall mystery person. Teigan replayed the memory, remembering how she had raised her voice at the intruder while trying to move the vase of flowers. Was that the secret?

"Move you DAMN RAKE!" she yelled while gripping the handle and flexing her arms with all her strength. Still the rake remained fixed where it was. She didn't think she could get breathless in a projection but there she was, gulping air through clenched teeth.

Maybe it wasn't not possible after all. Typically a rule-follower, Teigan's dislike for the strict way projections worked caused her anger to simmer. She should have considered herself lucky, but she wanted more. She wanted the ability to do *more*.

Then there was Jackson and the investigation that wasn't going anywhere. Teigan's anger boiled into rage and she lashed out.

"FUCK YOU, JACKSON!" She swung a fist at the rake handle and sent it flying onto the lawn next to the shed. She stared at it, not quite believing that she had succeeded.

But did it happen for real?

Teigan held her breath until her need for air pulled her out of her projection. She made a line to the ensuite bathroom, slid open the frosted window, and peered out at the back yard.

The rake, partially hidden in grass that needed mowing, lay near the shed. It was no longer leaning against the side of the shed.

"How...," Teigan whispered to herself before details began to meld and become clearer. It was her anger, rage, her release of raw emotion that had enabled a temporary projected super strength. For reasons she didn't quite understand, Teigan's ability to move objects in a projection was like a "get out of jail free" card.

To be used for emergencies only.

"Wild," she said.

"What's wild?" Mattix poked his head around the door frame.

Teigan thought fast. "The back yard. It's getting a bit wild." A lie or a half-truth. It didn't matter. They were both getting easier.

"It's on my chore list, when it warms up a bit more." Mattix kissed her shoulder. "Join me downstairs? Popcorn and Heartland?"

"Read my mind," Teigan said, immediately glad that Mattix didn't have that ability. Because he'd have questions. Lots of them. "I'll be down in five."

"Great." Mattix left to prepare their snacks.

Teigan regarded herself in the mirror. She had lots of questions, too. Now she possessed a way to get answers that rivaled any police investigation, and the only way to keep her secret safe was through lies. Lots of them.

$$- \ 55 \ -$$

TEIGAN WOKE FROM A DREAM of Newton, which on its own would have been a good way to begin the day. But it felt like she had just swam the first leg of a triathlon. Her entire body screamed with exhaustion. She rolled to her side to get out of bed and noticed the time: quarter past eight. She had slept in.

"Fuck." Teigan sprang out of bed, threw on her housecoat, and hustled down to the kitchen. "Sorry. Sorry."

Mattix and Elise looked at her with surprise.

"Nothing to be sorry about." Mattix sealed up a lunch bag and grinned at her. "Everything's under control."

"I *can* feed myself, yah know." Elise placed a hand on her hip for emphasis.

"You were really zoned out," Mattix continued. "Decided to let you sleep." He spotted Teigan's eyes shift to the corner of the kitchen where several small appliances sat, including the coffee machine. "And yes, there's fresh brew."

"Thank you." On her way to the coffee machine, Teigan planted kisses on Mattix's and Elise's cheeks. Then without deviating from her one-track path, she grabbed a coffee cup and filled it to the rim. She leveled her lips with the top of the cup and slurped the coffee down to a level safe for moving, just like a preschooler might do with their apple juice.

Teigan looked back at Mattix and Elise, both wearing looks of mild surprise. "What? I over-filled it."

Elise waved her off. "No worries, Mom. You do you."

Mattix found Teigan's eyes and locked gazes with her. "You going to be alright?"

Teigan took another long sip of coffee and sighed. "Now I am."

"Okay. I'll get Lise to school. Call me if you need anything."

Teigan nodded and watched them leave through the front door. The coffee was doing its job, pulling her out of the fog of last night's dreams.

Of Newton.

Teigan couldn't remember any details except that Newton had figured prominently. It was strange. She could remember any detail from her waking life or a projection, but most of her dreams had always remained elusive, dissipating like woodsmoke.

In a few more days it would be two weeks since his overdose and almost a week since Teigan had stopped her daily vigils. She refilled her mug and made her way back upstairs, not to her bedroom or her office, but to Newton's room.

It was the first time she had set foot in his space since the accident. His room was generally tidy (Newton would have argued that it was *spotless*). Teigan collected a few books and papers and set them on his desk in a neat pile, then forced herself to stop.

Newton's going to be home soon. He can do this.

Teigan scanned the shelves, noting all the books Newton had acquired during his life so far. His collection varied widely, including subjects like video games, DIY fix-it manuals, music and film history, and fiction. He still had a shelf devoted to Archie Double Digest comic books that he read voraciously in elementary school. Teigan pulled out one of the Archie comics, its cover dog-eared, and flipped through it wondering if he still read them.

Her eyes settled on part of a shelf devoted to his high school yearbooks. Teigan pulled out his most recent yearbook, Grade 11, sat on the edge of his bed, and flipped it open.

Even today, the yearbooks still smelled the same as she remembered them, a sharp scent of petroleum. She flipped through the pages carefully. Compared to her own yearbooks, all the images were printed in full colour. Hair and clothing styles had changed, but the poses and attitudes of students had mostly stayed the same.

Teigan moved through the pages and tried to identify kids she knew. She failed miserably. Near the middle of the yearbook, a small stack of folded purple paper slid out.

She unfolded one and realized at once that it was a letter from a secret admirer, written with a silver paint pen. It was hard to force herself to stop reading. Instead, Teigan skipped to the bottom of the page. There was no signature except for a small heart shape with a curled tail at the bottom and she recognized it immediately. It was identical in style as the one she had seen drawn in purple on Newton's left hand. And the odds were good that whoever drew it was at the afterparty as well. But who?

Maybe there'd be a clue further on in the yearbook. Teigan continued flipping through the publication. There were many farewells written in messy teenage cursive between photos and along the margins, but no heart with a curly tail. However, on almost every page with a photo of Newton, a single word stood out all on its own, like "Hawt!," "Smokin!," and "Sexxxy!," all of them written carefully so that there would be no mistaking what they said.

By the third instance, Teigan noticed a familiar pattern with the letters, particularly the writing style of the "e".

Like a backwards "3."

Teigan set the yearbook on the bed and ran to her office. She pulled out the sheet of paper with "Newton Coleman Radcliffe Crescent" written all over it and returned to the bedroom.

The "e"s matched. So did the "a"s and "n"s. Page after page, the words written in Newton's yearbook next to his many photos matched the cursive style on the sheet of paper Teigan held in her hand. The same person had written both.

But whose handwriting did I emulate?

She flipped back to the Grade 9 section and moved forward through the pages. They were mostly unmarked, which she expected considering Newton didn't hang with a younger crowd.

Teigan flipped into the J-K-L-M section and one photo stood out from the others. It had a small heart drawn in the upper right corner. Haislee Kirkland, with her blond hair and big blue eyes, stared back at her.

"I wonder…" The gears in Teigan's mind began to turn. She left everything on Newton's bed and went to Elise's bedroom. Compared to Newton's room, it looked like a bomb cyclone had hit. Teigan began a precise and challenging game of Eye Spy.

She was careful not to move anything unnecessarily and the objects she did move, she returned as close to their original location as possible. Elise's room might look like a mess to everyone else, but she probably had a recognizable system of organization.

It took several minutes to find Elise's Grade 9 yearbook buried on a shelf next to her desk. Teigan flipped it open to the A-B-C section of the Grade 9 students and saw her daughter's picture right away. Elise had worn a modest black halter top with wide straps that only exposed her bare shoulders. Teigan remembered the fight they had had on picture day. She had wanted Elise to wear a T-shirt, but Elise had stood her ground. Looking back now, the fight had been unnecessary. Elise looked classy and elegant for a fourteen-year-old. And she stood out from all the other teenagers on the page. Chalk one up for irrational parental fears.

Next to Elise's photo was a written message from Haislee, which read, "To my bff 4 life, love your #1 fan." In the top right sat a small heart. The "a," "e," and "n" were all written the same way as in Newton's yearbook.

The details were easy to put together. They wouldn't stand up in a court of law, but Teigan didn't need them to. She knew Haislee had had a crush on Newton for a long time and didn't try very hard to hide it. Now Teigan knew that Haislee had been at the afterparty, and she had lied to everyone about it.

And if Haislee was at the afterparty, there was a chance that others within Haislee's and Elise's circle of friends had gone too. Teigan matched the write-ups in Elise's yearbook with their corresponding names and photos as best she could and took photos with her phone. She carefully returned the yearbook to the spot where she had found it and returned to Newton's room.

Teigan followed the same procedure with Newton's yearbook. She was surprised at the number of write-ups Newton had. She had no idea that he was that popular at Diamond Bay. From the eyes of a parent at home, it didn't seem like he had many friends. But with the rise of smartphones, she knew that some kids formed entirely online relationships. It seemed sad in some ways, losing the in-person contact, but at least the kids were staying connected enough to sign each other's yearbooks.

Teigan wished there was a quality rating for the write-ups so she could prioritize who to talk to first. However, a lot can change in eight months. It was anyone's guess if the kids that signed Newton's Grade 11 yearbook would do the same this year.

Two kids that would be at the top of her list, even if they had bad quality ratings, would be Richard Baum and Dustin Stoaks. It was clear that Newton had had a falling out with them at some point between the summer after Grade 11 and now. But they still hung out occasionally.

It was all very confusing for Teigan, especially since Newton kept his cards close to his chest. He took his privacy very seriously. And now she sat on Newton's bed, violating his space.

Teigan returned Newton's yearbook to its spot in his bookshelf, with the secret admirer letters tucked back inside. She was again reminded that she still didn't know for sure who had written them. She filed that nagging detail in the back of her mind for now, grabbed her coffee cup, and returned to the kitchen.

A trip to Diamond Bay High School was on her to-do list today, and if she played her cards right, she'd get the answers she needed.

– 56 –

TEIGAN PARKED HER RENTAL a few blocks down Edgerton Street and slunk down in her seat so that she could see the red bricks of Diamond Bay in the distance just over top of the steering wheel. Reducing the chance of anyone spotting her was foremost in her mind.

Teigan had limited knowledge of Diamond Bay High School, even with two kids in attendance. Over the past four years, excluding her recent meeting with Principal McCarthy, she'd rarely visited the school except for parent-teacher meetings and special events held in the gymnasium. Most of the hallways and classrooms were a mystery... but not for long.

The digital clock on the dash of the Honda Civic read 11:05am. She pulled out her phone. Half an hour should be enough time to memorize the small collection of faces she had taken from the 2023 Diamond Bay yearbook. Then another half hour to roam the hallways and familiarize herself with the layout of the school.

Teigan locked the car and walked the short distance to the school while flipping one last time through pictures on her phone of the kids she wanted to talk to.

The memory of her meeting with McCarthy a few days ago took anxious bites at her psyche as she pulled open one of the doors to the front entrance. Her first and only priority was to scope out the school and talk to her list of kids, while simultaneously avoiding suspicion. She didn't need McCarthy or a nosy teacher on her case.

Teigan decided to start on the second floor and work her way down. She veered left, took the stairs, and followed the hallway on one side, one slow step at a time, peering into the classrooms with open doors. She must have looked like a lunatic to the students who happened to see her pass by, gawking through the doorway.

There was a chance that Elise or Haislee would spot her, or even Richard and Dustin, before the lunch bell rang. But there was little she could do about students staring aimlessly out the classroom doors. She shelved the thought and continued her reconnaissance operation, hopefully without raising suspicion.

Teigan paid particular attention to the locker numbers, fulfilling the secondary goal of her visit. Whatever information she was unable to uncover directly might be available through a projection. She knew the classrooms and walls would be a blurry mess in a projection, much like Jackson's office had been, but lockers might hold valuable information. It wouldn't take much effort to study a combination lock in a student's hand.

She reached the end of the hallway on the second floor, crossed to the opposite side, and repeated her maneuver with the remaining classrooms. Teigan took the stairs to the main floor and realized that the layout of classrooms was different. There was an additional hallway that led away from the main entrance. The main office was located at the nexus of the two hallways and the only reason she could come up with for forgetting its existence was her anxiety meeting McCarthy earlier. Even though she had an eidetic memory, her anxious state had locked it temporarily in her subconscious.

Teigan pulled out her phone. The time read: 11:45am. The

remaining twenty minutes was barely enough time to orient herself to the detail in one hallway, let alone two.

She quickened her pace and started with the hallway next to the stairs, an identical layout to the hallway above. She scanned the lockers, their numbers, and the accessible classrooms, finishing both sides of the hallway in twelve minutes. Teigan worried that her increased speed might affect the detail in a projection later, but she had no other option. She had to finish before class let out.

In the eight minutes that remained, Teigan worked her way down one side of the central hallway and up the other. Two banks of lockers and one classroom remained when the lunch bell shattered her concentration. And as she passed the main office, she spotted Principal McCarthy talking with the receptionist in the anteroom. He cast a glance out the door and Teigan shielded her face by returning her gaze to the lockers.

Please don't let him see me. Please...

Teigan walked to the nexus between the two ground floor hallways as students filed out of their classrooms. Immediately she faced a dilemma. Everyone was moving too fast, and all at once, which was completely normal at a high school. She may have a fantastic memory, but she had failed to run the plan through her head.

If it had been a projection, all of the faces she had memorized would stand out like shining avatars compared to the other nondescript, blurred, and distorted suggestions of faces. But she couldn't talk in a projection. In hindsight, this should have been a plan with multiple stages: identify locker numbers through projection, leave a note for further contact, and talk to the students one by one. But time was ticking. Teigan was here now, and she would make the best of the situation.

Picking out one or two people from a moving crowd is one thing. Identifying a dozen or more is quite another. In fact, impossible. Teigan decided to keep her eyes open until she positively identified one person she could direct her questions to.

And that person just happened to be...

Richard.

She made a direct approach and pulled his locker door all the way open, banging it flat against the locker next to him.

Richard took a step back, startled. He was unprepared for Teigan's intensity and looked around the hallway to see if anyone was watching. "Uh, Mrs. Coleman. What are you doing here?"

"I need to talk to you," Teigan said.

Richard directed his gaze into his locker. "About what?"

"I think you know."

Richard balked.

"We both know you were at the quarry." Teigan tried to make eye contact, but Richard kept turning his head away. "Were you there when Newton was drugged?"

"Look, Mrs. Coleman," Richard said. "I've got to go."

"Why didn't you help him? Newt has been your best friend since Grade 6."

Richard grabbed his backpack from inside his locker and hung it off one shoulder. "We grew apart, *okay*? End of story."

Teigan stared at him, her hand still propped on the locker door, preventing Richard from closing it. "What happened to you?"

Dustin appeared from behind Richard and rested his hand on Richard's shoulder. "He met *me*. Now, respectfully Mrs. Coleman, you're going to fuck off."

Teigan threw all her weight on the locker door and glared at the two teenagers. Richard tried to hide his panic and failed but Dustin returned a smug grin. She wanted to rip it off his face.

"Is there a problem, here?" McCarthy inserted himself between Teigan and the boys.

Teigan took her hand off Richard's locker door. He closed and locked it immediately. "No problem," she said.

"Actually, we *do* have a problem." Dustin narrowed his eyes at

Teigan and scowled. "She's getting in our faces and asking bullshit questions. Sorry for swearing, sir, but it's the truth."

"The only one swearing here is Dustin," Teigan said.

Dustin laughed. "You should have heard her, sir. M-F-er this and A-hole that. She even threatened us." Dustin nudged Richard. "Ain't that right?"

Richard nodded, his face showing less concern and more anger.

"That's a total lie," Teigan said.

Dustin stepped forward. "Bullshit. You just—"

"Enough. Mrs. Coleman..." McCarthy placed his hand on Teigan's arm and pulled her away from the boys, but Teigan yanked her arm out of his grasp.

"Don't *touch* me." Teigan saw Dustin snickering to himself and rage boiled up inside her.

"Please leave, Mrs. Coleman," McCarthy said, "or I'll be left with no choice but to call the police."

"Do it." Teigan daggered her eyes at the principal. "Ask for Detective Konishi."

Hearing Jackson's name made Dustin dial back his glee. He knew Teigan was serious.

McCarthy watched a small crowd begin to form around the four of them. "Mrs. Coleman... please."

Teigan spotted Elise and Haislee descending the stairs from the second floor. "I'm here to see my daughter. Or do you have a problem with that too?"

McCarthy crossed his arms against his chest. "Do it outside."

Teigan marched across the hallway, waved, and beckoned. Her face mirrored her current mood. "Lise."

Elise rolled her eyes and whispered something into Haislee's ear. Neither of them laughed this time.

"Mom." Elise spoke low through gritted teeth. "What are you doing here?" She glanced over her shoulder to see if anyone was watching.

"I'm not trying to embarrass you, if that's what you mean," Teigan said.

"Too late for *that*."

Teigan shot a look a Haislee. "Can I talk to you?"

"Me?" Haislee swallowed hard and took a quick, nervous look at Elise before facing Teigan. "What about?"

"Over here." Teigan directed Haislee to a small alcove next to the stairs that housed one of the school's many public water fountains.

Haislee followed, watching Teigan for any clue that would explain this unexpected interaction. Elise crossed her arms a short distance away, glowering at Teigan.

The two women stood close, their eyes on each other. "What's wrong, Mrs. Coleman?"

Teigan lowered her voice. "Can you be straight with me?"

Haislee nodded. "Yes, of course."

"Why did you lie about being at the afterparty?"

"I..." Haislee blinked at Teigan, uncertain. "I didn't. I had a stomach—"

"Haislee," Teigan said. "I know you were there. And I can prove it. Why did you lie?"

"I... I didn't want to get in trouble." Haislee cast a glance of confusion at Elise. "But Lise knows what happened. I told her everything."

"What did you tell her?"

"I stayed. I did CPR until help arrived," Haislee said. "Then I ran."

Teigan took a step back, as if the wind had been knocked out of her. She narrowed her eyes at Elise and approached her.

Elise's aggravation melted away to fear and she dropped her arms to her side.

"You *knew*? And you said *nothing*?" Teigan glared at her daughter, the heat of her anger burning back her tears. "Newt's your brother, *goddammit*. Why would you do that?"

"I'm sorry, Mom," Elise said, fighting back tears of her own. "I guess I thought telling you wouldn't help."

"Everything helps at this point."

"Hazy saved Newt's life." Elise shook her head trying to process the conversation. "Now he's in the hospital. How does knowing about what Hazy did help *anything* now?"

Teigan saw the sorrow etched into Elise's face. She took her daughter in her arms and held her close. In a school setting, Elise would normally have resisted such a display of affection, but she wrapped her arms around Teigan as well.

"Because I'm going to get the bastards that did this, hon." Teigan spoke softly as she turned her head to look across the hallway to where Richard and Dustin had been standing. She half expected them to still be there, watching her with their entitled eyes. "That's why everything helps." She stepped back and wiped Elise's tears away with her thumbs. "Okay?"

Elise nodded.

"No more secrets, okay?"

Elise smirked a sideways look at her.

Teigan corrected herself. "At least no more secrets about Newt. Deal?"

"Deal," Elise said.

Teigan looked back at Haislee. "Sorry for putting you on the spot."

"It's okay, Mrs. Coleman."

"Now that I've thoroughly embarrassed both of you, my job here is done." She reached out and squeezed both girls' hands and headed for the main entrance.

Back at the car, Teigan slid down in the driver's seat to hide her face from view, embracing what Elise would call an "epic fail." The only successful part of her hastily conceived plan was scouting the location. And in the safety of her fire engine red Civic, there was no time like the present to see if it worked.

$$- \ 57 \ -$$

TEIGAN RELAXED HERSELF with cleansing breaths and closed her eyes. Projecting to places was becoming easier with each trip. She pictured herself in the middle of the entryway, at the nexus of the two main hallways of the school. Being the middle of lunch break, the school was still busy with students, some perched on the stairs eating from their bag lunches, and a few sitting against their lockers reading or playing on their phones.

They all wore the same ensemble, gray shirts and pants, and their faces held blank, smeared visages. Teigan kept her eyes open for the kids she had wanted to talk to earlier, but didn't let it distract her from her current mission.

Teigan roamed the hallways of her projection, walking a normal pace, starting on the second floor, then the first, and followed by the central hallway. The classrooms appeared just she had expected, a generalized impression of a classroom built from her recce today merged with every high school classroom she had ever visited in her life. The locker numbers were clear and readable. Her plan hadn't been as much of an "epic fail" as she originally thought.

As she followed the central hallway back toward the entrance of the school, Teigan passed the main office on her left. Curiosity got the better of her and she stepped inside.

The typical sounds of the office, fingers on keyboards, filing cabinets opening and closing, laser printers whirring and spitting out paper, were noticeably absent. Teigan figured they were all eating lunch in the staff room.

She followed the winding path to McCarthy's office. The door stood ajar, allowing her to hear conversation float out from inside. The gap was also just wide enough for her to slip through.

McCarthy's office hadn't changed much since the last time she had been there. This time he had a sandwich laid out on sodden wax paper. Smells didn't transfer through a projection, but it looked like tuna salad. He had opened his thermos and filled his "World's Best Principal" cup with coffee. He sat reclined in his chair with his feet propped up on the corner of the desk, his phone to his ear.

"Yeah," McCarthy said. "I almost had to throw her out. I mean I get that her son's in a coma, but that doesn't give her the right to come in here and harass my students."

"I didn't harass anyone, dipshit." Teigan positioned herself in front of his desk, looking down on the portly man. Knowing that he couldn't see or hear her filled her with crazy glee.

"Totally." McCarthy took a bite of his sandwich, then continued talking with his mouth full. Teigan saw bits of chewed sandwich fly out of his mouth and stick to the phone's receiver.

"Even the smart ones overdose," he continued. "I read about this genius student in Boston, knew the effects and chemical makeup of every pharmaceutical out there. He made the mistake of assuming the drugs he bought would be clean. But nope. Laced with fentanyl. End of story."

Teigan felt her anger rising.

McCarthy took a sip of coffee. "The Coleman kid, forget his name—"

"His name is Newton, you asshole."

"Exactly. Bad supply," McCarthy said into the phone. "But she can't come in here like she owns the place. A story like this is bad enough. If she uncovers something else, something worse, it could be very bad for the school, and more importantly, bad for *me*. I tell you, if she shows her face here unannounced again, I'm calling the police from the get-go."

Teigan couldn't take this man's self-centered apathy any longer. She stood, braced herself on the front of his desk and leaned forward until she was a foot away from his face. Everything about McCarthy repulsed her.

"The kid better survive, for my sake at least." McCarthy began to laugh.

"Fuck YOU, you worthless piece of SHIT!" Fueled by rage, Teigan pushed her hands forward and the sound of the Civic's horn snapped her out of her projection.

At that same instant in McCarthy's office, his thermos, mug, and sandwich shot forth, soaking his crotch with a slurry of coffee and tuna salad, the mug smashing on the floor by his chair.

Back in the car, Teigan waited for her pulse to return to normal. Part of her wanted to drop by McCarthy's office unannounced to confirm that he was wearing his lunch, but she had a good feeling that she didn't need to. What she really needed was to check on her son.

$$- \ 58 \ -$$

RICHARD REMAINED QUIET for the remainder of the day. His run-in with Teigan had dug up old feelings, ones of lost friendship, frustration, and guilt. But why should he be feeling guilt? He hadn't done anything wrong.

Except throw Newton under the friendship bus.

There was that. Looking back on it now, after shunning Newton for most of their Grade 12 year so far, Richard held no pride in what he had done. Had it been a mistake to focus on his own life for a change? To seek out new friends and experiences? Richard hadn't thought so at the time, but tragedy put a different lens on things. Could he have just let his friend group get larger? Maybe.

After class, Richard grabbed everything he needed for homework and split for home. Usually he waited for Dustin and the two of them would cruise the neighbourhood looking for girls to chat up, or go to Tim Horton's for coffee and doughnuts and girls to chat up. Not today. He had other plans. He left the school, his head down and focused on the walk home. The fewer people he saw (or saw him) the better.

As he turned up Meridale Lane, he saw the familiar black Escalade in his driveway. Richard groaned and prepared for an onslaught of Dustin Stoaks. Sometimes it seemed like he was Dustin's only friend, an often exhausting title.

It was never like that with Newton. He allowed Richard to breath, to exist, and have space for himself when he needed it. Dustin, although loud and obnoxious, opened a world of experiences to Richard that Newton couldn't match. And there wasn't enough room in Richard's life for both of them.

Even though he didn't hang out with Newton one on one anymore, and definitely not in any other substantial way, Richard hadn't expected Newton's absence to affect him as much as it had. He had wanted Newton to continue to be part of his familiar background, a footnote.

As Richard approached the Escalade, Dustin leaned out the driver's side window, tapping his hand on the outside of the SUV's door.

"Hey butt plug," Dustin said. "Why'd you run off? Thought we were gonna play GTA 5. Kill some hoes, eh?"

"I've got other plans." Richard intentionally didn't face Dustin, because he'd see through the lie immediately.

"Oh yeah? Like what?" Dustin eyed Richard as he headed to the front door of his house and powered down the passenger window. "You got a hoe of your own I don't know about?"

"No." Richard took out his keys. "Just last minute plans." He unlocked the door and opened it. Richard looked back at Dustin framed in the passenger window and hoped he was far away enough that Dustin's bullshit meter wouldn't go off. "See you tomorrow."

The two stared at each other for a moment, then Dustin started the engine of the Escalade. "Suit yourself. I got a date with Candy and Trixie and..." Dustin continued to rattle off names of sex workers in Grand Theft Auto 5 as he backed out of the driveway.

Richard closed the door. That had gone better then he had predicted. Keys still in hand, he threw his backpack on the floor and stepped into the garage. His Norco 21-speed mountain bike hung off the back wall.

He hadn't gotten his bike out onto the road in months. That was something he used to do with Newton. Dustin had driven him around for most of the school year so far. The streets were clear of snow and ice which meant he wouldn't be risking life and limb to get to the hospital. He carried his bike out the side door, locked it, and started his journey.

Richard had missed the self-sufficient feeling of propelling himself under his own steam, the cool air in his face. However, the time away from his bicycle had taken a toll on his body. He had lost his stamina and was soon sucking wind. His pace slowed, but he carried on. Nothing would deter him from his mission today.

Forty minutes later, Richard rolled into the parking lot of Cherry Mills Medical Centre. He locked his bike and found the information desk. After inquiring about Newton Coleman, the admin on staff directed him to the intensive care unit on the second floor.

He stepped out of the elevator and walked to the reception desk of the ICU. "I'm looking for Newton Coleman."

Betty handed him a clipboard. "Please sign in."

Richard balked for a moment, then wrote down "L. Mario" and returned the clipboard. *Luigi Mario.* Back in Grade 6, Newton and Richard had discovered that the characters from *Super Mario Bros.*, their favourite video game, had the last name of Mario. They adopted the names when playing the games, but it became a running joke. Newton was Mario Mario and Richard was Luigi Mario. Only Newton would know the significance of the name and he was in a coma.

"Room 223." Betty offered a small smile as she buzzed the lock to the ward.

The room numbers on this end of the looped corridor of the ICU counted down from 226. Hospitals gave Richard the creeps at the best of times. Passing by the doorways of people of all ages clinging to life didn't help him feel any better.

He stood at the threshold to Newton's room. Wires and tubes partly obscured his face, but Richard knew it was Newton from the way his hair flipped up at the front, an unintentional pompadour.

Nurses had dimmed the lights to the room and drawn the window blinds. The pulse monitor, a small desk lamp (like Pixar's *Luxo*) beside the bed, and a nightlight above the counter facing the foot of his bed combined with spill from the corridor, gave Richard enough illumination to navigate the room without bumping into things.

Richard walked forward and stood by the right side of the bed. He looked at the fluctuating numbers on the pulse monitor. The ventilator hissed and popped rhythmically beside it in sync with the rise and fall of Newton's chest. Everything was real and inescapable now. And despite all the dust-ups and angst he and Newton had faced over the past year, Richard found himself wishing, hoping...

Please don't die.

Richard placed his hand on Newton's right hand, surprised by how warm it felt. "I'm sorry." He felt tears rise up and although they did not fall, he had not expected to get this emotional.

The ventilator began to make a different sound, almost echoing each mechanical breath. Richard took a step back, all at once aware that the additional sound was not coming from the ventilator at all, but from someone else breathing.

From behind Richard a voice spoke. "Don't turn around. And don't do anything stupid."

Richard felt panic rise in the back of his mind. He half expected the barrel of a gun pressed into his back. "What? I'm here to see a friend."

"You're not Newton's friend," the voice said.

"What would you know about it?"

"I've seen things."

Richard began to turn his head when he heard the person behind him take a step forward.

"What'd I say?" The voice spoke calmly and firmly. "Don't."

"What do you mean you've *seen* things?"

"Does the L. R. Wilson lecture hall at McMaster ring a bell?"

Richard's guts felt like they had liquefied inside him. "Don't know what you're talk—"

"Your *asshole* friend pushed Newton," the voice said. "Don't deny it. I was there. I have proof."

"He never pushed him," Richard said.

"Bullshit," the voice said. "That *asshole* started shoving people, which ended up causing Newton to fall."

"He never intended to hurt him."

"Yet he did. You stood by and did nothing. And now *this*."

"I never did *this*." Richard's panic morphed into short-lived anger. Then the steady, heavy breaths behind him raised the hairs on the back of his neck.

"Sure about that? You and your *asshole* friend better watch yourselves," the voice said.

"Or what?"

"Or I'll push back," the voice said. "You don't want to mess with me."

Richard had had enough. There was nowhere to go but out. With his pulse quickening at this unknown person behind him, he took a deep breath, tensed all his muscles, and turned to leave. Towering above him, backlit from the light in the corridor, his face shrouded in shadow, stood a tall man in a navy blue hoodie.

It was impossible to know the age of the individual from where Richard stood. He pushed past the mystery person, who made no attempt to stop him, and hustled down the corridor, looking back once. The person had stepped into Newton's room and out of sight.

He ignored Betty's wave as he passed the reception desk. She may have said something to him, but Richard was so focused on his exodus he didn't hear a thing. He took the stairs to the foyer and ran through the doors of the main entrance, barely letting them slide open before squeezing his body through.

Richard found a bench near the doors and had just sat down to catch his breath and let his heart slow to a normal pace, when someone pulled him up by his jacket.

"What the *fuck,* man?" Dustin pinned Richard against the brick wall. "Seriously, what the *fuck* are you doing here? This is your so-called 'last minute plans'?"

Richard pushed back. "I wanted to see how he was doing. Newton was my friend for a long time."

"And now he's *not.*" The veins on Dustin's forehead looked like they were going to pop. "Get over him."

"Why are you so mad? I didn't do anything wrong."

"That cop is still on the prowl, idiot," Dustin said. "Plus dipshit's mom, too. They're going to want to check up on anyone who visits him. Probably used your real name, right?"

"Fuck you," Richard said. "Give me some credit."

"I'll give you *something.*" Dustin raised his hand as if he was going to hit Richard, then backed off. "We're going. Get your bike."

Richard did as he was told and they secured the bike in the back of the Escalade. Dustin pulled out of the parking lot, turned the radio on, and cranked it.

Richard turned the volume down. "Look, I got to ask you something."

Dustin ignored the question and turned the volume back up.

Richard punched the power button and silenced the radio. "Stop being an asshole. You're acting like you've got something to hide."

"What?" Dustin kept his eyes on the road. "Don't be stupid."

"Do you remember everyone going to McMaster?"

"How could I forget?" Dustin laughed. "That was where Newton fell and broke his ribs. Fuckin' klutz."

"That's 'cause you pushed him," Richard said.

Dustin's grin dissolved. "I didn't push *anyone*. WE pushed some *other* fuckwit who just *happened* to fall on him."

"So you didn't do it on purpose?"

Dustin narrowed his eyes on Richard long enough to make him uncomfortable. "What's all this 'you' bullshit. WE pushed the fuckwit because WE don't like being pushed around. It's not our fault that Newton fell down like a baby."

Richard cast his mind back and tried to recall the day the class spent at McMaster. "I don't remember pushing anybody."

"Well, you did," Dustin said. "I remember 'cause you really gave it to the guy. I was impressed."

Richard shrugged back at him. "Don't remember that."

"What's wrong with you today?" Dustin took his eyes off the road long enough to give Richard a once-over. "You gettin' Old Timer's disease, you *McMasterbater?*"

Dustin cackled at his joke and Richard couldn't help but join in. Dustin's laugh was sometimes the funniest part of what he said.

"Here's an idea," Dustin said. "I drop your bike at your place, then we go back to my place and play some GTA 5—"

"And kill some hoes," they said in unison.

"Yeah, sure," Richard said.

"Alright." Dustin held out his right hand, made a fist, and Richard bumped it with his own. "Let's get our dicks wet... *virtually* that is."

Both teenagers burst out laughing again. Richard thought about sharing his experience in Newton's hospital room from earlier, but decided to keep it to himself and see if the mystery person followed through with his threats.

– 59 –

TEIGAN PULLED INTO THE VISITOR'S parking lot at Cherry Mills Medical Centre and immediately began scanning for an empty space. But she couldn't help but notice the big black SUV that rolled past, music blasting out the driver's side window.

A Cadillac Escalade.

Just before the SUV rolled beyond her sightline, she recognized Dustin at the wheel and Richard riding shotgun. That made sense since Dustin was the only teenager in Cherry Mills to drive a decked-out Cadillac. But why would they be here?

Teigan found a parking space on the opposite side of the lot from the main entrance. When she went to grab an elevator from the main lobby, the doors closed on her just before she reached them, despite people standing inside watching her approach. It felt like some force was conspiring against her, to delay her, and a swell of uneasiness rose within her.

As she waited for the next elevator, Teigan mulled over the day, focusing on her run-in with Richard and Dustin at the school, followed by crossing paths with them at the hospital. Cherry Mills was a small subdivision of Hamilton, but the odds of that happening would surely be low.

Teigan stepped out of the elevator on the second floor still deep in thought. She headed toward the ICU, passing a few people going the opposite direction.

Betty looked up at her and smiled. "Teigan! You're back." She grabbed the visitor clipboard. "Oh, by the way, your mystery visitor was here again."

Betty's words pulled Teigan out of her perseveration. "What do you mean?"

Betty pointed back at the elevator. "And he used a name this time."

A tall man wearing a navy blue hoodie pulled up over his head approached the open elevator.

"Hey! Wait!" Teigan ran back towards the elevator. Halfway there the doors started to slide closed. She could see the person standing at the back of the car, his head down and hidden the shadow of his hood. "Wait!"

The elevator doors closed. For a moment Teigan considered taking the stairs and giving chase, then Betty's voice replayed in her head.

He used a name.

Teigan hustled back to the ICU reception desk. Betty had the visitor clipboard ready for her. Teigan quickly signed it and noted the name right before hers.

First this person's name had been *Aye Friend*. Now, in the same handwriting style the name read: *Nick Bee*. Same as before, the name held no clues. Teigan took a photo of the signature for her files.

"Ring any bells for you?" Betty asked.

Teigan shook her head as she signed in.

"There was someone else here today too, about half an hour ago." Betty took the clipboard and scanned the list with her finger, tapping the name when she found it. "L. Mario."

Teigan nodded slowly as she worked at her memories. "Luigi," she said to herself. Then to Betty, "One of Newton's friends."

"Nice to know they care enough to visit," Betty said.

You don't know the half of it. "Any change in Newt?"

"Only that he keeps getting more handsome as the days pass," Betty said as she buzzed open the door to the ICU.

"You're very kind." Teigan sensed a hint of sadness behind Betty's smile. She followed the familiar corridor to Newton's room and stepped inside. The sheets were a slightly different colour today, changed out to prevent bedsores and maximize comfort.

Everything else remained the same, and it was that realization that snuck up on Teigan and hit her with overwhelming emotion. She walked around Newton's bed and collapsed into a chair, her hands covering her tears and muffling her sobs.

She placed one hand on Newton's left. "Oh, my beautiful boy. Please come back to us."

Teigan felt a twitch under her hand and pulled it away as if she had touched a hot ember. She stared at Newton's left hand and saw no movement, then shifted her gaze to the pulse monitor's screen. No anomalies displayed in the on-screen data. She pressed the call button anyway.

Almost instantly Teigan could hear rapid footfalls hustling down the corridor. A few seconds later, Betty appeared. "What is it?"

"Newt moved his hand," Teigan said. "I felt it, I swear I did."

Betty gave her reassuring smile. "That happens occasionally. Unfortunately, it's not a sign that Newton is coming out of his coma. It's merely reflexive. But it's a good sign too. His brain is still working, testing his limbs."

Teigan nodded. "Thanks. Sorry to bother you."

"No problem at all," Betty said. "Buzz me any time." She returned to the reception desk.

Teigan slid back in the chair and let her eyes drift over Newton's form under the covers. The mystery person had stood on the opposite side of the bed just moments ago.

She moved hastily to where she imagined the young man had

stood and attempted to imagine what he would do from that spot. Teigan pulled out her phone and took a photo as if that might spark her imagination. But the view wasn't much different.

She opened the camera roll and a grid of images displayed before her. Teigan tapped the screen to call up the most recent photo. Frustrated, she deleted it. The next most recent photo slid into view, the visitor sign-in sheet.

Teigan pinch-zoomed the image to focus on the hoodie's signature.

Nick Bee.

The name still meant nothing to her. Beside the signature, Betty had written the room number: 223. Teigan moved the photo down a few names until she saw the room number again.

The name beside it: L. Mario. That name held meaning. She kissed Newton's forehead.

"Richard was here, wasn't he, hon?" Teigan knew there would be no response. She returned to her chair.

It appeared that Richard still had a heart left, after all. Maybe it was her talk with him at the school that inspired his visit. Whatever the reason, Richard might know more than he had admitted to earlier.

But who was the tall, dark, and hooded person?

Teigan held space beside her son and resumed searching her seemingly limitless memory for the name Nick Bee. For someone to visit Newton's room multiple times, there had to be a connection somewhere.

– 60 –

THE NEXT DAY just before lunch, Teigan returned to her parking spot further up Edgerton Street with a new plan. Projection made surveillance a piece of cake and today she had one goal. She walked to the parking lot at Diamond Bay and scanned the student lot. It took no time to spot Dustin's Escalade. There was also a row of windows on the end of the building that appeared to belong to the library. Most had their blinds closed but a few were open and raised, allowing full view of the vehicles parked outside.

Teigan decided that walking with purpose would look less suspicious. She approached from the rear of the Escalade, walked to the driver's side window, and peered into the cab. She spent no more than a few seconds orienting herself to the interior, the driver's seat, passenger seat, and the bench seat behind.

She walked around the front of the Escalade, her eyes focused on the interior behind the windshield the whole time. Teigan finished at the passenger window, memorizing details with every glance. The remaining tinted windows would take more effort to look through. She was exposed enough as it was, and purposeful walking only went so far. Less time here meant less chance of getting caught. Her quick survey of the Escalade's interior would have to do.

Teigan returned to her red Civic to find a note slipped under a wiper blade. The unfolded note read, "talk to Killa Scrip." She looked past the car, then back the way she had come. There was no one around.

The handwriting was in purple ink and it looked like a girl's cursive, but that didn't mean much these days. The handwriting of youth today left much to be desired. Teigan was well versed in Haislee's particular cursive, and this didn't match at all.

Teigan jammed the note into her pocket, settled into the driver's seat, prepared herself to project, then decided to move the car first. The same car parked in the same spot two days in a row in a neighborhood it didn't belong would look suspicious. She started the engine and drove home. It didn't matter where she parked. Physical distance did not affect her memories or her projections. Her only enemy was time.

She found herself reclined on the couch in the living room of her house. It was easier to relax when she was safe, secure, and unseen. It was ten minutes until lunch break. Newton had once told her that Dustin and Richard usually hung out in the Escalade during this time, eating, listening to music, and watching (harassing) girls. Her plan relied on their predictability.

With each deep and cleansing breath, Teigan pictured the interior of the Escalade. She placed herself sitting on the bench seat behind the driver and front passenger seat and faced the console.

The many details missing inside the cab and in the parking lot shimmered as they tried to pull more information from her vast past memories. But a lack of detail didn't matter in this case. She was here to listen.

The lunch bell rang and students began to exit the school, some finding places outside to sit and eat, and others taking their cars to the local A&W or Tim Horton's. After ten minutes had passed, Teigan began to wonder if Dustin and Richard had changed their routine. Newton had shared his intel several months ago.

She considered another location, but that would involve breaking the connection with this projection and forming another. The process was getting easier for her, but it did take some time. Teigan decided to wait it out.

Twenty minutes into the lunch break, Dustin and Richard appeared. Richard had his backpack hanging off one shoulder. Dustin unlocked the doors with his key fob and both of them climbed inside.

Dustin grinned with anticipation. "So, what you got for me today?" He held out a hand.

Richard sighed, opened his backpack, and pulled out a thermos and something long and hastily wrapped with plastic.

"Well?"

"I'm getting to it." Richard unscrewed the top to the thermos and saw lukewarm chili. Inside the plastic wrap were at least half a dozen strips of bacon. It was difficult to tell as they were all stuck together. He poured some chili into the thermos lid and broke half of the bacon on top.

Teigan watched Dustin take the food greedily and shovel it into his mouth with the built-in spoon. Richard gnawed on the bacon and tilted the chili into his mouth as if he was drinking it.

Dustin looked at him, annoyed. "What are you doing?"

"Eating my share," Richard said. "Otherwise you'll eat it all. I'm not going to starve."

Dustin slurped his chili. "Small price to pay for my company."

"What a narcissist." Teigan leaned forward over the console so she could watch their conversation more closely. She knew that they couldn't see or hear her, but occasionally it felt like they could, and it raised the hairs on the back of her neck.

Richard swallowed the mouthful he was chewing. "There was this guy in Newton's room yesterday, after I got there."

Dustin paused eating long enough to mutter, "So?"

"He said you started the pushing at McMaster that eventually caused Newton to fall," Richard said. "You said it was both of us. Honestly, I didn't see who started it."

"Not this again." Dustin sucked the remaining chili out of the thermos cup. "Like I told you before... WE did it. Both of us."

"Richard, you're on to something," Teigan said. "Keep going."

Richard stared back at Dustin. "I don't remember it that way."

"That's your problem." Dustin turned in his seat. "Who is this fuckin' guy, anyway?"

"Didn't say," Richard said.

"What'd he look like?"

"He was behind me. Didn't see him."

"Keep going, Richard," Teigan said.

Dustin screwed up his face in disbelief. "Was he a fuckin' ghost or what?"

"He was real," Richard said. "He was tall, too. Over six feet. Taller than you. And he said he had proof."

Teigan smiled. "Bingo."

Dustin narrowed his eyes. "What proof?"

"Didn't say."

Dustin waved off the conversation. "It's all bullshit."

"It's not," Richard said. "He knew who *I* was. That means he knows who *you* are."

"What did he want?"

"He told us to watch our backs," Richard said.

"And you believed him." Dustin shook his head and laughed. "You gullible fuck. The guy was bullshitting you."

"He sounded pretty convincing to me."

"WE pushed people," Dustin said. "The fact that he said *I* did it makes him a liar."

"But he said he can prove it. He probably has video." Richard stared at Dustin across the console.

"Say it, Richard," Teigan said. "Find your balls and say it."

"And if he *does* have video," Richard continued, "would it make *you* a liar?"

Dustin's neck and cheeks flushed red. "It would show us, *both of us,* pushing people. End of fuckin' story." He swallowed, his throat clicking dryly. "I need a coffee. Let's hit Timmy's before we go back."

"Yeah, sure," Richard said, but Dustin had already started the Escalade's engine. Teigan could see doubt creep across Richard's face.

As Dustin reversed out of the parking stall, Teigan held her breath, but she did it too late. She slid forward off the bench seat and felt her body compress uncomfortably against the console and transmission of the SUV.

Teigan gasped and opened her eyes. Above was the familiar pattern of her ceiling. She gripped the cushions of the couch and waited for her breathing to settle.

Although she hadn't gotten the information she wanted, she had a lead. The young man she kept seeing at the hospital was either a classmate or a student from a nearby school. It wasn't a great lead, but it was one she could follow up on.

$$- \; 61 \; -$$

THE LUNCH BELL had rung and students filled the hallways looking for food and places to eat. Elise opened her locker and dug out her lunch bag. Peeking inside, she half expected the hastily prepared peanut butter and jam sandwich she made in the morning to be magically replaced with something more decadent, like an A&W Teen Burger and fries.

No such luck. Elise turned up her nose and secured her locker. She spotted Haislee running down the hallway toward her.

Haislee skidded to a stop just in front of her, the excitement on her face clearly evident.

Elise shook her head at Haislee and stifled a laugh. "What's got into you?"

A sly grin slid over Haislee's lips. "Wanna break the law?"

Elise stepped closer and lowered her voice. "What do you mean?"

Haislee placed her hand in her coat pocket and pulled out a joint, then flashed her eyebrows. "Wanna?"

"Where the hell did you get *that*?"

"Doesn't matter where I got it from," Haislee said. "What matters is it's *real* and I wanna smoke it."

Elise placed her hand over the joint to conceal it. "I thought you were smarter than this. We could get expelled."

"If we get *caught*. Come on, Lise. We could go to my place. It's closer." Haislee leaned in almost nose to nose with Elise and fluttered her eyelashes. "Please please *pweeeeeze?*"

That was Elise's kryptonite. She couldn't hold back her smile now. "Okay. Let's go."

The two of them hustled to the first floor and out of the school, following Edgerton to Tipperary Street and into Haislee's house. They emerged from the sliding door at the back of the house and onto the covered porch.

Haislee wasted no time. She placed the joint at her lips, dug out a lighter, and ignited the end. She drew in a breath, then coughed it out a couple of seconds later.

She handed it to Elise. "Your turn."

Elise hesitated for a moment, then inhaled in much the same way. Both had limited experience smoking marijuana, but it was fun to do something taboo together. She passed the joint back to Haislee, pulled her sandwich out of her lunch bag, and took a bite.

"You know what's weird?"

Haislee had just inhaled so she just shrugged and shook her head before exhaling.

"This train wreck of a sandwich actually tastes good now," Elise said. They both began to giggle.

Elise took the joint and inhaled the smoke, then blew it out. "Where did you get this, anyway? I feel baked already."

"Promise not to get mad?" Haislee took the joint and inhaled.

Elise gave Haislee a sideways look.

Haislee exhaled. "Promise me."

"Okay," Elise said. "I promise."

"Stoaks."

Elise's eyes widened. "You bought drugs from Dustin? Are you crazy?"

"No, I'm *stoked*." Haislee laughed. "I couldn't resist. He gave me a mega discount. I think he likes me."

Haislee handed the joint to Elise, but she waved it away. "Who cares? We've talked about this. Stay away from that dirtbag."

"Jesus, Lise. I just bought a joint from him," Haislee said. "It's not like I sucked him off for it." She inhaled again, the ember of the joint getting close to her fingers.

"What if this was laced with fentanyl? Buy your joints from someone else. Please." Elise took a bite from her sandwich. "Better yet, don't buy drugs at all. Okay?" She offered her sandwich to Haislee.

"Okay." Haislee took a large hungry bite. "Damn. You're right. This sandwich tastes awesome."

Elise glanced at the time on her phone. "We should be getting back."

Haislee looked at Elise and began to giggle again. "You think we'll be able to walk?"

An image of Newton bedridden in his hospital room popped into Elise's head. Newton couldn't walk. He may never walk again. A surge of guilt and shame flooded her.

"I hope so," Elise said.

The two of them helped each other to their feet and they started the short and wobbly walk back to the school.

– 62 –

THE NOTE THAT HAD BEEN LEFT on Teigan's car was burning a hole in her pocket, but the more pressing task was finding out who Nick Bee was. That meant visiting the schools that had been involved in the field trip to McMaster University.

Teigan sat in her office, faced with two choices: call Diamond Bay administration and see if they had a list of all participating schools, or call the university that hosted the event. The thought of having to talk to Grey McCarthy turned her stomach. That left McMaster University, which was probably the best choice anyway.

She called the university administration office. Using a fabricated story of a lost piece of jewelry at the event and after a few call transfers, Teigan was connected with Kate Harris, one of the presenters and a director of university admissions. Teigan remembered the woman's voice.

"I remember the day vividly," Kate said through the phone. "Most excitement we've had in quite some time."

"I'm the mother of that young man," Teigan said. "We spoke. You let me know Newt was in the hospital."

"Ha! I thought your voice sounded familiar." Teigan could hear Kate's smile. A good sign. "I hope your son is doing alright."

"I, uh..." Teigan balked for a moment. Bringing up his current condition wouldn't be appropriate. "Yes. Newt's all healed up. However, I'm calling for an unrelated reason. A student from Diamond Bay found a piece of jewelry at the presentation. I'm not sure why we're finding out this now, typical teen procrastination probably, but as a member of the parent auxiliary I've been tasked to find the rightful owner."

"And you need a list of the schools that attended, correct?"

"Yes. Just school names," Teigan said. "I'll take it from there."

"Daunting task, if you ask me, but you're in luck," Kate said. "I can dig up that list for you and email it, if you like."

"Actually, if it's not too much trouble, could you tell me now over the phone?"

"Absolutely. One moment." Sounds of keyboard taps and mouse clicks filtered through the phone line. "Here we are."

Teigan grabbed a sheet of paper and jotted the names down as Kate recited them.

"Thank you so much, Kate. You've been a great help."

"You're welcome," Kate said. "And please let Newt know that he's more than welcome to attend McMaster if he chooses to. He can ask for me by name."

"He'll be happy to hear that. Goodbye, Ms. Harris." Teigan hung up the phone and burst into tears. The cruelty of recent events had disrupted Newton's future and it had all snuck up on her. But as soon as the tears fell, she managed to wipe her eyes and carry on. The pursuit of those responsible helped keep her focused.

She looked over the list of other schools that attended the McMaster event back in February: Eastdale Secondary, Fernwood Secondary, Balfour Park Secondary, and Waterton Secondary. She took a photo of the list and filed the paper in a desk drawer.

Teigan still had half the day, more than enough time to visit the schools in question. She grabbed her keys and hit the road. Operation Yearbook was a go.

Using the same lost jewelry story she had used with Kate at

McMaster, the librarian of Eastdale Secondary directed Teigan to where past yearbooks were shelved. She pulled last year's yearbook out, found a seat at a nearby table, and began flipping through the photos of that year's student body. Students studying at the table gave her a curious eye.

Even though the name she was looking for, *Nick Bee*, would be listed early in the alphabetized pages, Teigan looked through all of the names of all grades, just to be sure. *Nick Bee* could be a nickname, a middle name, part of a name, a reversal of names, or an anagram. There were too many possibilities to leave the search to just the students with last names beginning with "B." The added time required to search the entire student body would be well worth it if she identified the mystery person.

Teigan continued with the remaining three schools, following the same story and procedure as she had at Eastdale. She ran into a snag only with Waterton Secondary. The librarian there had asked to see the jewelry in question. Obviously, Teigan didn't have it on hand.

"I didn't want it to get lost again," she had told the librarian.

Teigan promised the librarian that she'd look through the yearbook at the checkout counter so the librarian could oversee her actions. Deemed acceptable, the librarian presented Teigan with a copy of *Waterton's 2023 Yearbook*.

The librarian eyed her. "Are your hands clean?"

Teigan nodded. "I skipped lunch today. I can wash them right now if you like."

"No, that's fine," the librarian said. "Please be careful. It might not seem like it to you, but these are important historical documents that must be kept in optimal condition."

"I understand." Teigan took the yearbook, opened it carefully to the Grade 9 students, and began her search. She didn't hold out much hope. There had been no clues from the previous three schools. The odds of finding an answer were diminishing with every turn of the page.

Halfway through the Grade 11 students, Teigan came upon a name she hadn't heard in years: Benjamin Littleton.

Benjamin had been good friends with Newton all through elementary school, but their paths diverged in Grade 6. His parents moved him to a middle school that emphasized sports, and Waterton's academic/sports hybrid program was the next logical step. Time marched forward and they lost touch as kids do.

The young man in the photo looked nothing like the Benjamin she remembered from elementary school. His short dark hair framed an angular face and a strong jawline. If the sports track his parents had set up for him panned out, Teigan could see Benjamin in front of television cameras answering post-game interview questions. She made a mental note to mention him to Newton once he was out of his coma.

Teigan continued scanning names, but no further clue of Nick Bee's identity presented itself. Maybe this was a wild goose chase. Maybe Nick Bee was a made-up name, just like Aye Friend had been.

Although disappointed, Teigan was pleased that she hadn't left this particular stone unturned. Now she could dig deeper into the note that someone had left on her car and who *Killa Scrip* was. But as she drove home, Teigan began to second-guess herself.

She was certain that Nick Bee wasn't a student at any of the schools she had visited this afternoon, but had she been thorough enough with the students of Diamond Bay? Luckily, she could solve that problem easily.

Once back at home, Teigan made a beeline back to Newton's room and picked up last year's yearbook from his shelf. She flipped it open, preparing to examine the student body, when she heard the front door open and close.

It can't be Elise. She normally gets home closer to dinner time.

Teigan slipped the yearbook back into the shelf and padded

out of Newton's room and into her office farther down the hall. "Hello?"

"It's just me," Elise called upstairs.

Teigan appeared at the top of the stairs as Elise ascended. "You're home early."

"Don't feel well," Elise said. "Gonna lie down for a bit."

Teigan stepped back as Elise passed her quickly at the top of the stairs. The acrid smell of marijuana smoke clung to her daughter's clothes like an oil slick. Moving quickly did nothing to evade spreading the odor.

"Have you been smoking?" Teigan thought of asking about smoking marijuana specifically, but let it ride. She was curious what Elise would say.

"Second hand." Elise continued toward her room without looking back. "Was hanging with some friends and they lit up. Musta breathed some of it too 'cause I'm feeling woozy."

That was as close to the truth as Teigan was going to get. "Pretty gross, isn't it? Need a puke bucket?"

"It's not that bad." Elise stepped into her room and closed the door. "I'll be down for dinner," she said from inside.

Teigan considered going back into Newton's room and grabbing his yearbook, but now that Elise was home, she didn't want to be caught or even suspected of any breach of privacy. Tomorrow would have to suffice. Back in her office, she tucked the note under her desk blotter.

$$- \ 63 \ -$$

DUSTIN AND RICHARD SHARED a morning Chemistry class. Richard was the designated note taker and Dustin made copies afterward. Dustin demanded "sharing of the notes" and offered Richard "perks" in exchange, like free rides and unlimited video games and snacks. It was a pay-to-play system that Richard had never attempted to challenge.

Dustin reclined in a desk at the back of the class, gnawing on the eraser of a pencil. He leaned toward Richard in the desk next to him. "They need to teach us something useful."

Scribbling a note, mid-sentence, Richard didn't answer immediately.

Dustin tapped his shoulder. "You listening to me?"

"Let me finish first." Richard's annoyance came through loud and clear, but Dustin ignored it. "These are your notes too, remember. Don't want to fuck them up."

"Whatevs." Dustin motioned to the chalkboard filled with chemical equations. "She needs to teach us about things that matter, like what's in drugs and how they work. I'd be all over that. But instead, it's balancing stoichiometric equations or some shit."

"Gotta know the foundation," Richard said without looking up from his furiously written notes.

"Don't fuckin' start, dude." Dustin tilted his head back and yawned. "Friday can't come soon enough. You gonna bring a date this time?"

Richard shrugged and continued writing. The bell rang and Dustin threw what little was on his desk into his backpack.

"I'll see you outside," he said. "Don't be long." Dustin was one of the first out of the class.

Richard gave his head a subtle shake and continued writing notes. He knew from past experience that the consequences of incomplete notes were worse than Dustin's annoying rambling. He'd stay as long as needed to finish, or until the teacher kicked him out.

Dustin hated the fact that he had to go up a flight of stairs to get to Chemistry, but a class on the second floor meant exposure to a higher number of younger students in the hallways between classes. Good for business and for parties.

Dustin's parents would be out of town again over the weekend, and he never failed to seize those opportunities to host his self-titled "epic parties." After inviting and adding them to the official "party group chat" he'd already set up on Instagram, he'd ask them to post an introduction. People would know who was going and it helped build up momentum to ensure "epic" attendance.

Dustin had been in prospecting mode the entire week and word was spreading nicely about Friday's party. He spotted Haislee at her locker without Elise, her usual plus one.

Haislee got on Dustin's nerves most of the time, but her attractiveness and bubbly personality counted for a lot, especially at a party where single guys were looking to score. It was those guys that spread the "epicness."

She wasn't on his official invite list yet. Dustin took this opportunity to rectify that. He strutted across the hallways and leaned against the adjacent locker.

"Hey Hay-*zee*. What's up?"

Haislee looked up at him and Dustin swore he could see her blush a little. She leaned a little closer and lowered her voice. "Still coming down from that joint I got from you yesterday."

Dustin grinned. "You liked that, huh?"

She blinked her large blue eyes at him and tossed her hair to one side. "Holy shit bruh, it nearly wrecked me, but *yeah*."

He pulled open his coat to reveal an inner pocket. "There's more where that came from. But you might want to hold out for Friday night. Epic party. My place."

Haislee's jaw dropped a bit, and she glanced around her as if she was looking for someone. "An official *Stoaks* invite? Not some prank?"

Dustin shook his head. "Hundo percent legit."

Haislee thought about it for a moment. "Does everyone need an invite, or can I bring someone?"

"You mean Elise? Yeah sure, bring her. And anyone else, as long as they're just as pretty as you." Dustin was sure he saw her blush this time.

"I'll be there."

"Cool," Dustin said. "You got my Insta handle?"

"Uh, yeah. I, like, follow you."

Dustin smiled. "Of course you do. I got a link to the group chat in my bio. Join and post something. Introduce yourself. It's gonna be..."

"Epic!" they both said in unison.

Richard approached the two of them with his Chemistry book and binder under one arm. He nodded at Haislee. "Hey."

Haislee looked away from Dustin along enough to respond. "Hi, Richard."

"See you on Friday, *Hazy*," Dustin said and headed down the stairs to their next class, Richard close behind.

Dustin's phone chimed. He pulled it out to see a notification that Haislee had joined the party group chat. A second later another notification popped up, a message request from Haislee. "Follow me back?"

Dustin smirked slyly and turned to Richard. "Friday's gonna be epic."

$$-\ 64\ -$$

TEIGAN SAID GOODBYE to Max and Elise and locked the front door behind her. She had the house to herself. She finished her breakfast and followed it with a strong cup of coffee. She retrieved last year's yearbook from both Elise's and Newton's room.

Leave no stone unturned.

Teigan pulled the note out from under her desk blotter and set it beside Elise's yearbook. She studied the note, as a whole and as each individual letter.

Going through Elise's yearbook took a while longer than the yearbooks she had perused yesterday, as she was looking for both Nick Bee and handwriting that matched the Killa Scrip note. She came up blank on both accounts.

Teigan returned Elise's yearbook to her room and felt her anxiety lift a little. If anyone would notice a day-to-day shift in the things in their bedroom, it'd be Elise, and not because Newton was in the hospital. Elise saw the little details and remembered them. Teigan had often wondered if Elise had a touch of eidetic memory. It would make sense considering her own abilities.

She returned to her office and began the search process on Newton's yearbook. Because the yearbooks were identical, she'd only have to look for similar cursive writing. Teigan paged through the entire student body and could find no handwriting that came close to the style used on the note.

She continued into the section of the yearbook that featured groups of students, covering sports teams, musical and dramatic ensembles, and clubs. The signatures and little notes on these pages were more sporadic, written by students Teigan had already dismissed.

She continued past the center of the publication, past the secret admirer letters, and nothing matched the note. Teigan had begun to lose hope. There was always the option of trying to find who Killa Scrip was on her own, but she didn't like the odds or the danger that option presented.

Teigan closed the yearbook, pushed it aside on her desk, and slumped back in her office chair, frustrated. She scanned the edges of the yearbook, the purple pages of the letters peeking out from the center. She'd have to tidy those up before returning the yearbook to Newton's room.

Someone knows and *they go to Diamond Bay.*

Teigan refused to give up. She grabbed the yearbook and flipped through its pages again, naturally landing on the center spread where Newton had placed the secret admirer letters. She ignored her inner voice about invading her son's privacy and unfolded the letters.

Instead of the words, she examined the individual letters and found that focusing on the characteristics of the writing helped her overlook the content. Maintaining privacy in some small way was still important. Teigan realized at once that the *same person* had written the letters and the note. She went through all the letters, comparing them to the writing until she was a hundred percent certain. But a name still evaded her.

Teigan collected the secret admirer letters and placed them back in the center spread of the yearbook, which happened to open on music ensembles. She went through the faces one more time in case someone stood out for her.

She flipped through the pages one last time. Music. Math Club, Debate Club, Art Club, Earth Club...

Something clicked in Teigan's head. She flipped back to the spread on the Art Club. Instead of a group photo like many of the other clubs, a collage of notable art pieces spanned both pages. On the right page, in the bottom corner, a picture featured a girl holding her painting proudly in front of her. The painting, a close up of a bouquet of hyacinths, was the same colour as her hair: purple. Her signature at the bottom corner of her painting stared back at Teigan: a heart with a curly tail.

The photo's caption read, "Juniper Thomas wins 2nd place at Cherry Mills Art Festival with 'Grape Expectations.' "

A detail tugged at Teigan's memory. She flipped back in the yearbook and found Juniper's Grade 11 photo, still with purple hair. She flipped the pages forward again, the yearbook falling open to the secret admirer letters and music ensembles.

She unfolded one of the letters. At the bottom of the page sat the author's signature. A drawn heart with a curled tail stared back at her and Teigan recognized it immediately. Somehow she had missed that detail the first time. It was the same doodle she had found on Newton's left hand almost two weeks ago. Scrutinizing the doodle further, the curly tail under the heart could be described as a capital "J". It made sense.

"Juniper Thomas," Teigan whispered to herself. She refolded the letter and placed with the others.

Looking for a student with purple hair made searching a piece of cake. Juniper stood out in the group photos like hyacinth in the grass. She was a member of a few of the music ensembles and one photo showed her holding up a pair of drum sticks in a victorious pose. Juniper played percussion.

Teigan grinned. It had been a long time since she had experienced what felt like a real win. She knew the music ensembles practiced in a portable annex by the side of the school but had no idea when. However, after helping Elise pick her classes this year, it was clear that music was extracurricular. That meant practices took place in the morning, during lunch time, and after school.

She noted the time: 11:15am. Teigan had missed the morning, but if she hustled, she could observe who went to the lunch and after school sessions. Two out of three wasn't bad odds. Wasting no time, she fixed herself a bag lunch and hustled to Diamond Bay. She wanted to catch Juniper by surprise and her red Civic would be a dead giveaway.

Teigan arrived on Edgerton Street in front of the student parking lot with ten minutes to spare. From a bus shelter across the street, she was able to watch who went in and out of the portable classroom. She was hopeful that Juniper's purple hair would stand out enough to make her easy to spot.

The lunch bell rang and within minutes students began filing into the small building. Some redheads appeared but no one with purple hair. Teigan came to the sinking realization that Juniper may have changed her hair colour. The bus shelter was the perfect place to spot hair colour changes, but for faces, she needed to be closer.

Dampened music seeping from the portable walls reached her from where Teigan sat waiting for lunch to end. When the afternoon session bell rang, she launched herself from the bus shelter and hurried across the street toward the portable building. Teigan dug out her phone and began recording video. She enabled wide angle mode and tilted the phone down as much as she could while keeping the exodus of students in view. It had been a spur of the moment idea and she hoped it didn't look obvious. To complete the ruse, she moved her finger up and down over the screen to make it look like she was scrolling social media.

Teigan sat on the grass and continued recording until the teacher locked the door to the portable and headed to the main building. She scrubbed the video slowly, looking for any girl that looked like Juniper, but came up with nothing. It was possible that Juniper wasn't at school today, but Teigan decided to stick it out for the after school session.

With two hours to kill, she walked to a nearby Tim Horton's and ordered a coffee and cruller. Normally Teigan didn't drink coffee this late in the day since it messed with her sleep, but she had a feeling she wouldn't be sleeping much tonight anyway. The cruller filled a sudden craving that she couldn't ignore. She took a seat next to the window and pulled out her phone.

As Teigan ate her caffeinated sugar bomb, she searched the Internet for combinations of "Juniper Thomas," "Cherry Mills," and "Diamond Bay." Despite memorizing the photo from Newton's Grade 11 yearbook, Teigan wanted a more recent photo, one that might give a hint at what Juniper's current hair colour was.

The majority of the limited image search results led to Juniper's second place win in last year's Cherry Mills Art Festival and featured a photo similar to the one in the yearbook.

A couple results linked to her Instagram profile. Teigan tapped on one and the Instagram app launched. To her surprise, Juniper's account was not private. There were images of last year's art festival, plus several images of art pieces in the process of creation. Teigan found the timelapse videos of Juniper's work the most fascinating. There was so much unseen time and work that went into a drawing or painting.

The girl was talented and Teigan could see why Newton had formed an interest. However, after digging into her posts, Teigan discovered that the account had been inactive for almost a year. It appeared that Juniper enjoyed sharing her creations, then it all stopped. That kind of abrupt change usually happened for a reason. Teigan couldn't help but wonder if there was any connection to Newton.

She finished her coffee and donut and headed back to the school, but her unfamiliarity with the class schedule caused her to arrive later than desired. The end-of-day bell had already rung, and the grounds bustled with students heading home. The door to the music portable had already closed and she could hear music emanating from within. She had one more chance to find Juniper today.

Teigan retreated back to the bus stop across the street and revisited Juniper's Instagram profile. She scrolled through the images and read the sparse comments, looking for any clues that might provide some answers as to why Juniper stopped posting.

She clicked on commenters' names to see if their accounts were public (most weren't). Those that were public, Teigan made a conscious effort to not go too deep down the Instagram rabbit hole. She could see how easily time could disappear into these social apps.

As if to prove her point, the door to the music portable opened and students began leaving. Just over an hour had elapsed while Teigan had been exploring Instagram. She pocketed her phone and ran toward the portable.

This time around Teigan wasn't going to take any chances. She stood near the concrete landing at the bottom of the wooden steps leading inside the portable.

"Excuse me," Teigan said to a couple of emerging students. "I'm looking for Juniper Thomas."

One of the students hooked their thumb back up the stairs. "She's inside."

"Thanks." Teigan breathed a sigh of relief in the knowledge that she'd finally found Juniper. She focused on the door framing the students leaving the portable and pictured Juniper's face in her head.

After what seemed like dozens of students passing by, Teigan began to worry that perhaps she had missed her. Then a girl with long jet-black hair, black lipstick, and a black shirt and jeans stepped out of the door. She wore a pair of black silver-studded wrist straps and gripped a pair of drumsticks in one hand. Had it not been for the drumsticks, Teigan wouldn't have recognized her.

Juniper waved goodbye to someone inside, presumably the teacher, and headed down the steps. Halfway down, she spotted Teigan waiting for her. There was a flash of recognition in her eyes.

Juniper turned to go back, but the teacher was already locking up. "Forget something, June?"

"Nah." Juniper shook her head and continued down the stairs, flipping her hair to shroud her face.

Teigan approached her at the base of the stairs. "Are you Juniper Thomas?" She saw one of the girl's eyes narrow on her, uncertain.

The teacher stepped up behind Juniper and gave Teigan a once-over. "You okay, June?"

"Yeah, yeah," Juniper said.

"Okay." The teacher kept her eyes on Teigan as she walked away.

"Can I talk to you?"

Juniper propped herself up against the exterior wall of the portable and crossed her arms, one hand still gripping her drumsticks, the wood pitted at the ends from countless rimshots.

"My name is Teigan Coleman—"

"I know who you are," Juniper said.

Teigan nodded slowly. "I know. You left the note about Killa Scrip on my car."

Juniper shrugged.

"I also know about the letters," Teigan said.

A look of fear mixed with embarrassment crossed Juniper's face.

"I didn't read them, if that's what you're wondering. I just looked at them enough to compare handwriting. Do you believe me?"

Juniper slid a length of midnight hair away from her face, recrossed her arms, and maintained her cautious stare.

"Look, I'm not trying to get you in trouble," Teigan said. "Clearly you and Newt have a connection. I just want to know… what happened at Pyckman Quarry?"

"I wasn't there," Juniper said.

Teigan gave her a sideways look. "Come on, Juniper. That special heart you drew on Newt's hand? It's at the bottom of all your notes. I know you were there."

"What if I drew that heart before, at the dance?"

"Would you swear on Newt's life that's what actually happened?"

Juniper sighed. "Okay, I *was* there. I talked to him for about five minutes. Then I left. Too many people."

"What did you talk about?"

Juniper paused to think for a moment. "Nothing memorable."

"Did you see anything? Like someone spiking his drink?"

Juniper shook her head. "We actually swapped beers and I drank what was left of his. I was fine."

"I know Dustin was there. Did you see him?"

"Yeah." Juniper spoke with an air of disgust. "He's unfortunately hard to miss. That asshole and his fat fucking mouth. I can't stand that creep."

Teigan felt both frustration and gratitude. She had one more piece of the puzzle, but the rest of the story was still locked up. "What can you tell me about Killa Scrip?"

"He's a drug dealing thug, targets schools," Juniper said. "Not the kind of person you want to mess with. But he might know about the drugs that were used on Newton."

"Where can I find him?"

"No one deals with him directly." Juniper had begun to relax. "Some think he doesn't exist, but I think that's bullshit. Ask around at Pearson Square. But be careful. These people are super sketchy."

"Thank you, Juniper. I will." Teigan smiled and held out her hand. When Juniper didn't reciprocate, Teigan made a fist. Juniper returned a small grin and held out the hand gripping the drumsticks. They bumped fists.

Teigan turned to leave, then looked back at Juniper. "I hope to see you again under better circumstances. If you haven't visited Newt yet, please give it some thought. I'm sure he'd appreciate it."

"I will," Juniper said.

Teigan began the walk back home, with some of her questions answered and new questions forming.

– 65 –

AFTER ARRIVING HOME and finding Teigan out, Max took the reigns of preparing dinner. His recipe repertoire wasn't expansive and he had limited cooking skills, but he wasn't scared to get his hands dirty in the kitchen either. His trusty (and tasty) standby was spaghetti with meat balls, plus salad and garlic toast if they had the ingredients. Tonight, they'd have to do without the sides.

Max called up to Elise to let her know dinner was imminent. He checked the time on the range.

The blue numbers facing the cooktop glowed back at him, "6:44 pm."

Where are you, Tee?

Elise strolled into the kitchen. "Smells good, Dad."

"Glad you think so." Max strained the spaghetti. "Could you set the table, please?"

Elise grabbed for the plates. "Is Mom out tonight?"

Steam from the hot pasta filled the kitchen. "I don't know where your mom is, but set a place for her anyway." Max and Teigan had shared their locations with each other for safety reasons. When he checked it earlier, it had shown that here at home, specifically parked out front, was her last known location. Either her phone was dead or she had turned it off.

"Maybe she's at the hospital again," Elise said as she set plates and cutlery on the table.

"Great minds think alike," Max said. "I called right before starting dinner. Not there, and she hadn't been there all day."

Elise barely reacted. "I'm sure she's fine."

"Yeah, you're probably right." But Max was trying to calm the alarm bells going off in his head and hoped it didn't show. Working in IT, he knew that sometimes the technology worked a little too well. Knowing where a person was at any given time, especially a loved one, offered a feeling of reassurance, a feeling that he came to rely on. When a technical problem or the deliberate act of powering off made that knowledge unavailable, worry and anxiety took its place. Of course that's what smartphone makers wanted, and knowing someone's location was just one more incentive to keep them on their device.

Max checked Teigan's location one more time and saw the same result, her last known location, the time, that insidious spinning gear. He tapped out a quick text to let her know that dinner was ready and hit send. The message didn't fail, so that was something.

Elise served herself some spaghetti, took a few meat balls, and smothered everything in tomato sauce and Parmesan cheese. "You okay, Dad?"

Max put his phone into standby and pocketed it. "Yeah. It's just not like your mom to ignore a text." He plated his meal and joined Elise at the table. "I guess I'm worried about her doing what should be left to the police."

Elise shrugged. "Someone's gotta do it. And Mom kicks ass. She'd probably do a better job anyway."

"That is true," Max said. Teigan was the only woman he knew that was proficient in Brazilian Jiu-Jitsu, earning her blue belt. It had been a running joke between them that if Max ever got out of line, she'd put him to sleep with a rear naked choke hold.

Max twirled spaghetti on his fork. "What was the best thing about your day?" He smirked at Elise and began to chew.

Elise thought for a moment, then launched into a vivid description of some of the "tragic" presentations in her history class today. As Max listened and ate, knowing in his heart that his daughter was more of a writer than a STEM girl, Teigan parked her Civic a block away from Pearson Square.

– **66** –

THE AFTERNOON SUN had already begun its track toward the horizon, casting the streets of downtown Hamilton in a mix of blues and oranges. Pearson Square covered almost six square city blocks and sat raised above street level as a way to provide a community gathering space and thoroughfare above the businesses and parkades below. Plus, it allowed additional access to business on the top level.

Surrounding the central nexus of the square rose a few featureless glass and steel office towers supported on monolithic bases built of red brick. A Cineplex theatre and an auditorium faced the towers. All of the structures around the square, as well as the square itself, lacked any architectural imagination.

The half-dozen staircases that led to the square would quickly become a gauntlet with any crowd that happened to gather after seeing a movie or a live event. And the square was big. Including the buildings surrounding it like turrets, the space was equivalent to sixteen football fields, four across and four deep. It was an impressive if bland space.

If Teigan had one criticism, it was the lack of access (and escape). With a space this large, a person could exhaust themselves running from one side of the square to an exit staircase. On the chance that undesirables had blocked the stairs, the options for finding an alternative safe escape were slim.

Ironically Pearson Square was located within a few blocks of the Investigative Services Division of Hamilton Police. Teigan wondered if Jackson was still at his office and how quickly he could arrive if she needed help.

Probably not quick enough.

As Teigan approached the stairs, she spotted a man positioned at the base of the staircase with a phone to his ear. He watched her pass by with a pointed stare.

She ascended a few steps, then reversed and approached the man. She had no time to waste. His eyes never left her.

"Where can I find Killa Scrip?"

The man covered his phone against his chest and waved his free hand at her. "Fuck off, lady." Teigan detected a foreign accent mixed with his street dialect.

She didn't press the man for answers. Once at the top of the stairs, the interlocking concrete bricks opened out offering few places to hide if needed. Teigan glanced backward and saw that the man was still watching her from the bottom of the stairs, still on his phone.

She ventured forth toward the center of the square, on the lookout for anyone who fit the description of a drug dealer, although these days anyone could fit the bill. The natural light had dimmed since she had parked her car and the shadows rising from the surrounding buildings gave the square an oppressive feeling.

Teigan pressed on, passing a couple of pedestrians walking with intent toward the theatre. For the size of Pearson Square, the lighting was sparse. With the many nooks and crannies and the ever expanding shadows around them, it became clear why dealers used the area after dark. In an ideal world, Teigan would find the information she needed before nightfall, but it was the night that brought out the kinds of people she was looking for.

She crossed the square on hurried footsteps without success, then reversed back the way she came. Regret seeped into Teigan's mind as the skies darkened futher, always quicker than she expected. This excursion felt like it was destined to fail.

As she neared the epicenter of the square, a man holding a smartphone to his ear emerged from an alcove buried in the side of the Cineplex building. He walked with a limp and appeared to be white, but the fading light made that detail debatable. He wore a black leather jacket over a dirty baby-blue T-shirt and a red do-rag adorned with skulls contained his greasy hair.

"Hey." The man waved at her. "Hey, you need some help?"

Teigan's first instinct was to answer "No" and carry on her way. But her task pressed back on her fear.

She stopped. "Maybe." Teigan maintained a safe distance. "I'm looking for Killa Scrip."

The man slipped his phone into an inner jacket pocket and narrowed his eyes. "You lookin' for drugs? I got drugs." He took a step forward.

Teigan mirrored his move and took a step back. "I just want to talk to Killa Scrip. Where can I find him?"

"You a *cop*?"

"No," Teigan said. "Just a mother wanting information."

"A *hot* mama, too." The man grinned. Smoking and poor oral hygiene had stained his few remaining teeth a revolting brown. He let his eyes roam over her body. "I got the info you want. And you got somethin' *I* want."

"I don't want it that bad." Teigan turned to walk away, keeping the man in her line of sight.

"The fuck you don't." The man quickened his pace and closed the gap between them.

"Look I don't want any trouble," Teigan said.

"Anyone askin' about Killa Scrip is askin' for fuckin' trouble."

Teigan decided to cut her losses and bolted. She heard the man's laboured breathing and uneven footsteps as he pursued her. His apparent limp was slowing him down and every step Teigan made increased the distance behind her. She ran until she could no longer hear him.

Teigan risked slowing down to glance behind. The path was abandoned. There was no sign of her pursuer. She inhaled deeply to calm her heartbeat back to normal and scanned the square for any other surprises. The importance of talking to Killa Scrip took a backseat to her safety.

She made a move to turn around and a strong arm snaked around her neck while a hand grabbed her left hand and held it firmly behind her back.

"Nosy bitch." The man's breath reeked of warm roadkill and his voice sounded familiar. He wasn't the slimebag she had just ditched, but the one she had passed on the stairs heading into the square. His unique accent gave away his identity.

"Only stupid *cops* ask for Killa Scrip," the man said. "Killa Scrip don't like *cops*."

The two thugs were in on it. The first one had been in contact with the other. Teigan had been a mark from the moment she had entered Pearson Square.

"I'm *not* a cop." Before the thug behind her could respond, Teigan stepped wide with her right leg, moved her left leg behind the thug's right, and twisted her body left. Now on one leg, the man lost stability and hit the pavement on his left side. Teigan used the moment to slip her head out from the thug's grip, place one elbow in front of his throat to apply even pressure on his neck and locked it in place with her other arm behind his neck. This was the first time she had used the rear naked choke hold in a real situation. It was also one of the first moves she had learned in Brazilian Jiu-Jitsu.

The lack of blood flow to the man's brain was already having an effect. Teigan loosened her grip slightly.

"Where can I find Killa Scrip?"

"Fuck you, *bitch*." The man struggled helplessly against the hold.

Teigan found the man's body odor nauseating. She cinched the grip tighter to reduce the struggle. "Two things can happen. You either pass out and I let go, or you pass out and I hold tight. In three minutes your brain dies." She slackened her grip. "What's it going to be?"

The thug blubbered out his words. "I don't wanna die."

"Then tell me what I want to know," Teigan said. "Killa Scrip. Where?" She tightened the hold again. "I want an address."

The man said nothing.

"You're choosing to die?" Teigan gritted her teeth and held her grip. She had no intention of ending the man's life even though she knew he wouldn't have thought twice about ending hers. But she maintained her ruse. "Address. Now."

The man caved. "Bantor and Agate."

"If you're lying, I'll find you and finish the job." Teigan loosened her grip again. She'd rather not be in this position in the first place, but she discovered part of her was enjoying this inversion of power.

The man gasped, his arms flailing at his side. "I swear. I swear. Bantor... Agate. Please... don't..."

Teigan cinched her grip tight and in less than ten seconds the thug passed out. She released him and pushed his body onto his side and into the recovery position. He was an asshole but didn't deserve to die. He'd wake up in half a minute or less. She dusted herself off and headed for the stairs. A few minutes later she was back in her rental and on her way home.

Teigan felt fucking invincible. Killa Scrip's address was just the icing on the cake.

$$- \ 67 \ -$$

HAISLEE HAD DRIVEN through Rockwood West many times with her parents. But she never thought she'd have the opportunity to step inside any one of the massive houses that populated the affluent suburb.

"Nice digs." The taxi driver rolled to a stop in the circular driveway of Dustin Stoak's massive house. There were at least a dozen cars already parked along the edge of the driveway. "Yours?"

Haislee thought for a moment, then grinned slyly. "My boyfriend's parents, but mine some day."

"Nice." The driver held out a handheld payment terminal and Haislee tapped it with her phone. The driver nodded at her. "Thanks. Have a good night."

She stepped out of the taxi and looked up at Dustin's mansion, past the porte cochère and along the massive front windows. She could hear the lower bass tones of music playing inside. Haislee imagined what it would be like to live here and in a moment, she'd get a little taste of that life. She was so immersed in her fantasy that she didn't hear the taxi drive away.

She held up her phone, took a photo of the house, then twirled a one-eighty to take a selfie with the mansion in the background.

Haislee tapped the red record button. "My house is gonna be like this, peeps. Just sayin'... Hazy Daze out!"

The evening temperatures in April could still be a little cold. Haislee had decided on a beige open long cardigan on top of her white babydoll T-shirt. A blue flared skirt, the hem floating just at her knees, completed her Stoaks "epic" party ensemble. While a mini skirt would have turned some (all) heads, comfort was her main goal.

Haislee looped the thin strap of her clutch across her body. She stepped up to the front door and rang the bell. A moment later a familiar voice floated from the intercom speaker.

"Hazy's in da house!" Dustin said. "Just a mo."

Haislee took out her phone which had a screen protector that doubled as a mirror. She barely had time to check her makeup before the huge wooden front door swung open, rotating on an offset pivot instead of the usual hinges.

Dustin stepped into the doorway wearing a gray short-sleeved pique polo shirt and tan dockers. "Hazy..." He smiled warmly and held his arms out. "Or do you prefer Haislee?"

Haislee felt heat rise on her face. "Hazy's good."

"Not a state of being, I hope?" Dustin closed the door.

"Just a cool nick." She wiggled her phone in her hand. "Is your place *reel* friendly?"

Dustin didn't miss a beat. "Yeah, go ahead. Can I get you a drink?"

Haislee gave Dustin her best flirty face. "Surprise me."

"That'll be tough," Dustin said. "Follow me."

Dustin weaved his way toward the kitchen, with Haislee trailing close behind. Given special treatment by Dustin in his own home gave her a feeling of importance. Dozens of people milled about, some relaxing on the couches in the grand room, others perched against walls or on the stairs to the second floor, beers and mixed drinks in their hands. She felt the heat of their eyes on her.

Haislee spotted a few familiar faces, including Richard, but no one she'd actually talked to during the past school year. Most of the people here were strangers to her and she felt her anxiety spike. Richard gulped from his beer can, his eyes lingering on her as she walked by.

Haislee stuck with Dustin as much as she could. In this environment he was her safety net. He grabbed a beer from the beverage fridge and handed it to her.

"Talk later?" Dustin glanced around. "My job as host is never done."

"Yeah, sure." Haislee backed onto the wall beside the kitchen, cracked her beer, and slurped off the foam. From her vantage point she could see most of the first floor. She enjoyed watching people and the spot offered good coverage. The added bonus: she wouldn't seem so clingy. The music mixed with the chatter of conversation, and with the aid of her beer, Haislee began to relax. But she wished Elise was here.

"Huge party at Dustin's," Haislee texted Elise. "U comin?" She shot a video, panning across her view, and sent it as well.

"Dustin? Eww ick," Elise responded and added a barfing emoji.

"He's not that bad," Haislee texted. "Don't have to talk to him. Just in his house. Free food and beer. Good music. Lotsa cute guys."

"Can't. Visiting my bro," Elise's message back read. "But I want deets l8r."

Haislee felt a momentary pang of guilt for partying when Newton might not wake up. But she couldn't stop living. She tagged Elise's message with a heart emoji, then wandered through the crowd of partiers, working on her beer.

Many of the guys she passed by tried to get her attention, some even using lame pickup lines. The worst so far was from a guy who looked like he had just rolled out of bed. His shirt was dirty and his greasy hair hung in clumps. Haislee had an idea what he'd smell like before he got close enough to confirm it.

"Feel my shirt. It's made of boyfriend material," he had said, but it was the Cheetos stuck in his teeth that sealed his fate.

She noticed Richard had been shadowing her, not close enough for a conversation, but always within sight, nursing his beer. Haislee didn't get the impression that Richard talked to many girls, especially not at parties. Dustin, usually the leader of the duo, was busy hosting. Richard's awkwardness held him back.

Haislee recorded video reels of beer pong, shotgun competitions, and arm wrestling matches that got progressively sloppier with each shot of vodka. All of it destined for Instagram. Elise would have called them dick-swinging contests, mostly boring. But the reels got views and likes.

A mixed group played "Never Have I Ever" in a corner of the room. Haislee considered joining but the game wasn't as fun with people she didn't know. Some forgettable guy suggested she join a game of strip poker out in the poolhouse. Getting naked around strangers was an instant red flag.

If Haislee had known more people, this could have been an epic party for her. But she could watch only so many rounds of beer pong before her eyes glazed over.

She kept her eye on the second floor of the house. During her time roaming the party and recording video, Haislee had overheard Dustin bragging about his games room to anyone who would listen. She grabbed a bowl of snacks for herself, found a cozy spot at the end of the couch, and settled in to watch the party rage on.

– 68 –

"Hazy?" A voice from behind or beside or...

Haislee felt someone nudge her shoulder. She sat up, her eyes springing open, blinking. Everyone was gone. "What? Who..."

Dustin sat on the edge of the couch smiling at her. "You fell asleep. I guess the party wasn't so epic after all."

"No, no. I was tired," Haislee lied. She looked down at the empty bowl. "Plus it looks like I pigged out on snacks." Yawning, she asked what time it was.

"Just past four," Dustin said. "I can drive you home, or..." He glanced back at the front door. Richard stood there with his jacket on, his eyes focused on them.

"Or what?" Haislee shifted her gaze from Richard to Dustin.

"Or you could stay and play video games," Dustin said. "I've heard that you're quite a gamer. And I've got *all* the games."

Haislee leaned in a bit closer and lowered her voice. "Is Richard going to join us? He kinda gives me the creeps."

"I get that," Dustin whispered back. "I'll get rid of him." He walked over to Richard.

Haislee pulled out her phone and panned it left to right, recording video of the now-empty room. She watched the two of them exchange some words and share a brief bro-hug followed by a tap of each other's fists. Dustin ushered Richard out the front door.

"It's just you and me, now." Dustin beckoned her forward with a wave. "You'll love my games room."

Haislee stood and followed him. "I've heard the stories."

"Really? From who?"

"Well..." Haislee snickered. "From *you,* actually."

Dustin shook his head, self-conscious. "Yeah, okay. I talk about it a lot. I'm just super proud of the space."

"Can I record a reel or two?"

"Go for it." Dustin turned to face her phone's camera. "This week on MTV Cribs, yo!" he said as he flashed horn signs.

"Wait..." Haislee looked around at the afterparty mess. "Can I help you clean up first?"

"Don't worry about it," Dustin said. "I've called the housekeepers already. They'll be in tomorrow morning sometime to deal with it all."

"Must be nice."

Dustin shrugged. "You got parents. I got housekeepers." He started up the stairs to the second floor. "What's your favourite game?"

Haislee recorded the entire journey up the stairs panning around to capture it all. "The Legend of Zelda."

Dustin glanced back at her. "Tears of the Kingdom?"

Haislee grinned up at him.

"You're in luck," Dustin said. "Ever played it on a 200-inch flatscreen?"

"What?" Haislee caught up to Dustin on the second floor. "No way. Show me."

Dustin led Haislee into his bedroom. It was at least twice the size of hers. He turned on the sleek wall sconces that ran the length of each wall and cast a surprising amount of light. The headboard of his king-sized captain's bed sat centered against the far wall, the mattress above two sets of drawers on the left and right side. Blue LED running lights followed the bed's base along the floor, similar to those lining the aisles in an airplane or movie theatre, casting an eerie glow on the hardwood.

To the left of the bed was a door, presumably to the bathroom. Several finely milled bookcases lined the adjacent wall. Not books, but plastic and die-cast replicas of cars, planes, superheroes, Lego sets, and more that Haislee didn't recognize filled the shelves. It was like a museum catering to pop culture.

Against the wall and facing the foot of the bed sat an expansive desk housing a computer workstation with one large, curved screen, easily the width of three flat panel monitors side by side. The computer had an illuminated keyboard that cycled through colourful patterns, its own Sennheiser speakers, and a subwoofer on the floor. An ergonomic office chair made of one piece of woven carbon fiber and shaped like the driver's seat of a sports car sat on wheels in front of the desk.

To the right of the bed stood a long wardrobe, no doubt filled with expensive clothes, probably sorted by season, colour, or both. On the back wall between the bed and the wardrobe stood a full length mirror.

Framed supersized posters of video game art covered the little remaining wall space. Grand Theft Auto featured prominently.

Haislee took in the space with awe. "Your room is amazing." She panned her phone to capture the entire room and ended the video on herself. "Stoaks is *stoked!*"

"This is nothing," Dustin said. "Wait 'til you see the games room."

"You mean this isn't—"

"Fuck no." Dustin beckoned her to follow. "Come on." He stood in front of the mirror, their faces awash with blue light reflected from the bed's running lights. Dustin found Haislee's eyes and locked onto them. "Ready?"

Haislee beamed at him and nodded. She started a new video.

"Behold, peeps. Introducing the legendary Stoaks games room, where many fear to tread."

Dustin laughed. "You're badass." He slid the mirrored door open and turned on the lights. Lights at half their intensity faded up, giving the room a theatre ambiance. The leather couch and coffee table, the racing simulator, another computer, and more framed posters emerged from the darkness under their own sets of pot lights.

Haislee glanced out the door she had just stepped through, then back at the computer in the games room. "Another desktop?"

Dustin hooked a thumb at his bedroom. "That's work." He ran his hand across the computer desk in the games room. Three monitors and another glowing keyboard seemed to respond to his touch. "This is play."

"Sick." Haislee slipped her phone into clutch as she looked at the shelves of game consoles. "Holy shit. How many consoles do you have?"

Dustin looked pleased. "*All* of them."

"Seriously?"

"Well, most of them," Dustin said. "There's a few I haven't been able to find, like—"

"The Halcyon?" Haislee strolled by the consoles on the shelves, lit from above like they were in a museum.

Dustin did a double take. "Yeah. You know your stuff."

"Thanks," Haislee said. "I doubt you'll ever find one. They're super rare." She turned to him, tossing her hair over one shoulder. "Have you ever played Dragon's Lair? That's the system the Halcyon was based on."

"No."

"Me, neither. But my dad has. I've just seen vids." Haislee glanced at the big 200-inch screen. "So... are you going to boot up Zelda?"

"Yeah, abso-fuckin-lutely." Dustin strolled toward the bar. "Can I get you anything first? Drink? Snacks?"

"A drink."

"Beer? Coke?"

"Definitely a Coke," Haislee said.

Dustin reached into the bar fridge, handed her a chilled can of Coke, and set a beer down on the coffee table for himself. He went to a glass-fronted cabinet in a corner of the room and dug through it. A moment later he pulled out the game discs for Zelda: Tears of the Kingdom.

Haislee cracked the seal of her Coke and took an ample drink and sighed. "God, that's better than sex."

Dustin laughed. "Good to know." He brought a Nintendo Switch to the coffee table and pressed a hidden button. A port on the top of the table popped open, revealing all the cables needed to hook up any platform to the TV.

"It's a temporary solution," Dustin said. "What I want to do is have my main consoles hooked up all the time."

"This works." Haislee took another drink from her Coke, then swapped it for the Switch controller. "Can I go first?"

"Be my guest," Dustin said.

The game began with a cut scene of Zelda and Link descending a dark tunnel beneath Hyrule Castle. Haislee moved Link forward in the game until another cut scene began.

"I love the look of this game," she said.

"The graphics are good," Dustin said, "but Grand Theft Auto blows this out of the water in terms of realism."

Haislee laughed quietly. "It's fantasy, you doof. They weren't going for realism."

"You realize that this game takes a long time to complete, right?"

"You can save my game..." Haislee blinked. "Then maybe I could come back... you know... to finish." She held the controller up. "Want to play for a while?"

"Sure." Dustin took the controller and directed Link farther into the dark recesses of the castle. Haislee slurped her Coke and watched Dustin play.

"It'd be cool... to work at a company like Nintendo," Haislee said. "I'd love to do... the art."

Dustin worked the controllers, making Link run, jump and swim on the massive screen. "Yeah, that'd be super cool." He directed Link to a precipice and jumped into the clouds.

The 3D graphics and immense screen made Haislee feel dizzy. But it was more than that. She felt as if she was crashing.

A sugar high maybe?

"Whew. Maybe some... snacks would be... good," Haislee said.

"Okay." Dustin put the game into pause and rooted around at the bar. "Potato chips sound good?"

There was no response.

"Hazy?" Dustin walked back to the couch. Haislee had slumped over. He kneeled in front of her and gave her shoulders a gentle shake. "Haislee?"

Haislee groaned. "So... tired."

"I've got just the thing." Dustin slipped one arm under her knees and the other under her arm and around her body. He lifted her off the couch easily and carried her to his bed, laying her down on one side of the king-sized mattress. Her hair smelled faintly of flowers. He slid her purse strap from around her body and laid it beside her on the bed.

"Hazy?" Dustin gave Haislee another gentle nudge. "I've moved you to my bed to sleep. Is that okay?"

Haislee mumbled something resembling words. In her mind everything swirled in and out of orange and blue and black. Whatever she was lying on was soft and warm. Everything felt just right, except for a faint tickle, like fabric moving up her thighs, perhaps a blanket or the duvet cover.

Dustin's just tucking me in. He's not all bad.

– **69** –

ELISE LEFT A NOTE for her parents and took a bus to Cherry Mills Medical Centre. Even though she had been to the centre's ICU only twice before, she found her way to the reception desk on the second floor like she had been going daily. She took the sign-in sheet from the nurse at the desk, wrote down her name, and handed it back.

The nurse glanced at the name. "Elise Coleman, as in daughter of Teigan?"

Elise raised a brow and nodded.

The nurse extended her hand. "I'm Betty." The two of them shook hands. "Your mom and I are like this." She grinned and crossed her fingers. "Here at the ICU that is. Although I haven't seen her as regularly now. Everything okay?"

"She's trying to find out who did it…" Elise looked past reception with an awkward moment of silence. "You know, to my brother."

Betty nodded. "He's getting better. Every day. I should know."

Elise looked at the clock on the back wall of the reception area. It read quarter past seven. "I know visiting hours go until eight. But if I—"

"Not to worry, Elise," Betty said. "We'll make an exception if you need it." She buzzed the lock on the ICU door.

"Thanks." Elise walked down the corridor and found Newton's room before realizing that she didn't know the room number. The corridor, the room, Newton's bed, and the machines keeping him alive had burned a permanent spot in her memory.

After all this was over, she hoped to never visit the hospital in any capacity for the rest of her life. Elise stepped inside Newton's room.

"He's getting better," Betty had said moments earlier. Elise would have to take her word for it because the room looked – Newton looked – exactly the same as he had looked on the first day he had been admitted. The same machines, whirrs, and beeps.

Elise felt the impending sting of tears at the back of her eyes but fought them off. She walked around the foot of the bed and sat in one of the chairs.

"Newt," Elise said in a low whisper. She didn't know what words came next and instead of speaking, she placed her hand gently on his arm, careful to not jostle the IV line.

She heard her phone chime in her pocket. Elise grabbed it with her free hand. A text from Haislee displayed on the screen, followed by a notification of a sent video.

Elise tapped play and the handheld vertical video played back with talking, cheering, yelling, and music playing so loud it all mixed together into incomprehensible noise. This kind of display wasn't Elise's scene at the best of times, but she still felt left out. If Haislee had suggested accompanying her to the party earlier, she might have gone. Haislee could be very convincing. Finding a cute boyfriend had been a dream of Elise's ever since starting Grade 9. But right now Newton took priority, not because of guilt, but because she wanted to be there.

She texted Haislee back, expressing her disgust, but wanting details later. As much as she disliked these kinds of parties, she would never pass up details. Elise pocketed her phone.

"Come back to us, Newt. We miss you." Her eyes welled, then in a low whisper, "We love you."

Newton's arm twitched. Elise pulled back her hand like she had been poked with a pin. She turned to look at his face and caught his eyelids sliding closed.

"Betty!" Elise pushed back on her chair and bolted out of the room and back up the corridor. "Betty!"

Betty emerged from the reception area and met Elise halfway. "What's it is? Tell me." She placed a hand on Elise's shoulder as she walked her back to Newton's room.

"He moved... and..." Elise was vibrating, her excitement mixed with anxiety and fear of the unknown.

Betty prepared to respond when Elise added, "And he opened his eyes."

"Are you sure?"

"I saw his eyes," Elise said. "Just for a second."

Betty guided Elise back into the room.

Elise studied her brother closely. "His eyes are closed now, but they weren't a second ago. I swear."

"I believe you." Betty's serious eyes scanned Newton and his connected machines.

"Is that good?" Elise waited on tenterhooks.

Betty nodded. "It's very good." She pulled her stethoscope from a pocket and measured Newton's pulse and blood pressure, comparing it to the data displaying on the vital signs monitor. She jotted a note onto the chart at the end of the bed. "It's an indication that Newton may be waking from his coma. But that doesn't mean he'll be conscious just yet. We need a doctor to perform a detailed examination to be certain of what's going on."

"But he's okay?"

"It appears so." Betty looked at Elise kindly. "You two must have a strong bond."

Elise smiled sheepishly and shrugged. "I guess."

"Would you like me to contact your parents, or would you like to share the news?"

"I'll do it. Thanks."

"Any time, Elise." Betty left the room.

Elise pulled a chair close and sat, resting her body and arms on Newton's, as if hugging him from the side.

Fuck Dustin's party. Coming here had been the right choice. The only choice.

"Love you, Newt." A deep breath reassured her nose with the scent of clean – if institutional smelling – sheets. "Come back," she whispered, closing her eyes.

And, as if they were synced, Newton opened his eyes again. Just for a second before closing them once more.

$$- \; 70 \; -$$

Elise woke with a start around eight thirty, the ridges from Newton's top sheet temporarily lining her cheek with a web of random grooves. If Newton had been awake, he'd have gotten annoyed and pushed her off of him long before sleep took hold of her. Just being in his presence, hearing his heart beating, soothed her anxiety. She decided to visit more often.

Elise signed herself out of the ICU and thanked Betty for her help. She arrived home to find Mattix and Teigan cuddled in the love seat watching television and found herself hit with a flashback of the night Newton was admitted to hospital.

The afterparty.

Teigan glanced back at her. "How's Newt? Everything okay?"

Elise decided to hold back the news of Newton opening his eyes. She wanted that knowledge to be hers for a while. "Not much change, but Betty says he's making small improvements."

Mattix turned his head. "Like what?"

"His hand twitched when I was there," Elise said. "Freaked me out."

Teigan returned her attention to the television show. "Yeah, he did once when I was there, too."

"He probably did it on purpose," Mattix said.

"Yeah, probably." Elise headed up the stairs. It struck her as odd and somewhat sad how normal Newton's condition had become. She wanted the old normal back.

She checked her phone for any incoming texts she might have missed, but a clean, uncluttered screen with nothing but the time stared back at her. Elise slipped into her pajamas and a terry housecoat and threw her clothes into her hamper.

In her peripheral vision, she sensed motion out of her bedroom window. Elise turned her head and saw a person standing on the sidewalk in front of their house, the cone of light from the streetlamp casting a black shadow on the pavement. She didn't have much frame of reference, but the figure appeared tall and a dark hoodie hid the person's face. It felt like this strange person was looking only at her, *through* her.

She ran down the stairs, threw open the front door, and stood at the threshold.

"What is it, Lise?" Teigan said without looking away from the TV.

"There's some creep staring at the house."

That got Teigan's attention, and she met Elise at the door. "Where?"

Elise stepped onto the porch. "They *were* there." She turned to Teigan. "A second ago. I swear."

"I believe you." Teigan ran down the driveway to the sidewalk and scanned the street in both directions, then returned to the porch. "What did this person look like?"

"Tall. Couldn't see their face because of the hoodie."

Colour drained from Teigan's face. "Navy blue?"

"I don't know, Mom! It's dark out." Elise narrowed her eyes at her mother. "Are you okay? Do *you* know who that was?"

Teigan shook her head slowly. "No."

Mattix stepped to the door. "Everything okay out here?"

"Just a lame-ass porch party." Elise snugged her housecoat

closed, wrapped her arms around herself, and trudged inside and up the stairs.

Mattix sent Teigan a confused look. "What got into her?"

"She's spooked," Teigan said. "Anyone would be if they saw someone they didn't know staring at them."

"I can hear you, you know." Elise peered down from the pony wall on the second floor.

Mattix poked his head farther out the door.

"They're not there anymore." Elise slammed her bedroom door closed. "And I'm not crazy!" She flopped down onto her bed and could hear her parents' muffled talking through the wall and floor.

Elise rolled over and pulled out her phone. No notifications. She unlocked it and tapped out a text to Haislee.

"HayZ yo?"

No response, not even the thought icon with three bouncing dots.

"U OK?"

While waiting for Haislee to text her back, Elise switched over to Instagram. Haislee's account had been busy tonight. She had posted several photos and videos of Dustin's party, mostly of male posturing and drinking games, with the occasional selfie thrown in for good measure.

Elise typed a comment on one of Haislee's selfies. "Lookin hawt, Hazy! DM!"

She pinch-zoomed in on Haislee's smiling face. The old pangs of being left out tugged at the back of her mind. "Charge your fuckin' phone and text me back," she said in a whisper. Haislee always had a backup battery for emergencies.

Elise plugged her phone in on her bedside table. She closed her eyes and tried to picture Newton's hospital room as best she could. She caught a hint of the clean smell of Newton's hospital sheets still lingering on her shirt. Surprisingly, that stood out for her the most and it was enough to lull her to sleep.

$$- \; 71 \; -$$

HAISLEE WOKE TO DARKNESS, a mind-numbing headache, and a desperate need to pee. A slick film of sweat greased her skin. The heavy duvet spread over her wasn't helping. Her cheek stuck to her pillow, yet it wasn't a pillow exactly.

With one arm she pushed herself upright, sitting on the edge of the mattress. Her head exploded and Haislee winced, her fingers from both hands massaging her temples. Her shattered thoughts slowly coalesced and she realized she was in Dustin's game room. It wasn't a bed she was sitting on but the leather couch. She could see dim silhouettes of the Nintendo Switch controllers on the coffee table and had a vague memory of playing The Legend of Zelda. The rest of the evening was gone.

Had I really drunk that *much?*

Sitting upright with her bare feet on the cool floor helped reduce the throbbing pain in her head, as if gravity was pulling whatever it was in her head down and out of her body through her feet. Gravity pulled at her bladder too, overriding any feeling of comfort.

She stood up, bracing herself on the arm of the couch, and felt dull discomfort radiate from her groin. Fear replaced any residual headache she felt.

Have I been...

Instead of finishing her thought, Haislee reached under her skirt. Her panties were still on but maybe her period had started. After checking to make sure she was alone, she pulled her panties down slightly and looked at the gusset. The dimness did not provide much detail but there was enough light to confirm no dark patches resembling blood. She pulled her panties back up and felt cooling moisture on her skin. She tried to convince herself that it was just evaporating sweat, but something didn't feel right.

Haislee spotted her shoes close by and slipped them on. Glancing back, the sliding door to Dustin's room was half open. She stood and approached it, carefully peering into the bedroom.

The blankets on Dustin's bed were wrinkled and strewn about but Dustin was nowhere to be seen.

She pushed the sliding door open enough for her to pass through, walked around the bed and into the bathroom on the other side. Haislee sat and peed. The relief of internal pressure helped her relax which in turn helped her head find peace.

She dug her phone out of her clutch. It was powered off, not just in standby. She rarely turned her phone off and when she did, it was at home. Haislee held down the power button until the familiar logo appeared and returned it to her purse.

She wiped, flushed, and washed up. Normally she'd poke around the bathroom to see what things she could learn about Dustin. But this morning she just wanted to get home. Her parents would be worried.

Haislee opened the bedroom door. Bright sunshine bled out into the upper hallway and grand room from the floor-to-ceiling windows, making her eyes sting. She could hear utensils clattering below and smelled something good cooking, pancakes maybe.

She slipped off her shoes in order to tiptoe down the stairs without making a sound. There was no way to walk to the front door without passing by the entrance to the dining room and kitchen. Haislee took a determined breath and headed for the front door, imagining the taste of the spring air.

From within her purse a series of chirps sounded. She peeked at the screen and saw several texts from Elise sent last night.

"Hazy?"

Shit. Dustin had seen her, alerted by the text notifications. She heard his quick steps approach from the kitchen. "I was wonderin' when you were gonna get up."

Haislee stopped and turned around to see Dustin grinning at her.

"You were pretty wasted last night," he said. "You crashed right in the middle of playing Zelda. I didn't want to wake you."

"Uh, thanks." Haislee's phone chirped again.

Those fucking text reminders, as if she had forgotten.

Dustin motioned at her purse. "You need to get those?"

Haislee shook her head and hooked her thumb at the front door. "Look... I'm, like, just gonna go. My parents are probably freaking out."

"No. Stay," Dustin said. "I can call your parents. Plus Greta made waffles."

"Greta?"

"The hired help."

A guy who couldn't make waffles himself multiplied Haislee's desire to flee. "No, thanks." She pulled open the heavy front door and scooted through it, putting on her shoes at the top of the outer entrance.

Dustin jogged over to the door. "Seeya... *Hazy.*"

Haislee narrowed her eyes at him, trying to read his face but getting nothing in return. "Yeah, later."

She took the steps two at a time and followed the circular driveway out to the road, not looking back once. Once out on the main road and out of sight, she pulled out her phone and dialed.

The line trilled in her ear, then connected. "Lise...? Can you pick me up?" She knew the answer would be "yes" but needed to hear it. Both Haislee's and Elise's parents had long ago agreed that they'd always be available to pick them up any time, anywhere within reason, no questions asked.

Haislee breathed a sigh of hesitant relief and continued walking, knowing that she'd see her best friend again soon. One strange chapter of her life had come to a close. And while the discomfort in her body concerned her, the gap in her memory scared her more.

$$- \ 72 \ -$$

Elise loved Saturday morning sleep-ins. She dozed in bed, running scenarios through her head about why Haislee hadn't texted her back. The smell of coffee wafted under her door, and although tempting, the only things that would get her out of her warm comforter cocoon were bacon and waffles, in that order.

But a panicked call from her best friend sent her covers flying. "Of course we can pick you up." Elise scrambled for her clothes with the phone pinned between her ear and her shoulder. "Are you okay?" She pulled on her socks and jeans.

Staticky sounds of Haislee breathing on the other end of the line.

"Hazy?"

"I'm fine." Haislee's voice sounded a thousand miles away. "Just come get me. And Lise? My mom can't know."

"Okay. Text me your location." Elise threw on a shirt, pocketed her phone, and thumped down the stairs to the kitchen. "Mom?"

Mattix sat at the kitchen table, sipping a coffee and reading the newspaper. "She's in her office, but is there anything I can help with?"

"Thanks, Dad, but no." Elise reversed direction and headed back up the stairs. She knocked on Teigan's office door. "Mom?"

Elise heard movement, shuffling of papers, and a filing cabinet trundling closed. The door creaked open and Teigan appraised her daughter, first welcoming, then with confusion.

"Lise? What is it?"

"Can we go pick up Hazy?"

Her daughter's concern became her own. "Is she alright?"

"I think so," Elise said. "But…"

Teigan locked gaze with Elise. "But what?"

Elise blinked at her expectantly. "Her parents can't know. It's got to be our secret, Mom."

"What about your dad?"

"Probably, like, the less people, the better."

Teigan nodded. "Okay. Let me grab my purse."

The two of them headed back downstairs. Teigan pulled on a coat and slung her purse over her shoulder.

Teigan placed a hand on Mattix's shoulder. "Driving Lise to meet Haislee at Timmy's."

"Seemed urgent," Mattix said. "Not sure why I couldn't have driven her."

Teigan kissed Mattix. "It's a girl thing. I'll take the Civic."

Mattix shrugged and went back to his paper and coffee.

The two of them headed outside and buckled themselves in. Teigan looked at her daughter. "Where to?"

"Rosendale Road," Elise said.

"But whereabouts on Rosendale?"

Elise shrugged. "She's walking. We'll see her."

Once on the road, silence was the loudest passenger. Elise kept her eyes locked on the road ahead. Teigan tried to remain quiet as long as she could.

"What's this about, Lise?"

"I don't know," Elise said. "Hazy never said."

"If you were to guess—"

"Mom!"

Teigan sighed in frustration.

"Just be cool, Mom, okay?" Elise looked at her with eyes glistening with worry. "Please?"

"Okay." Teigan returned her focus to the road. She opened her mouth to say something else but thought better of it.

Elise spotted Haislee before Teigan did. She was following the sidewalk on the opposite side of the road.

"There she is!"

Teigan slowed and prepared for a U-turn. "She's coming from... Rockwood West?"

"I don't know."

Once Teigan pulled the Civic to a stop at the curb, Elise unbuckled and hopped out. "Stay in the car, okay?"

Teigan read the concern on her daughter's face and nodded, then killed the engine.

Elise closed the door and ran back to wrap her arms around Haislee.

"Hazy!" Elise whispered into her ear, "My mom's watching so we're gonna sit, okay?" She felt Haislee nod against her neck.

They parted and took a seat on the curb, now out of Teigan's line of sight. Elise felt relief at the increase in privacy.

"What happened?"

Haislee shook her head slowly while she worked at her memories. "I went to Dustin's party, which was meh honestly, but his house is amazing. Anyway, I was just mingling, watching, and posting shit."

"I know," Elise said. "I saw your reels. Felt like I was there."

"I'm glad you weren't. It was actually pretty boring. I fell asleep, and when I woke up, everyone had gone." Haislee wiped her nose with the sleeve of her sweater.

"Did you leave your drink unattended?"

Haislee shook her head. "Wait. No. Richard was there. He was just leaving. He was last to go. Then it was just me and Dustin."

"*Dustbin.*" Elise stared at her expectantly. "And?"

"And he was nice," Haislee said. "We went up into his games room. I drank a Coke, which *I* opened, and played Zelda. He didn't try anything. Then I woke up on the same couch I had been sitting on, but I felt weird."

"Do you remember anything?"

Haislee shook her head. "I guess I could have fallen asleep. I mean I was tired."

Elise narrowed her eyes. "You said you felt weird. Weird how?"

"It doesn't hurt exactly, but achy? Maybe a bit sore?"

"Downstairs?" Elise motioned subtly toward her groin.

Haislee nodded.

"Do you think you were assaulted?" Elise picked up a rock.

"I don't know why, but that was my first thought."

"Why?" Elise threw the rock across the road. "Because Dustbin's a *sleaze*."

"But I checked my..." Haislee lowered her voice and leaned closer. "I checked my underwear. It looked normal."

"Doesn't prove anything."

Haislee pulled her phone from her purse and unlocked it. The camera roll app displayed. "That's strange."

"What?"

"I never leave apps open." Haislee took a closer look. "And the photos and videos I shot last night are gone." She switched to the "Recently Deleted" folder. "They're gone permanently."

"Someone got into your phone?"

"I guess." Haislee stowed the phone. "There's no other explanation, unless I deleted them and don't remember doing it."

"Doubtful." Elise locked gaze with Haislee. "That asshole better not be responsible, or I'll fucking kill him."

"Don't do that." Haislee managed a small smile for the first time since meeting up. "He's better locked up for life instead." The two girls hugged.

"Let's get you home," Elise said.

They stood and both climbed into the back seat of the Civic.

Teigan glanced at them through the rear view mirror. "Everything good?"

"Yeah," Elise said. "If we could drop Hazy off, that'd be super cool."

"You could come back to our place," Teigan said. "Have some breakfast?"

"My parents are probably worried, so..."

"Right." Teigan started the engine. "Next stop, Tipperary."

– 73 –

As Teigan drove Haislee home, the car remained quiet. There was no hushed talking or shared watching of Instagram videos. Elise used an arm to hold Haislee close, her hand caressing her hair, and Haislee rested her head on Elise's shoulder. The picture was sweetness personified, but Teigan felt an undercurrent of unease. Something was wrong.

As her kids grew older and experienced problems in their lives, they began to turn more to their friends than to her and Mattix for help. Teigan knew that this was a natural development, a way to express their independence, but it still stung a bit. She was pleased that Elise had come to her this time, but wished she could be a bit more involved.

"Haislee?" Teigan glanced at the girls in the rear view mirror. "How are you doing, hon?"

Haislee sat up a bit straighter. "I'm okay."

Teigan probably should have left it at that, but when Newton's life was on the line she was like a dog after a bone. "Can I ask you something?"

Elise glared at her. "Mom!" she said through clenched teeth.

Haislee placed a hand on Elise to calm her. "It's fine. Go ahead, Mrs. Coleman."

"I know you were at the quarry that night," Teigan said. "You stayed with Newt and did CPR until the ambulance arrived. I'm so thankful to you for that." She paused to collect her words. "Was it you who called 9-1-1?"

"No. Not sure who did that." In the shaded back seat, Haislee looked like death warmed over. Her hair hung in tangled clumps and her mascara streaked down her face like bony black fingers.

"Did you see or hear anything that seemed sketchy?" Teigan alternated her gaze between the two girls in the back seat. Elise returned a scowl that meant she'd be giving Teigan an earful when they got home.

"Mom, watch the road!" Elise pointed forward.

"Sketchy how?"

"Like mention of tainted drugs or alcohol?" Teigan turned onto a side street.

"It was an afterparty," Haislee said. "There was drugs and alcohol there. No idea if it was tainted. I didn't drink that much, and I don't do drugs."

Elise and Haislee shared a quick knowing look.

"Did you see who gave Newt the marijuana?"

"Mom, stop with the questions," Elise said.

"I only saw Newt after he had... passed out." Haislee swallowed hard, her eyes misting up.

"How did you get to the quarry?"

"MOM. STOP." Elise clutched the backs of the driver and passenger seat and pulled herself forward. "You know the rules. No questions asked for emergency pickups."

"Lise, this is important!" Teigan raised her voice. "And it's not about last night."

"Doesn't matter."

"Don't you want to know who almost killed your brother?"

"Yes," Elise said, "but Hazy's not the enemy."

The car fell silent, except for Haislee's sniffles. Teigan glanced into the rear view mirror and saw her tears.

"Shit," Teigan said under her breath. "I'm sorry, Haislee."

"Maybe my Instagram videos caught something," Haislee said softly. "I posted a lot of videos that night."

Teigan pulled the car to the side of the road. "Will you show me?"

Haislee shared a knowing look with Elise.

Elise nodded. "But only if you want to."

Haislee pulled out her phone and positioned herself so that Teigan and Elise could see the screen. She launched Instagram and selected her public account.

"No, this isn't right," she said, frowning at the grid of images.

"What do you mean?" Teigan looked at them both.

Haislee exchanged a quick glance with Elise and scrolled through her posts. A seemingly endless train of images shot past the screen.

"They're not there," Haislee said.

"What isn't?"

Haislee switched into her Finsta account and scrolled through that. "All my photos and videos from that night are gone."

"I saw them last night," Elise said.

"Did you delete them?" Teigan asked.

"No, I—"

Elise cut Haislee off. "Don't be stupid, Mom."

Teigan struggled to control the flash of anger at her daughter's comment. "What did you say?"

"Nothing," said Elise.

"I will not be talked to like that." Teigan's jaw clenched on her words. "Do you understand me?"

A small nod from Elise.

"I don't, well, I *rarely* delete my stuff," Haislee said. "I just bury it with new stuff."

Teigan moved her gaze to Haislee. "How did they get deleted, then?"

Haislee shrugged and shook her head. "Maybe someone hacked my account?"

Teigan twisted in her seat to face the dashboard and the girls sank back in the passenger seat. Haislee tapped a few times and showed the screen to Elise. Teigan only saw the expression on their faces for second, but she was sure it was one of fear mixed with revelation.

"Find out anything?"

The two girls regarded Teigan in the rear view mirror with caution.

"No, Mom," Elise said.

"Looks like I *was* hacked." Haislee crammed her phone back into her purse then directed her gaze out the passenger window. "I'll fix it when I get home."

Teigan's gut feeling said they weren't being completely truthful, but she knew she wouldn't be getting any more information out of them.

$$- \ 74 \ -$$

Teigan let the Civic idle as she watched Elise walk Haislee to her door. The two friends exchanged brief words, rested their foreheads against each other for a moment, then hugged. Elise waved and walked back to the car. Haislee watched her go.

Elise hopped into the front passenger seat and rolled down the window. She leaned out and waved again. "Call me later." Haislee nodded, then stepped inside her house.

Teigan pulled away from the curb. "Do you have anything to tell me?"

Elise rolled her eyes and huffed in frustration. "No, *Mom*."

"Fine, but you could lose the attitude," Teigan said. "Chauffeuring you around on Saturday morning isn't my idea of fun."

Elise sighed and turned to look at her. "Thank you for driving me. But remember, this whole 'ask for pickup, no questions' idea was your idea."

"And Dad's."

"Right. So, if you want me to feel comfortable calling you, then, like, stand by the rules of the agreement you set up."

Teigan could feel the heat of Elise's stare.

"Which means *no* questions," Elise said. "Okay?"

It was a fair point. Teigan knew she had stepped over a line, but she was desperate for information surrounding Newton's situation.

"You're right." Peace had been restored between them, but only temporarily. Teigan couldn't leave things alone. "Can I ask you something else?" She saw Elise begin to wind up. "Before you freak out, it's nothing about today, or Instagram reels, or school, or—"

"What is it?" Elise's annoyance flipped to curiosity.

"What do you know about Killa Scrip?"

Elise's eyes widened for a second. "The better question is how do *you* know about him?"

"I was following a lead," Teigan said, "and his name popped up."

"Following a *lead?*" Elise smirked at her, holding back laughter. "What are you, a cop now?"

"The *cops* aren't doing anything." Teigan's knuckles whitened around the steering wheel. "I'm a concerned parent."

"Seriously, Mom. Leave the cops to deal with Killa Scrip."

"Humor me, oh daughter of mine." Teigan said. "What do you know about him?"

Elise shrugged. "What can I say? He's a scumbag dealer and he's dangerous. Avoid. Do *not* recommend."

"Have you ever met him?"

"What? Are you crazy? No." Elise sat up, concern on her face. "Besides no one actually, like, *meets* Killa Scrip. He has agents."

"What about Haislee?"

Elise shook her head. "Not that I know of."

"She doesn't buy her marijuana from him?" Teigan exchanged a knowing glance with her daughter. She hadn't forgotten smelling pot smoke on her clothes from before.

"I don't know where she gets her pot," Elise lied. "And that was just one time."

Teigan nodded and refocused her attention on the road ahead.

"Don't do anything stupid, Mom," Elise said. "I mean that in the most loving way."

Teigan gave her a side-eyed glance.

Elise crossed her arms against her chest. "Promise me." When Teigan didn't respond immediately, Elise pursed her lips and tensed her body as she leaned forward, insisting on an answer.

"I promise not to do anything stupid," Teigan said.

"Good. I don't want you to get hurt too." Elise relaxed back into her seat.

Teigan rolled up to the curb in front of their house, cut the engine, and shifted into park.

"Thanks, Mom." Elise already had the passenger door open. "Good talk." She closed it and strolled across the grass toward the porch.

I promised not to do anything stupid.

And she wouldn't. But in Teigan's mind, what she planned to do was not stupid, but necessary. She knew just the thing to help minimize her risk because her list of questions wasn't getting any smaller.

– 75 –

HAISLEE WAVED GOODBYE to Elise and slowly pressed the thumb latch on her front door. The size of her clutch was big enough for her phone and not much else, so she had forgone her keys the previous night. She hoped that it being late Saturday morning, one of her parents would have unlocked the door to get the morning paper.

The door creaked open. It was an unavoidable sound even with greased hinges. The scent of something baking, maybe muffins, rose to her nostrils. On any other day, her stomach would growl loudly, take control of her body, and lead her to the kitchen. But today all the wonderful smells did was remind her of Dustin's house. Her appetite disappeared.

"Haze?" The voice of her mother Grace floated out from the kitchen.

"Yeah, Mom." Haislee headed for the stairs.

"How was your night?"

Ever since Haislee and Elise had turned fifteen, their parents had rarely confirmed sleepover details with each other. If it was okay with one set of parents, it was okay with the other. But there was still a chance of it happening.

Haislee was half-way up the stairs and decided to play the

odds. "Good. We watched movies all night. Didn't get much sleep."

"Sounds like fun," Grace said. "Dad's making waffles—"

"Belgian style," Sam broke in.

"Want some?"

Waffles. Just like at Dustin's. N to the O.

Haislee could hear her mom approaching the stairs and quickened her pace. The last thing she wanted was to talk to or be seen by anyone. Her streaked mascara alone would have set off alarm bells. "I might. Got to shower first, though."

"Okay," Grace's voice said from downstairs. "We'll keep some warm for you."

Haislee stepped into her room, closed the door, and flopped onto the bed. If she stopped moving, she'd fall asleep, so she threw off her clutch purse, peeled out of her clothes and wrapped herself in her terrycloth robe.

She stepped out of her bedroom and into the bathroom at the end of the hall. Haislee examined herself in the mirror. "You look like shit, girl," she said to her reflection. The dark smudges of mascara made her look much worse than she actually felt and she couldn't wait to wash it off.

Haislee adjusted the water to a comfortable temperature and stepped into the tub, pulling the shower curtain closed behind her.

The warm water felt good on her skin, but nothing could rinse away the ache and her overwhelming feeling of unease. Haislee slid a hand down toward her groin and gently over her intimate areas. They were more sensitive to touch than they usually were, and she had no idea why. She hadn't felt like this yesterday. Could the blank spot in her memory be hiding the truth?

Suddenly and unexpectedly, Haislee burst into heavy sobs. She slid down the wall of the shower enclosure and sat in the bottom of the tub, her knees pulled close to her chest.

Something had *happened. But what?*

Hot tears ran in rivulets down her face and mixed with the shower water. And as she cried, her head cleared. If Haislee had to describe herself with one word, it would be *strong*. With two words: *strong* and *smart*.

She stood and quickly washed herself. Upon reaching for the shower curtain, an image of a fist locked around a handful of white fabric flashed in her head. Was this a clue? She thought it could have been her hand, but she wasn't sure.

Haislee cast her mind back to Dustin's house. There were no sheets in the games room. She was certain of that. She tried to picture his bedroom, but all she came back with were the ridiculous blue running lights along the floor of his captain's bed.

Her phone and the videos she had recorded during her tour would be of no help since they had all been deleted. But there was another way, because in addition to being strong and smart, Haislee was *prepared*.

$$- \ 76 \ -$$

TEIGAN SAT IN HER OFFICE staring at a pad of Post-It notes on her desk. On the top sheet she had written "Bantor and Agate." She pulled up Google Maps in her Internet browser.

Over the years, Teigan had used Maps often to covertly track her kids and explore the places where they hung out. She found the Street View particularly useful in determining the "sketchiness factor" of a destination.

If Teigan wanted to be absolutely sure of a location before a projection, scouting it out in person was mandatory. Maps might hold a new purpose for her now. Assuming the street view images were recent, she might be able to use Maps to collect enough memorable detail to aid her with a projection to the actual location. She loved having a superpower.

She pulled up the map for Hamilton, Ontario, and entered "Bantor and Agate" into the search field. Maps zoomed into the intersection of the two roads and placed a location pin.

A knock sounded on her partially open office door. "Tee?" Mattix peeked in. "I'm heading to Canadian Tire, then picking up some groceries. Need anything?"

Teigan switched tabs in her browser, although from Mattix's point of view, he couldn't see her screen. Better safe than sorry.

She thought for a moment, then walked over to face him, almost nose to nose. "How about a special dessert?"

"Like?"

"Surprise me." Teigan kissed him lightly.

Mattix nodded. "Okay." He moved to leave, then paused. "Are you okay? When I came in you looked a little... I don't know. Worried?"

"I'm fine," Teigan said. "Just concentrating on tax issues for GadgetGot."

"Yikes." Mattix narrowed his eyes and grinned slyly. "Need a break? Wanna come with?"

Teigan shook her head. "I'm good, but thanks."

Mattix gave her another look of appraisal, then planted a quick kiss. "Back in about an hour."

"Okay." Teigan listened to Mattix's footsteps as they descended to the first floor and out to the garage. When the garage door opened and the car started, she sat back down in front of her computer.

Teigan hoped she had acted convincingly. Mattix had always been very responsive to her moods and behavior. Lying to him was easy physically and extremely difficult emotionally.

She opened the tab with Maps loaded and dragged the little orange human icon to where the location pin sat. A 360° view of the intersection loaded on the screen. Teigan spent the next twenty minutes digitally touring the intersection in all four directions, memorizing house shapes and address numbers. Sometimes technology was magic.

Teigan switched to Instagram on her phone and loaded her "dark.angela2005" profile. She sent a friend request to both Dustin and Richard. Less than thirty seconds later, a message chimed from Dustin.

"What skool U from?" his text read.

Teigan panicked, then realized she could take her time replying.

She thought back to Operation Yearbook. "Waterton," she tapped back. It felt strangely exhilarating to be catfishing Dustin.

A moment later, "Cool. We should hang sometime."

"Ok." Teigan shot back. She stashed her phone in her purse and knocked on Elise's room. "Safe to enter?"

"Yeah."

Teigan stepped into her daughter's room. Elise was stretched out on her bed, phone in hand and earbuds installed in each ear.

"Just checking in," Teigan said. "Have you heard from Haislee since dropping her off?"

"No, but I'm sure she's fine." Elise's eyes remained glued to her phone.

"Okay." Teigan hooked a thumb behind her. "I'm going to lie down for a bit, or I might go for a drive. Haven't decided."

"To visit Newt?"

"Yeah, maybe." Another lie. Teigan knew exactly where she was going, and it wasn't to visit Newton. She pulled Elise's door closed.

"Mom?"

Teigan reopened the door enough to pop her head in and raised her brows.

"Are you okay?" Elise set her phone down and propped herself up on her elbows. "I mean, I know you're, like, trying to find clues, you know, about who drugged Newt. Can I help?"

"You already are," Teigan said. "Trust me."

Teigan closed the door and glimpsed a look of either concern, confusion, or both on her daughter's face. She retreated to her bedroom and stretched out on her bed.

She closed her eyes, relaxed her body, and pictured the intersection of Bantor and Agate streets. Compared to the few projections she had been on so far, where she had firsthand physical knowledge of the location she was visiting, the intersection she stood in now felt oddly flat and there was no sound. That made sense since she had trained her memory on a series of images instead of a 3D immersive experience.

Teigan worried that the Maps' Street View approach had been a waste of time. The vehicles and people in the images remained frozen. She tried to walk but nothing moved. All she could do was look in all directions around her. Which made sense considering the source of the images. Even "tapping" on the direction arrows in the images had no effect.

She held her breath, forcing the projection to end. She lay staring at the bedroom ceiling, waiting for her breathing to normalize.

Once calm, Teigan made several more attempts to place herself on the sidewalk, but she ended up in the center of the street each time. She couldn't seem to move from the spot she projected to.

Again, it made sense. The Street View images had been taken from the middle of the street and that's where she'd end up in a projection. As it turned out, her superpower had limitations.

She grabbed her purse and headed downstairs to get her shoes and coat on. "Heading out for a bit," she called out to Elise.

"Kay, Mom," Elise's voice floated out of her room.

Probably doom-scrolling Instagram.

Just as Teigan started the Honda's engine a text chime sounded from her purse. She peeked at the screen and saw that it was a message from Richard.

"Can't resist the dark angel, can you?" She laughed to herself. Teigan let the phone slide back into her purse. "Not today. I got bigger fish to fry." She pulled away from the curb and began the drive to the intersection of Bantor and Agate.

– **77** –

A FEW YEARS AGO, when Haislee started using Instagram regularly, she wrote a small app that checked for Instagram photos and videos that had been synced to iCloud. The app copied those files to a separate unsynced folder on her iMac's hard drive. She liked storing files in the cloud, but she didn't completely trust the process or the companies involved.

Haislee's hair hung in damp strands as she took a seat in front of her iMac. She logged in and selected her local backup folder. She opened a subfolder called "InstaBaked." A satisfied grin appeared on her face. All of the photos and video reels that she had taken of the Pyckman Quarry afterparty and Dustin's so-called "epic" party, the same ones that had mysteriously disappeared from her phone less than twenty-four hours ago, were all present and accounted for.

She scanned through the files and loaded the last video in the list. Haislee scrubbed forwarded until it displayed her entering Dustin's room. There it was, the—

For the second time in a day, an image of a fist clutching white sheets appeared clearly in her mind, then vanished.

Haislee refocused on the video as the view panned around the room. In hindsight, she wished she had held her phone steadier.

The camera's motion had blurred the detail, but there was enough to orient herself.

She clicked pause and the video froze.

There it was, confirmed. Dustin had white sheets. There was no way to be sure that the image she kept seeing was from his bedroom, but it was possible.

Haislee grabbed her phone and tapped out a text to Elise. "Got it all."

Elise responded immediately. "What?"

Haislee tapped back a single emoji, a purple smiling face with horns, and waited.

Her phone rang and she put it on speaker. "Eight seconds. You're getting slow, Lise."

"Ha ha, bitch" Elise said. "You got all your reels back?"

"All hail automatic backups."

"Sweet. Did you, like, find any clues about what happened to you last night?"

"Not really," Haislee said. "I remember pretty much all of it, except for the parts I don't."

"You should give copies to my mom," Elise's filtered voice said. "She asked me about Killa Scrip this morning, after we dropped you off. If you were drugged last night, that deadbeat is def possible."

"I don't like it."

"Why not? You posted everything to Insta anyway." Elise paused for a response and when none came, she continued. "You should be talking to the police anyway."

"Why?"

"Hazy! You were *assaulted.*"

"I don't know that for sure," Haislee said. "And there's no proof."

"Get a blood test or something."

"It's too late for that," Haislee said. "Date rape drugs disappear fast. And all the videos do is prove that I was there. Police never believe the victim anyway."

"What about Plan B? Or getting checked out by a doctor?"

"If I was assaulted, I think they used a condom," Haislee said. "There was, like, no... uh, you know, in my underwear."

"Jizz."

Haislee shuddered. She disliked that word. "And I already showered."

Elise continued. "Seriously bruh, you got to know for sure. You don't want to get knocked up."

"Alright. I'll do Plan B."

Elise sighed. "Okay. But I still think you should show my mom. She'd believe you. And *she* might find a clue in there."

Haislee stared at the freeze-frame of Dustin's bed on her iMac screen. The white sheets screamed back at her. "For your mom's eyes only... let me think about it. But one thing for sure. Dustin can never know I have these."

"Fucking right," Elise said. "Let that douchebag go on thinking that he has the upper hand."

"I'm going to go through these videos again to see if I can spot anything." Haislee picked up her phone and held it closer to her mouth. "Talk later, okay?"

"Yeah, okay," Elise's voice crackled. "Let me know if you find anything."

"I will." Haislee ended the call. But before going through the newfound photos and reels with a fine tooth comb, she had a more important task. She dug through a drawer under her desk, pulled out a memory stick, and plugged it into her iMac.

"Always be prepared," Haislee whispered to herself as she copied the files to the memory stick and watched the data flow.

$$- \ 78 \ -$$

TEIGAN DROVE DOWN BANTOR, then doubled back and repeated her reconnaissance along Agate, finally parking her Civic a block away from the intersection of the two streets.

Bantor Street featured many businesses, and she decided her chances would be better spotting Killa Scrip on a side street. Before getting out, Teigan sat in her car and watched, looking for any suspicious activity while trying not to appear suspicious herself.

Agate Market at the intersection corner did brisk business and Teigan recognized that the store could pose as a front. But she had a gut feeling that Killa Scrip wasn't that sophisticated.

After twenty minutes of surveillance, she spotted a house in her rear view mirror where a person had knocked on the front door, entered, then left a few minutes later the way they came.

That could be the place.

Teigan decided to wait a little longer to be sure. A grubby unshaven man wearing greasy clothes walked by the Civic, heading down the sidewalk behind her. For a split second she thought he was the same guy who had chased her at Pearson Square. No do-rag with skulls on it this time, and the chances of it being the same guy as before were slim. But she wasn't prepared to get out and possibly be spotted.

Instead, she watched and waited. The man stepped to the top of the front stoop and knocked before someone let him in. In less than two minutes the man emerged again and made the return walk. Teigan slumped in her seat and observed the man approach and pass in her driver's side mirror. Now able to see the man's face, she was positive it wasn't the same guy, but she didn't want to mess with him just the same.

When the sidewalk was clear, Teigan stepped out of the car. She took her phone out from her purse, tucked the purse under the driver's seat, and locked the door. If things went south, she didn't want Killa Scrip or any of his thugs to be able to track her down. Of course they could hack her phone, but that would require her passcode. She didn't do face recognition.

Teigan followed the sidewalk to the front walk of a small bungalow in surprisingly good condition, despite the neighborhood. The yard looked like it had been well kept the year before.

She climbed the stoop and knocked. Everything in her screamed *turn back,* except the mother. A small opening in the door slid back and an eye appeared.

"What the *fuck* do you want?" a voice growled from inside.

"I want to buy some roofies," Teigan said.

The eye squinted at as much of her as it could see. "Fuck off, lady." The small door slid closed.

Teigan pounded the door this time, even though her fear said not to. "And I want to talk to Killa Scrip." She heard movement and whispering inside, then the sound of two deadbolts disengaging and the door creaking open.

"Step the fuck *back.*" It was the same voice as before.

Teigan stepped off the stoop and two more steps down. A scrawny young man with bad acne, short bleached hair, and silver teeth stepped out of the house, closing the door behind him. His frame barely supported his clothes, making him look like a flag without wind.

"Are you Killa Scrip?"

The young thug scowled at her. "Look, bitch. Leave. *Now.* Before something happens to you."

"Not until I talk to Killa Scrip," Teigan said.

The thug stepped closer. Teigan could smell a mixture of cheap aerosol cologne, body odor, cigarettes, and rancid breath. "*No one talks to Killa Scrip.*"

Teigan took a fortifying breath. "I'm not leaving until I talk to him."

The thug pulled up his oversized shirt tail, grabbed the handle of his semi-automatic pistol, and held it in front of his crotch. "You sure about dat, bitch?"

This idea was getting Teigan nowhere except into more trouble. Her idea of talking rationally with a drug dealer had sounded better in her head.

The thug took another step toward her. "We got eyes everywhere. We'll find out where you live and take out your *whole* fuckin' family."

His black, lifeless eyes pierced right through her and Teigan felt her guts turn to water.

"Now *get* the *fuck* outta here."

Teigan nodded and backed down the steps and the walkway until she had returned to the sidewalk.

The young thug continued to scrutinize her with his pinhole eyes. He motioned with the hand holding the gun. Teigan averted her eyes and headed back to her car.

As she pulled out her keys and unlocked the driver's side door, she caught motion in her periphery. She turned to look and saw Dustin strolling down the sidewalk away from the intersection. He had his nose buried in his phone and was completely unaware of his surroundings.

The odds of them both visiting the same area of town, at the same time, were practically impossible. Still, there he was. The reason why must be the same. She launched herself at him, running at full speed.

When Dustin realized what was happening, it was too late. He had no chance of outrunning Teigan in his present physical condition, but he still made a weak attempt. Had he been more physically fit, he might have made it.

Dustin managed to run half a block before Teigan grabbed his collar and pinned him against the wall of Agate Market. His phone fell to the sidewalk.

"Strange part of town to be in for someone from Rockwood West."

"I could say the same about you." Dustin squirmed under Teigan's hold. "Let go of me."

"Why are you here?"

"Let go!" Dustin scanned the intersection for help or anyone he could yell to, but the vehicles or pedestrians he saw either kept their eyes forward or heads down.

"Sucks when no one's there to help you, huh? Leaving you for dead."

Dustin narrowed his eyes at her. Teigan's veiled reference to Newton at Pyckman Quarry was not lost on him.

"Why are you here, Dustin?"

He scowled. "Fuck you."

"*Why?*"

Dustin twisted his head to glance at the market's sign. "Buying stuff... at the market."

Teigan pulled Dustin back by his shirt collar and pushed him back against the wall with a solid *thud*. "Bullshit."

"Don't know what else to tell you." A smirk emerged on his lips. He knew he was getting under Teigan's skin. "Agate Market is the only place in this city where I can get certain things."

"What things?"

"THINGS."

Teigan knew she wasn't going to get the answer she wanted and loosened her grip. "I'm onto you, Dustin Stoaks."

Dustin shoved her backward and flung her hands away. "I don't give a fuck. You touch me again and your life is over." He straightened his collar and walked back the way he had come.

"Is that a threat?" Teigan watched the teenager trudge toward the intersection. "I know why you were here, Dustin," she added. "Don't forget that!"

Dustin didn't look back as he reached the intersection and turned up Bantor, past the front of Agate Market and out of sight.

She followed his route and peeked around the corner. Half a block up Bantor, Teigan saw Dustin pull himself into the driver's seat of his black Escalade. The engine rumbled to life and he threw the SUV into an immediate U-turn, causing drivers around him to send angry blasts of their horn.

As Teigan walked back to her car, an idea popped into her head. Dustin may have gotten under her skin, but she had riled him up as well. And the best time to strike was when the iron was hot. She started her car and turned left onto Bantor in pursuit.

$$- 79 -$$

Teigan rarely had a reason to venture into Rockwood West, but today was different. She needed to finish what she had started.

As she neared the excessive home of Dustin Stoaks, the familiar streets and signposts from picking up Haislee that morning stuck out like red flags. She hadn't put it together then, but Teigan realized that Haislee had been coming from Dustin's place.

She pulled her car into the circular driveway and parked beside Dustin's Escalade. Teigan looked up at the grandiose and ornate structure and had trouble understanding why a small family needed such a massive house.

She stepped up to the front door and rang the doorbell. Teigan heard electrical clicks from the intercom but no voice behind them.

"I know you can hear me, Dustin," she said. "We're not done." Teigan crossed her arms and waited.

A moment later, the intercom buzzed to life. "I'm callin' the cops," Dustin's voice said.

Teigan leaned in closer to the microphone grill on the intercom. "Good. I'll tell them I know what you did." It was a bluff based on circumstantial evidence and a hunch.

Silence.

If Dustin had called the police, what would she tell them? What if Jackson Konishi led the team? An awkward scene unfolding would be putting it mildly.

The front door swung open. Dustin stood in the threshold with one hand on the frame and the other on the door. He tilted his head slightly and gave her a sneer. "When are you gonna learn to mind your own fuckin' business?"

An image of Newton lying in his hospital bed flashed in Teigan's mind, unleashing a rage that she had never felt before. She charged the open door. "This *IS* my business!"

Startled, Dustin backed away, but Teigan kept pressing him as she walked into the house.

"I know what you did, you *bastard*." Her eyes blazed with fury. "I KNOW." Teigan stopped, now aware that she was inside the house. She paused, taking in all the open space and extravagance.

"I don't know what you're talking about," Dustin said.

Teigan couldn't accuse Dustin when she didn't have verifiable evidence. She couldn't overplay her hand no matter how angry she was. She strolled through the grand room. "I bet your bedroom is on the second floor, isn't it?"

"Time to leave, bitch," Dustin said.

Teigan walked between the fireplace and the coffee table, then ran her finger across the backrest of one of the many couches.

"It sure would be a shame if all this..." Teigan raised her arms and spun her body slowly. "Came to an end."

"You need to get the *fuck* outta my house." Dustin walked toward her. "Now. Or I *will* call the cops. I don't care if you tell them your crazy story, because I got one of my own and you're it. Trespassing. Assault. Give me more time and I'll think of more."

Teigan's anger cooled to a simmer. As much as she hated to admit it, Dustin had more of a case against her than she did against him. It was time to go.

As she strolled past, she raised her finger at him. "I will expose you, Dustin. Your luck is running out."

Teigan walked straight out of the house and down the steps to her car. She could feel his eyes on her the entire way.

Good. If I've rattled him, all the better.

She hated playing the waiting game, potentially endangering her own family, specifically Elise. But Teigan was desperate for results. If Dustin was involved, she had succeeded in planting the seeds of her suspicion in his head. Anxiety, worry, and perhaps panic was sure to grow, pushing out his common sense. Unless he was a true sociopath.

$$- \; 80 \; -$$

Mattix turned into the driveway and opened the garage door. Through the rear view mirror, his eyes locked on the empty space at the curb where Teigan's rental car was normally parked until the garage door cut off his view.

He unloaded the afternoon's purchases from the back of the Pathfinder and carried them into the kitchen. Mattix moved on autopilot, his mind preoccupied with the whereabouts of his wife, and while he trusted her completely, the not knowing grated at his nerves.

Elise bounded down the stairs and met him at the island in the kitchen. "Can I help?" When Mattix didn't answer right away, she asked again, finding his eyes with hers.

"Yeah, sure, honey." Mattix pulled items out of bags and set them on the counter. "You can be on pantry duty."

Elise nodded and got to work, transferring food and supplies that didn't require refrigeration to open spots in the pantry. To appease the "organization freak" in her dad, she did her best to store the dry goods efficiently.

Normally Mattix separated the groceries into dry and perishable groups and dealt with the perishables first, finding spots in the refrigerator and rearranging when necessary.

Today there were no groups. Randomly placed groceries and supplies cluttered the countertop. And Mattix had offered no feedback about how Elise was packing the pantry.

Elise noticed. "Dad? Are you okay?"

Mattix stopped unpacking and looked at her, confused. "What do you mean?"

Elise motioned at the counter with open palms. "There's no 'wet' and 'dry' piles." She "air-quoted" those words and continued. "And you haven't, like, said *anything* about my pantry packing skills."

"Do you want me to?"

"No, but normally I, like, don't have to ask."

Mattix shrugged. "Guess I'm a little distracted."

"About Mom, right?"

Mattix stared at his daughter, momentarily surprised by her perceptiveness. "It's that obvious, is it?"

"Kinda," Elise said. "I've been worried about her too."

"Tell me more." Mattix stopped unpacking to listen.

"It's like she thinks she's a detective or something," Elise said. "This morning she made Haislee cry by asking her all these questions."

"Questions about...?"

"You know, Dad. About Newton. And the party."

"She did this at Tim Horton's?"

Elise scrunched her brow in confusion. "Tim Horton's? What are you talking—"

The front door opened and Teigan called out. "Hello? Anyone home?"

"Yeah," Elise said.

Mattix remained silent but alarm bells were going off in his head. He distinctly remembered Teigan tell him she was taking Elise to meet Haislee at Tim Horton's this morning. Yet Elise knew nothing about it. Something was up.

Teigan dropped a box of doughnuts on the counter, planted

a kiss on Mattix's cheek, and put her jacket away in the closet just off the kitchen. She pointed to the doughnuts. "There's three crullers in there and my name is on one of them."

Elise pulled out a cruller and began wolfing it down.

Mattix resumed unpacking. "What have you been up to?"

"I met with Jackson," Teigan said. "Wanted an update on Newt's case."

"And?"

Teigan took a seat at the kitchen table. "What do you think?"

"Nothing?"

"You got it," Teigan said. "Nada. Big fat zip." She grabbed a cruller and took a bite.

Mattix looked at his wife gravely. Catching her in a lie had caught him by surprise. Now he couldn't help but wonder if Teigan was lying now. He had no way to prove she had met with Jackson other than contacting him directly, and he wasn't prepared to do that. Yet. There must be a good reason.

"Keep me in the loop with a call or a text next time." Mattix fought back his anger, his words coming out sounding robotic.

Silence descended on the kitchen as he folded and flattened an empty bag more than necessary.

Elise alternated her gaze back and forth between her parents. "Is... everything okay?"

Mattix grabbed the bag from Canadian Tire and carried it to the garage. He stopped, just in front of the door to the garage and out of sight, the conversation between his wife and daughter floating down the hallway to his ears.

"Your dad likes to be involved," Teigan said, "especially when it's about Newton."

"Yeah," Elise said. "I mean, so would I."

Mattix heard Teigan sigh. "It's my bad. I should have let him know. I'll make it up to him later."

"Eww, Mom. *Gross.*"

Mattix's anger cooled slightly.

"Hey! No more doughnuts," Teigan said. "Dinner's soon. You'll ruin your appetite."

"No, I won't." Elise talked through a mouthful of cake, muffling her words. She thumped upstairs.

Mattix overheard Teigan putting away the remaining groceries and he did the same with the tools and hardware from Canadian Tire. Things were shifting back to normal, but they weren't there yet. He filed the lie in the back of his mind and attuned his ears for more.

$$- \ 81 \ -$$

TEIGAN WAS UP before everyone else on Sunday morning preparing a breakfast of fruit salad, scrambled eggs, bacon, and waffles. On the surface, she wanted her family to see her as the caring mother. But guilt drove her underlying motivation. She hated keeping her family in the dark and the more time ticked by, the easier it became.

Mattix being home already when she returned yesterday from Dustin's house had thrown a wrench in her plans. She had tried to play it cool, and the lie about Jackson came easily enough. But she hadn't thought it through and her family wasn't stupid, particularly Mattix. He hadn't appeared suspicious, but after being married twenty-one years, you get to know a person's rhythms, idiosyncrasies, and habits. Something was off.

She hoped to catch Dustin saying or doing something to expose his involvement, sooner rather than later, because her deceptions needed to stop. Of course, she could choose to come clean this morning, over breakfast, get it all out in the open. But Sundays were meant for relaxing, and she had no intention of ruining the entire day.

The mingling warm smells of breakfast did their job. Teigan heard the familiar thumps through the ceiling of her family's sleepy steps. Normally the kids were last down, but this morning, both Mattix and Elise arrived in the kitchen at the same time.

Elise wiped the sleep from her eyes. "Waffles? Two days in a row?"

"What did we do to deserve this?" Mattix kissed Teigan's cheek and poured himself some coffee.

"I know I've been a little absent the past couple of days," Teigan said.

Elise raised an eyebrow at her. "A *little?*"

Mattix followed with, "Couple of *days?*"

"Come on, I'm trying here." Teigan opened the oven and pulled out a plate stacked with waffles. "Sit. Let's eat while things are warm."

The three of them took their usual spots at the kitchen table and began filling their plates with eggs, bacon, and waffles slathered with butter and syrup. Teigan had already placed bowls of fruit salad at each place setting.

Elise took a bite of her waffle and sighed. "We should have waffles every day. I'd, like, *never* skip breakfast."

"Be careful what you wish for," Mattix said. "Because someone has to *make* those waffles."

"Well..." Elise crunched a slice of bacon. "Me and Newt have school, and Dad works, so..." She propped her chin up on her hands, fluttered her eyelashes, and grinned at Teigan. "That leaves you, Mom."

"Hey, I work too." Teigan scooped up a bite of eggs. "Don't forget that."

The doorbell rang.

Teigan looked at Mattix. "You expecting someone?"

Mattix shook his head. "On Sunday? No." He took a gulp of his coffee to wash down his mouthful and headed to the front door.

Teigan cut her waffle into smaller pieces. "Probably Jehovah Witnesses."

"But it's Sunday, Mom," Elise said.

Sounds of the front door opening and talking carried back to the kitchen. Two voices, both male, one Mattix. The other one—

"Teigan?" It was Mattix.

"Yes, hon?" When there was no reply, Teigan set her fork down and walked toward the entryway. Her stomach dropped as Jackson came into view, standing next to Mattix at the door.

Jackson offered a halfhearted wave and virtually no smile. It was clear that he did not want to be there. "Hey."

Teigan shot a nervous glance at Mattix before settling on Jackson again. "What's wrong? Is it Newt? Do you have an update?"

Jackson sighed, reached into his sport jacket, and pulled out several pieces of paper, stapled and folded into thirds. He handed it to Teigan.

"What's this?" Teigan unfolded the papers and began to read. Her entire body went cold, and her goal of a relaxing Sunday began to swirl the drain. It was all her fault, too.

She didn't need to read the rest. Teigan folded the papers and placed them on the top of the newel post. She looked at Mattix's eyes and saw the flash of controlled anger.

"I didn't even touch him," Teigan said. "I swear."

"Whatever you did spooked him. And you did it at his place of residence." Jackson looked at her with disappointment. "Just so we're clear, you're not to talk to or approach Dustin Stoaks in any way for the next year. This peace bond carries with it a fine and if you violate it, Dustin is within his right to file charges."

"How did he... It's Sunday for fuck's sake."

Jackson shrugged and shook his head slowly. "His family's connected. That's my guess." He placed his hand on the doorknob. "Sorry for disrupting your morning."

"Wait," Teigan said. "Do you have an update on Newt's case?"

"No. Do you have anything you'd like to share with me?"

Teigan shook her head.

Quid pro quo, Jackson.

"Didn't think so." Jackson pulled open the front door. "I'll be in touch." He shared a mournful look with Mattix, before stepping outside and pulling the door closed behind him.

Elise stood behind Teigan, close to the stair's balusters. "What's going on?"

Teigan locked gaze with Mattix. "I can explain."

"Yeah." Mattix nodded at her slowly. "And you will. Right *goddamn* now."

– 82 –

ELISE, TEIGAN, AND MATTIX RETURNED to the kitchen table and sat. Mattix crossed his arms and focused his stony gaze on Teigan.

"Lise, hon." Teigan placed the peace bond next to her plate. "You don't have to be here for this if—"

"Lise has every right to stay if she wants," Mattix said. "The last thing we need in this house is *more* secrets."

Teigan nodded and stared at her plate of half eaten waffles, the butter congealing in the syrup. "First, I want to apologize. I never meant to hurt anyone." She considered her next words carefully, because even after Jackson had served her a peace bond, there was no chance she'd be telling Mattix and Elise *everything* she knew.

"I've suspected Dustin's involvement with Newt's drugging for a while now. But I have no proof. I've talked to him at school." Teigan's eyes flitted at Elise for a second. "I'm sure Lise remembers."

Elise nodded but averted her eyes and pushed her food around her plate.

Mattix shifted his attention to Elise. "So you knew, too?"

"She just saw me talk to him," Teigan said.

"Before McCarthy got in her face," Elise added.

Teigan placed her hand on Elise's and gave it a gentle squeeze. "Anyway, I wanted to try and scare a confession out of him. I went to his house and yelled at him, but I never touched him." She tapped the folded peace bond with a finger. "This 'fearing for my life' crap is complete bull."

"Dustin's a narcissistic asshole," Mattix said. "We know this. But that doesn't give you the right to harass him. Have you considered that he might *not* be responsible for Newt's situation? Because if *that's* true, this makes things so much worse for you."

Teigan nodded. "You're right."

Elise's phone chimed. She glanced at it then frantically picked it up, her finger madly tapping and scrolling.

"What is it?"

Elise grimaced. "Sorry Mom, but you're going to want to see this." She turned up the volume, placed the phone on the table so that Mattix and Teigan could both see it, and started the video.

Teigan's visit to Dustin's house yesterday, complete with her yelling, plays back for the three of them.

Mattix sighed and shook his head. "This is what I'm talking about. Jesus."

"The little bastard had a hidden camera," Teigan said.

"No shit, Tee. He's not stupid."

Elise put her phone into standby.

"But why would he do that?" Teigan leaned across the table toward Mattix. "He's got something to hide and wants me to look crazy."

"Or maybe he's doing the only thing he can to defend himself against your accusations," Mattix said. "You said it yourself. You have no proof. You need to let the police handle this. United front, remember?"

Teigan remembered all too well. She reached out to Mattix and Elise and took their hands. "I'm sorry." Shifting her gaze back and forth, she continued. "I promise to never speak to Dustin Stoaks again or approach him in any way. You have my word."

"You're going to be fined among other things if you do," Mattix said.

Teigan looked at him. "I'm serious. Dustin Stoaks is now off my radar. Okay?"

Elise nodded, then Mattix.

"But—"

"Jesus." Mattix rolled his eyes. "Here it comes."

Teigan felt anger bubble inside her but managed to keep a lid on it. "But I'm not going to stop trying to find answers. Until Newton is back with us again, this is the only way I can fight for him. Okay?"

"Just let the police do their job," Mattix said. "Don't do anything illegal. And keep us in the loop. No secrets."

Teigan nodded. "I promise."

Elise's phone chimed again.

Mattix groaned. "What now?"

Elise read the text and performed the usual finger gymnastics on the phone's display.

"Everything okay?" Teigan asked.

"Nothing's okay," Mattix said gruffly.

Teigan glared at him, then returned her attention to Elise. "Hon?"

"So, like, remember yesterday, when Hazy thought she had been, you know, hacked?"

Mattix alternated his gaze between Elise and Teigan and began nodding slowly, connecting the dots. "No one told me about Haislee getting hacked. I mean I wouldn't know anything about *that* subject, right? And let me guess. You never met with Haislee at Tim Horton's?"

Teigan and Elise had no words to offer.

"So much for no secrets."

"Dad, I'm sorry. I had no idea Mom said we went to Timmy's," Elise said. "But honestly, I didn't think you'd care. I mean it's *Instagram*. You literally *hate* Instagram."

"To be fair, that was yesterday," Teigan added. "No secrets from today forward."

"Fine." Mattix crossed his arms against his chest. "Has Haislee been hacked?"

"I don't know," Elise said. "But she got all her photos and reels back."

Teigan's eyes widened. "Really?"

"A teenager who doesn't rely on iCloud?" A small smile emerged on Mattix's face. "One in a million."

"This is good news," Teigan said.

"Yeah. There might be clues in the reels that could, like, tell us who drugged Newt," Elise said. "Hazy's going to put them all on a memory stick for me tomorrow."

"Videos of drunken teenagers recorded by drunken teenagers," Mattix said. "Great."

Elise recoiled, indignant. "Hazy doesn't get drunk. That's one reason I like her."

"Then I hope we find something." Mattix took his plate to the microwave to reheat it. "We deserve a win."

We certainly do.

Teigan recalled that she couldn't project into a static image, but a video might be possible. Monday couldn't come soon enough.

$$- 83 -$$

MONDAY WAS DRAWING to a close. Dustin sat in his First Nations Studies class on the first floor, concentrating to ignore the feeling of liquid fire moving through his gut. With any other class, he'd be fine to leave and relieve himself in the bathroom, maybe even take the rest of the class for a nice leisurely shit.

But he didn't like missing any of his First Nations Studies classes, not because he enjoyed it or wanted to learn about the Indigenous people of Canada, but because it was a requirement for graduation and attendance formed part of his grade. If he didn't pass, he'd have to come back next year.

Fuck that.

His guts had different ideas and taking notes in class wasn't one of them. If he didn't leave soon, he'd be on the front page of the *Diamond Bay Bulletin*. Eating leftover Taco Bell for breakfast had been a terrible idea. He collected his books and stuffed them into his backpack.

Dustin waited as long as he could, then excused himself to go to the bathroom and staggered into the hallway. The bathroom was less than a hundred feet away.

When he arrived at the door, he found it out of service and locked for cleaning. Panic crept into his head as his guts waged war on his insides. His closest option was the second floor bathroom, but he could hardly walk, let alone climb stairs. But he had no choice.

Dustin walked as quickly as he could manage, trying not to move his legs too much. He used the balls of his feet to hop from one step to the next until he arrived at the second floor landing.

The hallway was clear of other students, but in a few minutes it'd be packed, making navigation difficult.

Dustin shambled to the bathroom, pulled open the door and launched himself into the first empty stall. The anticipation of relief almost caused him to literally lose his shit, but he managed to get his pants down and onto the toilet just in time.

He relaxed and did his business, knowing he had dodged a very real bullet. The end-of-day bell rang and the sounds of students exiting classrooms and opening their lockers began to seep through the bathroom walls. Dustin finished up and washed his hands.

As he left, he spotted Haislee approaching Elise at her locker. Dustin slid back into the recessed entrance to the bathroom and watched the two girls. Haislee had been to one of his parties now. The challenge would be to get Elise to tag along to the next one. And Dustin loved challenges, especially if they involved girls.

As he brainstormed ways to convince Elise to attend one of his parties, he spotted Haislee hand her something small, pink, and oval. At first, he thought it was one of those pocket vibrators girls sometimes used. His brain almost derailed, but then Haislee did something odd. She pulled the top off the object and began waving it around emphatically.

Beneath the cap, the end was silver, rectangular, and instantly recognizable: a USB memory stick. Dustin's thoughts swirled, wondering what information it contained.

He waited for the two girls to make their way down the hallway to the stairs near the front entrance and disappear before following them.

Dustin descended the stairs and spotted Richard at his locker across the first floor hallway.

"Rich, I need your help."

Richard scrunched his brow. "With what?"

"You know Haislee and Elise?"

"Uh, yeah." Richard shifted on his feet. "What about them?"

"They have something of mine," Dustin said. "Get your shit. We need to tail them."

Richard grabbed his backpack, secured his locker, and the two of them headed out to the student parking lot.

"What do they have?" Richard asked.

Dustin provided no answer and instead strode toward the Escalade. "Get in."

He started the engine and turned to Richard. "Here's what we're going to do." He backed out of the parking lot and turned onto Edgerton Street, sharing his plan with Richard as he went.

– 84 –

DUSTIN SPOTTED HAISLEE AND ELISE walking on the sidewalk a block ahead. He slowed the Escalade to a stop. Richard unbuckled and got out. The two boys shared a knowing nod before Richard ran behind the SUV, across the street to the sidewalk, and began following the girls.

Dustin waited for Richard to get closer, then sped up to pass the girls. He made a hard left and bounced the Escalade's front tires up and over the curb, blocking the girls' path.

Richard grabbed Haislee from behind and twisted her arm behind her back.

Before Elise could run, Dustin grabbed the shoulder harness of her backpack and pulled her forward. "You got something of mine."

Elise yanked her belongings back, surprising Dustin and nearly pulling him off balance. "Fuck you." She glanced back at Haislee, pain evident on her friend's face, then to Richard. "Let her go!"

"When I get what's mine." Dustin pushed Elise face first onto the lawn and straddled her from behind.

Elise squirmed and yelled as loud as she could. "Get *off* me you *asshole!*"

Dustin ignored her and unzipped her backpack and dug through it, tossing the contents out onto grass.

"I'm gonna get you for this," Elise cried out.

"Stop it!" Haislee struggled against Richard's grip, but he lifted her arm in response, increasing her pain. "You're hurting us!"

Dustin threw out pens, a ruler, books, remnants of a bag lunch, and a binder onto the grass, then found what he was looking for. He pulled out a pink, elongated memory stick with soft rounded edges. He leaned and placed his mouth next to Elise's ear.

"Your friend is probably a shitty lay," he whispered, "But I'd bet anything that you *really* fuck." Dustin pushed himself up, using Elise's back as a launchpad. He motioned at Richard. "Let's go."

As Richard loosened his grip, Haislee lifted one leg and propelled it back, landing the heel of her shoe against the shin of Richard's leg. He cried out and stumbled back. Haislee ran and dropped to her knees beside Elise.

Back in the Escalade, Dustin yelled back, "Rich! Move your ass!"

Richard hobbled around the back of the SUV and climbed aboard. Dustin threw the vehicle into reverse, then forward, peeling out and leaving a cloud of blue, acrid smoke.

Inside the cab, Richard twisted in his seat to see Haislee and Elise through the back window, shrinking in the distance, until they disappeared from sight.

Dustin glanced at Richard with a smug grin and held up the pink memory stick in one hand. "And *that's* how it's done."

$$- \ 85 \ -$$

Haislee kneeled on the grass next to Elise and watched Dustin's Escalade drive away. She helped Elise collect her things. "Are you okay, Lise? Did he hurt you?"

"Not really." Elise repacked her backpack and brushed herself off. "But that fucking paint-on cologne he had on might take a while to fade."

Haislee leaned in and sniffed. "Ugh. What is that?"

"Probably Grind Body Spray," Elise said. "That shit is terrible."

"Wait." Haislee squinted at her. "How do you know what Grind Body Spray smells like?"

Elise gave Haislee a sideways glance. " 'Cause I got a brother who, like, tried it once. *Once.* It reeked so bad that we all threatened to kill him in his sleep if he used it again. It took, like, *forever* to get it out of his clothes."

They both laughed. Haislee stood and extended her hand to help Elise up.

"He told me I'd be a good fuck," Elise said.

"Eww. Perv. Did he say anything about me?"

"Actually, yeah. He said you'd be a bad fuck." Elise shrugged. "Sorry."

Haislee crossed her arms against her chest. "What the hell does *he* know anyway? We're both *great* fucks."

Both girls giggled.

"He probably uses one of those rubber dolls," Elise said.

Both girls looked at each other. "Ewww!" they said in unison, then burst into hysterical laughter.

"That asshole ain't got nothing on us," Elise said.

"But we got shit on him."

"What was on that memory stick, anyway?"

A sly grin formed on Haislee's face. "Just the photos. I wanted him to think that he had still kinda succeeded in deleting my content." She pulled another memory stick out of her pocket, the same rounded shape, but blue in colour.

"This one has *everything*." She handed it to Elise. "And of course I have everything on my computer at home. They're in the cloud too, just not iCloud."

"Don't mess with the tech goddess." Elise slid the memory stick into her pocket and they both resumed their walk home. "Can I still give these to my mom?"

"Totally." Then Haislee fell silent.

After several moments, Elise looked at her. "You okay?"

"I'm sorry, Lise."

"Huh? Sorry for what?"

"I had a feeling we were going to get jumped."

Elise reached for Haislee's arm, her face a big question mark, and they both stopped walking.

"I was totally baked at the end of Physics today," Haislee began. "I happened to see Dustbin walk past the front door to our class. I watched the rear door and... no Dustbin. That meant he must have gone to the bathroom across the hall."

Elise shrugged. "So?"

"I wanted to give you the memory stick," Haislee said, "but I also wanted him to *see* me do it."

"Sneaky bitch." Elise smirked. "That's why you were waving it around like a lunatic."

Haislee nodded. "I figured he might be watching, and I knew he'd know what it was. I was hoping that he'd think the memory stick had shit on it about him."

"And he did." Elise laughed. "The prick is so predictable. I'm glad he got the one you wanted him to."

"Yeah, me too." Haislee said. "I just wish I had seen something in those reels. Something to explain what happened at the party."

"Maybe my mom will see something. She's trying to be, like, a P.I. or something."

"Cool," Haislee said. "She'd be good at that."

"You really think so? All she's done so far is, like, get into fights with my dad."

The two of them reached the part of their journey where Tipperary split off from Radcliffe.

Haislee stopped. She could feel Elise's eyes on her.

"Want to come to my place for dinner?"

Haislee shook her head. "I got homework."

Elise kicked a stone out into the road. "Yeah, me too."

"Text me later, kay?"

Elise nodded and the two friends parted ways. "We'll get the motherfucker, Hazy. I just know it."

Haislee returned two thumbs up. She wanted to believe Elise's sentiment, but she didn't see it happening.

$$- \ 86 \ -$$

THE LITTLE PINK MEMORY STICK was burning a hole in Dustin's pocket. The longer it sat there, the angrier he became. If the memory stick held the information he thought it did, that meant Haislee had outsmarted him. And no one outsmarted Dustin Stoaks.

He dropped Richard off at the shack he called a home and sped back to Rockwood West.

Once back at his mansion, he kicked off his shoes and ran upstairs, two steps at a time. He flicked on the lights in his room, dumped his backpack on the floor, and rolled his office chair in front of his computer. The screen lit up when he wiggled the mouse and clicked.

Dustin typed in his password and the desktop appeared. He took the memory stick from his pocket and plugged it into an open USB port. The file browser popped up listing the stick's contents.

Dustin looked over the files and grinned, opening them one at a time. They were all images. "Dumb bitch," he said to himself, laughing. "I win again."

He unplugged the memory stick and took it down to the garage. With a hammer from his father's extensive set of tools,

Dustin smashed the stick on the concrete floor of the garage, exploding the small device into a thousand pieces of silicon, metal, and pink plastic.

To celebrate, he headed back up to his games room and loaded up Grand Theft Auto 5. He had a desperate need to "kill some hoes."

$$- \; 87 \; -$$

TEIGAN HAD JUST RECLINED on the couch in the living room with the latest *Jack Reacher* novel when Elise returned from school looking a little rough around the edges. Her hair hung in tangled knots at the back of her head and Teigan thought she saw grass or dirt stains on Elise's jeans.

"Tough day at school?"

Elise tossed her backpack halfway up the stairs and kicked off her shoes. "What?"

"Nothing," Teigan said. "Just looks like you got dragged through a hedge backward."

"Gee, thanks."

"Sorry," Teigan said. "Didn't mean to offend."

Elise trudged into the kitchen to grab a granola bar and returned to the stairs. She gave Teigan a sideways look.

Teigan glanced up from her book. "What is it, hon?"

Elise slipped her hand into her jeans pocket and removed the blue memory stick. "This is from Haislee, for your eyes only. No police, okay?"

Teigan took the memory stick and rotated it with her fingers, noting its smooth surface. "No worries. Newt's case with the police is on the back burner anyway."

"How is Newt, by the way?"

"I was there briefly this morning to check in, and things are looking very good. Brain activity and nerve responses are good. Newt could wake up any day now."

Elise approached the couch, dropped to her knees, and wrapped her arms around Teigan. "I'm so glad, Mom."

Caught somewhat by surprise, Teigan returned the hug and they let the embrace linger. "Me too, honey."

Elise pulled away and started toward the stairs. "I got some homework."

Teigan held up the memory stick. "And now I got something more important to look at. Thank Haislee for me?"

"Yup," Elise said from the stairs.

Teigan noted her page with a bookmark and followed her daughter up to the second floor. She paused at her door and gazed at Elise. "Look at us, each doing work in our own offices."

Elise smirked back at her. "You're weird, Mom."

"You know it." Teigan stepped into her office and closed the door. She took a seat behind her computer, logged in, and inserted the memory stick into a free USB port. The file folder window popped up, populated with thumbnails of images and videos. She went through everything, scrutinizing each with fresh eyes.

There were more images of the party at Pyckman Quarry than anything else, even some that hadn't been uploaded to Instagram. Teigan watched a video three times of Richard handing Newton a beer but couldn't spot anything off.

After quickly browsing a bunch of videos and pictures from Diamond Bay that held no relevance, Teigan reached the videos from Dustin's party last Friday night. The antics on screen made her nostalgic for her high school and college days. As stupid as they were, those parties were fun and memorable. She understood why Dustin enjoyed hosting.

The final videos in the list took the viewer on a tour of Dustin's house. Teigan recognized the gathering area on the main floor where she had yelled at him, although the point of view from a teenager's phone was quite different. Still, she was impressed at how steady and clear Haislee's video clips were.

From her computer monitor, Teigan watched and listened as Haislee's tour ascended up the stairs and into his bedroom, finally ending in Dustin's game room.

That little prick could sure turn on the charm when he wanted to.

Teigan sat back in her chair. The video had been clear as day, almost like she had taken the tour herself. And she *had* been there, at least in the main gathering area. She wondered if it would be enough to *aid* a projection. But there was something else bothering her.

She reviewed the images and videos of the afterparty and settled on the video of Richard handing Newton a beer. Nowhere else had she seen Newton consume any alcohol. She knew her son didn't drink to excess and would have stopped at one or perhaps two beers.

Teigan watched him open the can and take a swig. Had Newton left his open can of beer unattended and someone spiked it? It was possible, but there was no visual evidence of it. She scrubbed back on the video's timeline and paused it at the hand-off, Richard to Newton. Once best friends, could Richard be involved in some way? There was no way for her to know for sure, unless Richard confessed.

An idea popped into Teigan's head. She knew the layout of Richard's house almost as well as she knew her own. Six years of friendship meant a lot of pickups, drop-offs, and invariably an invitation for coffee by Peter. Teigan felt a shudder of disgust shoot through her.

She extracted the memory stick and stored it safely in a desk drawer. She returned to the living room, laid down on the couch, and pictured the inside of Richard's house.

Projection was becoming easier for Teigan, and after a few minutes of relaxed breathing, she found herself standing in the front foyer of Richard's house. The environment wasn't perfect, but it provided enough detail to move through the house unencumbered.

She entered the hallway and saw flickering light coming from the living room.

Maybe Richard was watching TV?

She ventured forth and passed the entrance, poking her head inside. To Teigan's surprise and horror, the big screen TV displayed what she could only describe as blurred pornography. Bodies and blobs of colour were moving in suggestive ways, but nothing was clear and distinct. And in the reclined La-Z-Boy directly in front of the TV sat Peter, headphones on, furiously masturbating beside a box of tissues.

Teigan felt her gorge rise. It was something she'd never be able to unsee. Throwing up in a projection was something she had yet to experience and hoped she never would. Back in the hallway, she calmed herself and moved forward through the house.

She tilted her head to one side and listened. Someone was using the bathroom to shower. Since there was only one bathroom in the house, there was a chance that it was someone Peter knew.

Someone else into porn?

No matter who it was, that'd be one more thing Teigan couldn't unsee. She considered stopping her projection right then and there.

But the odds were good that it was just Richard showering. The bathroom door was closed and Teigan couldn't get in, so her only option was to wait. He'd have to leave eventually.

Ten minutes later, Richard opened the door wearing a towel around his waist and walked to his room. His shoulder passed through Teigan on his way by, reminding her of the unpleasant tingling sensation she felt when her projected body and a real body occupied the same space.

She stepped into the bathroom, not knowing what she was looking for. The space was a mess, with a pile of moist, dirty towels hanging in a corner. Personal hygiene products cluttered the counter and a hair drier hung off the edge by its cord. A cloud of steam hovered around her head and made her skin prickle.

Though the top half of the mirror was obscured by fog, Teigan realized that she had no reflection. Then an idea, so elegant in its simplicity, popped into her head.

She leaned in and touched a fogged part of the mirror. The condensation coalesced into a drop and made the tip of her finger tingle. Pulling back her finger, the drip on the mirror remained.

Teigan heard noises from Richard's room down the hall. Eventually he would return to blow-dry his hair. She wasted no time and placed her finger on the fogged mirror, hastily dragging her finger across it.

– 88 –

MATTIX TURNED INTO THE DRIVEWAY and collected the Chinese takeout that he had carefully placed on the front seat of the Pathfinder. There was something about the familiar smell of takeout food filtered through brown paper or cardboard that made his stomach rage. It didn't matter what kind of food it was.

He carried it to the front door and let himself in. "I've made Chinese tonight."

"Be down in a mo," Elise said, her voice muffled through her bedroom door.

Mattix casually glanced into the living room and spotted Teigan snoozing on the couch. He went in to greet her, setting the bag of food on the floor. Mattix leaned down, aiming to kiss her forehead, then stopped.

Teigan had her eyes closed, but she was grinning in a way that Mattix recognized as mischievous. Then she raised her hand, and with her index finger extended began wiggling it in the air, as if scribing a secret message only she could see, one letter flowing over top of the next.

Mattix sat on the edge of the couch, grabbed the bag of food, and fanned the open top. He nudged her gently and wafted the warm smell toward her nose.

Teigan's eyes fluttered open, at first surprised, then with warm recognition. She smiled at Mattix and stretched. He swooped in for a kiss.

"Strange dreams?"

Teigan scrunched her brows. "What do you mean? Why?"

"You were writing in the air with your finger," Mattix said.

"I was?" Teigan rubbed her face and yawned. "Weird." She sniffed and smiled at him. "Is that what I think it is?"

Mattix nodded. "Fried rice, Singapore rice noodles, ginger-fried broccoli, almond chicken, and of course, fortune cookies."

"You're a mind reader," Teigan said.

"What can I say? I got the knack." Mattix stood and offered his hand to help her up. "Come on. Let's eat."

Teigan took it, stood, and leaned in, placing her mouth next to his ear. "I might have to have you for dessert."

"Great idea," Mattix said. "Then you tell me more about your weird dream. I'm dying to know what you wrote."

Teigan reached for plates, her back to him. "I'd tell you right now if I could remember, but it's gone."

Mattix couldn't see her face, but he detected an edge to her voice.

"I've got a great memory," Teigan said, "but dreams never seem to stick. You know that."

Mattix did know that, but he wasn't sure if he believed it anymore. For a moment he thought Teigan might be lying again, but chose to dismiss it. Promises had been made. Lies were a thing of the past. Or so he hoped.

— **89** —

RICHARD ENTERED HIS ROOM and pulled some clothes from his dresser. His style had changed since becoming friends with Dustin, for the better he thought. He dropped his sodden towel on the bed and pulled on underwear and socks. His current go-to attire was jeans and a T-shirt, with a button-up thrown on top. He modeled himself after Michael J. Fox's character Marty McFly from *Back to the Future*.

Dustin was full of tips (opinions). One tip favoured putting on his shirt before drying his damp hair.

"Why dry it and style it, then wreck it by pulling a shirt over top?" he had said.

Same went for applying deodorant. It was a simple, obvious tip, one Richard hadn't thought of earlier, but it served him well. He had noticed more girls were checking him out.

Now dressed, Richard returned to the bathroom to finish up his after shower routine. He grabbed the hair dryer and plugged it in. With his thumb on the power switch, he looked at himself in the mirror.

Condensation had collected on the top quarter of the glass and staring back at him were the words, "HE KNOWS."

Richard dropped the dryer on the floor, knocking the switch

to on. The hot air burned his feet and caused him to stumble back.

He pulled the plug out of the wall by the cord and stared at the mirror, his jaw hanging slack with surprise. Without a second thought, he reached out and smeared the misty letters into one large water droplet.

"Dad?" Richard called out.

There was no response.

Richard called out again and after a moment, he heard movement from somewhere in the house, followed by footsteps. Peter rounded the corner of the hall, cinching his belt tight around his waist.

"You weren't in the bathroom when I was showering, were you?"

"What? No," Peter said. "I don't get my rocks off staring at *your* scrawny bod."

"Right. Thanks." Richard pushed the bathroom door closed, but Peter blocked it with his hand.

"Why you asking?"

"Never mind." Richard closed and latched the door. He picked up the hair dryer and turned it on. The dryer rattled like something had broken inside and the hot air flowing out the nozzle carried an acrid odor with it.

Richard contemplated telling Dustin, but convinced himself that it must have been his imagination. Either that or it never happened at all. He didn't realize it, but he was gaslighting himself.

He grabbed his coat and wallet and headed to the front door.

Peter poked his head out from the kitchen. "You're leaving? Aren't you going to eat?"

"I'll grab something while I'm out." Richard slammed the front door behind him, glad to be free of his own home. He headed to the nearby Tim Horton's where Dustin said he'd be picking him up. They had a night of carousing planned, maybe followed by Grand Theft Auto 5. The night was young and full of possibilities.

– 90 –

TEIGAN FELT DISTRACTED all through dinner and the rest of the evening. She imagined what Richard's reaction to her message would have been. Shock? Worry? Fear? She hoped he was feeling all those things. Richard was weak. If he was involved, she had a feeling guilt would eat him alive and cause him to slip. But she couldn't rely on hope.

Mattix suggested a family movie night after dinner, but the only thing on Teigan's mind was projecting to Dustin's house. Would Haislee's videos she watched earlier have any impact on her projection?

She couldn't share her true desire with Mattix, so she agreed to the movie idea. Elise, who frowned on most family gatherings like everyone had the plague, decided to hang out with Haislee for the evening.

Mattix and Teigan had the evening to themselves. Instead of the movie, Teigan suggested visiting Newton.

"He's almost back with us, Matt," she had said and Mattix had agreed.

The trip to the hospital and back took almost two hours, getting them back to the house just before nine o'clock. Elise was not home yet.

Mattix took their coats and hung them up. "When do you think Newt will wake up?"

"Soon, I hope," Teigan said, her voice full of hope. "Betty was very optimistic."

"She was." Mattix wrapped his arms around her from behind and gave Teigan a hug. "We still got time for a movie. Interested?"

"Definitely."

They settled into the love seat and started up the latest action movie.

Ten minutes in, Teigan turned to Mattix with surprise on her face. "I forgot something!"

Mattix shrugged. "What?"

"Dessert!" She leaned in and kissed him hard.

The TV was off a second later and the two of them moved the party upstairs to their bedroom.

Later, both warm and sated, Mattix drifted off to sleep. The best sleep was sleep after sex. Teigan could have easily done the same, but she resisted. Once Mattix was fully within sleep's grasp, she proceeded with her next mission.

Teigan closed her eyes and projected to Dustin's house, positioning herself within the large grand room. It looked just as it had when she had visited Dustin two days ago. She doubted the house changed much at all considering that Dustin's parents were usually absent, tending to their business dealings across the country. A teenager with access to a huge house, practically unlimited funds, and no supervision was a recipe for trouble. Teigan meant to settle the question of Dustin's involvement once and for all.

And to see if good video actually helps a projection.

Teigan couldn't see why it wouldn't. She was already in the house, and she knew what the upstairs, and specifically Dustin's bedroom and games room looked like, all thanks to Haislee's excellent camera work.

She proceeded to the stairs and placed her foot on it. It

supported her weight, so she took another step followed by another. Twenty steps later, she stood on the upper landing that ran the length of the house and entered into several bedrooms, one belonging to Dustin.

The view of the gathering area below shimmered in the places where she had not directly viewed them and the hardwood floor at her feet had adopted a digital feel, somewhat pixelated but still solid.

Behind her, in areas where Haislee's videos had not reached, details were gone and the floor faded away into blackness. The environment reminded Teigan of a visual effects documentary she had seen recently where a room had been scanned with LIDAR in order to reconstruct it in a computer. While inside the room, things looked okay, but venturing beyond the scan, the room fell apart visually, allowing a view through walls and objects that led to empty space. Teigan made sure to avoid the faded areas. She didn't trust their structural integrity and they would be dangerous to investigate.

Although this is a projection. I'm pretty much invincible.

There was only one approved route to go, and those were the areas captured by Haislee's video. She followed the upper hallway into Dustin's room, not venturing away from the path Haislee had taken.

Teigan could see his bookcases, computer, captain's bed, and wardrobe. The mirror between the bed and the wardrobe remained closed, and as she discovered at Richard's earlier, there was no reflection of her.

Sounds of the toilet flushing. The door on the opposite side of the bed from the mirror opened and Dustin strolled out in a T-shirt and boxers. His pudgy frame left much to be desired.

Dustin sat in his office chair and logged into his computer. Teigan walked up behind him but not quick enough to see his login password keyed into his keyboard. Blurred and shifting images of light and dark fluctuated on his screen. Just to the right of the keyboard sat a mug with assorted pens and pencils in it.

The tidiness of Dustin's desk surprised Teigan. She expected a scattered mess like Newton and Elise. And even though she hadn't spotted any clues, the experiment had been a success. Haislee's videos had worked as an extension to her own memory of Dustin's house, but the details lacked a crispness that her own memories had. Still, it was a definite additional superpower.

Teigan stepped back, taking in Dustin's room as seen by Haislee's videos. Pleased with her experiment, she momentarily let her guard down. Her left foot entered a void in the floor that Haislee's video hadn't reached. The pull on her body increased, up her left leg and spreading over her body. It felt as if she was being stretched and drawn into a hole too small to fit through. She had no control and it terrified her. Instead of holding her breath, every gasp of air was squeezed from her lungs as she was forced farther into the void. Blackness enveloped her until—

Teigan woke with a jolt. She shot a look at Mattix beside her, not knowing if she had cried out as well before waking. He was deep in slumberland, sawing logs.

Stars danced in front of her eyes and her stomach churned, turning itself inside out. She leaped from the bed and stumbled into the ensuite bathroom, kicking the door closed. Teigan grasped the toilet just in time to catch her partially digested Chinese food from dinner. She sat on the bathroom floor in a cold sweat until her dizziness and nausea passed.

Note to self: Avoid unformed areas in projections. No shit.

Teigan rinsed and wiped her mouth, then padded woozily back to the bed, tucking herself next to Mattix's warm body. Her head still pounded dully but sleep had a way of conquering everything.

As she drifted off, Teigan worked out a new plan and Haislee's videos would play a key role.

– 91 –

DESPITE ATTEMPTS TO CONVINCE himself that he had been seeing things, two words had fractured Richard's sleep.

HE KNOWS.

The impossibility that Newton might know something shifted into something possible and took root in the back of his mind, where it began to grow.

He had overslept this morning and ended up running out the door for school, skipping breakfast. By the end of Math, his second class right before lunch, his stomach raged loudly and unforgivingly.

Richard's phone chirped. He shifted his backpack under his seat and moved deliberately slow. Getting caught using a phone in Mr. Barker's class meant a hundred percent chance of immediate confiscation for a week, plus a good chance of Mr. Barker pegging him in the head with a well-aimed piece of chalk.

He set his head down on his desk like he was both tired and ill, which was mostly accurate, and extended his hand into his backpack. He pulled out his phone, switched it to silent mode, and looked at the display.

"I KNOW WHAT U DID 2 NEWTON COLEMAN," the text read in all caps and Richard's blood ran cold.

"TF is this?" he tapped back.

The reply was immediate. "KARMA."

He dropped the phone back into his backpack and sat straight up. He craned his neck trying to get Dustin's attention. After the first week of second semester, Mr. Barker had them pegged as shit disturbers and separated the two of them, which made learning easier but communication difficult.

Richard had trouble concentrating on the remainder of the lesson and counted down the minutes to the lunch bell. Who was this person and why were they accusing him?

The bell rang and the class began to leave. Mr. Barker raised his hands. "Sit down. I'm not finished with you all yet." He waited until all eyes were on him, then held up the class textbook. "Chapter seven, linear programming, questions one through twelve, on my desk first thing next class." He paused for emphasis and to exercise his ego. "Okay, now you can go."

Richard threw his backpack onto his shoulder and pushed his way across the room to where Dustin was collecting his things. "Dude, we got a problem."

"Yeah, linear programming," Dustin said. "Twelve of them."

"No." Richard grabbed Dustin's arm, his grip tighter and more abrupt than what Dustin was used to.

Dustin stiffened and pulled his arm away. "The *fuck's* your damage?"

Richard extracted his phone from its designated spot in his pack and showed him the text. "Someone knows something."

"Bullshit." Dustin hoisted up his backpack by the grab handle.

Richard stepped closer, lowered his voice, and spoke through clenched teeth. "We gotta find out who this is."

Dustin glared at him. "Not here." He headed for the classroom door with Richard close behind. The two of them stopped at Dustin's locker. "What are you, *stupid?* You need to shut the fuck up."

"I know, but—"

Dustin bared his teeth and clenched Richard's shirt with one fist. "Stop talking if you want to live the rest of the day." He released Richard quickly so to not draw unwanted attention.

Richard brushed himself off. "Someone fucking *knows*."

Dustin laughed. "Who? Dark Angela? Probably someone trying to catfish you."

"When I got out of the shower yesterday, the words 'HE KNOWS' was written on my mirror."

Dustin's face burned with anger, and he worked his free hand into a whitened fist. "Your *dad* knows?"

"No, someone else."

"Listen to yourself." Dustin shook his head slowly. "You sound fuckin' crazy. Someone *other* than your dad wrote on your bathroom mirror? Fuck that."

"They did," Richard said. "I'm not making it up."

Dustin motioned at Richard's phone. "Show me a picture. You were smart enough to take a picture, right?"

"I... I wiped it off. I was scared."

"You're an idiot," Dustin said. "Now calm the fuck down. Newton doesn't know anything. Just like—"

"What if he does?"

"Just like *we* don't know anything," Dustin said. "Besides, I wiped that chick Hazy's phone. There's nothing that points to us. And she couldn't restore her videos."

"But what if Newton *does* know something?" Richard fought to keep his panic from showing.

"He's a fuckin' vegetable." Dustin's eyes darkened. "But if he knows something, I guess you better take care of it."

Richard leaned in. "What? Why me?"

"Because *you* gave him the beer."

Richard looked like he had just had the wind knocked out of him. "I gave him the beer *you* gave *me*."

"Your word against mine," Dustin said. "Now, I got shit to

do. If you really believe your crazy story, you better hustle. Make sure he doesn't talk again."

"What does *that* mean?"

"You're a smart kid." Dustin grabbed Richard's shoulder and shook it as a friend might. "You'll figure something out." He began to walk away from Richard, then stopped and returned, stopping almost nose to nose with Richard, a sneer on his face. "If you throw me under the bus, you're coming with me." He tapped Richard's cheek and walked away.

Richard stumbled to his locker in a daze, opened it, and promptly forgot what he wanted. His stomach had fallen strangely silent and instead buzzed with anxiety.

Despite Dustin's disbelief, Richard knew what he had seen written on his bathroom mirror had been real. Newton knew something and that knowledge couldn't get out. Ever.

He pulled on his coat and secured his locker. He threw his pack over his shoulder and left the school. He rarely skipped school, but today Richard had a good reason. He had Cherry Mills Medical Centre in his sights, and he had to figure out a plan before he got there.

– 92 –

Teigan sat at her desk working on administrative tasks for GadgetGot. Necessary busywork she had called it. But her brain kept going back to Haislee's videos and her exploratory projection from the previous night. She wanted to go back and really dig into Dustin's space, particularly his games room, but some things took precedence. Making sure her business continued to run smoothly was one of them. The work would take only a few hours.

A little after two-thirty in the afternoon, she made a late lunch of tomato soup with cheese toast, one of her comfort foods.

Halfway through lunch the phone rang. Teigan swallowed her bite and picked up the handset. "Hello?"

"Teigan?" The voice of Betty from the hospital buzzed in her ear.

Teigan's stomach dropped and she almost threw up her lunch. "Oh God." She didn't want to ask her next question because she didn't want the answer to be bad, but she *had* to ask. "Is everything alright?"

Please say yes. Please.

"More than alright, Teigan," Betty said. "We are seeing signs of Newton waking. If you'd like to be here when that happens, I'd recommend getting here sooner rather than later."

Relief washed over her and Teigan burst into tears. "Oh, thank you."

"Don't thank me," Betty said. "Thank your son. He's a fighter."

Teigan wiped her eyes and sniffled. "We'll get there as soon as possible. And Betty? We won't forget the kindness you've shown us."

"Glad to have helped. Will see you soon, then."

The line clicked and Teigan ended the call. She immediately redialed Mattix and told him the news.

"I knew he'd beat this, Tee. I just knew it," Mattix said. "I'll leave now, pick up Elise, then you, then we can all get to the hospital together."

"Yeah." Teigan's voice was barely above a whisper. "Hurry, love." She cried tears of joy until her eyes were dry, then finished her lunch, which tasted better than ever now.

Teigan texted Elise the plan and stepped outside to wait on the porch steps. She took in clean air, observed the sky painted blue, and noticed leaves budding out on the surrounding trees and plants. Everything felt new.

Teigan tried projecting to Newton's hospital room to pass the time, but found she couldn't relax enough to make it happen. She'd have to wait like any other normal person, which was always the hardest part.

$$- \ 93 \ -$$

RICHARD ARRIVED HOME close to twelve-thirty. The last person he wanted to see was his dad, so he let himself into the detached garage and began to pace between the cluttered and clumsy piles of his dad's worthless possessions.

The entire walk home, his thoughts focused on what he didn't want to do but knew he had to. He was graduating in a couple of months and with his grades so far, it would be with honours.

But all that would be over if rumour got out. There was no way he could let gossip destroy his future. He'd worked too hard.

Richard paced and tried to focus, but his hunger was back. Instead of going into the house, he dug through the shelves that contained his dad's Costco binges and found a giant package of cashew clusters. He hated cashews but it was better than nothing.

He tore open the bag and shoveled the bite-sized nuggets into his mouth. He was able to focus a bit better now that his stomach had stopped its protest. But he had still wasted almost two hours in an indecisive limbo.

If Newton woke up, it'd be game over. Richard had to make moves now. He gave up on a plan, emptied his backpack onto the floor, and threw in some of his dad's tools – a box cutter, hammer, and wire cutters. He grabbed his Norco off the wall and set off for the hospital.

No plan with a thoughtless collection of random tools.

"The ride will clear my head," Richard tried to convince himself. "I'll know what to do when I get there."

Except the ride did nothing but exhaust him, both mentally and physically. He locked his bicycle and headed to the ICU. Having visited Newton once before, he found his hospital room easily and quickly enough.

It looked like things hadn't changed at all since the last time he had visited. Newton remained hooked up to his ventilator and vital signs monitor as it recorded his life slowly ticking away.

Richard stared at Newton, someone he had once considered a good friend, and felt nothing but rage. He was convinced that Newton held his future in his hands. He couldn't allow that.

He slipped off his backpack and looked inside. The tools he had brought sat in the bottom like anchors of dread. Richard dismissed the box cutter immediately. First of all, it would be too messy, and he didn't like the sight of blood. Plus, despite his anger, he couldn't see himself stabbing Newton. It was too real.

The hammer was an even worse choice than the box cutter, although that gave him the option to smash the ventilator. However, doing so would make too much noise. Getting caught was not part of the plan.

He grabbed the wire cutters. Richard had two options: cut Newton's ventilator tube or the ventilator's power cord. His thoughts clarified. Fixing a cut air tube was easier than repairing a cut power cord.

Power cord it is.

Richard approached the right side of Newton's bed where the ventilator stood on a pole. He could see the power cord emerge from the side of the unit and arc down to a power outlet behind the head of the bed.

He reached toward the cord with his wire cutters open, ready to slice through the plastic sheath and wires inside, but stopped short of squeezing the grips.

Wait. Will I be electrocuted?

He looked at the rubber handles and wondered if they'd insulate him. Richard didn't know the answer and didn't have time to contemplate it.

He moved slowly, as if he didn't want to wake Newton up, even though Richard was ignorant to the fact that waking a coma patient was next to impossible. He positioned the blades around the power cord, ready to cut.

Richard glanced back at Newton one last time, watching his chest rise and fall in a steady rhythm. His vital signs continued to track across the monitor's digital screen. Newton's face looked peaceful, which made cutting the power cord easier.

Then Newton opened his eyes, turned his head, and locked his gaze with Richard's.

Startled, Richard dropped the wire cutters and stumbled backward. He crouched to retrieve them, but they had fallen too far under the bed.

"What the *fuck* are you doing?" a voice said from behind.

Richard spun around to face a tall young man in a navy blue hoodie pulled up over his head. He had run into this person during a previous visit, except today he could see the person's face. But that made no difference because he didn't recognize the person at all.

"The fuck?" Richard said. "You following me?"

"Just looking out for my friend," the young man said. "Which is more than I can say about you." They flicked their eyes toward the wire cutters under the bed.

"You don't know SHIT." Richard took that moment of distraction to attempt escape. He launched himself forward toward the door, but the young man caught him with his left arm and spun Richard toward his chest, snaking his arm around Richard's neck. He placed his right arm behind Richard's neck to complete the beginnings of a sleeper hold.

Richard knew it would be lights out in less than twenty seconds. Instead of struggling, he reached into his backpack still clutched in his left hand and pulled out the box cutter. He slid the blade out with his thumb and ran it across the young man's left forearm, slicing through the fabric and into skin and muscle beneath.

The young man yelped and pulled his arm away, allowing Richard just enough room to break free and bolt down the corridor.

The cut to the young man's arm must have been painful, but it didn't slow him down much. As Richard burst through the ICU doors and rounded the corner that led to the elevators, he saw his pursuer gaining on him.

Several people had boarded the elevator ahead. "Wait!" Richard called out.

One of the people inside held their arm against the elevator door. Richard flew into the elevator car and pounded on the "close door" button.

The young man rounded the corner, past the reception desk, as the elevator doors began to slide closed. He ran toward the doors, grasping his left arm with his right hand to staunch the bleeding.

Come on come on come on…

The doors sealed and the elevator car jerked into motion. Richard's mind raced. He knew this young man would take the stairs. His only chance at escape was to disappear. But that would be impossible if his pursuer beat him to the first floor.

Several tense seconds that felt like dozens ticked by. Finally, the elevator doors began to move and Richard forced his body through the partial opening.

Beside the elevators and opposite the stairway exit was a gift shop. It would have to do. He crouched behind a rack of magazines and waited, pretending to tie his shoelaces. First one shoe, then the next.

Richard stood up slowly and checked the corridors for anyone he recognized, especially someone in a navy blue hoodie. When convinced he was in the clear, he followed the corridor that branched away from the entrance and toward other departments of the hospital. There was more than one way to get out of a hospital. He walked away from the elevators as calmly as he could without looking back.

As far as his pursuer was concerned, Richard had simply disappeared.

– 94 –

MATTIX ROLLED INTO THE PARKADE at Cherry Mills Medical Centre and found a stall close to the entrance. Teigan and Elise piled out of the Pathfinder before he had fully stopped.

"Hey, let's not injure ourselves before we get there," Mattix said.

Teigan and Elise stood at the back of the SUV and glowered at him. "Not the time or place, hon," Teigan said.

Mattix nodded and locked up. "Fair enough. Let's go." He led the charge through the parkade to the main entrance.

"Watch for cars, hon!" Teigan called back at Mattix, snickering. She grinned at Elise and held out her hand, not expecting her daughter to take it. When Elise grabbed hold, Teigan's heart swelled. She savored the feeling knowing that it would be fleeting.

The three of them walked hastily through the front entrance. Although navigating the hospital and the ICU wasn't a new experience, Teigan knew the way by heart. It had been her home away from home for half of the past seventeen days.

"Come on." Teigan quickened her pace, reaching the elevator first. She punched the up button.

A moment later the elevator doors slid open and the three of them stepped inside. Teigan selected the second floor and waited for the doors to close, her hands tapping her thighs nervously.

In the foyer, Teigan spotted a young man in a navy blue hoodie. He was clutching his left arm, and even with his hood pulled up there was enough light to see his darting and searching eyes. His face looked both pained and panicked, like he had lost something important.

I know him!

The elevator doors started their slow slide closed and Teigan stepped out, holding the door with her hand.

"Tee?" Mattix looked at her confused. "What are you doing?"

Teigan glanced behind, then faced Mattix again. "Gonna grab something at the gift shop."

"I'll come with you," Elise said.

Teigan saw her daughter's eyes flicking to something *or someone* in the foyer, and back.

Shit. She knows.

"No, you stay with Dad." Teigan stepped out of the path of the elevator doors, allowing them to close.

Elise didn't argue. Instead, she locked her eyes onto Teigan's, burning through her until the elevator doors blocked their intensity.

Teigan turned and scanned the foyer for the young man in the navy blue hoodie, but he was no longer standing in the spot she had seen him last.

It was Teigan's turn to scan the crowds of people walking in and out of the hospital. There was no distinctive hoodie in the corridors branching away from the elevators. That left the outside.

She ran past the sliding doors of the entrance. Teigan shielded her eyes from the sun and scanned the open area spanning from the emergency entrance, across the ER parking lot, to the doors to the parkade.

No one with a navy blue hoodie was in sight.

Except...

A person headed toward the intersection adjacent to the hospital. They wore a dark top. At this distance it could be navy blue or black. That was good enough for Teigan. She burst forth after the young man, weaving between parked vehicles.

"Wait!" Teigan called. "You in the hoodie. WAIT!"

The light turned green and the walk signal flashed at the intersection. Teigan gave every ounce of strength she could muster to her legs, but her energy waned.

"BENJAMIN!"

Halfway across the intersection, the young man in the hoodie turned and looked back.

Teigan reached the corner and beckoned him toward her.

The young man gave her a sideways glance, then began to walk back. Teigan braced herself on the traffic light standard while she caught her breath.

He joined her at the corner. Teigan looked up at him and shaded her eyes. "Benjamin Littleton, right?"

Benjamin nodded. "Most people call me Ben or Benji now."

"You know who I am?"

"Of course," Benjamin said.

"I would never have recognized you if I hadn't seen your picture in Waterton's 2023 yearbook."

Benjamin raised a brow at her.

Teigan shook her head. "It's a long story." She glanced at his left arm and noticed the fabric had darker patches. Then she spotted red smears on his hand.

Blood.

"Are you okay?" Before Benjamin could respond, Teigan had taken his arm in her hand and carefully examined it. A two-inch gash along his forearm slowly oozed blood. "Jesus."

"It's not too bad," Benjamin said.

"What happened?"

"It's a long story."

"How about we take care of this right now." Teigan motioned

back toward the hospital entrance. "I hear hospitals are great for these kinds of things."

Benjamin smiled. The young face of Newton's first and best friend from Grade 5 shone through, bringing with it a flood of good memories.

"What about Newt? You're here for him."

"Let's get you fixed up first," Teigan said. "Then we can both watch him wake up."

Benjamin's eyes widened. "Really? He's coming out?"

"The doctors think so." The two walked back toward the hospital and Teigan continued. "I'm pretty sure I've seen you here before. Why not say hi?"

"News of what happened spread super fast," Benjamin said. "I wanted to be there for Newt just as fast, but it's been so long since we hung out." Benjamin shrugged. "Didn't feel right. I didn't want to intrude."

Teigan shook her head. "You wouldn't have intruded."

"It's been almost seven years, Mrs. Coleman," Benjamin said. "It's gonna be awkward."

"Maybe at first. Newt's a good guy, like you. The awkwardness wouldn't have lasted long." Teigan looked around for a nurse but realized they had a better chance at the ER.

"You know, Mrs. Coleman," Benjamin said. "It looks like my arm's stopped bleeding. It can wait."

"You sure?" Teigan eyed him with concern. "We're right here and—"

"Nah, I'm good."

"Okay." Teigan motioned to the elevators and Benjamin nodded. "I have to ask... Nick Bee? That was you, right?"

Benjamin sported a wide grin. "Yeah. We used to make up names for gaming sites. One thing we did was to use our middle name as our first name and the initial of our first name as our last name."

Teigan looked at him, doing her best to follow along.

Benjamin continued. "So that made me Nicholas Benjamin. Or Nick B."

Teigan laughed. "So simple, but I couldn't figure it out."

"Did you even know my middle name?"

Teigan thought for a moment. "I guess I didn't. I'm never going to forget it now."

Both of them laughed as they retraced the route they had taken fifteen minutes earlier, both wondering what they would find back in Newton's room.

– 95 –

MATTIX AND ELISE ARRIVED on the second floor and headed for the ICU. Betty recognized them at once, unlocked the door, and waved them through without signing in.

"Will Teigan be joining you?"

Mattix placed his arm on Elise's shoulder. "She'll be up in a few minutes. Got to get a hospital stuffie to complete the hospital experience." He looked down at Elise. "Right?"

Elise shook off his arm. "Whatever you say."

Mattix shrugged and exchanged a knowing look with Betty. "Thanks for everything."

Betty smiled warmly despite Elise's black cloud. "It's my job."

Mattix and Elise turned down the familiar corridor that would soon become a distant memory. Halfway to Newton's room, Mattix stopped and faced his daughter.

"What's up with you?"

Elise shook her head. "Nothing. Come on. I want to be there when Newt wakes up." She continued walking, then stopped and looked back. "Are you coming or not?"

There *was* something up with Elise, Mattix could feel it, but he had no intention of rocking the boat now. Whatever it was, it could wait. He caught up to her so they could both enter the room together.

Nothing had changed. The bed, the monitors, the ventilator, even Newton himself looked the same. It was like the universe had placed their memories into pause while they were away from the hospital, and it took a bit of Mattix's spirit with it.

Elise placed her hands on the railing at the foot of the bed. She looked up at Mattix, her eyes welling with tears. He took her in his arms and held her until they both felt ready to sit.

"It's going to be okay," Mattix said.

"Is it?" Elise turned away from him to watch the vital signs monitor. "What if it's not the same Newt?"

Mattix understood his daughter's reaction and worry, but held steadfast onto the mantra in his head.

It's going to be okay.

Haislee appeared at the open door, surprised to see Elise and Mattix. Her eyes darted between Elise, Mattix, and Newton.

"Hazy?" Elise furrowed her brow. "What are you doing here?"

Haislee took a step forward into the room. "I don't know. I... Sorry, I—" She raised a trembling hand to her lips, then turned and bolted from the room.

Elise wasted no time going after her.

Mattix looked around the room. "Looks like it's just me and you, son." He reached out and placed his hand on Newton's left forearm, careful not to disturb the IV cannula.

Newton's skin was warm, alive. This made perfect sense, yet Mattix was surprised by the sensation. He set his elbows on the mattress, clasped his hands, and raised them to his forehead as if praying. In a way he was, as he continued his internal mantra.

‐ 96 ‐

ELISE RAN DOWN THE CORRIDOR, peering into rooms as she went. Betty waved at her as she passed the reception desk.

"Are you looking for..." Betty scanned the sign-in sheet. "Haislee?"

Elise nodded.

Betty pointed down the other branch of the corridor that formed the ICU loop and lowered her voice. "She's in the chapel."

Elise followed the corridor to a small room, like many others in the ICU. The cramped space accommodated a few rows of chairs, and the dimmed lighting helped it feel more welcoming. Religious symbols and plaques from multiple faiths hung on the walls, and a rudimentary podium stood front and center.

Elise saw Haislee sitting to the left of the center aisle, midway down. She spotted a box of tissue sitting on the donations table by the door and grabbed it. She took a seat across the aisle from Haislee and offered the tissues.

Haislee took the box and pulled out a tissue, wiping her eyes. She hung her head and sighed heavily.

"What's going on?" Elise asked.

Haislee met Elise's gaze. "I had to say goodbye." Hearing the words were too much and she began to cry again.

"Goodbye?" Elise crossed the aisle, took the chair beside Haislee, and placed her arm around her friend's shoulder. "Hazy, Newt's not going to die."

Haislee looked at Elise with disbelief. "What?" She took another tissue, wiped her eyes again and blew her nose. "I thought... because you and..."

"The doctors told us he might wake up today," Elise said. "That's why we're here."

Haislee covered her face with a hand. "I just saw your dad picking you up at school and driving away really fast, I just thought the worst. Sorry."

Elise pulled her into a hug. "It's okay." She let the hug last as long as it felt right, then pulled back. "Also, how'd you, like, get here so fast?"

"Called my mom. She dropped me off."

"Totes appreesh," Elise said. "Newton does, too."

"I'd do anything for Newt." Haislee looked at Elise, her face clear of sorrow. "Like *anything*."

Elise cringed at her.

"I like him, Lise," Haislee said. "I always have. I know you're not down with that, but I can't ignore my feelings. That's why I freaked out."

"My brother *dating* my best friend?" Elise scrunched her nose. "That's a bit gross."

"Why? If we're both happy, why is that so bad?"

Elise shrugged. "I guess it's not. But what if he's not into you?"

"I'll stalk him to the ends of the Earth." When Elise's eyes bugged out, Haislee laughed. "Kidding... I'll deal. You know I've crushed on other guys before. Not quite like Newt, but..."

Elise considered the scenario, then smiled. "If you two ended up, like, dating somehow, I'd be cool with it I guess."

The two girls hugged again, then Haislee pulled out her phone.

"Who you calling?"

"My mom," Haislee said. "She told me she'd hang around for a bit if I needed a ride."

"Stay. Be there when Newt wakes up. He'd like that."

Haislee hesitated. "Are you sure? I mean—"

"I'm sure. We can drive you home."

"Okay."

Both girls stood and made their way back to Newton's hospital room. As they walked Haislee called her mom to tell her that she'd be staying a while. Betty offered a small wave as they passed by the reception desk.

When Elise entered Newton's room, she saw that her mom was still absent. The inner turmoil that she had felt before in the elevator returned with a vengeance.

$$- 97 -$$

Mattix hadn't moved from his chair when Elise returned with Haislee in tow. He wiped his face in hopes that his tears wouldn't be obvious. But that was off the table with his ever observant daughter.

"Dad? What's wrong?" Elise stopped mid-stride, her eyes laser focused on him.

"Oh nothing," Mattix said. "The moment caught me unexpectedly."

"We can go, Mr. Coleman..." Haislee hooked her thumb backward. "If you want to—"

"No way," Elise said. "I'm staying."

"It's okay, Haislee." Mattix forced a smile at them both. "Newt needs all the support he can get right now."

Elise continued into the room. "Where's Mom?"

"Getting a stuffie, remember?"

"Such bullshit," Elise said quietly to herself, but just loud enough to be heard. Haislee gave her a curious glance.

Mattix stood. "Here. You two sit. I need to stretch my legs." He walked to the window as Haislee took one of the chairs.

Elise remained standing. "Doesn't it bother you?"

Mattix faced her. "What?"

"Mom's acting all strange," Elise said. "She's disappearing for hours at a time, like, even now."

"Like I said, she's getting a something special for Newt. Plus she's been trying to find out who's responsible."

"And you believe that?"

Mattix crossed his arms. He felt anger rising within him but pushed it down. "I trust Mom. A better question is why *you* don't."

"Yeah," Teigan said from the doorway. "Why don't you trust me, Elise?"

Elise spun around and saw Teigan holding a stuffed beaver wearing a graduation cap on its head.

"I...you've been, like, all secretive," Elise said. "And the lying, even after you promised not to. Don't think we haven't noticed."

Mattix sighed, rubbed his temples, and directed his gaze at Teigan. "Maybe not do this now?"

Teigan held up her hand. "It's okay, Matt." She placed the beaver on Newton's bed and approached Elise. "You're right. I haven't been completely honest in the past. But I made a promise. No more secrets. And I've kept that promise."

"Really?" Elise crossed her arms in a fit. "Then who was that guy you just hooked up with?"

Teigan's eyes widened with surprise. "*Excuse* me? I've never *hooked up* with anyone except your father."

"Oh yeah? That guy you just met. Who is he?" Elise's eyes blazed. "It's the same guy I saw outside our house. He's the reason you stepped out of the elevator."

Teigan sighed. "You're right. I did meet someone downstairs."

Mattix's jaw dropped. "What?"

"And I'd like you all to meet him." Teigan walked to the door of the room and signaled to someone out into the corridor.

Benjamin stepped into the room, looking a little unsure of himself, despite being the tallest person in the room. He pulled his hood back to reveal a tousled mop of short brown hair.

"Elise, and everyone, this is Benjamin Littleton," Teigan said. "He was Newton's best friend in Grade 5. They ended up going to separate schools and lost touch. But he's been looking out for Newt ever since his overdose."

"Hey." Benjamin gave a small wave.

Elise stood dumbfounded. "Mom... I..."

"We'll talk about it later," Teigan said. "Make him feel welcome. You're probably going to see a lot more of him now."

"What happened to your arm?" Mattix asked.

Benjamin cast his eyes to the floor like he was looking for something. "Scratched it on my bike."

"Guys?" Haislee's voice was lost in the back and forth noise of conversation.

"Better get it looked at," Mattix said. "I mean, since you're here."

Haislee raised her voice a little louder. "Hey guys?"

Everyone looked at her.

Haislee pointed at Newton. "Someone's awake."

Newton blinked at them, his eyes working the room and the people in it.

Teigan grabbed the call button hanging from the bed and pressed it frantically. "Newt, darling. You're back!" She leaned over and kissed his shoulder. "Can you hear me? Blink twice for yes."

Newton began to blink, but the frequency was random and unrelated to the questions Teigan was throwing at him.

Betty hustled into the room and took a spot next to the bed. She noted Newton's vital signs, then made a call on the phone next to the bed. Afterward, she looked to the concerned faces surrounding his bed. "I know you all have missed Newton, but everyone needs to step back. Newton's going to feel disoriented and overwhelmed. Also, visiting hours will be ending early today."

Teigan took Betty aside. "I'd like to stay, if at all possible."

"I can't promise anything," Betty said. "Newton needs

monitoring and regular testing to determine his mental state going forward. He's going to require time to get back to the way he was before…" She lowered her voice so only Teigan could hear. "I hate to bring this up again, but there's a chance he won't be the same. You and your family need time to prepare for that possibility, and that's probably best done at home."

Teigan swallowed hard, nodded, and stepped back from the bed.

Mattix pulled her into a hug. "Newt's going to be okay," he whispered into her ear. "We're going to be okay."

Teigan buried her face against his chest. "Promise?"

"I promise." Mattix knew it was risky thing to say, but it felt right. He faced the rest of the group. "Let's let the doctors do what they need to do. Haislee, Benjamin, we can give you a lift home."

Haislee and Benjamin nodded their thanks.

Mattix and Teigan approached the side of the bed. "Looking forward to having you home, buddy," Mattix said.

Teigan placed a gentle kiss on Newton's forehead. "See you tomorrow, my sweet prince," she said softly.

Haislee paused bedside and waved timidly. "Glad you're awake, Newt." He managed a wink back, inciting Haislee to smile as her cheeks flushed rosy.

Elise placed her hand lightly on Newton's right hand. "Missed you, bro."

Finally, Benjamin approached the bed. "We got a lot to talk about." Newton made a weak thumbs up. Benjamin reciprocated, then made a fist and tapped the top of Newton's fist. Newton mirrored the move as best he could.

Teigan placed a trembling hand to her mouth. "Their secret handshake…" Mattix gave her a side hug and kissed her head.

The group took one last look before moving down the corridor to the elevator.

"I think I'll be missing work tomorrow," Mattix said.

"And school." Elise looked back at Mattix and Teigan, expecting some pushback, but none came. She nudged Haislee. "You can ditch too, if you want."

"Maybe," Haislee said. "I want to but…"

"Yeah. I get it." Elise placed her arm around Haislee's shoulder.

Benjamin remained quiet and followed behind the rest of the group. Teigan glanced back and extended her hand, beckoning him forward.

"How are you doing?" She patted his back gently.

"Good." Benjamin was a young man of few words.

"He remembered your secret handshake."

Benjamin chuckled. "Yeah. I think it needs updating."

Teigan nodded.

Mattix directed everyone into the elevator, then stepped in himself. Despite having to leave early, this was the best possible outcome that he could have imagined. But he knew they weren't completely out of the woods yet.

$$- \; 98 \; -$$

TEIGAN REMAINED SILENT for the entire drive home, including the drop-offs for Haislee and Benjamin. While she understood why she couldn't stay with Newton at the hospital, her anger continued to build, displacing her gratitude.

She hated feeling this way and hated *him* for causing it. Her son was facing his greatest moment of need in his young life so far, all because of Dustin Stoaks. She didn't know how all the pieces fit together, and solid proof eluded her, but she was sure of Dustin's involvement just as she was sure of the rage she felt toward him. This wasn't over.

Mattix had picked up A&W drive-thru for dinner and Teigan took it up into her office to eat. She fished out the memory stick Haislee had given her and inserted it into a USB port. The now familiar folder of images and videos popped up once again.

Teigan found the videos of Dustin's party last Friday and as she ate her Mama Burger and onion rings, she started to play them again, one by one, full screen and in great detail. Some she played at slow speed so she wouldn't miss a single detail. Others she paused to examine in closeup.

Time evaporated as Teigan immersed herself in Haislee's tour videos. Minutes turned into hours. A knock on her office door brought her out of her solitary focus. She instinctually minimized the applications on her monitor.

Mattix stuck his head in. "I'm going to bed. Sure would be nice if you were there too."

Teigan nodded. "I'll be there soon, hon. Let me wrap things up." She went to the door and kissed him. "Sorry for being a grouch. I've had a lot on my mind."

Mattix smiled wanly. "We all have." He closed the door.

Teigan returned to her chair and called up her video player. "One more run through," she told herself as she pressed play.

The final viewing for the night took almost an hour. Mattix would be asleep by now and probably pissed off. She powered down her computer and returned the memory stick to the desk drawer.

In the upstairs hallway, Teigan spotted light leaking from the bottom of Elise's door. Either she'd fallen asleep with the light on, which she was known to do, or she was working through the day's events in her own way, just like everyone else. Teigan thought of knocking and saying goodnight, then dismissed it.

Teigan placed her hand on the doorknob of the master bedroom, then hesitated. She glanced back at Newton's darkened room and new anger began to swell within her.

"Fuck it," Teigan said under her breath. "Fuck *him*." She grabbed her phone, purse, and jacket and tiptoed to the garage. Buckling herself in as the garage door slid open, she started the Pathfinder's engine and rolled out as soon as the door was open.

If the garage door hadn't woken Mattix and Elise, the sound of the Pathfinder's engine surely would have, but Teigan didn't care. Dustin Stoaks would answer her questions and this time she wasn't taking no for an answer.

– 99 –

THE ROADS WERE MOSTLY CLEAR at this hour of the night, and ten minutes after leaving her home on Radcliffe Crescent, Teigan found herself approaching the long driveway to Dustin's elaborate house.

What about the peace bond and fines? Filing charges?

"Fuck it," Teigan said again, her voice resonating in the cab of the SUV. Fines and charges were all inconsequential compared to finding who had almost killed her son.

But she didn't want to tip her entire hand yet. Teigan slowed, rolled past the end of the driveway, and peered out of the passenger side window.

The driveway was circular but held a more teardrop shape such that one could see the mansion and its porte cochère from the main street. Security lights flooded the grounds and made an unseen approach impossible. But the lights also revealed that Dustin's Escalade wasn't there.

Teigan decided to wait. She drove further down the street, then made a U-turn and parked less than half a block from Dustin's driveway. To pass the time, she loaded up the playlist she had made with Newton.

I'll wait all night if I have to.

It didn't take all night or even a few hours. Twenty minutes later Teigan spotted the black Escalade turn into Dustin's driveway. She ducked down in her seat to avoid the headlight beams and waited until the Escalade disappeared behind the dense hedges on both sides of the driveway.

Teigan stepped out of her Pathfinder, latched the door quietly, and ran crouched across the street to the hedge. She skirted the edge of it and scanned the curved portion of the driveway leading to the porte cochère.

She spotted Dustin step out of the Escalade, but instead of heading inside, he ran around to the passenger side and opened the door. A girl with long, dark hair emerged. He held her hand and led her to the front door.

"Shit." Teigan didn't care about charges or fines, but other witnesses were a dealbreaker. "But..."

There was another way.

Teigan hustled back to her Pathfinder, stepped in, and locked the doors. "I can project instead," she said to herself.

It was an infinitely better option, and her anger had almost led her astray. Surveillance couldn't get much better than invisible.

$$- \ 100 \ -$$

Teigan eased the driver's seat back and closed her eyes. It was time to revisit Dustin's house. It wasn't breaking a promise if she visited through a projection, was it? Surely not.

Calming herself, she pictured the grand room in Dustin's mansion where she had last stood. One thing she had learned about her superpower was that she could only initiate a useful projection to a physical place she had occupied once before.

Dustin's house was dark, except for a sliver of blue light slipping through his bedroom door on the second level. Teigan could also hear music. She walked to the stairs and followed them up. The music became clearer. It was Britney Spears singing "Gimme More." Teigan always knew who the latest pop singers and songs were and which older songs had staying power, an advantage of being a parent of a teenage girl. In this case the song was almost as old as Newton.

Teigan worried that the gap in Dustin's door might be too small to slip through, but it was open just enough. She exhaled and moved sideways into his bedroom. The music was coming from the games room, the one place she hadn't had a chance to check before, and the blue running lights at the floor of the captain's bed led the way.

Dustin and a girl she recognized from the many yearbooks she had studied last week were playing video games. However, her name eluded Teigan.

The game's jewel case sat on the coffee table: Just Dance 2024. Once Teigan saw the game's logo, the blurred rush of colours on the massive flat panel flipped into focus.

Elise has this game!

By parental default, Teigan knew all the songs in the game as well. The display featured a neon-coloured dancer making dance moves on the screen. The girl hopped and flung her arms and hips about, matching the moves and scoring major points.

Teigan peeked behind the bar. Haislee had not taken her camera here, resulting in an incomplete rendering of the space. The floor was transparent, an area she needed to avoid. Some known objects (soda and beer) appeared in full detail through the glass-paned refrigerator door, while others were imaginings of what the back of the bar should look like. The detail there was spotty due to the source being video. Because of that there were no clues either.

Teigan stood behind the couch and watched the two teenagers. They had pushed the coffee table to one side to allow the game to *see* their entire bodies. When the song ended, the girl took a bow, then flopped onto the couch.

"Score! 10,548 points," the girl said between breaths. "Beat that, twinkle toes."

"Before my turn, you want a drink?" Dustin raised a brow at her. "Beer? Pop?"

"Yes. A pop would be great."

Dustin hurried to the bar and Teigan shadowed him. She wasn't going to let him out of her sight.

Dustin opened the small windowed refrigerator. "Coke, Sprite, or Orange Crush?"

"Orange Crush," the girl called back.

Dustin grabbed the pop and a beer for himself. He set his beer on a side table. "Can I open it for you?" He motioned at her fingers. "Spare your nails?"

Jesus Christ. He's really turning on the charm.

The girl held out her hands and fanned her fingers, admiring her long and bright red nails. "They're just press-ons, but sure."

Dustin cracked the seal on the Orange Crush, causing it to foam a bit at the top. "Sorry about that," he said, and handed her the drink.

"No worries." The girl sipped from the can, taking care of the bubbles on the top. She took a few long gulps, then burped. "Oops. Sorry."

Dustin laughed. "I got to go to the bathroom real quick. Pick the song you want me to dance to."

The girl picked up the game controller and began searching the directory of songs as Dustin headed back toward his room. Teigan followed, hot on his heels.

Dustin walked around his bed, then peeked back into the games room. The girl was still searching for the next song.

He pulled open a bottom drawer from his bed, lifted up a false bottom, and selected a small memory card. Dustin reset the bottom drawer, picked up the mug of pens and pencils from his desk, and opened it up.

It was a prop!

The bottom fell away. Inside sat a GoPro video camera perched on a small pedestal. He pulled a side flap open and inserted the memory card.

Teigan's stomach dropped as she realized what might be happening.

Dustin turned the camera on, started it recording, and resealed the bottom, hiding the camera within. He set the fake cup back on his desk.

"Did you find my song yet?"

"Yup," the girl called back. "And don't bother asking what it is 'cause it's a surprise."

Dustin ran to the ensuite bathroom on the opposite side of his bed, flushed the toilet, and ran the water. As he passed by his desk, he adjusted the position of the hidden camera slightly and snugged his office chair against the front of the desk to ensure an unobstructed view. He pulled back the covers on his bed and returned to the games room.

Teigan bent down low to get a good look at the hidden camera. The mug was black and glossy, and there was no indication that it contained a hidden camera. Of course, that was Dustin's plan. Sam Smith's "I'm Not Here to Make Friends" began playing and Teigan hurried back into the games room.

Surprisingly, Dustin had moves. And the girl was having a great time watching him dance and cheering him on. To Teigan or to anyone else, it would have looked like two teenagers having a great time together.

The song ended and the points were tabulated.

"11,109! Take that." Dustin cracked his beer and took a long swallow. "I believe that's two all. Care for a tiebreaker round?"

"Fuck, yeah." The girl stood, stumbled, then corrected herself.

Dustin selected "Can't Tame Her" by Zara Larsson. "Ready?"

The game started playing the song, indicating the upcoming dance moves as the iridescent dancer on the screen strutted her stuff. The girl matched the moves on screen, scoring a couple *perfect* dance steps in a row. Then she made an uncharacteristic misstep. The girl tried to correct herself and maintain the beat of music in her movements, but she slowly became more erratic. Finally, she gave up and fell back onto the couch, nearly missing the cushion.

Dustin ran to her side. "Shit, are you okay?"

The girl rubbed her forehead and her eyes. "I... what the... feeling dizzy."

Dustin scooped her up in his arms, carried her back to his bedroom, and carefully laid her out on his bed.

"Rest a bit here," Dustin said. "You're going to be fine."

The girl's eyes had closed, and her mouth worked at words that failed to come out.

Dustin sat next to the girl and stroked her hair, her arm, then moved to her breasts, feeling them through her shirt. He pulled up the hem of her shirt, exposing her bare midriff, then ran his fingers down her form fitting jeans.

"Don't you do it, you *fat fuck*," Teigan said, frustrated and angry that he'd never hear her.

Dustin popped the button on the girl's jeans and slid down the zipper. With both hands, he gripped her jeans at her hips and pulled them all the way down to her ankles, exposing her red panties.

"Huh. They match your nails." Dustin pulled a condom from his back pocket and set it on the bed, then unbuckled his belt and pulled off his pants.

"Don't fucking do it!" It was long past the point of no return for Teigan, but she had to know for sure that Dustin would follow through.

Dustin tore open the condom wrapper, reached into his boxer shorts, and applied the condom. He pushed the girl's knees apart and lowered himself on top of her.

That was all Teigan could take. "Get off her you FUCKING PSYCHO PERVERT!" She raised her hands and shoved Dustin with all her strength. She felt his body move and—

In an instant she was back in her Pathfinder staring at the SUV's roof. She tried to project back to Dustin's bedroom but couldn't connect. Her heart raced as she reset her seat back upright. She pushed open the driver's side door and bolted toward Dustin's driveway.

Following the road in, Teigan picked up a fist-sized rock in her hand, its sharp edges digging into her palm. She ran across the lawn and past the ridiculous fountain.

When she was close enough to ensure that she would not miss, Teigan wound up and threw the rock at the back window of the

Escalade, exploding it into a cascade of small glass nuggets. They reminded her of uncut diamonds.

The Escalade's security alarm blasted through the night with an eardrum-splitting *whoop whoop*. The headlights and taillights flashed in unison.

She regretted her actions immediately. If she had been thinking clearly, she would have worn a dark hoodie like Benjamin's. There were likely security cameras around the house recording all comings and goings. Teigan would be easily recognizable. So be it. This was important.

Teigan wasted no time sprinting back to her vehicle. She belted herself in and sped away, hoping that the broken window had been enough to interrupt Dustin's assault.

– 101 –

Teigan buzzed with adrenaline, and it took the entire return trip to calm herself. Once back at home, she secured the Pathfinder in the garage and crept back upstairs.

Elise's bedroom light was out, and the house echoed back only her own harried breathing. All she could think about was the helpless girl at the hands of Dustin.

And he was *recording* it.

That sick bastard.

The broken window would have spooked Dustin, but had it been enough?

Teigan entered her office and closed the door. She took her phone out of her purse and dialed Jackson. She was not surprised to get his voicemail, considering it was well past midnight.

"Jackson. It's Teigan Coleman. I need to talk to you. About Dustin Stoaks. It's important."

She hung up and sent a text. "Important. PICK UP."

Then she called again. This time the line clicked and Jackson's weary, sleep-cracked voice answered. "Teigan... I guess you know what time it is?"

"Late," Teigan said. "Besides you told me to call you, any time, if something came up. Your exact words."

Jackson sighed. "What is it?"

"You need to arrest Dustin Stoaks. He's drugging and raping girls, right now, in fact! And somehow it's related to Newt."

"Whoa whoa whoa," Jackson said, his voice instantly more alert. "How do you know this?"

Teigan stammered. "I just do. I have sources."

"Who?"

"I can't say," Teigan said.

"What about proof?"

Teigan gritted her teeth in frustration. Her hopes that her call would go somewhere positive was over. "I don't have proof. But you have to believe me. He's got video recording equipment and—"

"How do you know all this?" he repeated.

Teigan fell silent. "I can't reveal my source."

"Look," Jackson said. "Teigan. I agree that Dustin's a Grade-A asshole. But without hard evidence of assault, there's nothing I can do."

Teigan leaned back in her office chair, her mind reeling at the thought of that girl alone, unconscious, with Dustin. There had to be something she could do. Arguing with Jackson wasn't it.

"Alright," she said. "Good night." Teigan hung up knowing the rest of her night would not be good at all. Jackson's probably wouldn't be either.

Teigan left her office and crept into Newton's room, closed the door, and turned on the light. The mess of a normal, well-adjusted teenager sprawled in front of her. She made a line for his Grade 11 yearbook and began flipping through the photos of the students. It didn't take long to find the girl she had seen at Dustin's house.

"Mom?" Elise was standing at Newton's door. "Where were you?"

Teigan gazed at her daughter and decided to let truth lead the way. Most of the truth. "I was at Dustin Stoaks house."

"Mom!" Elise immediately lowered her voice. "Why?"

"I was angry," Teigan said. "But he didn't see me and I didn't talk to him... I just threw a rock through the back window of his beloved Escalade."

"Holy shit." Elise took a seat next to Teigan on the bed. "Like, are you serious?"

"Totes serious." Teigan grinned at her.

"Bruh...," Elise said. "That's badass."

The two sat in silence for a moment.

Elise pointed at the yearbook. "What are you doing with that?"

Teigan flipped to another page of the yearbook. "I've been reminding myself of what Newt's life used to be like."

"What do you mean 'used to'?" Elise closed the door to the bedroom and returned to her place next to Teigan on the bed.

Teigan closed the yearbook and took Elise's hands in hers. "There's a chance that Newt won't be the same... cognitively."

"Like, he won't be able to talk properly, or...?"

"Maybe," Teigan said. "His personality or mannerisms might change. He might walk or run differently than he used to. No one knows for sure, not even the doctors."

Elise sat for a moment to process Teigan's words. "Everyone changes. Newt will roll with it. He's just being upgraded. Newton 2.0, the best version ever."

Teigan placed her arm around Elise's shoulder. "You are amazing, you know that?" She kissed the top of Elise's head, then stood in front of Newton's bookshelf, her eyes lazily roaming the titles. "If you or Haislee were ever sexually assaulted, you'd go to the police, right?"

Elise's eyes widened. "Whoa, Mom. Where'd that come from?"

"I've been having dark thoughts lately." Teigan returned the yearbook to the bookshelf and faced Elise. "Would you report it?"

"Yeah," Elise said.

"Would you tell *me*? Or Dad?"

Elise stood and wrapped her arms around her mother. "Probably you first, but of course."

"Good." They both stepped to the door and Teigan continued. "Thanks for the chat. I feel much better."

Teigan turned off the light and said goodnight to her daughter. She crept back into her bedroom as quietly as she could, brushed her teeth, undressed, and slipped into her night shirt. She pulled open the covers on her side of the bed, careful not to disturb Mattix. She slid between the sheets and pulled them up to her chin.

Mattix's hand reached for her under the covers, squeezed her hand, and released. It felt good.

"Everything okay?" Mattix whispered.

"Yeah." Teigan snuggled up next to him, allowing the warmth of his body to lull her towards sleep. And as she drifted off, an idea came to her, one that sleep would not be able to erase.

$$- 102 -$$

Teigan, Elise, and Mattix left for the hospital at nine o'clock the next morning. Betty was not surprised to see them all back so quickly.

"Where's the tall one?" Betty asked.

"It's family only today," Teigan said.

Betty smiled and nodded as she handed Teigan the sign-in sheet. "Newton had a good series of tests yesterday."

Teigan glanced at Mattix and Elise. "I'm so happy to hear that. So, Newt's going home today?"

"No guarantees," Betty said, "but things are looking good."

Teigan gave Elise an extra side hug. "We're going to..." She motioned excitedly toward the corridor to Newton's room and Betty buzzed them through.

Across town, at the Hamilton Police Investigative Services Branch, Jackson had just returned to his office from an early morning briefing. He sat at his desk and spotted the red "new email" notification on the task bar of his computer.

He opened up his mail program. At the top of the list, bolded and unread, the subject line read, "*ATTN: Hamilton Police - Re: Dustin Stoaks.*" Jackson opened the email, which was short and to the point.

"To whom it may concern," the email read. *"Dustin Stoaks, who resides in Rockwood West, has been drugging and raping girls. It is unknown how long he has been committing this crime. The most recent assaults have happened at his home, in his bedroom and games room."*

Jackson hovered over the sender of the email. The sender's name appeared as *"Silent Voice,"* which was not a valid email address. He contemplated looking into the originating email servers for clues, but suspected they'd lead nowhere.

The email continued. *"His method of delivering the drugs is unclear, but the following are known facts. A fake mug of pens and pencils on his desk contains a hidden video camera and there is a false bottom in a drawer of his bed that contains memory cards. However, you'll need more than that to secure a warrant to search his house."*

The email concluded by naming Dustin's last victim, a senior attending Diamond Bay High School.

Jackson's mind whirled. After Teigan's frantic call last night, then this email, he had to do something. If the information contained in the email was true, he couldn't ignore it. He grabbed his coat from the back of his chair and sprinted out the door.

– 103 –

JACKSON'S FIRST STOP was Diamond Bay High School. The second academic block of the day was still in session, resulting in barren hallways with limited student activity. Although the word "POLICE" did not emblazon the back of his jacket, the less commotion the better. He reported to the office, flashing his badge and requesting to speak with the principal. The secretary at the administration desk directed him to take a seat.

A moment later, Principal McCarthy emerged. Jackson stood and identified himself.

McCarthy regarded Jackson casually, almost dismissively. "How can I help you, Detective Konishi?"

"Is there somewhere we can speak privately?"

McCarthy shot a quick glance at the secretary, then motioned towards the maze of hallways that served Diamond Bay's administration. After a few quick twists and turns, McCarthy led Jackson into his office. "Have a seat."

"I'd rather stand," Jackson said. "This won't take long."

McCarthy eyed him curiously. "Should I be concerned?"

"Any time the police show up unannounced should be cause for concern," Jackson said. "But for now, can you tell me if Chelle Morelli came to school today? If so, I'd like to speak with her."

McCarthy called up the school's administrative website and searched the daily attendance record. "Our system shows her absent today."

"I assume giving me her home address is out of the question."

"Yes," McCarthy said. "Not without a warrant."

Jackson nodded. "Thank you. I'll see myself out." He turned and pulled open the office door.

"Wait. Detective…" McCarthy stood up behind his desk. "What's this about?"

"I'm just running down a lead," Jackson said. "If it amounts to anything, you'll know." He retraced his steps and left the school office, thanking the administrative secretary as he passed by.

Once at his car, he pulled out his phone, called up the White Pages, and searched for "Chelle Morelli."

Zero matches.

Being a teenager, the search had been a long shot. Teenagers subscribing to a land line were as rare as a Hamilton snow squall in summer. He tried the search with just "Morelli" and received a list of results. Jackson refined the search to matches within ten kilometres. Five address matches displayed, sorted by distance. He started the Camry's engine and worked his way through the list.

At the first address, an older woman answered the door and curtly told Jackson that no one named Morelli lived here. She had moved in close to a year ago, a fact that cast doubt on the entire list of results.

But Jackson caught a break on the second address, an apartment complex. He buzzed the intercom and a young man responded over the crackly speakers.

"Chelle Morelli? Who's askin'?"

"Hamilton Police," Jackson said. "Who am I speaking with?"

"Dante. What this about?"

"I'd like to question Chelle regarding an ongoing

investigation." Dante paused but Jackson could still hear his breathing. "Hello?"

"What's the investigation about?"

Jackson closed his eyes and pinched the bridge of his nose in frustration. "Sorry, but that's confidential. Is Chelle Morelli there or not?"

"Yeah, sorry man," Dante said. "She's my kid sister. Just being protective."

Jackson stepped back and glanced up toward the apartment, wondering what floor Dante lived. "Look, I'll show you my ID. Through the glass. You won't even have to open the door. Or you can buzz me up."

"Nah. That's okay. Kinda busy."

For a second Jackson's curious mind wondered why a person likely in their mid-twenties wasn't at work and why they didn't want to meet face to face. Could be dozens of reasons.

Dante continued. "She still lives at home with my ma and pa." He gave Jackson the address.

"Thanks, Dante."

"You're not going to arrest her or something, are you?"

Jackson shook his head even though Dante would never see it. "No. On that you have my word." He returned to his car and noted the address Dante gave him didn't match any of the search results.

Either Dante was full of shit, or the search results were out of date. Jackson chose to believe the latter.

He arrived at a modest split-level bungalow, circa mid-70s. Jackson estimated a five minute drive to the school. He parked and climbed the concrete steps to the stoop. He pulled open the aluminum storm door and knocked on the wooden front door behind.

A middle-aged woman answered. "Yes?"

"Good morning, ma'am." Jackson held out his ID. "Detective

Konishi, Hamilton Police. I got your address from Dante. Is Chelle Morelli home?"

"Why?" The woman's eyes revealed concern.

"I have some questions for her that might help with an ongoing investigation."

"I don't think—"

"Mom... It's okay." A teenage girl with dark brown hair stepped out from behind the shadow of her mother.

Jackson put on his softest face. "Chelle?"

The girl nodded.

"Chelle..." Jackson recognized the vibe of repressed trauma immediately. "Do you know Dustin Stoaks?"

Jackson had barely finished his question when tears filled Chelle's eyes and ran down her cheeks. She had put on a brave face for as long as she could. She looked to her mother for reassurance, then nodded to Jackson.

Chelle's mother opened the door wider to let Jackson in.

– 104 –

DUSTIN SAT IN First Nations Studies class, marking time. The day was almost over and he couldn't wait to leave. He thought it was dumb to make this course mandatory for graduation. It was history. Move on already.

The announcement speaker in the corner of the room crackled to life, preceded with a single tone to garner attention.

"Would Dustin Stoaks please report to the office," the speaker broadcast. "Dustin Stoaks to the office, please."

Several of his classmates taunted him with "Ooos" and "Ahhs."

Someone in the corner said, "Someone's in *trou-ble*." The rest of the class snickered.

Dustin placed his notebook and supplies in his backpack. "It's the secretary," he said. "She can't keep her hands off me." More laughter, this time at his joke, as he pushed his way out the door and into the hallway.

He strolled toward the main foyer and veered left to the office. Another student that he didn't recognize held up his fist to bump. "Give 'em hell, Stoaks."

Dustin tapped knuckles. "Fuckin' A!" He approached the main office doors and entered the anteroom to see McCarthy leaning over the desk of the receptionist, looking over a sheet of paper.

Another man stood next to him with his back to Dustin, and he felt a vague rush of familiarity.

McCarthy spotted Dustin enter and straightened up. The other man turned and faced him.

"Dustin Stoaks," Jackson said. "Remember me? Detective Konishi from Ham—"

"I know who you are." Dustin let his eyes jump between the three adults standing before him.

"Do you know why I've called you here?"

Dustin shook his head and spoke with a scowl. "No fuckin' idea."

"Do you think Chelle Morelli could help jog your memory?"

Dustin clenched his jaw in anger.

Jackson stepped forward. "Dustin Stoaks, I'm placing you under arrest for the drugging and rape of Chelle Morelli."

The receptionist audibly gasped and McCarthy scolded her with a stern glance.

Jackson continued. "You have the right to retain and instruct counsel without delay. You also have the right to free and immediate legal advice from duty counsel by making—"

"Don't need that shit," Dustin said.

"By making free telephone calls to the following numbers. Do you understand?" Jackson handed Dustin a business card with toll-free phone numbers printed on it.

Dustin took the card, ripped it into four pieces and threw it on the floor.

Jackson narrowed his eyes at the teenager. "Do you *understand?*"

"Yeah, whatever," Dustin said.

"Do you wish to call a lawyer?"

Dustin laughed. "No."

"You also have the right to apply for legal assistance through the provincial legal aid program," Jackson said. "Do you understand?"

"You're joking right? I'll be out by the end of the day."

Jackson finished up. "I wish to give you the following warning: You need not say anything. You have nothing to hope from any promise or favor and nothing to fear from any threat whether or not you say anything. Anything you do or say may be used as evidence. Do you understand?"

"Yes," Dustin said.

"Place your hands behind your back," Jackson said as he unhooked his handcuffs.

Dustin did as instructed, and Jackson secured his wrists with the cuffs.

Jackson turned to McCarthy. "Thanks for your cooperation," he said before leading Dustin out of the office, through the foyer, and out of the school.

A few students who were roaming the halls or returning from bathroom breaks watched in awe, pulling out their phones to record video. The word would be all over the school before the end-of-day bell.

Jackson led Dustin to his Camry and opened the rear passenger door. Dustin stepped inside and sat.

"What about *my* car?"

"Don't worry about it," Jackson said. "It'll be impounded and secured later today." He backed out of the parking lot and began the trip back to the station.

Dustin sat in the back seat and brainstormed ways to make Chelle pay for ratting on him. "Whatever that bitch told you, it's all fuckin' lies."

Jackson shot an icy glare at Dustin through the rear view mirror. "It's not just what Miss Morelli told us. It's what we *found.*"

They couldn't have found anything. He was too smart for the police and his hiding places were genius. "You're bluffin'. You haven't found anythin'."

Jackson ignored him and kept his eyes on the road. Dustin's

anger melted into panic and, for the first time in his young life, doubt crept into his mind.

$$- 105 -$$

AN HOUR BEFORE DUSTIN'S ARREST, Jackson arrived at his Rockwood West mansion with three extra officers, one seated beside him, and two in an additional Hamilton Police cruiser. He led the charge up the steps to the front door and rang the doorbell.

He expected the intercom to chirp on. Instead, a housekeeper pulled open the giant door. She looked at Jackson and his entourage, alarm in her eyes.

"Yes? Can I help you?" the housekeeper said.

Jackson revealed the badge clipped to his belt. "Hello, ma'am. Is Mr. or Mrs. Stoaks available?"

"I'm afraid not. They're away on business." The housekeeper eyed the other officers. One rocked on her heels as if in anticipation. "Is this about Dustin?"

"Why would you ask that?" Jackson peered past the housekeeper and into the grand room behind her. He could see the staircase leading to the second floor.

"I, uh..." Flustered, the housekeeper searched for the right words. "Dustin's the only other person who lives here."

Jackson pulled a slip of paper, folded in thirds, from his inside jacket pocket. "We have a warrant to search the premises." He handed the paper to the housekeeper. "What's your name, ma'am?"

"Greta."

"We won't be long, Greta." Jackson stepped inside the house. The other officers followed.

Greta pulled out a phone and began dialing.

Jackson headed up the stairs. "Greta, make sure Mr. and Mrs. Stoaks know that we produced a search warrant." He pushed open a few doors until he found Dustin's room. "You know what we're looking for," he said to the others. Everyone pulled on rubber gloves and began combing through Dustin's room.

Within minutes, Jackson and his team uncovered the hidden camera on Dustin's desk and the memory cards stashed under a false bottom in one of his bed's drawers.

"What have we here?" Jackson held up two vials with clear liquid in them, one labeled GHB and the other Rohypnol. He placed them each into evidence bags.

Once finished with the bedroom, the search moved to the games room. The mysterious email Jackson had received had not mentioned the games room, so the team searched for anything incriminating.

Jackson moved to the bar to search behind the counter, fridge, garbage cans, and floor level cupboards. There was nothing worth noting. It looked like the housekeeper did a good job of keeping things tidy.

But the fridge stood out, not because it had a window in the door, but because Dustin had divided the canned beverages inside into two distinct groups. Jackson opened the refrigerator door for a closer look. Each group had approximately the same numbers and brands of drinks.

His gut told him that something was wrong, and experience had taught him to never ignore his gut. He collected the canned drinks and bagged them, making sure to keep each group separate.

An hour later, the search team arrived back at the Hamilton

Police Investigative Services building. Jackson grabbed his laptop from his office and gathered in the meeting room down the hall. His other cases could wait. He pulled out a memory card from an evidence bag and slid it into the port on his laptop. The contents of the card popped up on the screen.

One file. A video.

Jackson clicked on it and saw Dustin's room as seen from the hidden camera. He scrubbed forward and witnessed Dustin carry a teenage girl in a white T-shirt and blue skirt into his room and place her on his bed. The girl was visibly drugged and her blond hair spilled over the pillow.

That's not Chelle Morelli.

He scrubbed forward further. Dustin undressed and assaulted the young woman.

"Gotcha, you little fucker." He couldn't bear to watch any more but scrubbed the video timeline forward to the end to be thorough. What Jackson saw unfold on the screen next left him both surprised and outraged. He popped the memory card out and placed it back in the evidence bag with the others.

"Heads are going to roll," he said to himself.

– 106 –

As expected, word of Dustin's arrest spread through the school like wildfire. The incessant buzzing, chirping, and dinging dominated the last several minutes of every class in the school. Some students in classrooms that overlooked the parking lot were lucky enough to witness Dustin's "perp walk." Their videos joined dozens of others on Instagram competing for likes and shares.

Richard couldn't concentrate on Physics at a time like this. He texted Dustin, "Where R U? What's going on?" There was no reply to any of his texts even after repeated attempts.

The hallways buzzed with groups of students gossiping about what had happened to Dustin. There was no need to eavesdrop. All the conversations were generally the same.

By the time Richard had collected his belongings and stepped out of the front entrance of the school, he saw a tow truck hauling Dustin's Escalade from the student parking lot. The back window had clear plastic taped over it and red evidence tape secured the doors.

Richard checked his phone. Still no text replies from Dustin. Not knowing what was going on continued to eat away at his peace of mind and he felt a desperate need to get home. It had become his last remaining safe place.

He quickened his pace and tried to busy his mind with other thoughts. It didn't matter what it was, as long as it distracted him. Instagram was a bust. People posting reels about Dustin's arrest filled his feed. He switched to thinking about video games and how he could become a millionaire by creating a best selling mobile game.

The pinging alerts from Instagram kept pulling him back to his feed. Richard gave it a second try, thinking that he might be able to figure out what happened from the posts, reels, and comments that kept showing up. But not surprisingly it was all speculation and rumour. He was about to turn off his phone when a notification from "dark.angela2005" popped up on his screen.

He tapped it. One of the dozens of reels posted of Dustin's perp walk loaded. He had already seen this one. The highlighted comment popped up. "Dustin Stoaks drugs and rapes girls," it read.

Richard's blood ran cold and his stomach burned, like he had swallowed a red hot ingot. A group of students glued to their phones passed by and bumped into him, causing him to nearly drop his phone.

"Bruh!" said one of the students. "Watch where you're going!"

A moment passed before Richard realized that he had been standing in the middle of the sidewalk. He had no idea how long he had been standing there blocking the way. He powered down his phone and doubled his effort to get home. At this point even his father would be a welcome sight.

Twenty minutes later, Richard turned up Meridale Lane. His house was a few hundred steps away.

He hustled up his driveway and placed his hand on the front door handle.

Locked.

"Jesus, Dad," Richard said under his breath. Peter had an annoying habit of locking the front door during school days. Richard had long suspected his dad did it to give himself a few extra seconds to "clean up." Most days he was okay with that but today Richard just wanted to get inside without any effort.

He dropped his backpack and dug out his keys. As he selected the front door key he heard a vehicle approach. Richard glanced over his shoulder and saw a car pull into the driveway, one that he hadn't seen before. The glare on the windshield obscured the identity of the driver until the door swung open and a man stepped out.

Richard had seen this man twice, the first time at school soon after Newton had been drugged, and the second time on Dustin's security camera. He was a cop.

The man closed his car door. "Richard? Remember me? Detective Jackson Konishi from Hamilton Police."

Richard nodded as his arms went slack.

"Mind if I ask you a few questions?"

Richard shrugged. "I guess."

The dead bolt slid back into the door and Peter stepped out, wrapped in his threadbare housecoat. "Hey, son. What's going on?" He looked at Jackson and pointed at him. "I know you. You're that cop."

Jackson approached both. "Detective Konishi."

Peter glanced at Richard and saw something in his son that raised alarm bells. "What are you—"

"I have questions for your son." Jackson tried to lock gaze with Richard, but the teenager avoided his attempts. "Richard, do you know Dustin Stoaks?"

Richard nodded.

"You'll have to speak up, please."

"Yes," Richard said. "I know Dustin. But who doesn't?"

"I understand he's a pretty popular guy." Jackson shifted his weight on his feet. "What about Elise Coleman?"

Richard looked up at Jackson like the words he was saying were crazy. "Of course I know Elise. That's... Newton's sister."

"That's right," Jackson said. "And you were friends with

Newton for a while. Years. So you must know Haislee Kirkland, since she's Elise's best friend. Apparently, they're inseparable."

Richard hesitated, then, "Yeah, I know Hazy."

"Hazy?" Jackson raised a brow.

"She... likes to be called Hazy."

Jackson nodded, then pulled out his notebook and jotted a few words down. "Richard, have you had sex with Haislee Kirkland?"

"Hey, now wait just a goddamned second," Peter said. "That sounds personal. You don't have to answer that, son."

Jackson's eyes turned to stone. "You're right. Richard Baum, I'm placing you under arrest for the drugging and rape of Haislee Kirkland."

"Jesus Christ." Anger and surprise rose in Peter's voice. "That's some bull—"

Jackson slapped a warrant on Peter's chest. Peter unfolded it, his eyes flitting over the document.

"This has got to be a mistake," Peter said.

Jackson shook his head. "No. I'm afraid not."

"Rich?" Peter turned to his son to see him hanging his head down, tears streaming down his face. "Richard?" Peter had his answer in his son's silence.

As Jackson handcuffed Richard's wrists behind his back, he read Richard his rights, then led the teenager to the back of his Camry.

From inside the car, Richard watched his father stand motionless on the front landing, his mouth agape with horror and confusion.

Jackson reversed out of the driveway and began the thirty-minute trip back to the station. Richard didn't look back or say a word the entire way there. Instead, his head filled with panic and worries for which he had no answer, except for his guilt.

$$- \; 107 \; -$$

The wheels of justice typically move slowly but the case of the "Rockwood Rapists," a moniker bestowed by the media, had been expedited due to its sensitive nature.

It came out in the trial that Richard's involvement with Dustin's assaults began the summer before Grade 12, while Dustin had begun his dark activities two years earlier. The video evidence indicated that some of the assaults took place at resorts out of the country. International trials were pending. In total, Dustin had drugged and raped 29 girls his age or younger according to the video evidence. Richard actively participated with Dustin in eight of the assaults, including Haislee's.

Both Dustin and Richard were eighteen years of age for the most recent assaults and pled guilty in hopes of a reduced sentence. The compelling and detailed video recordings, plus the testimony of Haislee and Chelle, made sure they had no other choice. Richard had no knowledge that Dustin had recorded the assaults, but that didn't make him any less culpable. Dustin's methods were never released to the public.

In the time between Dustin's and Richard's arrest and graduation from Diamond Bay, Newton worked hard to get back into the same physical shape he had been in before his coma. His first week back, Newton used a wheelchair to get around. Taking the elevator to his Chemistry class helped reduce the inconvenience of immobility. He switched to crutches for his second week and found the transition encouraging. Propelling himself in his wheelchair had helped strengthen his arms, which in turn allowed him to place more focus on his legs. According to Newton, the crutches were his "backup."

He refused rides to and from school, insisting that he walk and use that time to increase his stamina. Being able to dance unaided at his graduation celebration was his ultimate goal. Soon a cane replaced the crutches, then no additional walking aids at all.

Running was still a bit of a problem. Newton found he couldn't sprint. His legs would get out of sync and cause him to stop. But he kept working at it a bit at a time.

Returning home from school on the first Wednesday in June, Teigan met Newton at the front door and hugged him, her eyes bright and grateful. Newton had noticed the change in his mother immediately since returning home from the hospital. She was more affectionate and attentive than before. In fact, his whole family had shifted their behaviours toward him. It was a little smothering at times, but it was better than the alternative.

Newton looked a question at her. Teigan shook her head. "No word yet, but I thought we'd celebrate tonight. It's been two months. How about pizza?"

Newton grinned. "I'm in." He cocked his head to voices from upstairs.

"Haislee's over," Teigan said. "I'm betting she'll probably stay for dinner."

"Cool. I'm going to lie down for a bit." Newton raided the pantry for a bag of Hawkins Cheezies and headed upstairs to his room. He sprawled across his bed and thought about how much had changed in the past year as he wolfed down his favourite cheddar-flavoured corn snacks. Despite what had happened, he still missed Richard at times and the friendship they once had. Dustin on the other hand, Newton felt no empathy for.

He imagined the jail cell Dustin had spent the last two months in. Was it difficult to sleep on those thin mattresses? Was it cold? Was there no window in his cell? Newton hoped all of that was true.

He wanted to reach in through the bars of the cell, get Dustin in a choke hold, and find out how he had drugged him. In his heart Newton knew it had been Dustin who was responsible. The same date rape drugs had been found in Dustin's bedroom, yet he had no idea how Dustin had pulled it off.

Newton could hear himself yelling at him as he tightened his grip on Dustin's neck. "How did you do it, you bastard! Tell me! Tell me or I'll kill you!"

Dustin never spoke and Newton always let him go just before his lights went out. Even in his mind, Newton couldn't follow through with threats like this. Perhaps empathy or mercy was the essential difference between him and a psychopathic narcissist like Dustin.

Newton blinked and realized a couple of hours had passed. Sometimes his imagination mixed with dreams. He preferred the scenarios involving girls, because this last episode left much to be desired.

The smell of warm pizza floated up from downstairs and instantly made his stomach rumble. He hopped off the bed and made his way down to the kitchen, leaving behind an empty Hawkins Cheezies bag and a scattering of orange crumbs.

Mattix, Teigan, Elise and Haislee sat around the kitchen table, all eating slices of pizza. Newton waved hello as he opened the oven and pulled out a pizza box.

"Finally," Teigan said. "Was just about to go rouse you."

Mattix twisted in his chair to get a look at Newton. "No cane at all this week. How's it been?"

Teigan placed her hand on Mattix's arm and gave a subtle shake of her head. Mattix shrugged.

"It's been okay." Newton pulled three slices of deluxe from the Boston Pizza box and carried them to the last vacant chair at the table, which just happened to be next to Haislee. Newton glanced at Elise and she grinned and winked back at him. The placement of chairs had not been accidental.

He dug into his pizza, relishing every bite. Halfway through his first piece, Newton looked up and saw that everyone was looking at him.

"What?" he said.

Teigan reached over and gave his hand a quick squeeze. "It's just good to have you back."

"Thanks," Newton said through a full mouth. He chewed and swallowed. "I just want everything to get back to normal."

Elise's phone chimed. Then a second later, Haislee's. Both girls dug out their phones and looked at the displays.

"Holy shit." Elise's eyes widened.

"Lise. Language," Teigan chided.

"No, seriously." Elise presented her phone to Teigan. "Holy shit."

Newton perked up. "What is it?"

Haislee tilted her phone toward Newton. On the screen was an Instagram post from the *Hamilton Spectator*. The video showed Dustin and Richard, each handcuffed and led to waiting police cars.

The text below read, "After less than four hours deliberation, Dustin Stoaks and Richard Baum found guilty on all counts. Both could face twenty-five years in prison."

"Twenty-five years?" Newton looked at his parents.

Haislee's eyes darkened. "Those fucking *assholes* deserved life." She glanced at Teigan. "Sorry, Mrs. Coleman."

Teigan dismissed it. Haislee had every right to speak her mind.

"I don't know why it took four hours of deliberation," Mattix said. "Seemed like the evidence spoke for itself."

The doorbell rang. Teigan glanced at Mattix, then everyone else. "Is anyone expecting anyone?"

"Just those sex toys I bought online," Elise said without taking her eyes off her phone. Haislee covered her mouth and giggled.

Teigan leaned in and kissed the top of Elise's head. "Cool. Looking forward to seeing which one is your favourite."

"Mom!" Elise scrunched her nose up. "*Gross.*"

Teigan left to answer the door.

Newton swallowed a bite of pizza. "Who do you think it is?"

"Probably some reporter," Elise said.

Mattix topped up his wine glass. "Good guess. Wouldn't be surprised."

"They've been camping out on our street." Elise continued to doomscroll. "Pretty obvious if you ask me."

Mattix straightened up in his chair. "Really? I had no idea that—"

"We have a visitor." Teigan returned to the kitchen. Jackson followed her. "Everyone know Detective Konishi?"

"Yeah," Elise said. "He's the one that did jack to find out what happened to Newt."

"Lise!" Teigan's eyes flared at her daughter. "That's enough."

"Well, it's true."

"Yeah." Jackson's expression indicated contrition. "It kind of *is* true." He set his eyes on Newton. "I should have given your case more attention, and for that I'm sorry."

Newton looked at him. "Overworked and underpaid?"

"Something like that," Jackson said. "No excuse, but..."

Silence blanketed the kitchen, and all eyes were focused squarely on Jackson. If he hadn't felt the scrutiny of the Coleman family yet, he surely did now.

Elise crossed her arms against her chest. "Why are you *here*?"

Teigan moved to respond when Jackson waved her off. "It's

okay. It's a fair question. I'm here to share a theory and maybe some answers. Due to the publication ban on the details surrounding the Rockwood... case, I know some things that the public doesn't. These things may help you understand what might have happened to you. But it's confidential and circumstantial. If it appears in the wild, I'll know someone here leaked it. Can I trust you all?"

Teigan was first to respond. "Absolutely. A hundred percent. Right, everyone?"

Mattix nodded, followed by Newton and Haislee.

"Lise?" Teigan narrowed her eyes at her daughter.

"The jury knows," Elise said. "They could talk."

Jackson nodded. "You're right. So, I guess what I'm asking is that no one here say anything to anyone outside this house."

Elise considered for a moment. "Okay."

Teigan gave Jackson her full attention.

"I'll assume you've all been following the Rockwood R—" Jackson stopped himself short of saying the word "rapists" in consideration of Haislee, who had provided testimony. "The Rockwood case. As you know, Dustin had been using date rape drugs to subdue his victims. But the videos we collected and used as evidence against the boys never showed *how* Dustin drugged the girls. I wanted to know how."

Newton sat very still. "We all do. It's probably how he got me."

Jackson paused to look at them. "I think I've got something, but it's just a theory. We'd need a confession from Dustin to confirm it, and that won't happen." He took a breath. "When we were searching his games room, I looked in his bar fridge. There were two distinct rows of assorted drinks without any discernible reason why. I took them as evidence and on a whim, I had the cans tested for drugs. They came back positive for GHB and Rohypnol, but only the cans on one side of the fridge. It appears that Dustin pre-dosed the cans—"

"The tops," Newton said. "He put roofies on the tops, and when you opened the can and took your first sip... game over."

Jackson nodded. "Roofies are colourless, odorless, and tasteless. A few concentrated drops on the top near the opening would look like water. Got any aspirations for crime investigation, Newton?"

Newton managed a grin. "No. Not really."

"Fair enough," Jackson said. "Anyway, that's the current explanation. The prosecution used the theory, but it was circumstantial. Thankfully the videos alone were enough to convict."

Haislee fumed. "So when that *asshole* handed me a Coke, and I opened it myself, thinking I was safe, thinking that this guy wasn't so bad..."

"I'm so sorry, Haislee," Jackson said.

"They should have gotten *life*." Haislee made fists on the table. "What they did will affect *me* for the rest of *mine*."

Elise piped up. "And what *good* person just happens to have *roofies* on the top of pop cans in their *own fridge*? What other explanation is there other than that person was going to rape someone?"

Jackson sighed. "I agree."

"I drank one beer at that party," Newton said. "*One*. Not even a whole one. Just a few sips. And they made sure it was the *special* one."

"Yeah, that's likely. In your case, Newton, Dustin put a little too much on the can," Jackson said. "Maybe he forgot he had dosed the can already and dosed it again."

"Or maybe he really did want me to die—"

"Okay, stop." Teigan stood and paced into the kitchen. "I think I've heard enough."

"They're sick fucks." Mattix caught Teigan's warning glance and shrugged. "They are."

Teigan pulled a pizza box out of the oven and offered Jackson a slice.

"Thank you, but no." Jackson checked the clock on the stove. "Crap. I got to go. My wife's due at any moment." He waved goodbye.

"I'll see you out," Teigan said and followed him to the front door.

Mattix regarded the three teenagers. "One more thing to worry about, eh? Jesus. You sure have to have your wits about you these days."

"It's even worse for girls," Elise said.

A moment of silence hung in the room. "I'm glad they're going to prison," Newton said. He felt Haislee's hand give his knee a supportive squeeze and oddly he had no issues with the gesture. In fact, he found he liked it.

As he ate his pizza, he felt like his world was right again. Newton had survived a cowardly attack by bullies, and he finally knew *how* they had done it. His puzzle was almost complete. The only missing piece was Juniper.

– 108 –

TEIGAN WALKED JACKSON to the front door where he kneeled and slipped on his shoes. "Boy or girl?"

Jackson quickly tied his laces. "A girl, God help us."

Teigan sighed. "With this terrible rape trial, that hits hard."

Jackson stood. "Yeah, but still, we're super excited."

"Good."

"Plus who messes with a police detective's daughter?"

Teigan raised a brow at him. "Psycho assholes with wealthy parents?"

"Good point."

Teigan opened the door and walked Jackson to his Camry in the driveway.

"Thanks again for going out of your way," she said.

"It was the least I could do considering how I dropped the ball with Newton's case."

Teigan smiled and nodded. "By the way, I think your theory is sound. The important thing is the two are behind bars."

"And they're going to remain there for a long time. That video evidence was irrefutable." Jackson pulled open the driver side door and paused. "Can I ask you a question?"

Teigan leaned against the porch support. "Of course."

"Do you have any idea who 'Silent Voice' is?"

Teigan thought for a moment, then shook her head. "No. Why?"

Jackson stepped closer and lowered his voice. "You didn't hear this from me, and if it gets out I'll deny it, but I got an email back before this whole rape case started. It described everything we needed to look for in Dustin's house. Without it, the case would have fallen apart."

"Why are you asking me?"

"I know you had your own unofficial investigation going," Jackson said. "Thought you might've heard something."

"Nope. But I'm glad they talked to you."

Jackson returned to the open driver's side door. "One more thing... the night before Dustin's arrest, his SUV was vandalized, the back window smashed out."

Teigan shrugged. "He's got lots of enemies. Did you catch them?"

"No," Jackson said. "We couldn't get an ID from the security video." He smirked and narrowed his eyes at her. "They lucked out, if you ask me."

"Maybe it was your friendly neighbourhood Spider-Man." Teigan struggled to contain a nervous laugh building in the back of her throat.

Jackson chuckled and waved her off. He slid into the driver's seat, reached across the console, and rolled down the passenger window. "Goodbye, Teigan. I hope we meet again under better circumstances."

Teigan nodded and waved back. "Say hello to your wife and daughter for me."

"Will do." Jackson started the Camry's engine and reversed onto the street.

Teigan remained motionless as she watched him drive down the street and out of sight.

Silent Voice.

Teigan wondered if that would be the last lie she'd tell a police officer. It looked as if he had bought it. The details in the email were so specific, it couldn't have possibly been from someone who was never there. And Teigan was never in Dustin's room... not *physically.*

She didn't give her ponderings a second thought. Instead, she pictured Dustin spending all his time in prison trying to figure out how the police knew *exactly* where to look. And as Teigan strolled back inside with the knowledge that her family was safe and whole again, a satisfied smile formed on her face.

$$- 109 -$$

As the limousine pulled up in front of Juniper's house, Newton realized that in all the time he had known her, he had never visited her home.

And the first time dressed in a tux. Hard to top that.

Newton stepped out of the sleek black sedan dressed to match, complete with tails and coordinated purple bow tie and cummerbund. He walked to Juniper's front door using a new black cane to help prevent any stumbles, although he knew that she wouldn't care. His ego, on the other hand, was still a bit fragile. He held a wrist corsage made from a purple rose in his other hand.

He took a steadying breath with the knowledge that he might not have seen this day come to pass. Newton had been lucky, and he hoped that luck would continue tonight. He reached out and rang the doorbell. The chimes echoing within the house set his viscera vibrating with nervous energy.

A tall woman with brunette hair opened the door and Newton could see the resemblance immediately. "Newton Coleman! It's great to finally meet you. And a limo! *Classy.*" The woman extended her hand. "I'm Cat." She ushered him inside.

"June! Newton's here!" Cat called upstairs, then leaned closer to Newton and lowered her voice. "She's a little nervous."

"So am I, to be honest." Newton fiddled with the corsage box until the vision of Juniper on the second floor landing distracted him. Cat took a step back to watch.

This had been the moment Newton had been waiting for ever since his final year had begun. And he had almost missed it.

Juniper's hair, now brunette with purple highlights, was tied behind her head with a slender purple ribbon. Her dress reminded Newton of the one she'd worn at the Winter Formal. This time the dress was strapless and hugged her body more. Instead of tiny diamonds covering the fabric, they began at the hemline and faded away halfway up to her waist. She descended carefully down the stairs in sparkly purple shoes that Newton compared to Dorothy's ruby slippers from *The Wizard of Oz*.

"Wow." Newton blinked at her. "You look amazing… beautiful. Amazingly beautiful. Beautifully amazing… uh… all of the above." He felt the heat of embarrassment creep up his neck but owned it with a smile.

"Thank you, Newton." Juniper met him in front of the stairs. "You look very handsome too."

Newton held up the corsage. "I know purple's your colour so…" He swallowed nervously. "It should go on your wrist, but you don't have to wear it if you don't want to."

Juniper held out her left wrist. "Please."

Newton had studied videos on YouTube on how to attach a wrist corsage and tied it to Juniper's wrist like a pro.

"Not too tight?"

Juniper ran a finger around the ribbon holding the corsage to her wrist. "No. It's perfect." She admired the floral arrangement, then glanced at her mom. Cat held a white boutonnière by her side.

"I have something for you." Juniper took the boutonniere from Cat and lifted it out of its clear plastic container. "White goes with everything." She stepped close to Newton and pinned the flowers to his lapel. He could smell the warm sweetness of her skin.

"Picture time!" Cat pulled out her phone.

"Mom!"

"Sorry, but this is non-negotiable." Cat held up her phone and framed Newton and Juniper on her display. "Alright. Say *safe sex!*"

Newton grinned immediately.

"Aww." Cat held up her phone. "You two make the *cutest* couple."

"Okay, we're going, Mom." Juniper grabbed a small black clutch with a string strap hanging on the coat rack near the door. It was barely large enough to hold her phone. "Bye."

Cat followed the two teenagers to the door. "Have fun. I'm only a call or text away of you need anything."

"I know, Mom. Thanks." Juniper focused on the limousine. "Is *that* for us?"

"It's all ours," Newton said. "For as long as we need it tonight."

Juniper's eyes widened as Newton led her to the passenger side of the limousine, using the cane only when he needed to.

"Me and my parents split the cost."

"Wow, Newton," Juniper said. "This is... so cool."

"I wanted a memorable ending to an... interesting year." Newton pulled open the door and helped Juniper inside, then took a seat beside her. "Do you want to go straight to the school or drive for a bit?"

"Let's be fashionably late," Juniper said.

Newton instructed the driver to take them on a drive that would get them to the event centre twenty minutes late. As soon as the driver commenced his route, Newton raised the privacy panel.

"Don't worry," he said. "I'm not going to make a move on you. I know we're going as friends. I just wanted privacy."

"Thanks."

An awkward silence descended over them.

"I miss our talks... and hanging out," Newton finally said. "Like we did last summer."

"Me, too." Juniper touched the ribbon securing her corsage. "I'm sorry."

"Sorry? What do you mean?"

"Like, for ghosting you," Juniper said. "Then your coma happened and..."

"But you wrote me those letters." Newton narrowed his eyes at her. "You *did* write me those letters, right?"

"Yeah, that was me. But I'm still a bit mixed up," Juniper said. "The trial brought back a lot of bad memories."

"The... Rockwood trial?"

Juniper nodded.

Newton studied her face. "Did he...?"

Juniper fought back tears and nodded again.

"Oh, Jesus. I'm so sorry." Newton held open his arms, offering a hug. "As friends, if you want it."

Juniper nodded once more and Newton took her in his arms and held her as long as she felt comfortable. She pulled away and faced him. "You're such a good guy. I wish I had met you sooner... I still have so much shit to work through."

"It's okay." Newton straightened up and handed her a tissue from the limousine's central console. "Maybe our paths will cross again in the future... in a different way."

"Yeah," Juniper said, but Newton knew from the faraway look in her eyes that it probably wouldn't happen any time soon, if at all.

Another casualty of Dustin Stoaks.

"Well, we're here for a good time," Newton said.

"Not a long time." Juniper blotted her eyes and smiled at him.

Newton's eyes lit up with surprise. "You know Trooper?"

"Of course," Juniper said. "I may be a hermit, but I don't live under a rock."

Newton pulled out his phone and cued up the song to play through the limousine's wireless speakers. The two of them sang to the song as the side streets of Cherry Mills passed by their windows.

One song led to another and soon the limousine pulled up in front of Club Montview, a posh event centre and golf club that straddled Cherry Mills and Rockwood West. Newton opened the door, stepped out, his cane in one hand, and offered his free hand to Juniper. Muted rock music echoed from within the main building.

"Let's go have a blast," Newton said.

"You're on." Juniper took his hand and the two of them headed inside the club, as friends, to dance the night away.

– 110 –

Teigan and Mattix stood on the front porch, each with a glass of wine in their hands. They had just seen Newton off to his graduation dinner and dance in his rented black limousine. They had taken many photos and videos, probably too many. Newton's excitement at going was clear. He took the parental paparazzi all in stride and did not complain once. Teigan and Mattix were eternally grateful that this moment hadn't been stolen from them.

Five minutes later, Elise burst out the front door, not even slowing for a kiss goodbye. The contrast between brother and sister was eye-opening sometimes. She carried a backpack on her shoulder.

"Going to Hazy's," she yelled back from the driveway. "Back late."

"No later than midnight, young lady," Teigan called back.

Mattix chuckled. "She hates it when you call her 'young lady.' "

Teigan grinned and sipped her wine. "I know."

"You think she'll be home at midnight?"

"Probably not," Teigan said. "But it'll be close."

"Asserting her growing independence?"

"Something like that."

They clinked glasses.

"It's not often we get the house to ourselves," Mattix said. "But I've noticed it's happening more often."

"It's the inevitable passage of time. Families change." Teigan swirled the wine in her glass.

Mattix smirked at her. "Deep. Do you charge by the hour?"

"Don't tempt me." Teigan looked up at the man she had married twenty-one years ago and threw caution to the wind. "Hey, can I run something by you?"

"Of course."

"What would you say if I became a private investigator?"

Mattix looked at her with surprise. "What... like Magnum?"

"Yeah."

"Would you carry a gun?"

"No," Teigan said. "Uh, wait. Maybe?" Noticing Mattix's scrutiny she defaulted to her original answer. "On second thought, no."

"You sure?"

"Yeah, I don't like guns."

"Would you sell GadgetGot?"

"God no," Teigan said. "I'd run it in the background. It practically runs itself anyway." She watched Mattix roll the idea around in his head as he sipped his wine.

"Where'd this idea come from?"

"Oh, you know, I did a lot of digging for Newton, to find out the truth about what happened," Teigan said. "And even though I ultimately failed, I think I'd be good at it."

Mattix looked at her and slowly nodded his head.

"What?"

"If there's one thing I've learned about you, Tee, in the time I've known you, it's that you can do anything you set your mind to," Mattix said. "But there's going to be more secrets, isn't there?" His eyes carried a more serious tone now.

Teigan shrugged. "Yeah. Probably. Goes with the territory. But I promise to tell you everything I can."

"You've put a lot of thought into this, I see."

More than you'll ever know, my husband.

"Look, Tee, I just want you safe."

"Me, too." She locked her gaze with his. "Is that a yes?"

"Of course," Mattix said. "You'll always have my complete support. A hundred percent."

Teigan kissed him then hugged him tight. "Hey, you know, we've got the house to ourselves tonight."

"Yeah, I heard. Got any ideas?"

"I got a few."

Mattix flashed his brows. "I know something that requires investigation."

"Do tell."

They finished their wine and Mattix led Teigan into the house, closing the door behind them.

September 2, 2024 - March 12, 2025
Victoria, BC

Afterword

Like it? Rate it. Share it.

If you enjoyed *Every Move They Make*, please rate it and spread the word. With your rating, you take part in this book's success. If you're interested in learning more about my books or connecting with me on various social platforms, please go to LeeGabel.com/links or visit his bookshop at Bookshop.LeeGabel.com.

Note from the author

My eleventh novel represents a shift away from my usual genres. I've been reading more mystery stories lately. I'm not sure if that aligns with growing older, but I've found that mysteries engage my brain more. So, it was inevitable that I try my hand at writing one. If you have been entertained, I have done my job. I do have plans to write more Cherry Mills mysteries. Look for the next book in 2026.

To be honest, the writing process wasn't as different as I thought it would be. Most of the work took place during the outlining stage, making sure secrets, reveals, and twists were properly spaced and made sense.

While still a mystery at its heart, this story has unconventional elements. Since you've finished the book, I'm sure you know what

I'm talking about. I like taking a genre and introducing an unexpected aspect that pushes a story in a different direction.

This marks the first time one of my stories has been based in Canada. In light of everything that has transpired in my country over the last several months, I am glad for that. I used my own experiences as both a parent and a high school student to model my central characters. My high school days were not... optimal. There was lots to draw from. I hope you, the reader, enjoyed the ride.

Many thanks go to my wife and editor Sheila. I couldn't do this without her, nor would I want to. To my son, thank you for your courage and for being you. And as always, to my family and friends who supported my decision to quit my job to write full time back in 2016, you were right. I am *your* number one fan now.

About the author

Since 1992, Lee has worked within the visual and dramatic arts landscape as a graphic designer, illustrator, visual effects artist, animator, screenwriter, and author. He's contributed to an Emmy award and once walked 63.5 kilometers in 13 hours. Traditionally trained as a screenwriter, Lee has moved to writing books in order to share his stories.

Lee has spent most of his life living on an island in the Pacific Northwest and he writes in multiple genres that interest him. Why? In his own words: "Writing is magic. I'll never understand how it works the way it does, but I do know if I put energy into writing, it rewards me in strange and wonderful ways. Even if I know where I'm going in a story, often I'll end up being pulled in directions by my characters that I least expect. What ends up on the page never ceases to surprise me, and that's super cool. Writing continues to be one of the most difficult and most rewarding aspects of my life."

Find Lee on the Internet:

Want to join Lee's Reader Group or find out more about Lee and the books he writes? Please go to:

LeeGabel.com/links or visit his bookshop at:

Bookshop.LeeGabel.com

Note from the author: If you liked this book, may I ask three things? **First,** *please rate this book. I appreciate your opinion and what I focus on next depends on you, the reader.* **Second,** *please consider joining my reader group at LeeGabel.com/join. Once a month I share little details of my life (the fun stuff, that is) and keep you informed of future books. Plus, I'll give you a* **15% discount** *on all my ebooks.* **And third,** *if you liked this book, please recommend it to your friends. You can also ask your local library to order it for you if they don't have it yet. My sincere thanks.*

One more thing: *This book features music references. For a playlist of all music, please go to: LeeGabel.com/music*

LEE'S BOOKS

CHERRY MILLS MYSTERIES
Every Move They Make

DREAMWAKER SAGA
Lucid Bodies
Lucid Revenge
Lucid Fate

DETEST-A-PEST SERIES
Vermin 2.0
Arachnid 2.0
Molerat 2.0
Tentacle 2.0

STANDALONE
David's Summer
Snipped
Tied

Dreamwakers are like fire... they burn when they're hot. And some are a living nightmare.

By accident, sixteen-year-old Wynter discovers her power to summon dreamwakers — people born from dreams that exist in physical form. Her friends have trouble believing her power exists, until she makes herself a boyfriend.

But dreamwakers come with rules and free will... and everyone knows teenagers and rules don't mix. Before Wynter can figure them out, her new boyfriend goes rogue and hooks up with Jezebel, the town psychopath.

Every day Wynter and her dreamwaker remain apart chips away more of her life force. Her friends help her wage a battle of brains versus brawn... but Jezebel has the luck of the devil on her side.

Navigating between dreams and reality is harder than it looks, and the fight may leave Wynter a prisoner of her own mind.

Lucid Bodies, Dreamwaker Saga #1 (410 pages)

Controlling a rogue dreamwaker holds an addictive power. But those adrift in a mind-altering limbo can still unleash payback... with a little help from their friends.

"Find me..."

Cash can't ignore Wynter's last words before her mind trapped her between dreams and reality. He would do anything for Wynter but finding her means finding her dreamwaker boyfriend. Cash must balance jealousy and loyalty or risk fracturing a lifelong friendship.

Jezebel continues her reign of terror, with Wynter's dreamwaker boyfriend enslaved at her side. After realizing his error, the dreamwaker makes amends with Cash and Wynter's friends, and forms a plan to reunite with Wynter.

In retaliation, Jezebel targets Wynter's family with an act of extreme revenge that devastates the neighborhood.

While the town sheriff builds his case against Jezebel, Cash picks up the pieces left by Jezebel's fury and sets into motion the plan to find Wynter and reunite her with her dreamwaker. But no plan is perfect, especially when Jezebel doesn't get what she wants.

Lucid Revenge, Dreamwaker Saga #2 (320 pages)

Everyone makes mistakes, even psychopaths. This time, the mistake is murder, and the evidence may lie in plain sight.

Free from her mental prison but with her sanity crumbling, Wynter and her friends take advantage of Jezebel's injuries and double their efforts to reunite her with her dreamwaker boyfriend.

Despite her vulnerabilities, Jezebel discovers that she can wield her dreamwaker power from beyond her hospital bed. But she forgets to acknowledge a dreamwaker's free will.

When a mysterious murder rocks the town, the sheriff discovers the murder weapon holds the answers he's looking for, until it disappears in front of his eyes. Running their own investigation, Wynter's friends unlock Jezebel's secret and use it against her, gaining a much needed advantage.

Together once again, Wynter, her dreamwaker boyfriend, her friends, and the sheriff formulate one last plan to connect Jezebel to her crimes, a plan perfect in its simplicity.

But evading consequences is Jezebel's specialty... and she has no intention of peaceful surrender.

Lucid Fate, Dreamwaker Saga #3 (410 pages)

An infestation of supersized vermin with a hunger for raw meat? CHECK.

An estranged son staying for the summer? CHECK.
An intense fear of rats? DOUBLE-CHECK.

Sam Shaw's life has flipped upside down. Pets and tenants in his Bronx brownstone begin to disappear. Left behind is a wake of carnage.

All evidence points to a hybrid colony of vicious white-tailed rats that has moved into the basement – genetically superior with intelligence to match.

When his ex-wife dumps his son Bradley on his doorstep, Sam must switch into protection mode, if his son will let him.

Faced with impossible odds, Sam hires Bertha O'Connor from Detest-A-Pest Exterminators Inc. She runs the only outfit brave enough – or crazy enough – to take the job.

With help from the Detest-A-Pest crew, Sam must face his fears or the white-tailed mutants will eat him alive. Because this horde of super-rats are smarter than anyone had bargained for...

Detest-A-Pest #1 (304 pages)

Spiders. Over 35,000 species. Every person on Earth eaten in one year. Now there's one more... a ravenous eight-legged hybrid thousands of years in the making and bigger than a dozen burritos.

After a summer of exterminator training in New York, Bradley returns home ready to face his senior year with renewed confidence. But fate gets in the way of his grand teenage plans – especially when eight legs attack instead of four.

And these aren't your typical, everyday spiders. Their newly acquired taste for raw meat has them casting a wide net over Bradley's sleepy San Fernando suburb. It doesn't take them long to scramble up the food chain.

Add a vengeful ex-girlfriend casting a web of lies into the mix, and things get downright sticky.

But Detest-A-Pest can't resist a challenge. Sam and O'Connor rejoin Bradley and his inventive friends as they wage war on an infestation of spiders poised to swallow not only the high school, but the neighborhood and everyone within...

Detest-A-Pest #2 (504 pages)

A playground for the rich. A genetic mutation a thousand years old. A relentless hunger for human flesh. What could go wrong?

Harry Harcourt has a problem. People are dying at exclusive golf resort Mar-A-Verde. As head greenskeeper, it's up to him to "fix" the problem and keep the course open... or face termination. But it's not one problem, it's a vast network of vicious problems, all under the turf.

As bodies pile up, resident doctor Daniela Trejo joins Harry in the fight. Together, they capture a creature unlike anything on Earth – acid skin and razor-sharp fangs with agility that matches its appetite. But the creature escapes.

Outmatched and outnumbered, Harry seeks outside help. No one wants to touch the job – no one except Detest-A-Pest. O'Connor, Sam, and Hope hit the road for what looks like an easy payday in a tropical paradise. What awaits them is a journey through hell that has gruesome death hiding in every shadow...

Detest-A-Pest #3 (340 pages)

A forbidden treasure awakens a centuries-old curse. An unexpected tropical threat. An ally hiding in plain sight.

To celebrate Bradley's high school graduation, O'Connor takes the Detest-A-Pest crew to Club Niho'gula on the remote and beautiful Hawaiian island of Lanai. But trouble tends to follow O'Connor everywhere she goes...

Strange creatures attack guests in broad daylight. The locals blame the attacks on the Legend of Pepehi Waapa – the boat killer. Someone or some thing has unleashed the curse behind it. Ignoring all warnings, O'Connor vows to find the culprit at any cost. But unseen by most, a clue lies just below the surface.

When Sam disappears without a trace, it becomes clear that something larger – more nefarious – is at work. The Detest-A-Pest crew and their new Hawaiian friends realize that they must work together – and fast – if they want any chance of finding Sam alive. Because the evil forces at work could easily send them all to watery graves...

Detest-A-Pest #4 (353 pages)

A family in crisis. An impossible choice. A race against time.

An unplanned pregnancy turns the lives of Deanna, her husband Max, and her teenage son upside down. But there's something else wrong...

After baby David receives a cancer diagnosis, Deanna drops everything to focus on finding a cure. Max has other ideas.

Based on his own troubled past, Max challenges Deanna to consider quality of life versus quantity. Their opposing opinions throw their marriage into chaos and Deanna seeks treatment options alone.

Caught in the middle, Alex must navigate this family crisis on his own. An unexpected friendship with a cancer survivor may offer the perspective he needs.

With the clock ticking, Deanna stops at nothing to save baby David's life... but her relationship with her family may not survive the process.

David's Summer (310 pages)

Two sisters. One wants in. One has a plan. But gang loyalty cuts family ties...

Jess works, spends time with friends, and earns good grades in school. But she's also sole provider for her drug-addicted mother... And she hates it.

Her sister Nova holds a high-profile position in the Dynamite Queens. Within her turf Nova enjoys fame, fortune, freedom, and respect – at a cost of family life.

But Jess wants what Nova has and is willing to do anything to get it. After one explosive argument, Jess joins a rival gang, a decision that leads her down a path of brutal consequences.

South Central L. A. erupts with violence as two gangs – two sisters – wage war on each other. For the winner, victory could be unforgiving...

Tied is a fast-paced look at family, friendship, betrayal, and revenge through the lens of tough Los Angeles girl gangs.

Note: This novel contains strong language and gang violence.

Tied: A Street Gang Novel (316 pages)

"Get snipped," they said. "It will solve all your problems," they said. Unfortunately, Ted listened...

Five years ago, it was love at first sight. Now, it's life on autopilot as tumbleweeds roll through Ted and Iris's bedroom. Their lackluster love life is driving Ted nuts. Iris's solution to their bedroom blues: get snipped.

Kunal and Ray, Ted's best friends and sworn enemies of Iris, agree with her for once. All roads seem to lead to a surgical solution, but Ted's not going there... until an explosive argument changes everything. A vasectomy seems like Ted's only play to win Iris back.

The antics of his precocious next-door neighbor complicates matters. Ted's ill-conceived decisions jeopardize everything important in his life, including his nuts.

But life was about to throw Ted a romantic curve-ball aimed straight at his heart...

Snipped: A Cutting Comedy (300 pages)